Wasted

Mikki Goffin was born in 1976 and graduated from Warwick University in 1998 with a degree in psychology and philosophy and a half-finished manuscript. Unlike many of the characters in this novel, she lived a wholesome and purposeful student existence and now resides in south-east London with a long-term boyfriend called Jez and a free-range budgerigar called Ernie. She is writing her second novel.

Wasted

MIKKI GOFFIN

PHŒNIX

A PHOENIX PAPERBACK ORIGINAL

This edition first published in Great Britain in 2001
by Phoenix, a division of Orion Books Ltd,
Orion House, 5 Upper Saint Martin's Lane
London, WC2H 9EA

How crazy craziness makes everyone, how irrationally afraid. The madness hidden in each of us, called to, identified, aroused like a lust. And against that the jaw sets. The more I fear my own insanity, the more I must punish yours.

Kate Millett, *The Loony-Bin Trip*, University of Illinois Press, 1990

Far from the Maddening Crowd

The coming of the night
Sleep again
Such sadness
Like the coming of
The grief
Found only in dreams

Waves of tiredness
Followed by the drowning
Of the mind
Into an abyss
Of inner things.

The poor busted junkie
She doesn't know
Why all dreams
Are sad
Why there's no more drugs

Why staying awake
Even in the silence
Seems like heaven
In comparison

The sleep
The coming of death
Heavy apostlement.

Lynette Steel, 'Tonight to Sleep', 1988

I

Prelude to Insanity

The world is becoming like a lunatic asylum run by lunatics.
David Lloyd George, 8 Jan, 1933

We all have to go through an in-between stage. At a certain age we need to come to terms with the death of childhood and the birth of adulthood. It is this teen-to-twenties limbo phase that gives us a final opportunity to renew our licence to be objectionable and tiresome on a full-time basis. All of a sudden, our lives take on new meaning: we gain direction, a purpose, a focus, a set of misguided but firm beliefs – and an attitude so savage it will reduce even the sternest of parents to tears. As the Future Generation, it is our responsibility to develop into prosperous, virtuous model citizens. For now though, we are apathetic, surly creatures, our bodies ravaged by hormones and our brains addled by television and popular culture and computer games. Although we have grown physically and are legally entitled to smoke, drink and copulate, our minds are in a constant struggle to keep up with the sense of maturity that these privileges bestow upon us. Despite demanding the dubious luxury of adult status, we are unable and unwilling to connect with the adult world while we still expect to be fed and nurtured by our parents – those absurd, wrinkly embarrassments who don't understand us. Our dear old parents: those stalwart martyrs whose sufferance by this stage has gone way beyond the call of duty.

We need to find an agreeable way of adapting ourselves to a

society that has so far only succeeded in moulding us into angry, ignorant youths. We need to reconcile our aimlessness with a growing sense of ambition. We want maximum success with minimum effort. We want to call the shots, to find out about *real* life, to sample its ups and downs without getting burned. In short, we need a trial run for adulthood. And so this is what a lot of us do: we go to university.

Your halcyon days start and finish here. You probably won't remember them, and that is undoubtedly for the best. You may find yourself in a grotty basement in a student hovel with eardrum-bursting music and neurone-numbing drugs and the possibility of getting laid and the certainty of getting drunk, surrounded by unknown people who essentially bore you and yet who you adore more and more in direct proportion to the amount you are drinking.

And this was where I was, or at least where I thought I was.

It was definitely a basement – there was just one tiny rectangle of a grimy window at the top of a far wall, dusty cobwebs hung in all four corners and the place was damp and smelled of mould and yeast and rotten apples. And it was definitely a hovel, the kind of squalid hovel only a student can live in and to whom the words 'environmental health' would never occur. I had a hazy recollection of being invited there earlier in the evening by someone in a bar whose name began with 'P' or maybe 'K'. In any case, he had been a student, there was no doubt about that. His T-shirt promoted the various touring venues and dates of an obscure indie band, and his red and blue hair extensions suggested he was probably not in full-time gainful employment. And this was most certainly a bona fide student's home, right down to the life-size cardboard cut-out of Darth Vader and the 'Take Me to Your Dealer' alien poster tacked diagonally to the wall, the budget bulk-buy beer cases and the strewn plastic bottles adapted into customised bongs, the dirt-encrusted carpet and the thick shroud of marijuana smoke and the general pervasive feeling of filth, affliction, sexual desperation and lethargy.

I was in a bad way. And it felt good. Somewhere in between

sobriety and apoplexy is a perfect haven for anyone suffering from existential angst and disillusionment, and I was there.

From Therapy? to Senseless Things to the Manics, the distorted music boomed from a battered pair of bombastic speakers; anguished and torturous lyrics swamped by over-amplified bass reverberated through my entire body. I felt exhilarated and bored and confused and sexy and ugly and invisible and popular and isolated. Where am I why am I here what am I doing who is this weird man looming towards me and why is he smiling in such a slimy and suspicious way? 'There you go, love, get that down your neck.'

A gangly, greasy-haired bloke I did not know or find particularly attractive and yet with whom I would shortly exchange personal details and saliva handed me a drink I did not want and yet promptly downed.

'Blimey, love, you're puttin' them away sharpish tonight,' he chortled, moving closer so I could feel his rancid breath on me, warm and beery. The bristles of his wispy beard scratched my cheek as he put one arm around me and cradled a six-pack of lager under the other. He had an accent I couldn't quite decipher, although even if I hadn't been pissed out of my mind the relentless brain-bruising thud of the background music was hardly conducive to any kind of meaningful discussion. He shouted something at me above the din that sounded like, 'So what are you studying then?' or something equally dull and inconsequential. A trail of slaver ran from the corner of his mouth to his chin; it glinted brown and foamy in the dim fluorescence of the electric light.

It's at times like this when people are compelled to lie – obliged, even. When you are a student at a student party, you're faceless, unimportant, tedious, fatuous, and yet it doesn't matter because all anybody gives a damn about is scoring, and if you're of approximately the right gender or you are in possession of drugs, consider yourself a welcome addition to the throng.

'French,' I yelled back at him over the din, my throat hurting from all the shouting I had done over the course of the night.

A lie, incidentally. I was (ostensibly) studying English Literature. That is, my course was based on reading many classic volumes of beautifully constructed prose and showing critical appreciation of them by scrawling lengthy arse-lick essays and bullshitting my way through seminars. For some reason, he responded enthusiastically to this. I'm usually quite adept at interpreting body language and anticipating a person's actions, but this one just lunged at me, all sink-plunger mouth and boxing-glove hands. Like an over-excited puppy, he lapped roughly at my face, then grabbed the back of my head and shoved his tongue into my mouth. At first I was shocked and repulsed, and kind of froze in horror. But then, the comfort of realising I was drunk and that this was a normal thing to do in the given situation calmed me into submission. I held my breath and made a concerted effort to enjoy it, letting his tongue flap around my tonsils for a while, and maybe even venturing my own into his mouth once or twice. After a while it did get a bit too boring and unpleasant, so I politely pushed him away and turned my head to the side, wiping my mouth discreetly with the back of my hand.

'Me name's Ant, by the way,' he breathed hoarsely in my ear, pawing at my thighs.

'I'm Abi,' I said, stupidly holding out my hand as if we were newly introduced business associates. Bemused, Ant ceased mauling my leg for a second and held my hand and shook it limply.

'Extremely fuckin' pleased to meet you, Abi,' he assured me. 'Voulez vous coucher avec moi ce soir?' He found himself amusing and threw back his head to let out a short burst of stentorian laughter.

Scouse. He was a Scouser. Brilliant. Just brilliant.

I gave him a *stop it, you're killing me* look, then anxiously scanned the room over his shoulder for any sign of Nadine or Alex or Marbles, or anyone I even vaguely knew. But all I could see was a kaleidoscope blur of faces and bodies, a milling mass of strangers made all the more strange by my impaired vision. I collapsed back against the wall and pulled my legs up to my chest, feeling nauseous in the pit of my stomach.

'Do yer want another drink?' Ant offered. I tilted my head towards him and tried to smile. His features swam in front of my eyes, wonderfully indistinct. When the senses are warped by alcohol, it is so much easier to convince yourself that the person you are flirting with is a beauty rather than a beast. There is probably no better reason to keep on drinking. I squeezed my eyes shut and took a few deep breaths.

'Can you get me some water, please?'

'Eh?' he leaned towards me, taking the opportunity to look down my top with minimal subtlety.

'Water, please,' I shouted straight into his proffered ear.

'*Water*?' he asked, incredulous.

'Yeah, you know, the wet stuff that comes out of taps.'

Ant shrugged, still taking great interest in my cleavage, which I had of course deliberately bolstered for the occasion. I puffed out my chest, while at the same time making sure my expression conveyed 'I am a woman, not a pair of breasts' indignation.

'OK, whatever,' he said. I watched as he disappeared into the crowd, realising with a terrible jolt that I had been openly intimate with a man wearing a faded Pantera T-shirt, a pair of gaudy Bermuda shorts and black plimsolls with white socks. I wasn't even *that* drunk for God's sake; I was just totally incapable of stringing together a coherent sentence of more than a few words and of accurately judging distances, faces, reactions, liquid quantities, and the passage of time. And of walking, as I shortly found out when I attempted to stand up in a quest to locate the toilet. I left the basement via a set of stone steps and stagger-crawled from one student-crammed room to another, one hand against the wall for support, the other flailing about erratically as I tried to regain my balance. I was at that stage of inebriety in which it seems quite normal to start talking to yourself. Doddering and disorientated, I consoled myself with foolish and meaningless mutterings which gave me enough encouragement to make it as far as the stairs.

I pushed past a straggling row of people on my way up the rickety steps, shouting, 'Ex*cuse* me,' when I was obstructed by a dumpy, dwarfish oaf with a goatee and pink spiky hair. He turned to me, his eyes wild and askew behind the lenses of his bottle-bottomed glasses and remarked, seemingly without irony, 'Why, what have we here? A fine filly, if ever I saw one!'

Sadly, I had neither the strength nor the quick-wittedness to give him the scathing retort he deserved, so I merely shoved him out of the way and ignored his lecherous play for my ascending backside. I got to the top of the stairs and discovered that the row of people I had just fought my way past was in fact the queue for the toilet – and 'the only damn bog in the whole place', according to the Chinese girl at the head of the queue who was clutching her crotch and hopping about in desperation. Dismayed, I turned and tramped back down, stopped once again on the way by the pink-haired goatee cretin. This time, his opening gambit was the shockingly crass, 'Fuck me if I'm wrong but isn't your name Helga von Winklehoven?' which even by student standards was hardly worthy of a standing ovulation.

The next thing I knew, I was dragged away by a bossy Irish girl called Leanne ('Fock this, my bladder's gonna burst at this rate so it is'), who took me outside into the back garden and squatted beside me over a weed-upon weed patch behind a disused woodshed while chirpily recounting a messy experience she had just shared with someone called Keith. I remember feeling wet soil on my knees and buttocks, a hot, damp sensation in my gusset, a craving for a cigarette and a packet of prawn cocktail crisps, and I think someone spilled a glass of blackcurrant punch over my skirt but after that I must have blanked out for a while, because I suddenly or maybe not so suddenly found myself in another room without knowing how I had got there or even whether I was still at the same party. Eerily enough, I seemed to be surrounded by completely different people, in a completely different environment. I blended myself into this new crowd with ease – this involved leisurely vegging out in an available area and smiling languidly at anyone whose barely open eyes made contact with mine.

It eventually transpired that I had somehow made my way into the attic, a small room at the top of the house painted jade and mauve, with sloping ceilings, wooden beams and floorboards and a skylight. According to a doped-out, beatific girl with whom I found myself in gibberish parlance, it was called 'The Peace Room', and was intended for all those 'disenchanted by society', and those who 'demanded a more meaningful and spiritual aspect' to their evening. In other words, it was Stoned Central. Soft 'ethnic' music oozed from tinny speakers to provide a soothing ambient sound, and a spaced-out, bushy-bearded man wearing flip-flops and a toga played a ukulele in the corner surrounded by cross-legged, doe-eyed vegan types who occasionally clinked their finger cymbals or dreamily bashed their organic tambourines in time to his mesmerised strumming. Others smoked from bongs of every shape and colour, sitting in happy throngs on beanbags and cushions and nodding sagely at each other, knowing nothing at all about anything whatsoever and not caring. Incense wafted in smoky drifts from several burning joss sticks – I detected jasmine flower and ylang ylang even through the potent hash haze. The lampshade was draped with orange organza for extra atmosphere, and candles burned precariously around the edges of the room, flickering light and shadow across the walls in waves of protean shapes. Wind chimes rattled and tinkled in the breeze. A kindly stranger handed me his joint and a tumbler of mystery liquid that I discovered, after a tentative sip, was wonderful, pure, plain water.

The next few hours (minutes?) passed like a dream, fuzzed-up and weird and desultory. An excitable pigtailed girl in a sequinned crop top with a sari around her waist and a glittering bindi between her eyes threw her skinny arms around me and proclaimed me to be a 'beautiful soul'. Jangling with metal bracelets and bells, she excitedly spoke in a meandering fashion about seemingly anything and everything from her knowledge of auras and chakras to her previous life as a seahorse to the importance of legalising cannabis – a gram of which she had in its purest form in a plastic bag that she produced nonchalantly from a pink silk purse on a string around her neck. She wittered on and on as her skinhead boyfriend industriously licked Rizla papers and demolished Rothmans and passed around king-size joints at a steady rate of two or three a minute.

My sensations of all that was happening around me were vague at best, downright surreal at worst. I couldn't even work out whether or not I was having a 'good time'. What defines a 'good time' to a student? Is the greatness of a party measured by how little you can remember of it the next day? If that was the case, I felt I must have been doing pretty well. It was like being in a film freeze-framed and fast-forwarded simultaneously – time passed in slow motion, and yet at confusing, jerky speed, like a stroboscopic effect; I saw my hand take a joint and then before I even felt it between my lips, the hot vapours were dragged into my scorched lungs, and I was already taking another one, sometimes one in each hand. Or, the power of coherent speech having long since left me, I would find myself chatting to someone, getting my joint lit or taken from me, maybe lying on the floor embracing one or two or more people, or suddenly alone in a different part of the room with only a tiny fragment of recollection as to what had happened just moments before. When I finally ventured out into the sudden bright light of the upstairs landing, the infamous refrain of Rage Against the Machine's 'Killing in the Name' at several thousand decibels provided a stark contrast to the peace-pipe fanfare I had been subjected to in the Peace Room. It was like emerging from a time capsule from the sixties straight into the nineties.

The party was just about winding down by then: unconscious bodies lay slumped on top of each other in a disarray of entangled, frenetically angled limbs like a scene in a nuclear fall-out, and a few die-hard try-hards still determined to get lucky were attempting last-ditch small talk with comatose women and other inanimate objects and wondering why they weren't getting responses. Every conceivable student type was accounted for at that party, from disgruntled anti-Capitalist to liberal bohemian; from unwashed, genuine crusty to fragrant and rich crusty; from fashion-conscious, coked-up, parent-pampered brats to fashion-unconscious free spirits who happily shared out their fags and gear. Simple people with complexes, inherently identical, desperate for both acceptance and individuality, every single one of us personifying everything that is wrong and sad and dull about students. Ant caught up with me eventually, just as a raucous fight was kicking off in the back garden. He seized me as if I were a piece of driftwood in a turbulent ocean and clung to me, asking me where the hell I'd been for the last six hours. It was gone five in the morning by then. He gave me an eighth of resin for a fiver and wrote his dealer's name and number on the back of a season ticket with the corner ripped out of it. Little was I to realise then that this would be the most considerate and romantic thing anyone would do for me for a very long time.

'You kipping over?' he asked, gesturing at a convenient patch of spare floor space, just about big enough for two people to get uncomfortably cosy. I shook my head. I was ravenously hungry, my mouth felt like my tongue had been dragged across sandpaper, and I needed the toilet again – as a matter of extreme urgency.

'I suppose a shag is out of the question?' he added hopefully, crushing a beer can in his hand and belching with gusto.

I belched back in retaliation, louder and prouder, sealing the fate of any potential sexual experience we may have shared that night.

'I need a slash,' I said flatly. 'Then I'm going home.'

I dropped my knickers in the nick of time just as the wailing began from Jasmine's room. But it was too late; I simply had to go. I straddled the porcelain and sighed with relief while the wailing intensified to a high-pitched scream. In a rising panic, I tried in vain to make the stream flow quicker and stretched out both arms to reach for the door. A brief grapple with Andrex in one hand and door handle in the other, I finally managed to fling the door open, teetering on the edge of the toilet seat just before losing my balance and falling off. The screaming continued. I scrambled to my feet, careered headlong and blindly into the doorframe, keeled over backwards, got up again, and waddled awkwardly to Jasmine's room, my ankles manacled by knicker elastic.

'Jas . . . ?' I knocked gingerly on my sister's bedroom door as the screaming subsided to a whimper. 'Are you OK?'

I pushed the door ajar and peeped inside.

As usual, the large bay window was festooned with great lengths of multi-coloured fabrics, and a narrow gap in the middle allowed only a small chink of morning sunlight to filter through, its hazy rays picking out a spiral of whirling dust particles and softly illuminating the haphazard chaos of Jasmine's disordered bedroom. I tentatively breathed in the pungent vapour of smoke and musty incense which hung in the air. Clothes were scattered around the floor, along with fag ends, crusty crockery, empty crisp packets, old tissues and an assortment of unidentifiable objects. I stepped inside after a moment's hesitation.

'Are you OK?' I repeated, slightly louder.

Abruptly, Jasmine sat upright in bed and stared straight at me, eyes blazing.

'Who the *fuck* gave you permission to come in?' she demanded, pulling the quilt around her.

'I thought you'd hurt yourself . . . ' I trailed off, knowing that I had violated the 'No Trespassers' rule. I blushed scarlet and backed out of the room sheepishly.

'No, it's all right . . . *damn* . . . hey, wait a second.' Jasmine fumbled around for a while and pulled on her dressing gown. 'Look, sorry to snap, sis. You . . . er . . . interrupted something.' She glanced over at me and smiled. 'Come here, there's someone I'd like you to meet.'

She swung her legs over the side of the bed and beckoned me over. Both suspicious and curious, I crept towards her, carefully side-stepping various obstacles along the way. As soon as I was near enough to see, she flung back her duvet to reveal our neighbour's son Darren in a pair of navy briefs and little else, curled up like a question mark on the bed sheet. As a child, I found his near-nakedness both gruesome and hilarious. I clapped my hand to my mouth in shock, suppressing a giggle. He pretended to be asleep, then 'woke up' with a start and blinked at me in confusion through a shaggy tangle of hair, as if I was the last person he expected to see.

'Oh! Er . . . mornin',' he waved at me feebly with two fingers and winked dozily. I was eight years old and my knowledge of sexuality was almost non-existent. I knew that men had 'thingies' and that women had babies, but I didn't know why or how. This didn't stop me from attaching great and ominous meaning to the presence of a semi-clothed, dishevelled man in my older sister's bed.

'W-why is Darren here?' I asked, not really wanting to know the answer. Jasmine ignored me and began desperately searching the assortment of empty Silk Cut and Marlboro packets that littered her dresser. She finally managed to find a half-smoked fag in a makeshift ashtray on the floor. She sparked it up, threw Darren an unwashed T-shirt, and regarded me with an ambivalent expression that I found unnerving. Darren scrambled into the T-shirt, a flurry of scrawny limbs and dreadlocks, cursing under his breath.

'Does Daddy know he's here?' I persisted, pressing myself into the corner of the room and staring at him, wide-eyed. I was absolutely bewildered. Jasmine had always described Darren as a 'sad, sad sack of shite' and yet, here he was, in her room, practically naked. I looked on with mildly sickened fascination as he blundered about looking for his trousers, his sockless feet occasionally happening upon the odd sharp implement – a drawing pin, and then a shard of glass, a small remnant from Jasmine's last temper tantrum. He swore loudly and shot me a malevolent look.

Jasmine drew back an edge of curtain and opened the window. 'Piss off,' she said, yanking at his sleeve.

Darren mumbled some more impolite words before diving out of the window, his graceless descent into the flowerbed below eliciting further swearing, more vociferous and fervent.

Jasmine calmly closed the window, sucking in her cheeks as she inhaled deeply on her cigarette. She appeared to be in a trance, gazing dreamily into the smoke. She was fifteen, well-developed, impulsive, wild and dissident. At that time I admired her with all my heart, to the extent that I aspired to be just like her when I was big. I crabbed towards the door, glancing nervously at her.

'No, you don't have to go,' she said, without looking at me. 'Close the door and sit on the bed.'

I watched as she smoked the cigarette right down to the filter and stubbed it out on the windowsill. I didn't really want to stay, but Jasmine wasn't the sort of person to be argued with. After wading through a festering pile of laundry, I perched myself obediently on the edge of her bed.

'Look, don't tell Dad, OK?' She crossed the room to flick through her cassette collection: Roxy Music, Suzy Quatro, The Stranglers, Blondie, the Velvet Underground, The Clash – if it was a classic seventies symphony, Jasmine probably had it. ' . . . And especially not Jane,' she added, selecting a Pink Floyd tape. 'She pisses me off, the way she tries to rule me.'

It upset me when Jasmine bitched about our stepmother. Jane was the only mother I'd known, but Jasmine remained stubbornly, although perhaps understandably, loyal to the memory of our real mother.

'Jane *does* love us,' I said.

Jasmine made a guttural noise and shoved the tape into her cassette player.

I shrugged and mumbled, 'They're both at church anyway.'

'Hypocrites!'

I didn't know what it meant but I nodded anyway. There was a long silence. I twirled my hair around my fingers and swung my legs back and forth nervously. 'Oh Abigail . . .' she said gently, kneeling down in front of me and looking me straight in the face. 'I don't mean to be so . . .' she trailed off mysteriously, and her eyes focused on the wall behind me. Finally she said, 'One day you will understand.' She took my hands in hers and smiled crookedly. 'One day.' Naturally inquisitive and persistent, I pointed at the window and asked, 'Why *was* he here though?'

She sighed, reached under the bed and pulled out a half-empty bottle of whisky. 'Well, I suppose you'll have to learn sooner or later.' She lay back on the bed and sprawled up against the headboard, her long, dark hair fanning out against the white pillows. She grinned at me as she swigged from the bottle, and I gazed back at her dumbly, not knowing what to expect next.

'And you may as well learn from me,' she continued, putting the bottle between her knees as she pulled her hair back away from her face and tied it into a ponytail with an elastic band. 'I think I'll be a good teacher. What say you, shortie?' She leaned over to turn up the volume on her stereo, and Dark Side of the Moon blared from both speakers. Although I was an eighties child, Jasmine had grown up in the seventies – or at least her best memories were all of the seventies – and her influence was bound to have a powerful hold over me, especially since I was always so desperate to impress her. Pink Floyd reminded me of Jasmine. Although I started off having little choice in the matter (they more or less provided the soundtrack to the first few years of my childhood), I ended up genuinely loving them, almost to the point of obsession. Their music was suggestive of halcyon days, of a time I couldn't quite remember but that was somehow vividly evoked merely by listening to the songs. Jasmine had recently smuggled me into one of their concerts, and her tallest biker friend wrapped me up in his leather jacket and lifted me up on to his shoulders so I could see better. And I sang my little lungs out along with the rest of them to 'We Don't Need No Education'. I even refused to go to school the following Monday just to prove that I understood the profundity of the lyrics. (Of course, the double negative eluded me until a pedantic school friend pointed it out some years later.)

'Can I have some?' I said eventually, looking at the whisky bottle curiously. 'You told me it makes you feel good when shit things happen.'

'No you fuckin' can't,' she snapped aggressively, taking another few gulps. 'And anyway, what kind of shit things ever happen to you? Spilt Ribena on your Postman Pat quilt cover? Lost your favourite teddy bear? Got told off by your teacher for not doing your piss-easy homework?' She screwed the lid back on and replaced the bottle under the bed. 'You don't know nothin' Abi, you're just a silly little kid.'

I felt myself burn with indignation, clenching my fists in useless defiance and glaring at her as she clambered back under the duvet and pulled it up over her head.

'Anyway,' I whined, 'I know why Darren was here and I think it's disgusting.'

'You don't know jack, pea-brain,' Jasmine's muffled voice retorted.

'I do, I do! I know all about willies and virginias. And Jane told me all about periods and tampering.'

Her head popped back out and she snorted with laughter. 'You're priceless, sis.'

'You *scared* me,' I whined petulantly. 'You were screaming. I thought you'd hurt yourself.'

She shuffled into a sitting position and held out her arms to me. I got up and collapsed into them, snuggling up to the warmth of her dressing gown, friends again.

'What have I told you about coming into my room, short arse?' she whispered into my hair.

I looked up at her and obediently recited Jasmine's concise version of Rules of my Room. 'Don't come in.'

'Unless . . . ?' she prompted.

'Unless you want to die.'

'Correct. Now please don't forget that.'

'I won't. I'm sorry.'

She cuddled me close to her and I breathed in her reassuring scent, now feeling more at ease. Jasmine had this strange ability to make me feel nervous and edgy, and yet at the same time, sort of . . . safe.

'It's OK,' she said after a long silence, 'you've probably done me a favour actually.'

We listened to the music together for a while, Jasmine humming quietly to herself, me resting my head against her chest and listening to the hypnotic thrum of her heartbeat. I felt my eyelids getting heavy and was almost on the brink of falling asleep when she finally stirred to glance over at her alarm clock.

'When are the folks getting back?' she asked, nudging me in the back with her elbow.

'Not for ages.'

'Well then, how about I give you a brief but all-encompassing lesson about the birds and the bees?'

'What's that?'

'Tell you what,' she said, rummaging in her bedside drawer,

'you go and make me a coffee, and I'll find some pens and draw some diagrams for you.'

I thought about this proposition, just for a second. 'Okay then.'

Then I got up to put the kettle on, unaware that my safely-guarded childhood innocence was soon to be tarnished, explicitly and mercilessly, by my most admired role model; by someone who should really have known better.

And so over the course of one Sunday morning I learned all about the adolescent subculture in which Jasmine was immersed. After telling me all about sex (all the ins and outs, no stone left unturned), she progressed quite naturally on to soft drugs, hard drugs, abortion and bondage, concluding with detailed advice on how to shoplift even bulky items without getting caught. All of this was described and explained in simple terms, and further demonstration and detail was provided by visual aids which Jasmine scribbled in biro in her spiral-bound notebook with varying degrees of accuracy. I was transfixed and overwhelmed. I couldn't wait to tell my friends.

Just as Jasmine promised me, with the kind of foresight only an older sister can have, I developed into a voluptuous (verging on plump) and naturally objectionable teenager, and hid a mildly hysterical fascination with the opposite sex. As also predicted, this fascination quickly soured to derision, and then neutralised to a more mutually agreeable indifference when puberty finally receded. But Jasmine turned out to be wrong about a lot of things, as well. During those delinquent years, I never once got caught by the police for anything (let alone for having underage sex in a supermarket trolley in Watford High Street, one of Jasmine's lesser misdemeanours). I never took hard drugs (although I had an unhealthy fondness for dope from a fairly early age), I never had an abortion, and I never stole anything – although I suppose I was an accomplice when my best friend Sylvie stole three Mars bars and a tube of Smarties from the school tuck shop and hid them in my coat hood. Nearly all my sexual fantasies were somewhere in the range of tame to boring, and I very rarely did anything outlandish or particularly adventurous – sexually or otherwise. I rarely deviated from the norm in anything I did or said. I suppose I was average, which must have disappointed Jasmine. She didn't want an average sister. She needed someone to understand her, because she was about as far from average as it is possible to be.

She was born on 18 May 1969, seven years before me almost to the day. At the time our mum was only seventeen, and was taking her liberated flower-child 'free love' ideals as far as possible. Our dad, older yet barely wiser by nine years, married her as soon as my despairing grandparents begrudgingly gave their blessing. Apart from his love of getting stoned (or perhaps because of it), he was a good father to us – patient, kind and loving, despite his frequent lapses from reality. They couldn't afford to have me but – so the story goes – my dad rushed in and saved me from the destructive grip of the terminator. Just as my mother was about to go under the anaesthetic, he had marched in proudly, a sudden and fierce attack of conscience compelling him to proclaim, 'Don't kill my son!' And so seven months later I was born, female yet normal, and I was carried around in an embroidered rucksack and spent my nappy-wearing years in a crumbling hippy commune in south London, surrounded by gladioli, psychedelia, stray animals and garish wallpaper. And abundant supplies of mind-altering substances. Jasmine was my mentor from day one. I was her 'most precious doll', her real life Tiny Tears, and she took care of me when our parents lay entwined in catatonic stupors, and on the rare occasions when the free love among the twenty or so of us who lived there had been temporarily exhausted or extinguished by the oblivion of potent home grown.

I was a repulsive child; piggy face and bloated cheeks and straggly hair in bunches, with stumpy limbs and sticky-out ears. But Jasmine was pretty right from the start – huge, gamine eyes with long curly lashes, lots of dark hair and a perfect heart-shaped face with skin that you'd expect to see on a soap commercial. She had boundless energy and a seething lust for life, and I followed her every move like a besotted puppy dog – sometimes wary, but unquestioningly loyal. She was anarchic and strong-willed, and she had guts. It was an explosive and formidable combination of traits and she certainly got herself noticed. Although our extended family may well have been more effluent than affluent, we were never deprived. We were loved not only by our parents but also by every other flora-wielding, peace-promoting beflared eccentric that lived in our eclectically furnished makeshift home. And Jasmine and I always had each other, if all else failed.

When our mum got bored with transcendental meditation and group sex, she went on a mission to 'find herself', and meanwhile our dad – now well into his thirties – took Jasmine and me with him to live with his parents in Scotland following a severe ultimatum from social services. He managed to wean himself off the evil weed, cut his hair and find a job, while our mum's far-flung mission took a new turn – she found alcohol, and lost interest in finding herself altogether. Or maybe she forgot to. She died on 5 October 1978, when I was two. Vodka and Valium were just two of the ingredients in the suicidal cocktail she had taken. While I was obviously too young to understand, Jasmine and Dad were utterly devastated. Although my dad never talked about it much, Jasmine's childhood memories of our mum are vivid and numerous, if slightly rose-tinted. She would regale me with endless stories of how amazing our mum was, how she fought fiercely for what she believed in, how her peripatetic and rather solitary childhood led her from one foster home to another while she tried to find refuge and a real family and home to call her own. I would never know quite how many of Jasmine's tales were hyperbolic, but from a very young age I was made aware that my mum was, in no uncertain terms, remarkable and totally irreplaceable. Jasmine gave me a picture of her, which I kept with me all the time. She looked nothing like me but very similar to Jasmine – striking, slightly Hispanic features and an elegantly curvaceous figure. I felt sorry I had never been given the chance to know her for myself instead of constructing my own unreliable image of her through others' recounted memories and two-dimensional photographs. Her name was Angel, but she was known as 'Dusty' to most of her friends. Jasmine said that if she ever had kids, she'd call the first one Angel, even if it was a boy.

We lived with our grandparents in West Lothian until Dad remarried in 1982, and I suppose that was the point at which the so-called 'normality' of my life began. Sometimes I wished Dad had never cleaned up his act and just continued living the alternative life he loved; but most of the time I was glad that his radical image – bird's nest hair, garlands of flowers, vile bell-bottoms and copious facial hair – was jettisoned in favour of a more responsible and orthodox one. In three eventful years, he transformed himself miraculously from John Lennon into Joe Normal, until he was perhaps best described as amiable and balding. The only real, tangible reminder of his former beatnik bohemia was the much-worn sheepskin waistcoat which lurked for years in the back of his wardrobe, reeking of mothballs and mould. Unofficially, he became a blaspheming 'occasional smoker' who sympathised with both agnosticism and pantheism. Officially though, he gave up smoking and found Jesus. This may have had something to do with the fact that Jane, his second chance at true love, was a born-again Christian. His name was once Tyran Pagan, but that self-imposed variation on his real name was promptly surrendered in favour of the more job-worthy Thomas Geoffrey Page. The enormous quantities of psychotropic drugs that he had consumed for almost two decades inevitably took their toll and unfortunately he suffered from mild narcolepsy and often had trouble remembering even the most basic things. So, from maelstrom to male menopause, our dysfunctional father was finally tamed and conventionalised by our vivacious and big-hearted stepmother, who, to her credit, took on a lot when she married him. Less propitiously, we also inherited a stroppy, infantile stepbrother called Lewis who was four months younger than me, and the sort of person nobody would ever live with voluntarily. But, considering we had such a shaky start, things seemed to have worked out well.

All five of us lived in a small semi in a quiet, anonymous road in a small town in Hertfordshire, surrounded by other families with similar houses, gardens, cars, lifestyles. Just like them, we were a normal, ordinary family in a normal, ordinary house. We blended in well. Everything slotted into place. That is to say, we seemed to get on with our everyday, average lives in the most sensible and rational ways possible, just like the rest of them.

Jasmine always believed in living for the moment. She tried everything. It all started when she was nine and had her first cigarette. Granny Page found out and gave her a damn good telling off. 'Smoking makes pretty girls look ugly and all the boys won't go near you because you'll smell and cough like an old hag.'

Little did we know that this marked just the very beginning of a seemingly endless downward spiral, and nobody could have predicted that Jasmine's reaction to our mother's death would have gone to such extremes. Jasmine didn't want to look pretty or attract the boys. She continued smoking, got more beautiful than ever, and had every boy in school lusting after her. Our grandparents must have been very relieved when Dad finally remarried and we left their Scottish cottage to go and live as a nuclear family in the city suburbs. At last a bit of stability, a chance to adjust to a normal life in a normal family setting. A fresh start, a new life. That's what we all hoped. That's what we all thought.

But Jasmine never settled down, no matter how much Dad and Jane cajoled and coerced. From my own standpoint, she seemed to become increasingly distant and cold-hearted, but it was only with the passage of many painful years that I came to realise the sense of helplessness and desolation she must have been experiencing. It was easy to resent her at the time, because *she* was the one causing my dad and my stepmother to cry, *she* was the reason my fragile new family had become a collection of individual wrecks rather than a unified team.

She hated her new school and bunked off to smoke grass with boys twice her age to prove it.

Then she started sniffing solvents.

Then she started coming home drunk every other night.

Then she started not coming home at all and keeping everyone up all night, sick with worry.

Between the ages of twelve and eighteen, Jasmine took various stimulants, hallucinogens and narcotics, ranging from the everyday taxable (nicotine, alcohol) to marijuana, mescaline, crack cocaine, magic mushrooms, LSD, speed and eventually, heroin. It got to the point where she needed speed to buck her up in the morning and then had to take diazepam in the evening to help her relax. With the stupefaction of amphetamines and the stultification of barbiturates, her life became like a dizzying merry-go-round, except of course there was nothing merry about it at all. Things were not good for a very long time. She became like a stranger, and it broke Dad's heart. He desperately stocked up on advice books and self-help leaflets with catchy titles such as 'What to do if your child is an addict', 'Getting through to your disturbed teenager', 'Coping with schizophrenia in the family', 'Learning to accept your child's mental health problem', 'Drugs: The Facts', 'Drugs: How to deal with them' (I thought that one sounded highly suspicious), 'Living in the shadow of paranoid schizophrenia' and 'Mental Illness: Nothing to be ashamed of'. He and Jane must have read everything on the market, but still they were none the wiser.

I was the only one Jasmine confided in, but for a while she refused to talk even to me. It was as if an invisible barrier had been drawn between her and the outside world. There was a time I couldn't even bear to be in the same room as her. She became a shadow of her former self, all her spirit and sparkle seemed to have drained from her, and her personality completely changed. It was frightening. Only with hindsight could we have interpreted the signs of impending tragedy; at the time we were just ignorant and scared. Jasmine's behaviour got worse and worse over the years, until she was completely out of control. Our mum's death seemed to have triggered something in her, something deep-rooted and destructive. Her drug taking, petty thieving and sexual indiscretions were cries for help interpreted as symptomatic of an obstinate and rebellious spirit, an untameable spirit that would soon get tired of rebelling and eventually settle down. A short-term phase. Her last school report described Jasmine as 'emotionally volatile, insecure and defiant'. She left school when she was sixteen (not that she ever attended on a regular basis anyway) with two O-levels and an attitude. She was caught by the headmistress fellating the caretaker in the PE cupboard one Monday evening. Jasmine was high at the time and allegedly invited her to join in the merriment. This was the last and most severe incident in an extensive series of mischiefs, and she was promptly expelled. My dad and Jane then received a stern letter suggesting an immediate course of remedial counselling. The caretaker lost his job, incidentally.

Over the course of the next year, Jasmine sank ever deeper into a dark world of drugs and depression, and a role reversal occurred. Whereas I once relied on her, she became dependent on me. And on an array of illegal substances. I grew up very quickly and became accustomed to her unpredictable mood swings and erratic behaviour, but there were some things I could not have prepared myself for. After a brief and intensely worrying spell of roughing it in London, she lived in a barely habitable squat in Dagenham with a barely human boyfriend for almost a year. He was on heroin and was prone to violent outbursts, and when Jasmine's parasuicides became more and more frequent, our dad insisted – with what little forceful authority he still had left – that she move back into the family home with us where she would be safe. She agreed because deep down and despite everything, she did have immense respect for Dad and even greater remorse for what she was putting him through, and also because she missed me just as much as I missed her. But even when I was with her, I missed her. She just wasn't the same. She used to cry in my lap like a baby, for hours, ceaselessly. Counselling didn't seem to work, and Jasmine's use of drugs as a means of escape rapidly turned into a full-blown heroin addiction.

My sister was a junkie by the age of eighteen. It was two years later that she was promoted to 'schizophrenic' and institutionalised for six months while doctors tried to stabilise her. I suppose it is impossible to know whether or not the drugs themselves had made her that way, or if she was born with some kind of predisposition to it. In any case, the drugs couldn't have helped.

We were just about coming to terms with her drug addiction

and then suddenly, our beleaguered family had a more terrifying word to deal with. A word even more terrible than 'addict', 'junkie' and 'heroin': *schizophrenia*. We were told that Jasmine was clinically insane, over the telephone, by a psychiatric nurse we had never even met. Just when we thought things couldn't get any worse, we were confronted with this final, earth-shattering diagnosis, and with the possibility that Jasmine would never get better. At least with the heroin there was always the hope – and a realistic hope – that she would get over it, that she would pull through. But with this bombshell, it felt like we'd reached a dead end, and there was no way out. Things became clear and confusing at once – all our questions were answered by this one dreadful, powerful word *schizophrenia*, and yet it was inadequate, as it only served to create yet more questions.

The strain on the family was incredible.

There is nothing so deafening and sinister as the shocked silence of parents who have returned unexpectedly early from a weekend away to find their home has been demolished overnight by a rioting gang of youths. It had been Jasmine's party, Jasmine's idea, but that didn't make me any less culpable. Dad and Jane had booked themselves a well-deserved weekend at a health farm and Lewis had sensibly gone to a mate's house, knowing from experience that Jasmine's otherwise indiscriminate party invites did not extend to ginger-haired stepbrothers.

The opportunity was there, and my devious sister took it. And I was just as eager. We had allowed ourselves enough time to clean up the incriminating evidence of the inevitably messy aftermath, so Dad and Jane would have been none the wiser. It was all planned perfectly, every contingent prepared for, every cleaning agent for every possible stain on standby and all necessary chores in the clear-up operation divided and agreed between us beforehand. Nothing could have gone wrong. In hindsight, I should have seen that Dad was fast approaching a nervous breakdown and needed to get away, even if only for two nights. If I had known the extent to which I was adding to his burgeoning unhappiness at the time, I might have behaved more like the supportive daughter he needed me to be, rather than the difficult teenager I sadistically enjoyed being. ('One tearaway in the family is enough please, Abi,' he had said to me on several occasions.)

When he and Jane got back on a Sunday afternoon rather than a Monday morning, I don't think anything could have prepared them for what they saw. They unlocked the door, smiling at first as it swung open wide into the hallway, hollering, 'Hello, girls! We're back!' only to be confronted with their worst nightmare. Their faces fell, crumpled in horror, as they stood on the threshold of a scene of unspeakable catastrophe.

I sat on the stairs rubbing my bruised knee (a mandatory random party injury) and trying to think of a way to explain the damage that had been inflicted on the house by uncontrolled droves of Jasmine's most notorious acquaintances, high or low on every and any drug they could get their law-breaking hands on. However, something prevented me from speaking – something called fear. Something called shame.

Jane was the first to speak.

'Why is there a motorbike in my hallway?'

Dad followed immediately with, 'Where is Jasmine?' His voice didn't sound angry, or sad, or anything really. I glanced at him guiltily. I was sixteen and only too aware of the fact that there was a naked twenty-four-year-old man upstairs in my bed rolling me a big fat joint of finest Dutch.

'Oh, hel*lo* you two!' I exclaimed cheerily, finding my voice at last and pitifully trying to pretend that nothing was amiss. 'You're back early.'

Dad marched towards me purposefully, his eyes now blazing. His shoes squelched and crackled with each step on the heavily soiled and cluttered carpet. '*Where. Is. Your. Sister.*' The top of his head had turned bright pink. He was not a happy man. I hung my head and continued to rub the unexplained bruise on my knee. Dad grabbed my arm and pulled it roughly until I yelped in pain.

'*Abigail,* where *is* she?'

I pointed towards the back door. 'Last I saw she was in the tool shed with . . . with . . .' I snorted with girlish mirth, and put my hand over my mouth, as Dad and Jane looked at each other in exasperation.

'I'll check out the back,' Dad said, turning to Jane, who was now occupied with picking up fragments of her favourite vase, which had been smashed to smithereens over a gatecrasher's head some hours before. 'You look upstairs, Jane.'

'Shit,' I said under my breath, getting to my feet to limp paralytically up the stairs, clinging to the banister.

'And check Abigail's room first,' Dad called out as the back door slammed behind him.

'No!' I cried desperately, falling forward.

There was a short silence while I made a mad scramble for the top stair and then Jane stopped me just as I was trying to decide whether to sort out the man in my bedroom first or the three men, one woman and illegal talcum powder supplies in the bathroom.

'I'm so disappointed with you.'

I looked over my shoulder and Jane was standing in the middle of the hall, a piece of vase in one hand, a soggy unwound toilet roll in the other, and tears in her eyes. 'How could you?' Her voice was quiet, so full of hurt, the words jolted me into deep sorrow and regret. I sidled down the steps on my bum, stopping half-way and leaning my head against the banister. I was hungover and needed sleep, but I felt overwhelmed with guilt – not just the usual begrudging guilt that teenagers often feel when they piss their parents off – this was *real* guilt.

I gave her a sheepish look. 'We were going to clear the place up before you and Dad got back,' I whimpered ineffectually.

'How *could* you?' she repeated, shaking her head sadly and glimpsing the words '*Come to Daddy*' and '*Revolting Cocks*' written in cerise lipstick on the gilt-framed hall mirror.

'I'm sorry. It got a bit out of hand. Er . . . it looks worse than it is,' I offered brightly. She didn't say anything, she just looked around in dismay at the wreckage of the house, her arms flapping at her sides as if she wanted to fly away.

'Your poor father,' she mumbled eventually. 'Your poor, poor father.' She wandered into the lounge, where the French windows led on to the patio. The patio could now be accessed directly without first having to open the sliding door, thanks to a particularly raucous guest who, in a fit of drug-induced pique, had violently projected a sizeable object straight towards, through and beyond the reinforced glass.

'Hey, it will be all right. It's not really that bad,' I yelled. 'Just need to push a hoover about, a bit of a dusting here and there . . .'

'Shut *up*, Abigail,' Jane snapped.

I clung to the banisters and watched from my safe vantage point as she surveyed the smashed ornaments and photo frames, the graffitied wallpaper, the carpet with its unique new pattern of footprints and fag butts and liquid splashes, the ripped and stained sofas, the abandoned drinking vessels and bottles left empty or half-full, the random collection of pixilated and exhausted bodies lying around and snoring boorishly in pools of vomit. Someone had drawn glasses and moustaches on the family portrait above the fireplace. It had seemed funny at the time. The night before, a Noah's Ark of lusty couples had arranged themselves with orgiastic vigour into strange, undulating obstructions on the floor and sofas, and various people had mistaken Jane's beloved yucca plant for a toilet. Jane was shaking her head sadly as she removed a condom from between the smashed doors of an otherwise bereft drinks cabinet.

'At least the telly's still in one piece,' I said. Miraculously, this was true.

Denzil the family cat wove stealthily between the battlefield of heads, bodies and feet, and sniffed inquisitively at the groin of a sleeping stranger, laid asunder across Dad's Turkish kilim.

Outside in the garden, a shouting match was going on, getting louder with each enraged exchange. I turned and hobbled to my room as Jane walked wearily into the kitchen to search for extra-strong bin-liners, rubber gloves and thick bleach. The pickled dung-heap of my brain buffeted the inside of my skull, the squidgy mass of useless cerebellum screaming out for a final mercy hit. I went to my room and got it, sleeping off my indulgence until Dad and Jane furiously wrenched me out of bed a few minutes later, turfing my caned and bewildered boyfriend out on to the street along with everyone else.

It took five gruelling days and substantial amounts of cash to get the house back to its former homely state.

It took much longer for Dad and Jane to finally forgive and trust me again.

The night before I left home for the first time, a suffocating spell of insomnia held me frozen in bed, eyes wide and glazed, limbs rigid. Every part of my body was innervated with dread and excitement, while my head spun with a continuous succession of unconnected and mostly irrelevant thoughts. After hours of restless tossing and turning, I looked up to see Jasmine silhouetted in the doorway. She was wearing one of Dad's hideous old shirts, Lewis's tartan slippers and a shower cap.

She murmured something incoherent to herself, and then moved towards me, clutching an old photo album.

'Don't go.' She crouched down slowly by the bed and looked into my eyes. She had been crying. 'Don't leave me, I need you.'

'Can't sleep either?' I mumbled groggily.

'Don't leave me, I need you,' she repeated.

'Oh, Jas . . . I'll still see you practically every weekend.' I turned and propped myself up on my elbow and reached over for the light switch, giddy with fatigue.

She grabbed my arm. 'No, leave the light off. Please.' She held on to my hand for a long time, not saying anything. After a few moments, she whispered, 'Do you realise what it's gonna be like without you here to stop me going mad?'

I looked her up and down with mild amusement. 'You *are* mad Jasmine. That's what makes you so interesting.' It was an unfortunate choice of words, but I had exhaustion as an excuse. I patted her head affectionately, and stroked her hair. It used to be long, very long, right down to her waist, but she cut it all off when she was first taken into care then shaved it off completely a year later. It was now just to her shoulders.

'Don't.' She glared at me then climbed in beside me, an

insecure child rather than a twenty-five-year-old woman. 'Don't take the piss.'

'I wasn't.' I took the photo album from her and opened up the static plastic pages. 'Anyway, it's not like I'm going for ever – and you can come and visit me whenever you like. Remember *you're* the one who finally convinced me I should go.'

She didn't speak for a long time. I put my night-light on to look through the photographs and she just stared at the ceiling, glassy-eyed.

Her mental condition was now somewhat curiously described as 'stable', and the experts who were paid to analyse her claimed she would remain stable for as long as she was taking antipsychotics (to reduce her schizoid symptoms) and methadone (heroin substitute) daily to prevent her from flipping out. Regular assessments confirmed she was well on the way to adjusting herself to a normal way of life and soon she wouldn't need any medication at all. She'd come a long way and it had taken a long time and a lot of pain and tears. Despite her claims to the contrary, I knew she was still over-friendly with Billy and Charlie, drank too much alcohol and smoked far too many roll-ups, but I was hopeful that the worst of it was over, and that it was only a matter of time before she made a full recovery.

As for me – now eighteen and theoretically an adult – I had decided, after gentle persuasion from parents and teachers alike, that I would choose the slightly less unattractive of the two options open to me after my mediocre A-level results. Rather than plumping for a McJob or embarking on any kind of worthwhile career quest, I was going to make that brave step towards quasi-independence and go to university to make my family proud of me. Maybe even to make *myself* proud of me. Up until a few months before, I had assumed that once exams were out of the way my future would just fall into place and all would become crystal clear without me actually having to do anything much to make it happen. I thought in the meantime I could maybe skulk around the house for a while longer, flicking idly through the jobs sections of local papers and circling the odd one or two that paid far more than I was worth, still expecting pocket money from my exasperated father for doing the square root of bugger all, still desperately yearning for things I could never have and not doing anything about it except feeling bitter.

But a pep talk from my form tutor ('You're a bright girl, but where is your motivation?') did get me thinking that maybe I was destined for better things than the dole queue and a lifetime of unfulfilling stopgap jobs. I had more or less resigned myself to that possibility, but then a totally unexpected lecture from Dad and Jane ('We'll be proud of you whatever you decide to do, but you have a good brain and it would be a shame to waste it,') followed by a verbal kick up the arse from Jasmine ('I will miss you, but for fuck's sake get out of this place and *do* something with your life,') finally clinched my decision. I couldn't just expect the way ahead to be mapped out for me for the rest of my life by parents and teachers and other responsible grown-ups; I was accountable for my own life and my own future and I needed to prove I could do it. So off went the UCAS form. Like most uninitiated students, I was under the cheerfully naïve impression that a university course would naturally make my future brighter and simpler, and my prospects so much better.

But of course, leaving home isn't easy when you've been looked after for most of your life and you barely even know how to heat up a can of beans, let alone how much a can of beans actually costs.

And when you have a sister who is needy and vulnerable it makes leaving home even harder. The allegiance between Jasmine and me was strong but her mercurial temperament often meant I could only guess at her true emotions. It's one thing to read all about the mechanics of an illness, the physiology, the whole myriad of symptoms, the possible causes, the strategies of coping, the treatments . . . it's something else entirely to understand and to sympathise when you feel the person you love has just become hostile and, well, *unlovable.* With most people, you are able to make pretty accurate inferences most of the time about how they are feeling, what they are thinking. With Jasmine this was very hard to determine. You just didn't know what was going on with her, even when she was apparently happy, smiling, getting stoned, at ease with herself, sharing a joke at a party. Or when she would rock back and forth with her head in her hands, crying and screaming about the voices that wouldn't go away, about weird, surreal things that seemed to mean so much to her and yet so little to us, the family, watching on uselessly. Sometimes it was just impossible to relate to her. The sad fact was, no matter how much love we gave her, no matter how patient and compassionate we tried to be, Jasmine was essentially alone. That was why leaving home, for me, was more than just a major step towards independence – it was a more important, and fearful, step away from a person I not only cared about deeply but also felt responsible for. Our relationship was a fragile and complex one and I couldn't help feeling apprehensive about how it would change when I left, after so many years of building up a special and irrevocable bond.

'It won't be the same, Abi,' Jasmine finally said, as I flicked through the pictures, charting our odd little family's history through almost three decades – from sepia snaps of Mum and Dad, the doped-out happy hippy couple, Jasmine as a baby, to the more recent ones of the Page family in joyous spirits last Christmas, Dad and Jane at Alton Towers, Jasmine and me in the garden that summer with our ex-neighbour Darren and his wife and new daughter.

Jasmine took off the shower cap and studied the psychedelic anemone design on it, biting her lip to hold back tears. 'It won't be the same,' she repeated, wistfully.

2

Ambient Jasmine

I sloped wearily downstairs the next morning to find Jane preparing a huge breakfast I didn't want, and Lewis sprawled across the lounge carpet with a copy of *Viz*, cackling sporadically and picking his nose.

'Good morning! How are you feeling, sweetie?' Jane beamed at me, slipping a fried egg on to a plate already stacked high with toast, beans, sausages and bacon.

'A bit weird,' I admitted.

'I thought I'd make you breakfast,' she explained, pointing her spatula at the greasy feast. I smiled weakly and sat in front of it, my stomach churning. 'Cheers, Jane. It looks lovely,' I mumbled. Like Jasmine, I had been a vegetarian for some years, but Jane sometimes forgot this. I stared at the fat-drenched rashers with some dismay.

'Tea?'

'Ta.'

I heard Dad whistling *Ode to Joy* in the hall and rustling through the collection of junk mail and bills which had just clattered on to our doormat. 'Jesus *Christ*,' he spluttered as he entered the kitchen, brandishing *The Times*. 'Sorry, love,' he mumbled at an outraged Jane, whose hand spontaneously flew to the silver cross at her throat, 'But you wouldn't *believe* what these people are trying to flog us.' He kissed the top of my head as he passed, and put his arm around Jane as he showed her a brochure full of over-priced, superfluous objects, apparently including a self-warming body muff and a remote controlled garden gnome.

He rambled and ranted for a while then seemed to suddenly remember that today was the day his younger daughter was leaving home. He regarded me over the top of his glasses before swooping forward and taking me in his arms.

'Oh *Abigail* . . . !' he exclaimed, 'I can still remember when you were small and pink and bald. Now look at you!'

'Big and pink and hairy,' I mused humourlessly, keeping myself upright in my chair and trying not to let my true feelings bubble to the surface.

'I can't believe you're leaving,' Jane said.

I nibbled on a slice of toast and shrugged.

'I'm ready,' I bluffed, with extra bravado for good measure.

Dad grabbed Jane around the waist and wailed in a mockingly dramatic voice, 'How are we going to live without our lovely little daughter?' Then he looked over at me with a smile and said, 'Still, we need to set you on the road to independence at some point I suppose.'

Lewis trudged in and started helping himself to my breakfast, after whacking me over the head with *Viz* and grunting his usual morning greeting.

'I think I'll manage just fine without her actually,' he garbled through a mouthful of fried pig.

I made a point of ignoring him. 'I'm only going to university, Dad. And it's hardly the other side of the world, is it?'

'More's the pity,' Lewis scoffed.

'*Lewis*,' Jane scolded ineffectually.

'And it's not like she's going to be independent, for God's sake,' he went on, 'she'll still expect handouts and come crawling back every weekend for food and stuff.'

I glared at him in disdain, suppressing the temptation to thump him. However, he was probably right and this infuriated me. It made me all the more determined to prove him wrong.

'He'll miss you too, really,' Jane said, as if such an utter lie would bring me any scrap of comfort. Lewis squirted tomato ketchup over my toast and eggs and dug in voraciously. I pushed the plate away and watched him with appalled fascination. Jane coughed quietly and stared at the teabags as she stirred them around in the pot. The phone suddenly started ringing, making us all jump, and Jane grabbed the receiver and tinkled a breezy salutation.

'Oh *Sylvie*, how are you, my love?' she chirruped at my oldest friend as if she hadn't seen her for years, when Sylvie had only been around the evening before with a pleasingly naff 'goodbye' present for me: to wit, a packet of 'Penis Pasta'. ('Your staple diet for the next three years!' she had said. I assumed she meant plain pasta.)

Jane handed me the phone and Sylvie's chatty, excited voice came gushing out as soon as I pressed the receiver to my ear. 'A bit of gossip before you leave, mate.'

'Yeah?'

Jane put a cup of tea in front of me and then, sensing I required some privacy, left the room, followed closely by Lewis (dragged by the collar) and Dad.

'I only just found out, Ben told me.'

Ben was Sylvie's boyfriend, an arrogant and pugnacious ex-public schoolboy with more than a passing resemblance to a pitbull, and, as far as I could tell, all the charm to match. For some reason, I was quite interested.

'Um . . . it's to do with Nick,' Sylvie said cautiously.

'Go on,' I urged, my interest rising, just a little.

Nick was my ex, similar to Ben in some ways, but without the ferocious canine features. On the contrary, he was fretfully suave and sexy, in his understated way. He had the kind of debonair wit that could charm any woman into bed, and he was almost two years older than me and quite well off. (When I first met him I was of the age when a boyfriend with a nice car and no spots was an enviable status symbol.) I had been with him for nearly two years and I knew it was love because I always used to read his horoscope before mine. I maybe felt a twinge of something at the mention of his name, but I was well and truly over him.

'Well, *apparently*, Sarah's having his baby.'

The statement, and the blasé way in which it was said, felt like a slap in the face. 'Having his *what*?'

Sarah King (slim, dim, outrageously attractive, lots of money and no scruples) had kindly offered her 'rebound' services to Nick just after he broke it off with me – or rather, she was the reason he broke it off with me in the first place. But I had no bad feelings about the matter; I was not bitter, cut-up and hurt. Not me. I took the receiver away from my ear and blinked at it confusedly. Sylvie babbled into nothingness.

'Abi . . . ? Hello? Are you still there?'

I looked helplessly at the solitary fried egg Lewis had spared and stabbed the yolk with a fork, for want of something more violent to do.

'God, Sylvie. Do you honestly believe I give a toss about either of those two?' I eventually managed to stutter. Minus points for conviction.

'Oh, I'm sorry. I just thought you might like to know. Have you seen him at all? Has he come around to say goodbye to you?'

'Look, I don't care any more. Sarah just took over where I left off. I'm not jealous. She's welcome to him. Bloody tart.'

'But have you *seen* him? I know he wanted to see you before he left, he just felt . . . I dunno, uneasy I suppose. He *does* still care . . .'

'*He's* the one who left *me*. After everything I did for him!' I was getting uptight, and I didn't want to, which made me even more uptight. 'I haven't heard from him since he dropped around to pick up his fucking CDs. That was ages ago, just after exams. The bastard didn't even ask me how I was feeling, it was just hello Abi can I have my CDs back, cheers, see you around. He knew Jasmine was still in hospital and he didn't even ask how she was. And *he's* the one who wanted us to remain friends. Some friend.' It was about five seconds before I added the qualifying, emphatic '*Bastard*!' to round it off.

'Mate. Calm down.' Sylvie's equable voice only made my mood worse.

'Look, I'm *leaving* today you know. I don't *need* this, Sylvie.'

'Well, I'm coming over before you go. I shouldn't have told you, I knew you'd get like this.'

'I'm not *like* anything!' I screeched, brandishing my fork in the air before using it repeatedly to attack the sorry-looking remnants of the fry-up. I watched the yellow yolk bleed into the orange sauce.

'I'm coming over,' Sylvie repeated coolly, before hanging up abruptly.

I replaced the receiver and took a few deep breaths before getting up.

'Just forget about him,' Jasmine said, as I shuffled dejectedly into the lounge. 'It's been months since you two split up, you've got to move on.'

She and Lewis were watching an unrelentingly cheerful Saturday morning TV show – the last thing I was in the mood for.

'Oh by the way,' Jasmine added, with blithe nonchalance, 'he called around last week, when you were down the pub. I forgot to tell you.'

I glared at her. 'What?! Why didn't you . . . how could you . . .' I trailed off and flapped my arms about in useless annoyance.

I knew she had deliberately 'forgotten', because she had hated Nick from the first minute she met him. Instead of the usual pleasantries that are exchanged during introductory meetings, such as 'What's your name?' and 'Where do you live?', she had endeared herself to my new boyfriend with the more probing questions 'What is your *species*?' and '*Why* do you live?' So they hadn't exactly hit it off. Jasmine was a very astute judge of character and, wise after the event, I did come to see her view eventually. But at the time, love-drunk and adolescent to the core, it had caused a rift between us.

'Sorry.' She smirked and proceeded to paint her toenails silverblue.

'Well . . . never mind.' I tried to act casual, like I didn't care. 'Did he say he was going to call round again by any chance?'

She shrugged. 'Dunno. Can't remember.'

'Well, it's a bit late now *anyway*,' I muttered, turning and marching up the stairs.

'You're moving away from this shithole now, so what does it matter?' Jasmine shouted after me.

In my room, I sat on the rumpled bed and looked around at the bare walls pock-marked with blue-tack, the cuddly toys filling my windowsill, the unfinished epic novel gathering dust on my bedside cabinet, the pile of university prospectus books in the corner, the calendar with today's greatly anticipated day highlighted in pink and yellow. The suitcases and bags packed full of my worldly possessions waiting just outside the door. My wardrobe, starkly empty apart from two plastic coat hangers. I suddenly felt overwhelmed by a wave of melancholia, mixed with nausea.

It's time for a change, I told myself. Time to fly the nest; time to find out what life was *really* like.

First, I had to phone Nick.

I raced for the phone and dialled his number in one second flat. It rang four times before the answerphone crackled to life. I listened patiently to Nick's father's polite recorded message and then my mind went completely blank just as the beeps started. Eventually, I managed, 'Hello, it's me. Just phoning to say bye.' Pause. 'Er . . . bye then.' I slammed down the receiver.

And that was it.

I was now responsible for one of the most pitiful answerphone messages ever recorded. I thought about calling again to try to put the situation straight: 'Ha ha! Sorry about that, what I meant to say is have a nice life, won't you Nicholas? Good luck with Sarah and everything, and maybe I'll see you around one day. Congrats about the sprog by the way, it's so good to hear you've decided to reproduce yourself.' My hand hovered over the telephone for a few seconds, then I changed my mind, cursing myself under my breath. I went back into my room and kicked out in frustration at one of my bulging suitcases.

I decided to have one last tour of my lovely, safe family home before leaving. I surveyed my room once again; it looked bereft and sad, stripped of all the things that had made it so uniquely mine. I walked down the dim landing, past Lewis's bedroom door (permanently closed due to his clandestine onanistic and video game habits). His Faith No More poster had been usurped by a full-length bikini shot of a semi-famous American celebrity, blown up and toned down in all the right places, static smile and posture perfectly captured. I moved on quickly and put my head around Jasmine's door to look into her room, which was shockingly bright and tidy. She was sitting at her dressing table, gazing blankly at her reflection in the mirror. 'People are Strange' by the Doors played quietly on her hifi and sunlight streamed in through the window, shimmering copper streaks in her hair.

'Hey,' she said, looking at me in the mirror.

'Hey,' I said back.

She turned in her seat to face me. 'Will you finish my toenails for me? My back's giving me gyp this morning.'

'Sure.' I sat on the end of her bed. 'Have you cleaned your room?'

'No. Just kicked a few things under the bed and opened the curtains.'

'It's looking nice.'

'Yeah. I s'pose.' She got up and handed me the nail polish, lay back on her pillows and put her feet in my lap. She rolled cigarettes and smoked and hummed to the music as I concentrated with the tiny brush. In my bleary-eyed, exhausted state, I managed to clumsily paint most of one of her little toes, but she didn't seem to notice or care.

'I'm just having one last look around before I go,' I said quietly, screwing the lid back into the pot. She moved her feet and waved them in the air to dry the nail polish and said, 'Whatever,' handing me the stub of her roll-up for one last drag. I puffed at it then extinguished it in a wax-congealed candle holder by her bed. 'I'll be moving on myself soon,' Jasmine mumbled, as I headed towards the door.

'Yeah?'

'Yeah. Maybe go and live with some old friends up north, or get a job in Brighton. Could maybe stay with you at your uni digs until I get sorted.'

'That would be nice,' I said, knowing it would probably never happen. I shut the door quietly behind me and Jasmine cranked up her music full volume.

I went down the stairs again, taking each step one at a time, studying the framed pictures on the wall on the way down with renewed fascination. I lingered for a long time over the photograph of Dad and Jane on their wedding day – a serendipitously sunny Saturday in April that still remained fresh in my memory even after twelve years. Jane had wanted Jasmine and me to be bridesmaids, and naturally I was delighted. My tomboy sister had donned the blush pink lace and silk with less enthusiasm, however. She chewed gum and blew bubbles and made faces throughout the ceremony, and refused to be in any of the photographs, much to Dad and Jane's chagrin. However, apart from Jasmine's obstinacy, the day was almost perfect. Jane was radiant and Dad couldn't wipe the euphoric grin from his face the entire day. I was overjoyed with my beautiful fairy-tale dress, my princess tiara, the flowers in my hair, my new shoes with grown-up heels that made an exciting clacking noise, the clusters of brilliant blooms and foliage that filled and fragranced the crowded little church, everything all planned and designed down to the very last detail by my new stepmother.

Dad reached rock-bottom about six months or so after my mum's death – he had already applied for and been rejected from countless jobs, felt useless as a father and desperately lonely as a young widower, and was overcome with shame at being dependent on his parents again. We were living hundreds of miles from London where we had all felt so at home, and although my kind and devoted grandparents adored Jasmine and me, we both felt unsettled – although I to a much lesser extent. I was of course very young and could only passively observe the behaviour and sense the emotions of those around me – it must have affected me on a subliminal level, but I can't remember ever feeling deeply unhappy. I just couldn't quite grasp why sometimes I would find Dad cradling Jasmine in his arms, and the pair of them would be crying their hearts out, for no apparent reason. Or why sometimes my grandparents would be talking in hushed, secretive tones around the kitchen table and then would suddenly brighten up when they saw me and draw me into their arms and call me a 'sweet and precious bairn' when I hadn't even been particularly well-behaved, let alone sweet and precious. Jasmine's stories about our mum fascinated me, but held little relevance in my world of dolls and hair ribbons and Sesame Street. Of course I noticed that other kids had a daddy *and* mummy, but Jasmine told me we were special because our mummy was in Heaven, and would always be with us wherever we went, our Guardian Angel.

Dad retreated into himself, became morose. He clung to Jasmine and me with a fierce and passionate love, feeling inadequate and helpless in everything he did. Sometimes just looking at Jasmine would prompt him to cry, because her looks and mannerisms and ways of saying things reminded him so much of the wife he had adored.

But then Jane walked into his life and things started looking up.

No matter who had come on to the scene to fill the void left by our mum, Jasmine would have felt ambivalent at best, downright hostile at worst. I was won over by Jane from the beginning, much to Jasmine's annoyance. She rather quaintly introduced herself as 'Ms Harris' and told me I had pretty eyes. She gave me a Milky Bar and offered Jasmine the more 'grown-up' gift of a chocolate orange. Jasmine had smiled coolly and said she didn't accept sweets from strangers. We were eventually introduced to Lewis, and my enthusiasm for my dad's girlfriend waned slightly. Our grandparents were overjoyed and enormously relieved by their only son's new happiness. They lectured Jasmine endlessly about accepting Jane into the family, and condemned her selfishness at refusing to make an effort. A truce of sorts was eventually called: Jasmine told Jane she would never replace our mum so she might as well not even try, Jane replied by saying she had no intention of replacing our mum and that she must always cherish her memories but that our dad deserved to be happy and we all had to move on. I remember her words well, and only came to realise some years later just how wise and brave and sincere she was and just how much she must have loved Dad to take on the near-impossible task of making Jasmine accept her. Trying to bring together two broken families to form one big happy unit is no mean feat even in the best of circumstances.

Over the years, we have been through considerably more than the average family, and Jane has remained steadfast throughout. It took a long time, and she would certainly never admit it, but even Jasmine knows that our stepmother has more than proved herself.

I slowly descended the last few stairs and walked into the lounge again, where Lewis was fiddling feverishly with his Gameboy and Dad and Jane watched the TV with increasing bemusement.

'When do you want to set off, love?' Dad asked.

'Soon. Just . . . taking a last look around.'

'OK,' he winked at me jovially, and I felt a surge of emotion well up inside me. I turned away, blinking back tears. Why should I feel so sad and scared and guilty about going away? I was taking the first step towards accepting responsibility for *myself* at last. I wasn't even *properly* leaving home – it was only a matter of time before I got hopelessly homesick and meekly returned to the reassuring bosom of my family, complaining of impending alcoholism, malnutrition and an exhausted overdraft. There was nothing to keep me at home any more, not really. And there was every reason to get out there and make my mark on the big wide world. Or to do a degree in English Literature.

On the doorframe at the entrance to the kitchen, our heights over the years had been recorded in three different colours: Lewis in blue, Jasmine in red, me in green. Each pen line had the date and the exact measurement scrawled next to it. Jasmine only had two entries: one at thirteen years old (153 cm), and another at fourteen (161 cm). After that, I think she must have lost interest in charting her growth pattern. As a child eager to grow at least as tall as her big sister, I had started off measuring myself religiously every week, so there were several messily etched green lines at about the 110 cm mark, with Jasmine's red ink viciously emblazoned over mine, '*Abi is a midget*', '*My sister is a dwarf*'.

My last entry was at age sixteen, level-pegging with Lewis. Out of mild curiosity, I pressed myself up against the doorframe and was genuinely disappointed to find that I hadn't even grown one centimetre since. If anything, I seemed to have shrunk. Lewis had meanwhile overtaken me by a good four inches. I was as tall as Jasmine had been at fourteen years old.

It wasn't until my dad and I had almost finished loading the car that Sylvie turned up, red-faced and windswept. She had Ben with her, who grunted a greeting at me and smoked stoically, looking a bit of a tit in a pair of yellow shades and baggy combats.

'Going already?' Sylvie looked even more flustered than usual, and gripped Ben's arm every so often as if it provided some kind of comfort.

'Looks like it.' I put my hands on my hips and shuffled impatiently, trying not to look vexed.

'How about I make you lot a cuppa before we leave?' my dad offered, slamming the boot and jangling his car keys.

'Yeah, that would be nice, Mr Page, cheers.' Sylvie accepted with her best courteous smile, and Ben shrugged and stamped on his cigarette.

As soon as we went inside and sat down, Sylvie flung her arms around me and made some blubbing noises. Ben shifted uncomfortably in the doorway, exchanging looks of embarrassment with Lewis.

'I'm sorry. It's just . . .' Sylvie reached into her pocket for an extremely old and ineffectual scrap of tissue which she tried to blow her nose on. 'It's just I'm going to miss you *so* much.'

Yeah right, I thought. Since she had been with Ben, I had been demoted from best friend to occasional drinking companion. I was just someone to fill in the little bits of spare time she had when she couldn't be with her darling boyfriend, around whom her world seemed to revolve.

'I'll miss you too,' I said, desperately wanting to mean it as sincerely as I would have meant it just a few months before.

Sylvie buried her face in my shoulder and I patted her back as she sobbed quietly, her phlegm flowing freely on to the absorbent fabric of my hooded jacket. She had been suffering from a particularly tenacious cold for a few weeks, and was obviously having trouble shaking it off.

My dad entered with a tray of steaming mugs and an assortment of biscuits, and Sylvie calmed down remarkably quickly. She stuffed her face with a chocolate chip cookie or two, wiped her nose, and began droning on about the latest gossip, including details about my ex-beloved's imminent sprog. God! It wasn't enough that I was discarded in favour of a vacuous harlot with no buttocks, now the only man I had ever loved had decided to *propagate his genes* with this unfeasibly slim wench.

'Hey, I know you're still a bit cut-up about breaking up with Nick and everything, but . . . just think about all those gorgeous men you'll get to meet at uni!' Sylvie added this as an afterthought, but with such conviction that I actually believed it for a second.

'I know someone who's going to Sussex uni, too . . . or is it Southampton? I'm not really sure. There's so many bloody universities around these days. I *think* it's Sussex. That's the one you're going to, innit?' Ben had suddenly found the motivation to speak, and the dull, monotone sound of his voice barely inspired me to look up, let alone take notice. Undeterred, he continued. 'My mate's . . . brother's, er – girlfriend's . . .' He paused and actually closed his eyes in contemplation, trying to work out what kind of relationship he had to this person, whoever they might be – and as if it would be of any interest to me. In the end he gave up and admitted, 'Well, I don't s'pose I actually *know* them as such, but anyway. Whatever. I've heard it's a pretty good place, and it's near the coast and stuff. Which is . . . like, cool.' He walked over to the French windows and feigned interest in our shabby garden outside, nibbling pensively on a bourbon.

'Well, thanks for that, Ben,' I said, dunking a ginger nut into my tea and wondering why my parents had stocked up on so many biscuits just before I was about to leave home. I decided that I was actually looking forward to leaving after all. Sylvie was a lovely person, and had been my closest friend since primary school, but lately she had been doing my head in and her devotion to this hulking neanderthal had caused many a difference of opinion. And I certainly didn't want to stick around while my ex-boyfriend re-created himself as 'Young Dad of the Year'.

Jasmine breezed into the room, giving a perfunctory nod to our cookie-engorged guests before spreading herself on the floor in front of the muted television set. She spread her medication out in front of her and began her daily pill-swallowing ritual. Ben gave me a startled look and began creeping towards the front door, making jerky head movements at Sylvie, who acknowledged his discomfort with a surreptitious glance and gesture over my shoulder. She took a deep breath before gulping down the last of her tea, then leaned over briskly and said, 'Safe journey, Abi. Stay in touch, won't you?' She gave me a final, brief hug as I garbled something about not being able to afford stamps or payphones. 'See you round, Jasmine,' Sylvie blurted out half-heartedly, not even glancing in her direction. She and Ben scampered to the front door without another word, slamming it behind them and leaving the room vibrating with an ominous silence.

'Hmmm, that was subtle. Was it something I said?' Jasmine pondered aloud.

'Don't worry about it. I think they just find you a bit ... intimidating.'

This was an understatement. Both of them were unequivocally terrified of Jasmine ever since witnessing one of her more tempestuous tantrums at my dad's fiftieth birthday bash the year before.

Jasmine made a disdainful noise. 'What do they know?' She dismissed them with a wave of her hand, swallowing her last pill and a small beaker of green liquid that looked like mouthwash. The dual-purpose medication she had been prescribed was to wean her off heroin and control her extreme mood swings. Most of the time it worked. The truth was, all my friends thought she was weird and even many of Jasmine's closest friends had deserted her, one by one, over the years. Her remaining friends, what was left of them, nearly all suffered from some personal affliction or other, whether it be homelessness, AIDS, drug addiction or familial or social rejection. Jasmine said she liked to surround herself with people who made her feel fortunate and humble. She told me her problems faded into insignificance in comparison. 'Sometimes you have to gain some kind of perspective in order to feel thankful for what you have got,' she once said to me. 'Gratitude and humility are two of the most underrated virtues in the world.'

Behind her hardened façade, she was the most caring and compassionate person I knew. Although she never had much money (all her habits were very expensive and she couldn't hold down a job for very long), she supported a number of animal charities and did regular voluntary work. She was disillusioned with the world, and her childish idealism was her way of responding to what she felt was 'an upside-down and sick society'. She never gave up on something once she'd started it, and she never compromised her beliefs.

And she never walked by a homeless person without sitting down next to them for a chat and a cigarette. I remember we went window-shopping in Oxford Street one freezing and wet December afternoon and saw a man huddled in a doorway, wrapped in a filthy sleeping bag and Salvation Army blanket. His beard was grey with dirt and age, and he was holding a scrap of cardboard that simply said 'Laid off, Pissed off'. Jasmine was immediately smitten. Ignoring the haughty antipathy displayed by most of the passers-by who all had safe, warm homes to go back to, and caring not a whit that the old man hadn't seen a bar of soap in quite some time, she bundled under his sleeping bag with him and they chatted spiritedly as if they were old friends. She gave him a fag, and he offered her a swig of his Diamond White, which she politely declined. Meanwhile I was left to lurk on the street corner, not knowing whether to feel embarrassed or proud. It took one derisory comment from a woman with an unsmiling facelift, conspicuous clanging jewellery and a genuine fox-fur coat to make me realise I should feel very, very proud. And from that moment on, I *was* proud of my sister; deeply in awe of her. It helped me see past the bad spells, the times when Jasmine slid into dark moods, the times when she would talk to me or aloud to herself about bizarre and meaningless things, theories and nonsense, when she became a stranger even to herself. But others weren't convinced of Jasmine's good nature. All the nurses and specialists and various mental health experts who tried to help Jasmine over the years had invariably reminded her: 'You are so lucky to have a family who support and love you, why can't you just stop hurting them?'

And they were right, and they were wrong.

The label *paranoid schizophrenic* seemed so negative and so final and powerful. And by paranoid, we're not talking 'Do I look fat in this dress?' It refers to something deeper, darker and much more sinister than I can ever truly understand. 'Schizophrenic' is such a stigmatised word; it has so much misconception and misunderstanding tied to it. It doesn't mean 'schizoid' and 'frenetic', because everyone displays schizoid and frenetic behaviour regularly without even realising it. It doesn't mean ambivalent or having two personalities because there are very few people who can honestly claim to possess clarity in all their everyday thoughts, and behave the same way in every situation. All individuals have different personas, but the mentally 'normal' have a certain degree of control over their thoughts, feelings and actions. In schizophrenia these are disconnected and disorganised to the extent that it often feels as if the mind or the whole body has been taken over and thoughts are transferred, played with or 'taken out' by an external, uncontrollable force. This, apparently, is the difference between the sane and the insane. Or one of many possible differences.

'I need a fix,' Jasmine sighed, stretching out on the sofa and exposing her midriff. 'This shit just zombifies me.'

'Jas, you know if you touch that stuff again you'll be carted off back to Rayneham before you can blink.'

'I know, I know.' She pressed her fingers to her temples and screwed her eyes shut tight, rocking herself back and forth. 'But you're leaving now, and it's crap around here anyway. It doesn't matter any more. I feel like shit all the time.'

Rayneham was the clinic (rehabilitation centre, mental home) where Jasmine had spent many months, on and off, for the last six years. I hated visiting her there; the other in-patients were vegetables or violent drug-users or maladjusted delinquents or severe autistics or demented psychos or children trapped inside adult bodies, all of them put under the same one-size-fits-all category as my sister – MAD, loopy, loco, barmy, gaga, insane, tonto, unhinged, barking, unbalanced, crazy. But Jasmine, in contrast to many of the others, was bright, pretty and full of life – at least when she hadn't been drugged up, or drugged down. She never shat the bed or had Napoleonic delusions or danced down the corridor to imaginary music; if indeed any of those behaviours are indicative of insanity, then Jasmine was of sound mind. Rayneham was so soullessly bleak: the brisk, faux-friendly staff who bustled around in their condescending droves; in-patients' paintings tacked patronisingly to the walls like a playschool; the dull, faded furniture in characterless rooms off long, intimidating hallways lit by fluorescent bulbs; the heavy and pervasive feeling of monotony, of routine gone mad. It was *One Flew Over the Cuckoo's Nest*, a modernised and sanitised and acclimatised set; every attempt had been made to make the mad feel at home but there was all of nothing to ease the suffering.

'Abi . . . promise me something,' Jasmine whispered, holding her arms out to me, her eyes brimming with tears. Taken aback, I returned her embrace. 'Promise me that you'll never do anything stupid. And don't let yourself get pushed around. Never forget all the things I've told you. I know that I'm a useless fuck-up but you can do things right where I went wrong.'

I pulled away and held her by the shoulders. She bowed her head and her hair fell forward. I pushed it back over her shoulder, and said, 'Don't talk like that. Don't be like this, Jas.'

She glanced up and a single tear ran down her cheek to the corner of her mouth.

'And I'm not promising you anything until you promise me *you* won't do anything stupid when I'm away. And you *know* what I mean,' I warned, clutching her wrist and turning her arm to display the faint silvery marks and bruises which dappled and dimpled the pallid skin around her blue veins, the enduring scars of the past.

'I don't want you to be ashamed of me . . .'

'*Promise* me.'

'I'll try. I promise.'

That was as good as I was going to get. There was little more to be said. We held each other for a few moments, and I inhaled her aroma, savouring it: she sometimes wore jasmine perfume, or patchouli, and there was always a suggestion of tobacco and marijuana, and the faintly musty smell of her clothes. It's weird how sometimes smells can conjure up the most vivid memories, sometimes even more powerful and real than those recalled by photos and letters and songs.

Five minutes later she was watching forlornly from the window as I got in the car with Dad. I forced a smile as the engine revved noisily, waving madly at Jane and proffering a slightly less congenial hand gesture to Lewis. I didn't cry.

3

Living it Up

Madness is something rare in individuals – but in groups, parties, peoples, ages it is the rule.

Friedrich Nietzsche, *Beyond Good and Evil*

The university was bigger, more daunting than I remembered: red-brick, modern architecture set in a backdrop of tranquil greenery abundantly peopled with a cosmopolitan mix of new and old students. I was unable to take in very much detail at first as my mind was elsewhere for the whole journey. A mind-bending succession of *what-ifs* raced through my mind at rapid speed. I drove there myself – somewhat less speedily – in our crappy D-reg Metro while Dad slumped drowsily in the passenger seat. Due to a variety of medical contraindications, he wasn't supposed to drive, but his medication (another pill-popping Page) kept him relatively alert. At least, as alert as is possible for a man as dopey and docile as my father. So he often insisted that he would be fine to drive himself, as long as he kept the radio on full volume and a flask of coffee by his side.

I parked the car in a wide, freshly tarred car park outside an old-looking building where a swarm of new students and their emotional parents were congregated in a valedictory ceremony.

We sat in silence for a few seconds before Dad turned to me, his bovine features set in an uncharacteristically grave expression.

'This is it,' he said, his tone suggesting that I was about to face execution, rather than three years at a very pleasant educational institution.

I took a deep breath and mumbled, 'Yes, I suppose it is.'

I took off my seatbelt and was about to open the door when he grabbed my arm, suddenly, almost alarmingly, and gripped it tight. 'I'm so scared about Jasmine,' he said, the words tumbling out as if he'd wanted to say them for some time. 'I just . . . don't . . . know . . . how things are going to be now you've left home.' I was unnerved to see a look of genuine panic in his eyes. He dropped his hands into his lap.

'Dad –'

'She's so much like your mother was. So impulsive. Your mum was only a year older than Jasmine when she –'

'Dad –'

'Please try to understand. I feel so . . . responsible. Like all this is my fault, like I should have *done* something, you know?' He leaned back against the headrest and there was another long silence. Eventually, he uttered the words I'd been dreading, his voice breaking with emotion half-way through. 'I don't know how much longer I can cope, Abigail. She's been over the edge so many times. She nearly died earlier this year. I love her so much and I feel so bloody . . . so bloody *helpless*.'

He hunched forward and I put my arm around his shaking shoulders as he wept on to the dashboard.

'You know how strong she is, Dad. She hasn't taken heroin or anything for months now, and the antipsychotics help make her . . . well, normal.' I winced at the word because it was so inappropriate, and so completely devoid of meaning as far as I was concerned. 'I mean,' I struggled to correct myself, fishing around in the glove compartment for tissues, 'she's held it together. She's overcome the worst of it. Things will only get better from now on.'

I stressed the words but I wasn't sure if I truly believed in them. Dad glanced over at me, his eyes puffy and tired.

'You really think so?'

I smiled and shrugged. 'They can *only* get better,' I mumbled, feebly.

'But it's the *methadone*,' he sobbed, 'and she's so unpredictable. I want her to be free of it all, I hate to see her like this. I hate the *not knowing*. I don't want her to be "stable", I want her to be happy and healthy, and to love life. Is that really too much to want for your daughter? For her to settle down, to be a normal twenty-five-year-old with aspirations and ambitions? It's just always *there* though, in the background. I want to be able to wake up in the morning and not have to dread the possibility of my daughter slipping away from me. Again and again. Over and over.' He gasped for breath as he clung to my shoulders, and I too felt hot tears spring to my eyes. For the first and last time that strange day, I allowed myself to cry out loud – not just for Jasmine, but for selfish reasons as well. I felt lonely, scared and bewildered, and wasn't sure I was ready to take on the heavy role of irresponsible student; not when I knew I had to try to keep so mature and sensible about much more important things.

We got through a pack of Handy Andies before we felt adequately composed and comforted, and then decided it was time to check out my assigned on-campus accommodation. Dad went from doleful and despairing to proud and sentimental as we were issued with my room key and struggled, laden with luggage, towards a block of student bedsits which would be my home for the next three terms. The narrow ground-floor corridor consisted of eleven identical, spartan rooms with a communal bathroom at the far end and a communal kitchen at the near end. My room was next door but one to the bathroom, and consisted of: an eight by eight space (barely roomy enough to swing a stunted rodent, let alone any kind of feline), with a child-sized bed spread with stiff, tightly-tucked sheets and grey and pale blue blankets which looked itchy. There was a tiny, skewed desk with a dusty lamp, a hand basin with a grimy mirror cabinet above it, a small and obviously ancient wardrobe with the handles hanging off, a coarse beige carpet dotted with burn-marks, and magnolia walls tinged nicotine brown. A curtain made from horrible thick orange material hung over the grubby sash window. The room smelt of teabags and mildew and second-hand shops.

'Aaaah . . . ! Perfect!' Dad appraised, dropping my bag to the floor and gazing around. He flicked a switch on the wall and the naked bulb bleached the bleak scene in urine-yellow light. I regarded the room with a lesser degree of rapture, still clinging on to my suitcase and seriously considering my escape plan already. We were offered cups of tea by a bumptious 'residential adviser' called Sue ('I'm here to make sure everyone lives in harmony and nothing illegal goes on,' she assured Dad, winking at me over his shoulder as if to say *Don't worry, little girl, I'll overlook the occasional midnight feast, so long as you save me a couple of sherbet dips*). After each being presented with weak teas in chipped, dirty cups, Dad and I sat on the knackered mattress in silence for a while, lost in our own thoughts. We eventually said our farewells, heavy-hearted but dry-eyed, and as I watched my father trudge back up the corridor, wave at me one last time before turning and disappearing out of the main entrance, the finality of the situation struck me. I was surrounded by, living with, ten people I had never met before. I was a hundred miles from home, but it may as well have been a thousand. I was, officially, a full-time, tax-pissing student of English Literature, and I was *way* out of my depth.

I spent the first twenty hours of student life confined to my new, strange room, enhancing my seclusion with the merry melodies of Joy Division and The Jesus and Mary Chain; poor, scratchy copies of Jasmine's albums. My dad's words stayed with me all night, and after listening to fellow hallmates I hadn't yet met chattering outside my door until the small hours, making friends and being human, I finally fell into a fitful slumber in a tiny bed that had obviously been designed for masochists.

Several hours later, I awoke to the sound of someone – or something – doing cow impressions and galloping up and down the corridor outside.

'Marbles, you're a cock-sucking piece of scum,' said a male voice, affecting a feeble South American accent.

Marbles? People were on crass nickname terms with each other *already*?

'Yeah well kiss my round, rosy ass, you son of a homo,' was the equally perplexing retort. The voice then moo-ed again and a pair of feet cantered heavily up the corridor, stopping just outside my door to ask, 'Does anyone live here?'

The voice seemed so loud it felt as if he – Marbles – whoever the hell it was – was standing right next to my bed. I froze. I suddenly felt panicky, shy, nervy. My heart soared into a frenzied, quick-beat rhythm, thumping in my ears. I turned my head to look at my radio alarm: nine-fifty. *Oh, God, what am I supposed to do*? I thought. Should I be up, bustling around, introducing myself, getting to know everyone, socialising furiously and putting on my best 'please-like-me' demeanour? I stuffed my head under the flat, synthetic pillow and breathed in the starchy smell of the cotton sheets. No, I will stay in bed and continue with my quest to be the world's most miserable student. I put my hand on my chest and tried to calm down my madly pumping heart with a few deep sighs, controlling what was rapidly turning into a mild panic attack. 'Marbles' knocked tentatively on my door and called, 'Helloooo-ooo . . . is there anyone in there?' He knocked again, louder, and barked, 'Answer me, goddamn you!'

Things suddenly felt surreal, awful: where was I? What the hell was I doing there, surrounded by farmyard animal-impersonating buffoons with stupid names, lying in a tiny cramped bed in a tiny grey room, feeling utterly pathetic? I hardly dared breathe until I was sure 'Marbles' had given up and sidled back down towards his own room. 'Hmmm . . . No one there . . .' I heard his voice drift off into the distance, '. . . or else it's someone very sad who doesn't want to talk to me.'

'Can't think why that would be,' said a sarcastic female voice with a heavy northern accent, and then a gaggle of female voices whispered and laughed further off down the hall.

I reached the conclusion that I could no longer put off the crucial preliminary introductions, which were likely to run along the lines of, 'Well, we're all in the same boat so let's exchange boring details about our lives to establish just how little we have in common.' So I ventured out of bed, hunched myself into my oversized dressing gown and, well aware that I didn't look my best first thing in the morning, threw a towel over my head and crept timidly towards the bathroom. This boasted the same class of luxury fixtures and fittings as my bedroom. It was basically a plain white-tiled room with three separate shower and toilet cubicles in private partitions and a once-white matchbox-sized bathtub with rusty taps behind a door with a busted lock.

Three minutes after my shower, back in my room, my cynicism proved unfounded. A gentle knock at the door was followed by an unfamiliar female voice. 'Hello? I don't think I met you last night . . . can I come in?'

I stared at the back of the door, then down at my dripping, naked body. I started rubbing myself down vigorously and yelled out, 'Just a minute!'

I blundered hurriedly into the clothes I had worn the day before and flung the door open with exaggerated exuberance, smiling broadly. A strikingly pretty, slender girl with perfect olive skin and bright green eyes smiled back at me with an air of self-assurance that was neither overbearing nor arrogant. I waited mutely for her to introduce herself.

'Er . . . hi. My name is Nadine,' she said. 'I'm in the room at the end. I arrived yesterday, just before you, but you didn't look like you were quite ready to . . .' she leaned across and tucked in the label of my creased T-shirt, '. . . join in with the inane chit-chat.' She walked in and sat on my crumpled bed.

'Great little rooms they've given us, innit?' she said, looking around at the glaring lack of decor. I was about to respond, but she continued talking. 'Well, I'm sorry we didn't meet last night; I just reckoned you needed some time to yourself. Hope you weren't feeling too lonely or anything.'

'Sorry,' I mumbled, 'I had a bit of a bad night. Feeling a bit . . .'

'Homesick?' It was more of a definite sentence-finishing than an enquiry. 'I think we'll all feel a bit weird for a while, but –'

I had a dreadful feeling she was going to use the expression 'we're all in the same boat', but she didn't. Instead she just gazed at me enquiringly until I came to my senses.

'Oh, God, sorry. Abigail. Abi.' I held out my hand and she pumped it vigorously, grinning broadly.

'All right, Abi. You're a Buzzcocks fan, I see.' She eyed my old T-shirt – or rather Jasmine's old T-shirt which I had inherited – with a look that could have been amusement or sympathy. I shrugged and folded my arms across my chest defensively.

'Nah, they're all right, I'm not takin' the piss,' she assured me. She then started chatting garrulously about her first impressions of everybody else on our hall, all nine of them. I had no recollection of seeing or hearing her arrive, or any of the others for that matter, but then the events of the day before still seemed hazy and unreal. I started combing my damp hair and was only mildly taken aback when she brightly offered to do it for me. I handed her the comb and sat beside her, having known her for one minute, and she fussed around my hair like Jane used to, claiming it was 'lovely and thick', in 'such good condition', in between telling me further details about our hallmates. I learned that Marbles was 'actually called – get this – *Maurice Venables*', and that, contrary to the cow impressions, he was actually pretty intelligent.

'Well, he must be, he's doing some weird shit course like molecular science or something.'

Nadine began plaiting my hair, and I figured she had a lot of hair-braiding experience, as her own hair was the longest I had ever seen, right down past her backside.

'Don't know why he calls himself Marbles, though,' she said, anticipating my question. 'Must be some weird kind of anagram, I s'pose. Got a scrunchie?'

'What? Oh . . . here you go.' I handed her a threadbare old ponytail band and she tied up my hair briskly before turning me around to look at me face on.

'There you go. Gorgeous.'

'Cheers,' I smiled, patting the back of my head and trying to remember the last time my hair had ever felt so well groomed. Usually I would have been annoyed or at least a little edgy about someone I didn't know suddenly bursting in and handling my hair, but strangely, thankfully, I felt at ease.

Nadine tucked her feet underneath her and chatted away. 'Obviously, I haven't met absolutely everyone in this block yet, but there's plenty of time for all that. We'll probably chuck a mega party soon so we can all get acquainted with each other, *nudge nudge wink wink*.' She bounced excitedly on the squeaking mattress and poked me playfully in the ribs.

'Anyway,' she went on, 'the boys on this hall seem OK, I think. Bit wanky, but that's what you come to expect, I suppose. Not sure that any of them rock my boat, to be honest. Hey, I tell you what,' she took out a packet of fags and offered me one which I declined out of politeness even though my body was screaming for one, 'why don't you finish getting yourself sorted out, then come down the hall and find me in the kitchen. I haven't had breakfast yet and I'm starving.' As if to confirm this, her stomach made a low growling noise and she let out a little laugh. 'Better make it a full English,' she giggled.

I watched her light up and take short little puffs from the cigarette, blowing out thin streams of smoke and tapping the ash heedlessly on to the floor. 'Anyway,' she said, 'I'll introduce you to everyone and we can all head down to the beach. It's not that far. All right with you?'

I looked at her in awe. She was acting like she'd just downed half a dozen Es with a gallon of Lucozade. I'd never seen anyone with so much energy and social buzz; it was like she was bursting at the seams with excitement. Maybe it was just her way of controlling her nervousness, she must surely have been feeling just as unsettled as I was.

'Why not?' I smiled at her again, relieved that there was at least one possible friend within the vicinity, but also mildly disconcerted by her enthusiasm and over-familiarity. 'Give me five minutes.'

'OK, I'll see you in a bit then.' She got up and, like a bat out of hell, she flapped out of the door. I heard her footsteps tramp down to the kitchen where she shortly demanded 'Who the fuck has opened my Rice Krispies?', then I pushed the door shut with my foot and stared at the wall for a few seconds, still trying to take in my new surroundings.

When I bravely ventured a look in the mirror I discovered to my horror that, apart from my well-groomed hair, I looked like an extra out of *Night of the Living Dead.* I practised my smile for a few seconds, slapped some make-up on and then, in a sudden fit of neurosis, emptied out my (still unpacked) suitcase on to the bed, reminding myself over and over how important first impressions are. I stripped off once again and searched the jumble for something decent to wear. In the end I decided on a pair of patchwork flares (another of Jasmine's hand-me-downs), a plain black top and a pink knitted cardigan, which I tied around my waist to hide my spare tyre. Finally, I shoved my feet into a pair of old Adidas pumps, brushed my teeth quickly and far too vigorously, subjected myself to one last look in the mirror, sprayed myself liberally with deodorant and perfume, grabbed my purse and ventured out into the corridor. I was ready at last to meet my hallmates, those with whom I was to share breathing space and toilet seats for the next year.

Over the course of that bizarre first Sunday, my fitting-in process went as well as I could have hoped, all things considered. The eleven of us initially introduced ourselves in a rather guarded and self-conscious fashion, all false smiles and hand gestures, not wanting to give too much away but not wanting to appear stand-offish. After some prolonged, stifled silences, we all went to a bar on the seafront called Gemini or Aquarius or something, and loosened up with the aid of alcohol and amusing anecdotes.

Nadine, as if I hadn't guessed already, was the feisty, indefatigable one who appeared to love everybody at first, seemingly without question. She was the kind of girl you'd expect to see in a particularly improbable Tampax ad, scooting skittishly down the road on rollerblades with the wind in her hair and a broad grin on her face: the antithesis of menstruating women everywhere. Alex Cheadle, self-appointed loyal sidekick of the already infamous Marbles, was unfortunately as good-looking as he was belligerent and racist. But he was soon put in his place when his deeply offensive joke about Indian girls and hygiene cast an uncomfortable silence over the group, causing even Marbles, the only one who laughed out loud, to blush and shut up. This was due to Nadine's well-timed announcement that she was half-Indian and her subsequent suggestion that Alex should go and stick his acne-deformed head up his well-sodomised arse. I decided, after my vague initial reservations, that I really liked

Nadine and the more I got to know her, the more I warmed to her.

Also among our happy throng there was a slightly strange 'eighties throwback' Morrissey clone called, strangely enough, 'Garston Trent Kearney'. He claimed to be stuck in the eighties ('I'm telling you, everything was cool about the eighties, from the fashion and the hairstyles to the music and the movies'), but was neither amused nor interested when I informed him that I lived near a crap little town called Garston. He was even less amused when I offered my definitive two-word counter-argument to his tenuous 'cool eighties' theory: 'Bucks Fizz'. He merely tugged at the flamboyant sleeve of his 'New Romantic' overshirt and scowled at me from beneath his quiffed hair. I think I managed to ingratiate myself however, when I pointed at his Gene Loves Jezebel T-shirt and uttered an exclamation of approval, albeit a half-hearted one.

The other girls were called Rachel, Juliet and Catherine, and they seemed pleasant enough – even though their conversations, littered with nervous and insincere giggling, focused mainly on fashion and facial cleansers and the cast of *Friends*. Juliet and Catherine looked like they had just stepped off a catwalk, all glossy hair and pearl-white teeth and peachy complexions and nail polish, with sit-up-and-beg physiques accentuated by blatantly expensive, figure-hugging clothes.

It emerged before too long that Rachel (blonde, slightly boyish-looking, very skinny, longish hair in a ponytail) was involved in a long-term full-on relationship with another of the boys, who was called Simon (blond, slightly girlish-looking, very skinny, longish hair in a ponytail). At first, both of them seemed absorbed almost entirely in themselves and each other and didn't really pay much attention to anyone else. It didn't take me long to realise that Rachel and Simon were the most unashamedly disgusting couple I had ever met. They were both wearing Smashing Pumpkins sweatshirts and matching his 'n' hers Nike Air trainers. They were both from Leeds and had met at primary school over ten years before. Having been more or less inseparable ever since, they had optimistically applied for the same course at the same university, living in the same halls of residence. Fortuitously – for them at least – they achieved all these goals in landing their places at Sussex. They were both enrolled on a Politics course and had been allocated rooms next to each other. Just as well, because they had vowed that if they couldn't stay together, they would have 'sacrificed' a degree altogether and instead bought a house in Newcastle and procreated copiously. I learned all this from a gushy, pie-eyed Rachel, who proudly and without irony showed me a miniature picture of herself and her beloved which she kept in a gold pendant on a chain around her neck. I just smiled and nodded politely whenever there was a gap in our one-sided conversation while she paused for breath. 'We were so lucky to get on this course and stay together. It means we'll never be apart!' she enthused besottedly to anyone who was listening, which was apparently just me. 'I mean, we just can't stand being away from each other. I know it sounds corny and everything, but we were made for each other.'

'Yes. I can see that,' I smiled back at her, feeling my stomach do an unpleasant lurch as she leaned over and kissed the back of Simon's neck, then he turned around and bundled on top of her, murmuring a series of pet names as they entwined their gangly limbs; a pair of craneflies mating. I wondered to myself: *Is this what true love is supposed to do to you?* I was not tolerant of lovey-dovey couples at the best of times but, still reeling from the news about Nick, the sight of Simon and Rachel made me feel positively homicidal.

There were two other blokes but they didn't have much to say, and frankly I couldn't really blame them for disappearing shortly after the formal first introductions. Yoshi (his real first name was unpronounceable, so he offered us this punchy alternative) was an intellectual computer-whizz from Japan, and was very meek and diminutive. I felt rather sorry for him, as it was clear from the outset that he didn't seem to have a single thing in common with any of the rest of us – for a start, he was intent on studying and actively avoiding nights of drug-fuelled debauchery. Although, credit to Nadine, she did try to bring him out of his shell by talking about her recent escapades around Japan with her sister during her year out. She even tried to strike up a conversation in Japanese, which impressed everyone except Yoshi, who made a few monosyllabic responses then some courteous excuses before leaving.

And then there was Murphy – who refused to disclose his first name – and he was the obligatory 'Really Freaking Weird One'. He was a bedraggled, deeply pensive and woebegone Goth (as if there were any other type), who decided after an hour or so that idle banter with an assortment of increasingly pissed strangers was substantially less enthralling than spending the rest of the evening in quiet contemplation with the Sisters of Mercy and Edgar Allan Poe. Upon his departure, Alex and Marbles exchanged looks of bafflement.

'What's with that miserable fucker?' Alex asked, with the typical tact and diplomacy we would all come to associate him with.

'He's a Goth,' Garston explained.

'That's no reason to be devoid of a personality,' said Marbles.

'That's the whole point of being a Goth. I should know. I've been there,' Garston confessed.

Marbles and Alex looked blank and said, 'Oh. Right,' in near-perfect unison.

We finally swayed out on to the beach, kicking our shoes off and daring each other to a skinny dip, and I was quite fuzzily happy and much more at ease by this time. Collapsing out on to the shingle shore, we continued our merry exchanges until evening fell around us. I got the impression that Garston fancied me, despite my earlier faux pas, and, more disturbingly, that Nadine was interested in Alex, whose unremitting breed of 'foot-in-mouth' disease had continued to offend just about all of us in turn. Conversely, Marbles and Alex had both reached the conclusion that Juliet and Catherine were 'professional lesbian cock-teasers', a label applied without hesitation when their crass chat-up lines fell flat. (They opted for the dual-attack approach, with Marbles trying the 'You know, if I were you, I'd have sex with me' line, and Alex firing on all cylinders with 'There's a quiet spot just over there where you could suck me off and nobody would notice.' Juliet and Catherine giggled and minced and pouted and flicked hair but ultimately disappointed the boys' valiant efforts.)

After checking out a couple more pubs, we ventured back to campus. The students' union, such as it was, appeared to have little real excitement to offer – but that didn't matter because the nightlife of Brighton was 'second only to London', according to self-proclaimed 'proud Southerner' Marbles. ('Especially if you're gay,' he had added, much to the disgust of Alex, whose idea of Utopia apparently consisted solely of white thoroughbred heterosexuals.)

I felt lucky, all things considered. My hallmates were an eclectic mix, and generally at least tolerable; as long as the Couple from Hell stayed out of my face as much as possible and Alex rationed himself to just one or two derisive and ignorant remarks per day. The scary thing was that while I was judging all of them, they were presumably judging me, and I really wasn't sure of the kind of impression I had made. I started off trying to make myself conscious of every nuance of my body language and speech, frantically monitoring my responses to questions and running to the toilets every ten minutes to check in the mirror that I hadn't transmogrified into something hideous. But of course this became exhausting before long, and in the end I just kept on drinking, getting more and more relaxed until I ended up not giving a toss. And, as Sunday night turned into Monday morning, I couldn't even remember what I had been so nervous about.

Back at our digs, we gathered around the kitchen table and discussed such erudite topics as the potential shaggability of our tutors, and whether we would sleep with them to get good marks, even if they were old and ugly.

'Student life begins here, guys,' announced Marbles, with the pretentious air of some kind of an intrepid adventurer, opening the fridge to reveal at least two dozen cans of lager. 'Let's live it to the max.'

'I'll drink to that,' droned Simon, opening a pack of 'Death' cigarettes and offering them around, as Rachel disappeared under the table, tanked up to the eyeballs.

Turning up for your first lecture with a hangover is not a good idea, especially when you are disorientated and vulnerable, and easy prey for rapacious second years. Nine-thirtyish Monday morning, head thumping, I found myself in a huge, badly lit theatre hall, squashed between a colossal black girl and a surly-looking bearded bloke with B.O. I was there for almost an hour before realising that the lecturer up at the front (shaggability rating nil) seemed to be warbling on about electromagnetic fields and chemical formulae and not 'Introduction to Medieval Literature'. Rather than make a quiet exit, I fell asleep until a waft of beardy bloke's armpits roused me hours, possibly minutes later. He was absorbed in scrawling some bizarre kind of complicated diagram on the spiral jotter pad in front of him. I tried moving as far away from him as was possible in the narrow wooden seat, but this meant edging towards the equally perturbing character on my right.

'Hey, I was about to wake you, girlfriend. You're missing all the interesting bits,' she whispered.

'Oh yeah, I'm in the wrong lecture,' I told her, by way of explanation.

Girlfriend?

'Oh well . . . never mind. Gives you an opportunity to sleep off your hangover, eh?' She grinned at me, revealing a formidable set of gnashers like a piano keyboard.

'Yeah,' I sighed, placing my head back on to my outstretched arms on the desk in front of me and closing my eyes. I couldn't be bothered to move, although if I hadn't felt so ill and lethargic, beardy bloke's armpits would have been impetus enough. I tried breathing through my mouth. 'What's this, then?' I mumbled at the girl, who was listening with one ear to a bland rap band on her personal stereo. 'Physics or something?'

She laughed. 'You a first year?'

'Isn't it obvious? Haven't I got "mock me" written all over my forehead?'

She leaned over close and whispered close to my ear. 'We're all first years in here. This is a "Welcome to University Life" introductory lecture. Some fucked-up boring idea of an initiation ceremony or something. You ain't missed much. You know, "Thanks for choosing Sussex, I'm sure you'll all be happy here, please make sure to study well and eat your greens and pass your exams and no sex or drugs in the interim if you can possibly avoid it thank you so much." That bloke down there with the flannels and the dodgy cardi and the silly specs is the wotsit bloke. Manager, or Assistant Chancellor, or something. He's just been explaining about how lucky we all are to be so near the wonderful Brighton coast, lovely fields, South Downs and trees and countryside and all, blah blah. Now –' she nodded towards the verbose man in the middle of the room and raised her pencilled-in eyebrows, 'now he's talking about financial constraints and budgeting. And academic excellence. Hey, did you know Neil from *The Young Ones* came here?'

'That's news to me,' I admitted.

So I was in the right place after all. Not that it really mattered. I looked around for Nadine, or any of the few others I knew, but my vision was still blurred and the room was absolutely bursting with first-year intake. I decided, after a moment's split-second contemplation, to return to my slumber.

'My name's Claire,' the girl informed me.

I was fast losing consciousness. 'Wake me up when it's over please, Claire.'

I was wrong about Garston; he wasn't interested in me. I was waiting by the payphone on Monday night (Dad had promised to call at exactly eight o'clock, it was ten past and I was beginning to get agitated), and Garston swept past me with an outlandishly statuesque, elegant brunette. Her clothes were stylish and perfectly fitted, and her perfume had been applied with such gay abandon it made my eyes water. She had not so much sprayed it as marinated herself in it. The pair of them together looked like wannabe supermodel meets Spandau Ballet reject.

'Oh, Abi, this is my girlfriend . . .' Garston called down the hall to me as he began unlocking his door. She shot him a withering look and placed a hand on her bony hip. 'Er . . . sorry, my *fiancée*, Samantha. Er – Sam, that's Abi.' He waved his hand about, apparently thinking that this constituted a formal introduction. The *fiancée* surveyed me with an unsettling arrogance that was wholly unwarranted, and when she was finally satisfied that I was not quite as aesthetically blessed or nearly as well dressed or fragrant as she was, she managed a nod of acknowledgement, a curtain of sleek auburn hair falling over her don't-smile-or-it-will-crack face.

'Pleased to meet you, Samantha,' I said, putting on my full-beam smile and wondering why Garston had neglected to mention this very significant other in his life the night before.

'She's come to stay for a couple of days. So make sure that we're not . . . er . . . you know, disturbed.'

Too late for that mate, you're already *well* disturbed.

'Sure,' I said. I watched them disappear into Garston's room and continued to linger by the phone, willing it to ring.

Dad did eventually call but it was a surprisingly brief conversation because Jasmine was out with a new 'friend', Jane was losing her voice due to a throat infection and Dad always hated talking into phones for longer than was absolutely necessary. I shuffled into the kitchen afterwards and dutifully informed everyone that Duran Duran's greatest fan was 'otherwise engaged' with a 'willowy fashion victim' for the foreseeable future, and was not to be disturbed under any circumstances. Nobody seemed to care very much, unsurprisingly.

Except Marbles. 'Lucky bastard!' was his exclamation. 'The sly old hound!'

Alex nodded in agreement, Simon and Rachel shrugged and fed each other toast cut up into soldiers, Nadine dug a plastic fork despondently into a Pot Noodle, Yoshi buried his head in a turgid economics book, and Catherine and Juliet adjusted their micro mini skirts and breezed off in a waft of eau de toilette on a determined mission to pull. *Fait accompli*, I mused grimly as Marbles and Alex followed in hot pursuit, salivating lasciviously. Minutes later, as Frankie Goes to Hollywood blared suggestively from Garston's bedroom, Nadine and I decided that the prospect of instant inebriation down at one of the union bars was an altogether more appealing option than sitting around a table watching Rachel and Simon dribble over each other and Japanese banker boy get excited about the exchange rate mechanism.

'God, I feel weird,' Nadine informed me en route, 'I've barely been here two days and I already have an alcohol problem.' She passed me a half-empty bottle of beer and I suffered one mouthful. 'You know,' she hiccuped, 'it's really quite sad that all of us feel the need to get shitfaced in order to get to know each other. Sure alcohol knocks down certain barriers and dissolves inhibitions and all, but it also turns you into a completely different fucking person, know what I mean?'

I nodded. 'Social anaesthetic,' I said, thinking aloud.

'Y'what?'

'Although saying that, I used to believe I could get pissed on water. My sister told me that if I gulped it down really quickly while holding my breath and counting backwards from a hundred, I'd end up sloshed.'

'And that worked?'

'In a weird placebo way, yeah, I think it did. I'd be rolling round on the floor laughing my head off after a few glasses of chilled Evian, and Jasmine would just be shaking her head in despair all the while at my gullibility.'

'That'd be right. I know all about older sisters. I've got two of my own.'

There was a brief silence.

'Anyway,' Nadine linked her arm in mine and drained the last of the bottle, 'I'm usually a nice person when I'm sober. Honest. It's just this stuff turns me into a right old bitch.'

I learned a lot of facts about Nadine over the next hour or so. That she was a bitch when pissed was not one that struck me. She was from Leicester, 'a right crappy place an' no mistake', and her mother was originally from Delhi 'once upon a time'. Her father had a very important and incredibly dull job with an obscenely high wage but she had never been spoilt. She had an older, married brother as well as two older 'desperate spinster' sisters. Her surname was Ferrell and her middle name was Grace ('my great-gran's name – and highly inappropriate I must say'), she used to believe in God, she loved all animals and hated her doctor ('a dribbling, incompetent perv who looks like a sack of spanners'), she liked her coffee strong and black (and didn't make the crap comment 'like my men'), was 'semi-vegetarian', had a savings account with £2.51 in it and thought *Monty Python's Flying Circus* was the funniest thing ever. Her first job was floor sweeping in a hairdresser's salon, which she held down for two Saturdays before losing her rag and lunging at her 'greasy Italian boss' with a broom handle and a can of industrial-strength hairspray. She loved travelling and had been to Sydney, Thailand, Morocco and Tokyo during her gap year, as well as European cities including Rome, Paris and Amsterdam ('*believe* the hype, the place is just awesome'). She could speak a little French and Japanese, and far too much English ('just slap me if I'm getting really irritating'), and liked to affect regional accents, Manchester being her favourite. She had never had a steady boyfriend, her best friend back in Leicester was called Charlotte but she had become 'dead boring' since settling down with a 'cretinous tosspot called Gary'. She ate too much chocolate (it didn't show) and her favourite film was *The Wizard of Oz.* She was at university to study law and to broaden an already wide-open mind, had achieved a near-perfect 26 points in her A-levels, was 99 per cent sure she wanted to be a solicitor 'or something like that', was heavily into dance music, voted Labour ('dunno why') and had a budgie called Woody and a chinchilla called Fergal.

When I managed to get a word in edgeways, I told her the basics of my life history – a special abridged version – and even felt comfortable enough to talk about Jasmine in more detail. But because I had met so few people who properly understood schizophrenia, I just said, 'We're very close but she took a lot of drugs and she's not quite right in the head.' Which was the most fitting euphemism I could think of at the time. Nadine responded with the usual, appropriate mixture of sensitivity and ignorance, saying something like 'Well, there's the price to be paid for a hedonistic lifestyle,' before launching into a spirited verbal attack on the way in which 'mentally disadvantaged' people are treated in society. I decided it was far too early to rely on her as a confidante when it came to Jasmine. Right from the start, I did feel a strangely powerful affinity with Nadine, though, something I hadn't felt with any of my friends from back home, even Sylvie.

I had no intention of getting drunk again that night, but sadly events took an unexpected (if not entirely unpredictable) turn. I had a definite early (i.e. pre-midday) lecture the next day – a proper one, with a qualified English tutor and everything. But when Nadine bought me a triple vodka and Coke, it seemed rude to refuse. Even ruder not to return the favour once we'd polished the first round off. It was about ten o'clock when Marbles swaggered up to us, dragging a near-comatose Alex by the collar, and jabbering nonsensically about helium balloons, sushi and leather thongs. They had apparently failed in their mission to obtain a willing female, but they didn't seem too bothered. It was about two minutes past ten when a self-confessed 'sex-obsessed third year' approached all four of us and invited us 'fuckable little freshers' back to his house in nearby Hove for a start-of-term celebratory party.

'My name is Matt. Remember it, girls, you'll both be screaming it later,' he said, gawping at my breasts, which were thankfully mostly obscured in the modest alcove of one of my more sensible bras, beneath a not-so-sensible silver vest top. He typified every third-year student – that is, an ordinary student who exudes three times the desperation. His T-shirt simply said 'Bollocks' and his pathetic attempt at a beard made him look like Shaggy from *Scooby Doo*. But, after Alex was sick on his shoes (this was a *favour*, they were suede slip-ons with *tassels*), we felt obliged to accept the party invite.

Now, I am not a party animal by any stretch of the imagination. I am quite content to curl up quietly on a sofa on my own with two litres of Pepsi and my own personal plantation of puff, observing everyone else around me enjoying their own definition of a good time. The first ever party I attended – that is, *proper* party: booze, loud music, random copulating bodies and no balloons or party hats – was Jasmine's twenty-first. Dad and Jane had reluctantly allowed me to join in with the 'adult' fun and revelry ('Just make sure you look after your sister,' Dad had yelled after us as we scampered down the road, already half-drunk and giggling like imbeciles. To this day I don't know if he was talking to me or Jasmine). The party was held at her then boyfriend's house, an eccentric French bloke called Jacques who walked with a limp and spoke with a lisp. His parents were filthy rich and had conveniently buggered off to Lyon for the weekend, leaving him, a newly rehabilitated Jasmine, my fourteen-year-old self and fifty-odd twenty-somethings to enjoy five-star accommodation at their sprawling three-storey luxury home. Needless to say, by the end of the night, 'luxury' was the last word that sprang to mind.

Jasmine spent the first few hours asking for Charlie, who until the age of twelve I had always assumed to be a particularly evasive friend of hers. That is, until I found out the truth: Charlie was of course not a geezer at all, but generally attended parties in little bags, and cost a lot of money. Jasmine made a concerted effort to avoid H out of respect for Dad, but also because she had only just got over a very bad spell – after more than three consecutive months as a committed in-patient at Rayneham, she had lost two stone in weight and nearly all her self-confidence. Still recovering from heroin and officially suffering from a chronic mental illness that may or may not have been a direct consequence, she was constantly on the lookout for the next thrill. Whatever would take her away from reality for a few blissful seconds, minutes, hours. She found Charlie and chopped him up into four white lines on the smoked glass coffee table using her National Insurance card. Being the youngest there and not really knowing anyone else, I had shyly hidden away in a corner behind an overgrown pot plant, and spliffed my brain numb until I was barely visible through the dense, aromatic smoke.

That night was the first time I actually threw up from mixing alcohol and cannabis. I still maintain that the triple cheese pizza, chocolate hash cakes and tortilla chips played a part, though. It was also the first time I saw a naked, erect penis. The event traumatised me so much I couldn't look a man in the eye for quite some time afterwards. The penis was – and presumably still is – attached to a hydrophobic, harmonica-playing hippy called Malcolm. I remember all too well the moment our eyes met across the smoky room. Someone with no talent had just assaulted the grand piano with their own stoned rendition of 'Chopsticks', while a large gang raided the fridge and cooked pizza and offered around various munchies: huge, bumper packs of crisps and snacks and peanuts and pretzels and popcorn, which spilled from the split bags on to the plush carpet to be hoovered up later by the ravenous hoards who were too stoned the first time round. There were enough snacks to feed a small country for a year – or rather, just about enough to satiate a houseful of dope-smoking youths for a couple of hours. I had just finished half a family-sized deep pan and started my third bag of 'crunchy maize snacks' – chilli sauce flavour, if I recall correctly. I looked up and a pair of brooding, dark eyes stared intently back at me. I made the mistake of returning the stare and holding it rather than sensibly backing away and retreating into the expansive garden to conceal myself in the shed or the gazebo for the rest of the night.

'You're Jasmine's sister, aren't you?'

Before I knew it, the staring man had got up and lurched towards me and was now standing over me. I tipped my head towards him dozily, and either he was swaying quite violently from side to side or my vision was seriously affected. I managed a nod.

'I can tell. You have her beautiful eyes.' His voice sounded distant and his spit sprayed me from above.

This was a needlessly unctuous comment that was quite simply not true anyway, but I nodded again, sensing the objects and people in my peripheral vision shift in and out of focus and the sounds distort into one great muffled noise around me. I wiped his spit away and said, 'Do you want a crisp?' offering up my half-empty packet.

And so we had sat together sharing crisps and more smokes and chatting about nothing of any consequence. He played a Levellers song on his harmonica and wove beads into my hair with coloured thread. He told me that although he was a bona fide hippy ('I was conceived at Woodstock, you know'), he hated most human beings because they are 'basically' ugly and evil. I remember thinking, how typical of me to be singled out of the crowd by a misanthropic hippy called Malcolm with scary eyes. He claimed to be 'bi-curious', a pro at tantric sex (in hindsight I realise he could have said 'frantic'), a lifelong member of Greenpeace and the drummer in a band called Chasm. Despite my diminishing enthusiasm for his company, we ended up in a passionate clinch. Or at least, we kissed for a while, I think . . . and then he just took it out, without any warning. I looked down and there it was, poking out of the front of his jaunty slacks as if to say 'Why, hello there!', winking up at me like some kind of demonic serpent. He cradled it lovingly then looked at me with those intense, bulgy eyes and whispered, 'Prepare to be amazed.'

It was at that point the pizza and various snacks chose to move the wrong way out of my digestive system. The lumpy mucus scattered over a wide area, the jaunty slacks were ruined, the message was got. Needless to say, Malcolm failed his cherry-picking conquest on that occasion.

Now a little older, I was sadly no less callow and unsophisticated. My first student party, such as it was, must have been a rip-roaring success, as I couldn't remember a single thing about it the next day. All I knew was that I wanted to sleep for ever, to stay in my room with the curtains drawn and not have to venture into daylight until my suffering had subsided. Nadine reliably informed me that I had spent most of the night gazing down the toilet, hugging the piss-splashed seat with desperate tenacity. Marbles had managed to cop off with a chubby, loud postgrad called Sonia, and Alex ended up in bed with a mystery blonde, although he was far too drunk to get a result.

This first party, an anonymous gathering, a meeting of minds for those who had no minds and didn't mind, was just the first of many barely memorable nights of intense partying. This was having a good time. Retching your guts up in a stranger's bog and drinking some more to blot it all out and bring it back up again; this was fun. Pills and poppers to loosen up, glory hits of cheap-cut cocaine for confidence and concupiscence, skunk to mellow out, beer to fight or fornicate; painkillers and persistent somnolence the next morning to assuage your suffering and recharge your brain and body. I wasn't used to living it up in such grand style, I didn't even *like* alcohol all that much. There *had* to be more to student life than cheap drink, cheap thrills, bad drugs and 10 per cent discounts. Surely.

'It will get better, you know,' Nadine soothed me, sitting on my bed and handing me a large blister pack of paracetamol. 'It's still early days yet; plenty of time to catch up with the big boys.'

I wondered what exactly she meant by this but my head hurt too much to say anything.

'Just take it slowly. You're being too ambitious, trying too hard. Don't worry.' She held a glass of water to my lips and ordered me to take the pain relief. I didn't need telling twice.

I gulped down two tablets, then groaned in agony and fell back on to the bed, my brain throbbing like it was bursting out of my skull. I closed my eyes tightly and tried to block out every bit of light, every cruel stimulus that ruthlessly impinged upon my raw senses. Nadine tutted at me and looked at her watch.

'I don't know about you, but I have a lecture in less than ten minutes.'

My eyes flickered open and I sprang up like a wind-up toy. 'Oh shit!' I exclaimed with genuine alarm, and then something whirred and clanked inside my head and I winced at the pain, mumbled 'Oh bugger and shit' under my breath, and didn't move a muscle. Missing a lecture was far less important than preventing my untimely demise, and I figured I'd need at least the whole day to recover from the indulgence of the night before.

How pitiful I was. I had been a student for thirty-six hours and already I was confined to bed.

My first official lecture therefore went unattended, despite my best intentions. I nursed my hangover until lunchtime then resolved to do something positive and went to explore the university and surrounding area in the cold light of day, by myself. I was hardly the picture of health; the whites of my eyes were red, my skin and hair had a greasy sheen and it felt like I was walking underwater; every step was a huge effort and all the while I grumbled like a decrepit, arthritic old lady. I only had myself to blame, which of course made it worse.

After queuing up to collect and cash in my paltry grant cheque, I went back to my room, unpacked my suitcase and hung my clothes in the wardrobe, then put up a couple of posters and lit a stick of incense. When I was satisfied that I had got my room into some semblance of order, I lay back on my bed, feeling the remnants of my headache ebb away as I enjoyed a brief moment's peace and solitude. I promised myself I *would* take my degree seriously, and wouldn't submit to the drunken debauchery of studenthood no matter how much peer pressure I was exposed to. Then I fell asleep again, believing it.

4

That Space Cadet Glow

Time is never wasted when you're wasted all the time.
Catherine Zandonella

'Fuck a Fresher' week mercifully passed most of us by without so much as a whimper. Garston's *fiancée* flounced off after a tiff on Thursday night, and Alex and Marbles continued to bewail their 'watermelon testicles', while Catherine and Juliet attracted and rebuffed plentiful male attention between them. Murphy managed to alienate himself even more from the rest of us by putting a poster on his door which said, 'Burn the Christians'. He reminded me of one of Jasmine's nicer ex-boyfriends, a curiously sweet and innocuous pagan called Seth who drove a Harley and bred exotic arthropods. I had liked him. But I didn't think I'd like Murphy at first. His aloof superiority over us God-fearing mortals and his refusal to fraternise with fellow students was all part of a façade to disguise a lonely and confused man who loved his mum and was racked by guilt over his sexual identity.

On Saturday morning, Marbles strode into the kitchen and announced, 'There's someone on the phone who's demanding to talk to a Francis. There's no one called Francis here, is there?'

There was a short silence. Murphy was spreading Marmite on a piece of cremated bread, and for the first time, I heard him speak more than one word, after quietly clearing his throat and looking down at his huge black boots.

'It's not my mother is it?'

The cadence was soft and very well spoken; he almost sounded posh.

'Er . . . ' Marbles looked around the room, the evil grin on his face widening, 'it's a woman of some kind.'

'Oh, *Jesus . . .*' Frank rolled his kohl eyes and vanished with a swish of his binbag pantaloons, leaving the rest of us in stunned silence. Nadine smirked at me from across the table, and shoved half a Pop Tart in her mouth. Marbles echoed the feelings of everyone in a single uncontrolled exclamation.

'He's fuckin' well called *Frank*!' he leaned against the door and cackled. 'I don't believe it! Frank the Goth!'

From then on, we could no longer feel antagonistic towards our resident Goth. He knew it, and he gradually started to make an effort to socialise more. This began with cautious invitations for us to accompany him to novelty Goth nights at various remote venues in Brighton's cosmopolitan clubland, which a few of us very occasionally accepted, and then his sociability progressed to letting us venture into the murky hollow of his bedroom and smoke his weed – which was surprisingly of very high quality. We eventually accepted him as one of us when it turned out that he had his very own marijuana plant growing in his room, bold as brass.

Jasmine sent me a very optimistic letter and a collection of her poems. She told me she had reduced her methadone dose and was feeling much better. She had been through the agony of heroin withdrawal more times than I could bear to remember, and I felt certain she'd never go back there after coming so far. She had even found a new boyfriend, whom she wrote about enthusiastically for two paragraphs, ending '*This is the one, sis! He's my soulmate, this is the real thing!*' Jasmine's track record for keeping boyfriends was pretty poor, so I remained quite sceptical, although glad that she had found someone who made her happy. She had never had much trouble finding boyfriends, of course, but she did have a tendency to attract and settle for those who were not just bastards, but bloody weird bastards.

She phoned me on Sunday, two weeks after I had started at uni.

'All right, how's it going then? I s'pose you've been busy.'

'Well, busy isn't quite the word I'd use.' I had forced myself to go to one solitary lecture out of a possible and more or less obligatory twelve, and had fallen asleep before the lecturer even arrived. Not a good start, by any standards.

'I've missed you loads, can I see you soon? Maybe bring Honey along too? He is just amazing, you'd love him, honestly.'

'Yeah, I'm beginning to get the impression you quite like him,' I muttered. Honey was of course the new boyfriend – a big, black, beautiful biker, according to my enamoured sister.

'So it is OK for us to come and visit you?'

'Yeah, I'd love to see you, Jas, but I'm just not sure . . .'

'Oh come on, Abi! I know you miss me too. You can't hold your drink and you smoke far too much weed to have the faintest idea of what's going on around you. You *need* me.'

'That's not true.' It was, I suppose.

'So, anyway – tell me. Are there any nice men down there on the southern coast? Has my little sister been playing yo-yo with her knickers or what?'

'Like hell. I'm yet to meet a single straight bloke who hasn't got a face like an arse. I heard a rumour that there was one hiding around here somewhere, but he's probably been ambushed and assaulted to within six inches of his life by a gang of desperate women already. The situation is dire, sis. Really, really bad.'

'You're a *student.* You're not supposed to *care* what they're like, it's immaterial. You just *shag* them. That's what students do, innit? Smoke, drink, shag, sleep . . . have I missed something?'

'Study?'

'Bollocks.'

'Well, anyway. I can't complain. The people on my hall are generally OK. Nadine is lovely. You'd like Nadine.'

'Yeah?'

'And the rest of the people in my digs are . . . uhm, interesting.'

'Interesting eh?' Jasmine mumbled something, and then trailed off, suddenly sounding bored, distracted, as if I were keeping her from something. 'Well, maybe I will come and see you soon,' she said half-heartedly.

'You'll have to give me some warning . . .'

'Yeah, bye.'

'Jasmine –'

She hung up before I had a chance to say anything else. I plonked the receiver down and slouched back to my room despondently. The conversation, brief as it turned out to be, made me realise how, in just a fortnight, I was beginning to lose touch with Jasmine and home. Suddenly disconnected from a familiar and safe family life, I felt vulnerable and pitiful, gripped by inertia, horrified at the thought of having to fend for myself.

Looked at dispassionately, university is just like doing your A-levels all over again except a little bit more intense and away from home. But there was a pervasive claustrophobia cramping me. Everywhere I went, conformity surrounded and smothered me like a security blanket. Or insecurity blanket. I *wanted* to move on, to grow up and break free and yet, like most of the people around me, I was scared and unsure of myself and of the direction in which I was supposed to be heading. Over the next three years, I was supposed to pupate from petulant post-pubescent to fully-fledged grown-up with a fresh set of ideals and the ability to reflect on past, present and future possibilities in a cogent and rational way. In the meantime, all I could do was merely hope or assume that the future would work out just fine, while silently crying out inside for the way things used to be.

'When I think about the future, most of the time all I feel is . . . numb. Not even unhappy, or scared, or anything like that. Just . . . nothing.'

I could smell antibacterial soap and disinfectant. I had really bad period pain and felt like I was going to throw up. The shiny happy framed family portrait on the desk to my left smiled out at me gleefully, mocking my discomfort. I focused on the carpet tiles: dark grey with moss green flecks. Everything else in the room was black or white. Mostly white.

'Why do you think that is, Jasmine?'

It was a cold but sunny day in September 1991. I was fifteen.

After Jasmine had not answered for a minute or two, I glanced over at the psychiatrist and said, 'I feel like that too, sometimes.'

The psychiatrist turned slightly in her seat, her pen still poised over her notepad.

'Well, I think all of us have moments when we –'

'Do you mind if I smoke?' Jasmine held up her cigarette packet and looked expectantly at the well-heeled, well-educated woman who had been psychologically assessing her for the past six weeks.

'This is a no-smoking building, Jasmine. You know that.'

'Well, hey. I won't tell if you don't.' She winked and sparked up and the psychiatrist hurriedly scribbled some notes in her pad, as if she had just received divine inspiration.

'Ummm . . . Dr Chambers?' I tipped my chair forward, holding my aching abdomen.

'Oh, call me Liz. Please.' Smile. Smile.

'Er . . . Liz, could I please be excused?' I glanced over at Jasmine, who was now arched back in her seat, bored to distraction, looking up at the plastic day-glo stars on the ceiling and blowing smoke circles at them.

'Of course. You know where the toilets are, don't you?'

I thanked her and left the unbearable brightness of the modern consultancy room in great haste, nearly tripping over my shoelaces as I went. This was the first, last and only time I had accompanied Jasmine to one of her counselling sessions. As part of a new remedial care scheme, members of the family had been advised to take an active role in this aspect of her analysis and treatment. The idea was that we'd all get a better idea of her feelings and motivations, and with the guidance of a qualified professional, we would ultimately be better equipped to help her through it.

It was a good idea in theory at least.

For most of the intensely uncomfortable one-hour session I sat in on, Jasmine had been uncooperative and rude, constantly and consciously contradicting herself and answering every other question with a tart retort such as 'How am I supposed to know? I'm mad, aren't I?' All I knew was that a supercilious woman in a smart suit who didn't know my sister was attempting to work her out by asking her some searching and spurious questions that had already been asked countless times before. I squirmed in my seat the whole time, in both physical and mental pain. I contributed little, if anything, apart from the occasional 'hmmm' and 'I don't really know' and 'yes' and 'perhaps'. I was a stroppy and selfish teenager, what more could I have done?

When I returned, Liz was standing with her back to Jasmine, staring out of the window through the crooked slats of the white venetian blinds.

'Ummm . . . I don't suppose you've got a paracetamol or something?' I asked hesitantly, shutting the heavy wooden door behind me and shuffling back to my chair.

Liz didn't respond to my request. Jasmine looked at me and mouthed '*Headache*?' and I shook my head and pointed at my stomach. She reached into her pocket and handed me a packet of wine gums. I took a lemon one and sucked it slowly. For a while the only noise was the terrible ticking of the clock on the wall above my head. Jasmine broke the silence just as I felt inclined to scream. 'Yeah,' she said, as if she was continuing from an interrupted discussion, 'sometimes when it gets really bad I just want to fuck myself over on drugs and I don't really think about the consequences. I just do it.'

There was another very long silence. Liz took a deep intake of breath before turning around. 'I see,' she said.

She walked stiffly over to a grey filing cabinet in the corner of the room and opened one of the drawers with a clatter.

'Can I just say, that is a lovely skirt you're wearing, Elizabeth,' Jasmine sighed. Liz ran a hand absently over the tweed fabric of her straight pencil skirt and said, 'Thank you.'

She flipped open a file and sped-read some pages and then took her glasses off and let them hang from the cord around her neck. She dressed like a fifty-year-old, but she was only about ten years older than Jasmine. They were both female and bored, and that was just about all they had in common.

'I want to go back to what we were talking about last week, when your stepmother was here with you,' Liz said, sitting back in her shiny leather swivel chair and opening a compartment in her desk. There was a rustle of a paper wrapper, and she popped a mint into her mouth and threw a box of Nurofen at me.

I just managed to catch it and opened my mouth to thank her, but her eyes were fixed on Jasmine as she continued talking. 'I know you're not comfortable talking about your feelings for your stepmother, but –' She clicked the mint against her teeth and smiled that superior smile; sympathy and condescension tinged with increasing impatience.

'I think you misunderstand. I love Jane. I'm not uncomfortable at all talking about her.'

I snapped out of my tedium upon hearing this. It was the first time I had ever heard Jasmine say she loved Jane; probably the first time she had ever said it.

Liz furrowed her brow and dug around in her pocket for a biro. When she found one, she removed the lid with her teeth and wrote one or two words on her notepad, then hesitated before writing a few more.

'Now –' she glanced over at the clock and gave both of us a wide and scarily genuine grin when she realised there was only five minutes left to go. 'To be honest, we haven't really made much progress today, and I have to say, I think it's because you're here, Abigail.'

'Me?'

'Don't worry, it's not a bad thing. I think I can see that you two have no secrets from each other.'

The only remotely insightful thing she'd said for the entire hour.

Jasmine smiled.

I smiled.

Dr Liz Chambers filed away some papers and stopped her Dictaphone tape and said, 'It was nice meeting you, Abigail. Just you and me again tomorrow, Jasmine.'

My sister lit up another cigarette and said, 'I can hardly wait.'

Things went smoothly, boringly so, right up to the penultimate week of the first term. I managed to attend a couple more lectures, despite my characteristic lassitude, and even managed to pen an essay of sorts. The getting-to-know-you tomfoolery of the first few weeks led inevitably to the formation of a number of 'cliques' – both within my own small hall of residence and the wider student community. On the macro level, there was the Elite No. 1 (the Very Wealthy and Influential and probably Not Very Intelligent), the Elite No. 2 (Tedious Intellectuals), the Nerds (computer anoraks who spent far too much time in the library), the Religious Nuts (otherwise known as the God Squad, who often ended up having more sex than the most stringent of agnostics, so long as it was with each other), the Internationals (a good cultural mix was implicitly encouraged, but in the event, those students who spoke little or no English hung around in isolated groups, refusing to mix), the Oldies (mature students and postgrads who either suffered the same unsociable affliction as the Internationals, or went too far the other way), the Drop-Outs (general drug users/dossers who slept all day and danced all night) and the Sporties (lacking the characteristic lethargy of most students, they expended their energy representing the university in its range of sport teams, or – in the case of rugby players at least – in excessive masturbation and baring their arse cheeks to unsuspecting victims). Naturally, there were miscellaneous others, but I found that these were the main ones, and generally had no problem identifying which group a person belonged to within seconds of first meeting them.

On a micro level, I identified the Vacuous Vixens (Juliet and Catherine), the Benign Pillocks (Marbles, Alex and probably Garston), the 'Two for the Price of One, for an Unlimited Time Only' (Simon and Rachel) and The Sociopaths (the painfully shy and taciturn Yoshi, whom we rarely saw as he often went back home or studied compulsively in his room; and Frank the Goth, although only to a certain extent). I suppose it goes without saying that I saw myself as one of the 'Drop-Outs', and I didn't intend to change that. I was quite happy to count myself among their disproportionately large number. I'm not sure what category would have suited Nadine; she had the intelligence of an Elite No. 2 without the tedium, the ethnic air of an International without the foreign language or insularity, the energy and vivacity of a Sporty without the sportiness . . . Yet I felt close to her and was able to identify more with her than anyone else.

As a student, I lingered somewhere midway between success and failure. That is to say, I had the potential in there somewhere, but I was not doing very much to actualise it, spending most of my days and nights in dope-induced torpor. Nadine would often tell me I was a waste of space, in the nicest possible way, and order me to get on with the boring things and 'put a bit of welly into it'. She had the enviable ability to make it look as if her degree was merely incidental to the fact that she was at university, even though she attended every lecture and seminar religiously, with baffling eagerness. Her essays were consistently excellent and churned out with seemingly very little effort. Yet she was always the life and soul of every party, and certainly the most sociable person on our hall. Always the first to get a round in, always the last to go to bed. I envied and admired her deeply. As far as my own coursework went, despite Nadine's chiding and the good example she set, I was typically and persistently lazy – one week I was supposed to be reading *Catcher in the Rye*, the next week, sifting through the finer aspects of *The Canterbury Tales*, while analysing Joyce's *Ulysses* and writing in-depth essays on *Far From the Madding Crowd*. I had so much to read and do, eventually I resorted to retiring to bed with a copy of Marie Claire, a family-sized bag of crisps, a large slab of Dairy Milk and two dozen smokes. The classic texts meanwhile remained on my desk, covered with Post-it memos and half-finished scrawled attempts at lecture notes, mostly blagged off other people on my course. My fellow English Lit colleagues were affable enough, and to my dismay all seemed to possess much greater motivation than I did. Feeling rather alone in my lax approach to the more academic aspects of my university career, I consoled myself with the thought that it was only a matter of time before I got into the swing of things. 'I just need to get used to some kind of routine, of discipline,' I told myself one lazy Friday morning near the end of October, as I crumbled the last scrap of my week's quarter-ounce ration into my last Rizla paper.

Nadine and I became firm friends in virtually no time at all – a counterattack to the thick-as-thieves comradeship of Marbles and Alex, who were almost like a comedy double act, except without the comedy. Marbles had the brusque but charmingly winsome presence of a born leader, making him popular with just about everyone – even those who may initially have been repulsed by his forthrightness. With less aesthetic pull but more charisma than the narcissistic Alex, Marbles frequently elicited the response: 'I like him, but I don't know why.' Nadine's opinion was the more specific 'a bit of a git with a lot of a personality'. Together, the pair of them looked as if they should have been in a boy band; it was only a matter of time before they were, alas. By the end of the third week of the first term, they had formed an 'alternative rock' group with a couple of Americans from the upstairs floor, with the emphasis on 'alternative'. Marbles was on guitar and vocals, Alex played the bass – badly – and wrote most of the 'songs', a lanky Yank called Gus was on drums, and 'JD' ostensibly served a backing vocals and percussion function, although his wild retro-style and tendency to say 'man' a lot, along with the fact he was always under the influence of some drug or other, meant he just *had* to be in the band, regardless of musical talent. He shook maracas and scratched vintage hiphop records on a makeshift mixer contraption in the background, yelled into a microphone ('Yo!' or 'Eat this' or 'Check it out') and waved his huge, frizzy hair around while the others fumbled for the right notes in search of a rhythm and a tune, or jumped and stamped about in their cut-off khaki combats and skateboarding trainers. All four of them were devoid of the tiniest glimmer of talent, and Nadine and I told them as much.

'You'll be on *Top of the Pops* in a couple of years,' Nadine assured them.

'Will you be our roadies?' JD asked, removing his purple shades and eyeing us drowsily through a mop of chaotic black ringlets.

'Fuck no, that would mean sleeping with you.'

He shrugged and lit up a cigarette. 'Fair enough.'

A decade of living in Britain had dulled his Californian twang, and his voice was loaded with the tired irony of those truly enlightened students who have finally managed to work out the inherent absurdity and pointlessness of their existence. I warmed to him immediately, not least because he was generous with his goods and often invited a huge gang of us to come to his room to get obliterated.

Their resulting unmusical ensemble was called The Space Cadets and their repertoire included such delightful ballads as 'Fuck You Sideways', 'Sorry I killed your Granny' and 'Spank my Funky Monkey'. Despite this, I had been curious to check them out, and after much protesting from Nadine along the lines of 'I'd rather perform oral sex on Bernard Manning . . . and *swallow*,' I managed to drag her to one of their rehearsals, or 'jamming sessions' as they liked to call them. Sure enough, it took two minutes of aural torture to reach the conclusion that 'Agadoo' wasn't such a bad old song after all.

The flirting/flunking farce of student life turned out to be everything I had expected, and more. Or maybe less. The stereotypical view of students as time-wasting, pretentious little wannabes was confirmed at every turn. The whole culture, such as it was, seemed to depend on an unwritten yet universally accepted law of conformity, and you were not generally considered a 'proper' student unless you adhered to one, or preferably all, of the central principles: (1) You must (at least pretend to) have regular, totally unsatisfying sex, preferably (often necessarily) when drunk and most definitely with a random assortment of profoundly unappealing partners, (2) You must drink cheap beer by the barrel, get pissed shamefully quickly and use this as an excuse for making a tit of yourself on a monotonously regular basis, (3) Don't forget to talk loudly with an air of self-importance that is wholly misplaced, (4) You must be into a particular genre of music and dress according to that preference so your peers are able to categorise you with ease, (5) Bullshitting must come as second nature.

Apart from number 5, which is a trait most students will have already picked up spontaneously with the advent of puberty, I was personally doing pretty badly. In fact, strictly speaking, I barely made the ranks of studentliness. This was not to say I was any less piteous than the rest of them, just in a different way. I had been through a 'wild and rebellious' phase several years earlier (being young and impressionable, I had followed Jasmine's example with conscientious loyalty, copying her exotic hairstyles and colours and fashion statements) so my various attempts at some silly semblance of individuality had already been stamped out in several Doc Martens, platform soles and thigh-high boots.

Assumptions about everyone had to be made purely on the basis of what they were wearing and how they carried it off. Students are essentially as deep as a muddy puddle.

My own assumptions largely remained unchanged, although my tolerance of people whom I previously perceived as intolerable did gradually improve. Garston the eighties throwback: quiff hairstyle, tight jeans, 'memorabilia' T-shirts, flouncey, 'poetic' shirts, subtle make-up, not-so-subtle *Now! That's What I Call Music* collection. Fairly quiet, except when drunk. Fairly interesting, except when sober. Frank the Goth: black rags, piercings, weird habits, deathly white face, sad panda eyes, berserk hair effects. Spoke only when he had to, reeked of patchouli, averse to bright lights and colour. Marbles the Beastie Boy Poseur: brightly coloured shirts often only half-buttoned whatever the weather, Calvin Klein underwear just visible over the sagging waistbands of his ridiculously enormous trousers, a few choice items of jewellery. Bit of a fitness freak, a lot of a show-off, listened to Snoop Doggy Dogg and Dr Dre and Cypress Hill and was an amazing dancer, although he knew it. Walked with a swagger, chain-smoked anything he could get his hands on, called women 'birds' or 'bitches', just to be argumentative. Yoshi the nondescript bookworm type: little round glasses, neatly pressed garments, unchanging expression of mild concern etched on his face. Never talked, but would probably have used words like 'extrapolate' and 'mensurate' if he did. Sexually inert or inept. Tape most likely to be in his walkman: Carol Vorderman sings The Bee Gees. Alex the highly polished mummy's boy: perfect teeth, tidy hair, expensive trainers, garish puffa jacket, ubiquitous designer record bag. Spoilt, vain, bigoted, ignorant, arrogant, predatory, pathetic, utterly irresistible to most heterosexual women.

It got me thinking: what was I? *Who* was I? Were my clothes nice? Did they reflect my personality? Was my personality nice? Were my favourite bands cool enough? Being a student is all about surrendering your individuality to become one of the masses. To find ourselves, we must first lose ourselves, and claim that *that* is part of the art of becoming a unique person. University is a safe haven for practising adults, a cocoon stage in our mental and intellectual development, a protective shell where we can sprout our metaphorical wings while naturally comparing ourselves to our contemporaries to establish whether or not our feelings, fears, emotions and preferences are normal.

It is well known that the sexual imperative is one of the things students particularly like to associate themselves with, what with being slaves to their hormones and all that. But sadly enough, for a long time the nearest I got to copping off was apple-bobbing with Marbles while stoned at a Hallowe'en party. I didn't think I was doing anything wrong. I had the kind of OK looks that don't intimidate or bewitch men, nor do they particularly impress them. I was easy enough to get on (and off) with, but my progress on the sex front was so far a bit of a non-starter.

As the shops started clearing out their window displays and eagerly replacing images of cackling witches and pumpkin lanterns with coloured fairy lights and shrines to everyone's jolly bearded favourite, Santa Claus, the festivities brought a new element to my fast-stagnating student existence. I was only dimly aware that I was 'lacking' something but then the realisation hit me like a bolt out of the blue on bonfire night, when Brighton beach was packed out and lit up and I sullenly observed that everybody seemed to be one half of a loved-up couple. All of a sudden, the neurotic part of my brain rattled with preposterous thoughts: here I was, the victim of an evil conspiracy, smug lovers versus lonely saddos. And I was in a minority. Just as the first fireworks began screeching through an asphalt sky, a gorgeous man thrust a sparkler into my gloved hand and gave me a gusset-gushing smile. He then scuttled off to embrace and snog his equally gorgeous girlfriend, flaunting their adoration of each other for all to see. Something sparked up in *me.* I finally decided, once and for all: I was a real woman with real urges and real hormones that were really raging. I could ignore my impulses no longer. It was about bloody time I had a bloody good shag.

Being a moderately choosy type, I needed a man to be both attractive *and* interesting. A rare breed indeed. But let's be realistic, this was university and I simply couldn't afford to be fussy. Ugly and dull would have to do.

So with a determined spirit and these exacting standards in mind, I went to a pub with Nadine.

The pub was called the Gherkin and Firkin, or something like that. To my joy and embarrassment, I was being very obviously eyed up by a pensive-looking bloke on the opposite side of the room.

'Don't look now, but I think someone over there is giving you the come-to-bed eyes,' Nadine pointed out, her usual loud, tactless style causing me to hide behind a beer jug and cringe.

'You're not very experienced, are you?' she laughed, and pulled at my arm. 'When did you last get your jollies?'

'W-what?'

'Oh don't give me that shocked look Abigail. Come on, let's go and introduce ourselves. He kind of looks like Mel Gibson in this light.'

'He does *NOT*! Shut up, will you?'

She lit a cigarette and looked askance at me. 'I'm picking up something from you . . . I believe it's called *sexual frustration*!'

'For crying out loud, Nadine, I'm just *not that desperate.*' A blatant lie, and we both knew it. I was gagging. Just walking past one of the boys in the bathroom – even *Yoshi*, for Christ's sake – made me all hot and flustered.

'You're such an unconvincing liar.'

'Leave me alone.' I glugged beer and hunched forward, grumbling to myself.

Nadine popped peanuts into her mouth and continued taunting me. 'You're telling me you have no desire to be lying flat on your back, panting with lust, hot flesh pounding on yours, groping wildly at a pair of perfectly honed, pumping buttocks?'

'God almighty, what are you *on*?' I felt that perhaps Nadine was doing the wrong degree. All that filthy imagination wasted on a law degree. I drank more beer, now feeling a bit sick, while surreptitiously sneaking glances at the brooding, staring bloke. OK, he had Mel Gibson's eyes, at least from this distance. But he wasn't anything special, just another scruffy student in a duffle coat with a pint of cider and an ugly friend to make him look better. He smiled at me and I changed my mind. It was pathetic; I felt as if I was thirteen years old again and was trying to get someone to dance with me at the school disco.

'I think you'd be doing yourself a favour if you sampled that one, my girl.' Nadine gave me a sly wink and blew a stream of smoke at me.

'Do you have to be so crude?'

'Do you have to be such a *prude*?'

'Look, I just came out here for a quiet pint or two and a little chat, that's all. I don't want you pairing me off with the first bloke who looks at me.'

She wasn't listening, she was actually beckoning him over, smiling lewdly like some kind of deranged pimp.

'That's it, I hate you. I'm going to the loo.' Mortified, I stood up and made my way to the toilet, ignoring Nadine's insistent cries of 'But you must have sex before it closes up!'

I was almost there when the bloke – the Bloke – stood in my way and casually asked me, 'Do you have the time?'

'Er . . . yeah. It's . . .' I glanced at my stupid, ancient Popswatch watch, not daring to look at him. 'It's twenty past ten.' I tried to push past him, the dawning realisation that I hadn't actually 'pulled' since splitting up with Nick suddenly terrifying me rather than adding to my motivation to do something about it. He remained in my path and with a flourish, he looked at his own watch and said, 'So it is.'

How crashingly unoriginal, I thought, my heart sinking with disappointment. What a wanker. I pointed at the door of the women's toilets and muttered, 'If you would be so kind as to let me pass so I can –'

'You didn't let me finish,' he persisted.

I sighed, sensing I would be even less impressed with what was to follow, but I waited for his chat-up line with as bored an expression as I could muster.

'I really wanted to know – do you have the time . . . to come back to my place and let me cover every inch of that gorgeous body of yours with my well-trained tongue and then give you the best sex you've ever had in your life?'

My mouth dropped open.

One less glug of beer and I would have been in the ladies like a shot and escaped out of the window. One less month of accumulated sexual frustration and I would have told him where to go. As it was, I just remained fixed to the spot, searching in vain for an appropriate reaction. I mean, the audacity of the man! As if – as if! Like I'd just let a total stranger invade my body for the sake of a little bit of carnal pleasure. The nerve of the man! The cheek of it! How dare he be so presumptuous! He could have been some weird fetishist or a psycho for all I knew.

'I've got loads of drugs back at mine,' he said, playing the trump card. Bastard, he had me.

'I'll get my coat,' I said.

His name was Craig and he was a third year studying History of Art. In other words, he was big on creativity and waffle, not so hot at engaging conversation. But it didn't matter. We had nothing in common at all except the most important thing: the thing that unites all sexual beings who haven't yet mastered self-control and discernment. Nadine had high hopes for me, but in the event, nothing actually happened that night after all. We went to the Concorde dance club, left at two-thirty, went back to his house and fell asleep in front of MTV after a brief grope and a rambling, dope-fuelled discussion about eugenics, suspension bridges, Renaissance art and *Fawlty Towers.* By that time, I was just too damn tired to feel any kind of insatiable urges. I think I dozed off just as he was in the middle of trying to unhook my bra

– he wasn't able to work out that it was a front-fastening one, so his attempts, spirited as they were, ultimately proved futile. We agreed the next morning over boiled eggs and stale bread that we would meet up again, and he drove me back to campus and told me he'd really enjoyed our night together, even though I was sure he couldn't have remembered much more about it than I did. I convinced myself that he was nice enough, not weird or pushy or obsessive or anything. I took his phone number and let him kiss me; a polite, civilised kiss with only a bit of tongue and the minimum of slaver. Quite nice actually.

'You mean *you didn't do anything*?' Nadine made no effort to disguise her disappointment. She had predictably come knocking on my door almost as soon as I got back, demanding all the sordid details, embellished if necessary to keep her overactive imagination satisfied. I was expecting her visit and anticipating her disappointment, so had a strong cup of black coffee and a couple of chocolate digestives waiting for her by my bed, by way of appeasement.

'I hardly know the man, and anyway, I just didn't really feel like it when it came to the crunch.'

'When it came to the *crunch*? Hark at yourself!' She rubbed at her eyes and stifled a yawn; she had obviously only just got out of bed, yet still managed to look sickeningly stunning. I did my best to avoid the mirror, as I was fairly certain the same could not be said of me at that moment. Sickening, maybe. Stunning, absolutely not.

'Get a grip Nade. I'll do what I want to do, when I want to do it.' I opened my wardrobe and searched for something decent and cleanish to wear.

'You know your problem? You smoke too much weed.'

I rattled some coathangers, my search proving to be something of a challenge.

'What's that got to do with anything for Christ's sake?' It seemed that whenever I did something crap or eccentric, my weed habit was to blame. No matter what the issue was: my lethargy, my forgetfulness, my frequent clumsiness, my incapacity for alcohol, my refusal of sex with a stranger – marijuana is the culprit.

'I just can't believe you didn't . . . you know . . . shag him.'

'Well excuse me, but you haven't exactly been putting it about yourself, have you?'

'Hmm, well that's different. I took a vow of celibacy.'

'You what?'

She finished her coffee and started looking through one of my textbooks with an exaggerated 'Oh, this looks interesting' expression. After a couple of seconds she had read more of it than I had, so I said, 'You do talk crap sometimes.'

'It's true,' she insisted. 'I take all my sexual energy and just turn it into something worthwhile, to use it for pursuits that won't result in having to be polite to a bloke who makes my stomach turn, or faking orgasms and having to constantly tell lies such as 'You are so funny' and 'Really, it's the biggest I've ever seen' just to keep a male ego fully inflated, or long, pointless and indescribably boring dinner dates with someone who I can't relate to or . . .'

I held my hands up in defeat. 'No, stop there. I'm convinced. I will also take a vow of celibacy. Let's both join a nunnery and be done with it.'

'You don't mean that.'

I turned to face her, my hands on my hips in defiance and disbelief. 'Do you honestly expect me to believe you are not . . . er – sexual, in any way?'

'Of course.'

This could have meant 'of course' she *was* sexual, or 'of course' she expected me to believe that she wasn't. I sighed and started rummaging in my underwear drawer.

'Well,' I said, holding a greying sports bra up to the light then throwing it back into the drawer in disgust, 'when did you last lie back and think of England?'

'Now that's where you and I are different, Abi. You may think of England. Each to their own. I think of . . . India.'

I gave her a quizzical look. 'OK then, when did you last lie back and think of India?'

She laughed. 'Darling, I do that nearly every night, with my trusty vibrating friend.'

My eyebrows shot to the top of my head. Nadine plaited her hair calmly, as if what she had just told me was no more revealing than telling me she played the flute, or supported Chelsea.

I decided not to press the issue. 'Well,' I said, after a long pause, 'if you can take a vow of celibacy, I see no reason why I can't.'

'Only it's not really celibacy, is it?'

'What?' I had a dreadful feeling Nadine did want to press the issue.

'Never mind.' She pointed to my jeans, crumpled and sad-looking in the corner of the room. 'Oh just wear them and be done with it, woman. You're giving me a headache with all this "Oh lordy, what shall I wear?" bollocks.'

'I *always* wear them though. They're boring. It's no good, I'm going to have to go to the launderette.'

'Steady on there, girl.'

'Well, it's Saturday. I want to look the part tonight, don't I?'

'What's the occasion?'

'How about one final meaningless sexual experience before I take that vow once and for all?' I pulled off my old clothes and kicked them under the bed then slipped a smelly T-shirt that had been hanging on the back of my chair over my head and stepped into an even smellier pair of haggard-looking trousers.

'Ha! That's the spirit, mate.'

'Yeah, and I'll thank you to keep your oar out of it if you don't mind.'

She gave me an innocent, wide-eyed look. 'Consider me suitably castigated and humbled,' she said.

I abused my armpits and the ozone layer with a generous blast of deodorant, which almost solved my stinky clothes problem, but not quite. I found a black sack at the bottom of my wardrobe and started filling it with my unwashed rags.

'So . . . maybe tonight will be the night I'll hear you screaming through the walls . . . ?' Nadine grinned hopefully.

'Yeah right. If you do, it will be screams of pure frustration at having been lumbered with yet another sad apology of a man who thinks a clitoris is an unusual species of flowering herb.'

She let out a brief peal of laughter and then her face went serious and she said, 'It's a stupid bloody word though, isn't it?'

'What?'

'Clitoris. I mean, have you never stopped to think about how utterly preposterous the word is?'

I paused as I lifted – or rather peeled – a particularly skanky garment from the floor. 'Er, no actually. I reckon there are probably better things to think about.'

Nadine obviously disagreed with me and went into one of her ruminative spiels. 'Eight letters and three syllables for something the size of a bean. Ridiculous! I mean, here we are, living, breathing, complex organisms with all these amazing body parts – brain, heart, lungs – all of those organs keep us alive and yet warrant only one syllable. Do you not see the irony?'

I sighed with impatience. 'Do you want my honest answer or shall I humour you?'

'It's like "labia". And "fallopian". And "uterus". All relatively small and non-vital female body parts and yet a man – yes, it must have been a man, it could *only* have been a man – took it upon himself to give them stupid, long-winded names. Now *penis* – there's a word.'

'Nadine, shut up.'

'I mean, it's onomatopoeic in a way, don't you think?'

'*What?*'

'Male parts are nearly all onomatopoeic. Scrotum. Glans. Or bell end, if you will.'

'Please stop.'

'Testes. What a fantastic word. So much better than *ovaries*, don't you think?'

'I don't care.'

I hurled one last item in my laundry sack. 'I'm going to the launderette now. Do you want to stay here wibbling to yourself about the wonder of etymology and the semantics of sex organs or are you going to join me?'

'Do you think my frail little heart will be able to take the excitement?'

'I don't know, but it sure as hell beats listening to you bang on about bollocks.'

'Fair enough, mate.'

So we spent another one of many Saturday mornings in the campus launderette watching my soiled smalls circulate inside an archaic, clunky washing machine, reading each other random passages from *The Female Eunuch.*

I lost my virginity when I was fifteen, in a rather sad quest to 'get it over with' before it was actually legal. Or, if I'm being honest, at a time when I was so passionately in love with the idea of being in love with the person I thought I was in love with, that it seemed like the natural and obvious thing to do. Predictably enough, the whole thing was set up by Jasmine, who had so many eligible male friends she could almost have set up a dating service. Well, in effect, she *did*, except I was her only client, and she was crap at finding an even vaguely compatible match. I had always thought that the main difference between my sister and me was that she was beautiful and remarkable and I was just ordinary. Tom changed my view. After several catastrophic set-ups, Jasmine struck gold when she introduced me to Tom. He was much older than me, almost nine years, but even with hindsight I don't think I could have chosen a better person to relieve me of the burden of my innocence. He taught me how to have confidence in myself, demonstrated in no uncertain terms that the multiple orgasm is not merely a myth, constantly told me I was beautiful ('utterly, stunningly sublime . . . exquisite'), had endless supplies of quality gear at his disposal, and wrote me reams and reams of profound love poetry (profound, because I didn't understand a word of it). Of course, I know *now* that the poetry was shite, but at the time I was captivated and deeply flattered by it and I thought he must have loved me to the same extent that I loved him. And I *did* love him – earnestly, completely, hopelessly, uncompromisingly, adolescently. He, however, for most of our eighteen-month relationship, was furtively sleeping with his ex-wife.

Being fiercely protective of me, Jasmine made sure that Tom was publicly humiliated as a result, but ultimately this didn't help me to get over it. I languished with a broken heart and so began my 'black' phase. I thought I'd never be able to trust anyone ever again, so I confined myself to my room, scribbled an angry journal about how shit men are and how shit life is, listened to Goth music on suicidal loop play, smoked my lungs black and became even more uncommunicative with my family, as is a teenager's prerogative.

My first sexual encounter as a university student was, as tradition would dictate, an unmitigated disaster. I met up with Craig again, determined to fling caution to the wind and allow him to ravish me as he had so eloquently promised. After ignoring Nadine's obscenely suggestive hand gestures, I left her in a bar with Marbles, Garston, Simon and Rachel, who were playing a puerile drinking game and arguing amongst themselves about the differences between a glockenspiel and a xylophone.

The truth is, students generally don't have that much sex, they only like to think they do. Everyone feels pressurised to hurl themselves into a succession of rampant one-night stands and yet the reality is that this only happens if you are a seriously deluded old slapper. And it isn't really sex, not strictly speaking. It's more like a hit-and-miss débâcle with no real passion in it at all; just two sweaty bodies pressed together in a haphazard attempt to fuse genitals and reach some kind of climactic conclusion. Rarely satisfying, but it narrowly beats going home and bashing one out over *Playboy*'s centrefold or making an emotional phone call to the boy/girlfriend you left back home and tearfully explaining how you've grown apart but you feel too guilty and dirty to sleep with someone else. I don't think it is any coincidence that 'fornication' (illicit sexual activity between consenting parties) is such a similar word to 'formication' (sensation of insects crawling on the skin). In the case of being a heterosexual female student, I discovered that they were one and the same thing.

Craig, eager and freshly shaven and in his own words, 'well up for it', proved true to his promise for all of thirty seconds. He took me back to his house and at first things went along pretty well; we were certainly hot for each other and his hands were all over me. The kissing was frantic and slobbery; we panted into each other's mouths and rolled about on the floor, wrestling with clothes, tongues lolling, glowing in each other's rising body heat.

Then, in true cavalier style, he took my hand and led me to his bedroom – a fetid cupboard with piles of dirty washing and battered old books and dozens of copies of FHM and mouldy plates and old socks and computer games, and in the corner, a bed just about big enough to accommodate a dormouse. I had become almost immune to squalor, but not quite to *this* degree of squalor, and found it something of an effort to hide my disgust. By now though I was more or less overcome with lust, melting into my M & S panties and burning with a mounting desire. He laid me down on the rickety bed, and I managed to overlook the spring that lodged itself in my back. Our lips stayed locked as we clumsily undressed each other. Unfortunately I had been drinking. 'Dutch courage' I had called it; 'A grave mistake' were Nadine's words. I was feeling light-headed but quite pleasantly so – drunk enough not to mind too much when he began gnawing at my neck in an effort to mark his territory with a hideous purple lovebite, but not so drunk that I let him progress on to other body parts. Or allow myself to be remotely beguiled by his 'alternative' foreplay techniques.

'God Annie, I could really snort a line off your tits.'

He pretended there was a long sliver of cocaine running along my chest and trailed his nose across the imaginary line, inhaling deeply. 'Fuckin' lovely.' He observed the oblique streak of snot he had deposited on my breasts and, thinking this had really got my juices flowing, proceeded to plant wet, totally unerotic kisses on my abdomen.

He no longer had Mel Gibson's eyes. They were horrible, slitty, reptilian. And I think it's fair to say the floodgates of Heaven had now been slammed shut. I was stricken.

'My name is Abigail,' I corrected him, looking down at the top of his ruffled head as he burrowed his face in my paunch.

He stopped slobbering for a moment and tried to focus on my face. 'That's what I said, isn't it?'

'No, you called me Annie.'

'Oh. Soz.'

If we had had an ounce of common sense between us, we'd have left it there, got dressed and maybe left the passion for another time. For me, the mood had vanished even quicker than it had arisen. But the thinking nucleus of Craig's body at that moment was a few degrees south of his brain, and it had stolen all the lifeblood from every other part. He was determined to get his oats. Like a blinkered donkey going for the dangling carrot, he sought out the obvious hot spots with ardour and ineptitude in equal proportions. Relentlessly, he made a dive at my crotch and started fondling my thighs. He was, as they say, 'going down'. I was now feeling about as sexually receptive as a sack of spuds.

I whispered as kindly as possible, 'No, please don't bother with that.' The mere thought of his over-zealous tongue resolutely trying to evoke an orgasmic response was just too much to bear.

He seemed offended. 'But . . . I'm *really* good,' he murmured, trying to lie down beside me on the bed and oafishly elbowing the side of my face as he struggled into position.

I turned my head and smiled at him. 'I'm sure you are, just – not now, OK?' He leaned over and nuzzled my neck. I moaned with boredom and despair. All lust had flown out of the window along with his cringingly naff warm-up script and his inability to remember something as basic as my bloody name.

My moan was, of course, interpreted as an open invitation to climb on top of me and make unconvincing thrusting movements while shoving his tongue down my throat.

'You do realise you've given me the major horn now, don't you?' he accused me huskily, showing all his teeth as he grinned down at me. That was almost on a par with the wretched phrase 'It's a shame to waste it.' He had me pinned down, his arms either side of my head and his bony hips levelled in on mine, with the few clothes we still had on acting as flimsy barriers between us and mutual nakedness. My stomach rumbled at me angrily.

'Hey . . .' Craig whispered in my ear, 'I just really, *really* want you.'

Nothing was half-measures with this guy. It was all 'really' this or 'really' that. I sighed deeply. Maybe if I concentrated hard enough, all that passion would come flooding back to me. I held out my arms to him lackadaisically and we kissed some more. *Maybe . . . maybe if I give him a wank – just a quick one, mind – I can then make my excuses and get the hell out of here,* I thought frantically to myself as our teeth clashed together and his spittle formed a little puddle on my chin. His hard-on could have cut glass. I felt it rub and grind against my inner thigh but it aroused no excitement in me whatsoever. Nadine's 'grave mistake' prophecy was beginning to clang true. I felt the booze churn around in my stomach, mixing with my earlier dinner of baked potato, beans and broccoli florets. Craig took his position between my splayed legs like an athlete on starters orders and proceeded with the old thrusting routine again, adding further fervour to his 'well up for it' state. I reached down to put a shaky hand on the obvious obstruction in his boxer shorts.

We fidgeted into a slightly less excruciating position and I made a conscious effort to look anywhere but down as he yanked the boxer shorts down past his knees and disposed of them with great alacrity, flinging them across the room with a flick of his ankle. My semi-pissed constitution meant I was able to ignore the mild sense of repulsion I was experiencing and to sportingly take the bull by the horns, so to speak. I groped blindly for his dick and held it limply, casting my mind back to my last sexual experience and trying to remember what to do and how to do it and how long for and with what degree of passion and firmness, etc. All the while we were snogging like fourteen-year-olds at the cinema, grappling at the lesser erogenous zones: nipples, earlobes, shoulders, buttocks. Slowly, cautiously, I began making all the accepted fist manoeuvres, stifling a yawn and craning my neck to look at the clock on the wall. After a few minutes, however, it was clear that Craig was not satisfied with my cack-handed handjob attempt.

'Annie, that's just great but – but . . .'

A sense of foreboding crashed down on me like a ten-ton weight.

'. . . Would you mind using your mouth?'

Pause.

'Er . . .'

Oh GOD! What had I done to deserve this? Was this the great sexual experience I had been anticipating for the last six months? Would I mind using my *mouth*? Er, like, *yes*. Yes, I bloody *would* mind. He's lucky I'm even handling the damn thing, but *sucking* it? Who the hell does he think he is?

I wasn't cut out for all this. I wanted to go home.

Feeling like I was setting the women's lib movement back a few hundred years, I said meekly, 'Well Craig, if that's what you want.'

'That *is* what I want,' Craig assured me, gently stroking my hair in a fleeting moment of affection before pushing my head forcibly down. I rationalised that a few moments of utmost disgust would at least get me out of that situation, albeit minus self-respect and dignity. OK, so the sex thing hadn't quite worked out as well as I'd hoped, but there may still have been *something* to salvage. So, I salvaged away.

There must be some rules when it comes to oral sex. I broke every single damn one of them that night. I refused to open my eyes right up to the last minute. Hazy memories of Malcolm the misanthropic hippy came flooding back to me as I inhaled the pungent aroma of student penis. At first, I admit, the repulsion was hard to bear, but before too long I was able to train my mind on to other things and mentally planned out my shopping list for my weekly trip to Asda the next day.

Two pints of milk.

'Oh yeah, that's good . . .'

A loaf of bread, not the cheap stuff, proper granary.

'Don't stop, oh that's just right . . .'

Two tins of beans, an iceberg lettuce, a pack of mature cheddar.

'That's amazing, you're amazing . . .'

A packet of brown rice, pasta shells, three Golden Delicious apples, two pounds of tomatoes.

'I. Am. In. Heaven . . . Hmmmmmm Heaven . . .'

Monster Munch. Diet Coke, cornflakes, pasta sauce, mushrooms, peanut butter. Spuds. Teabags, spaghetti, cottage cheese. Anything else? Biscuits – digestives. Not chocolate ones. Actually yes, chocolate ones. Mineral water. And Rizla papers! I think that's all. Jesus *Christ*, hasn't he come yet?

Sylvie once compared fellatio to sucking half-melted Camembert through a candle doused in salt with the wick taken out. At the time, I had humoured her, thinking that Ben must have had something seriously wrong with him. But that night in my hazy, crapulent state, her analogy held a dreadful truth. Usually, I am a spitter rather than a swallower, but most times I am composed enough to do so in an inoffensive and discreet manner. Not so on this occasion. When he finally reached the zenith of his fulfilment, ejaculating noisily, violently, copiously and totally without warning (except perhaps a slightly higher-pitched 'Oooh yeah you're amazing'), it was such a gruesome shock I was rendered temporarily insensible. The spit/swallow quandary was not an issue. Instead of doing either, I went for the ill-advised 'store in cheeks like hamster' option, which allowed my tongue to fully savour the taste, while the half-digested dinner in my gut gurgled and lurched upwards, aided on its way by the 'Dutch courage'. Despite my best efforts to prevent it, some of the semen trickled down my throat. Tidal waves of sheer nausea washed over me. I dribbled some and, for want of something better to do, gargled – *gargled* – the rest, before the full horror finally dawned on me. All the while, Craig lay in rapture, still trembling slightly from the force of his tremendous climax, and jibbering inanely to himself, eyes closed, face flushed: 'That . . . was . . . fan . . . tas . . .'

And then, quite naturally, my gagging reflex decided to kick in. And so the first and last rule of oral sex was violated in a vivid and violent outburst.

My vomit hit his testicles at great velocity just as he was finishing his sentence. '. . . tic . . .' Craig murmured, as the acrid stench of puke filled the room. I clapped my hand over my mouth, not knowing whether to laugh or cry, or to throw up again. Unfortunately, the latter option seemed imminent, and this time the technicolour jet sprayed through my fingers, smattering his stomach and his bed sheets. I think by this point Craig was rapidly descending from his fluffy little post-orgasmic cloud. His mumblings had ceased and when I ventured a glance at him – briefly, penitently, and with due mortification – the look on his face was probably best described as aghast. I lowered my head in shame as he opened and closed his mouth wordlessly; dumb-struck with what I could safely assume was total and complete abhorrence. For the first (and last) time, I ventured a look at his prone, withered organ which looked back at me blamelessly – small, sad, shrivelled, and slimed in vile, viscous liquid. In the horrified silence that followed, things went all blurred and I suddenly remembered one more item of shopping I needed to get. 'Vegetarian sausages!' I exclaimed, before passing out and rolling off the bed.

A face loomed towards me, and my eyes gradually rolled sluggishly in their sockets and focused until I was able to recognise it as Nadine's. 'Abi . . . ?' she said, peering into them like a doctor checking for signs of life.

'W-where . . . ?' I was utterly disorientated, and tried to sit up to take in my surroundings. 'Where am I . . . w-what's happ –'

'Shhh . . .' Nadine held my arm and pushed me gently back down. She looked around and whispered something to someone else, whom I couldn't see.

'What's happened? Where am I?' I groaned, finally getting the words out of my furred-up mouth.

'Bloody hell, mate,' she turned back to me and smiled reassuringly, pulling a blanket around me. 'We've tried everything to bring you around. Threw cold water over you. Slapped you. Marbles even donated his saggy old pants and we stuck them under your nose. Thought if that didn't work, you must have been dead.'

'Have I been resurrected then?'

'You've been out for the count for over an hour. I was worried. We've *all* been worried.'

'What the fuck have you been drinking?' Alex's voice suddenly demanded. He was standing behind Nadine, lurking in the shadows, wearing only the bottom half of his pyjamas.

'I thought you said you were going to stop drinking so much,' Nadine scolded me, leaning forward and brushing some sticky hair out of my face.

I was on my bed in my room. I recognised the cracks in the ceiling and the familiar smell. My head felt like something had shat in it and my tongue felt like it was coated with ectoplasmic gunge. I was paralysed from the waist down. I groaned again, and rubbed my eyes with my hands, which stank of vomit. This triggered some vague recollections. Then I remembered.

'OH GOD!!!' I grabbed the blanket and pulled it right over my head, quivering with regret, remorse and revulsion. Craig. Whisky. A hideously regurgitated spud. *What had I done?*

'I mixed my fluids big time . . .' I mumbled from beneath the blanket, hoping with all my heart that they weren't aware of the grisly details.

'Yeah, we gathered that. Your boyfriend brought you back and said you were in a pretty bad way,' Alex said. I tried to turn to look at him, to check for any smirks or knowing glances, but was only able to glimpse his bare feet out of the corner of a bleary eye.

'And we were like, "No shit, what the fuck have you done to her?" ' Nadine added.

'He was a right moody bastard, I'll tell you that much. He drove you back in his car and I found him in the corridor at about one in the morning, with you slung over his shoulder if you fuckin' please.'

'He brought me back here?'

'Yeah, he says for you to give him a call as soon as you're better.' Nadine motioned for Alex to leave the room and after he left, she put her face close to mine and whispered, '*What did he do to you?*'

'Really, I don't want to talk about it.'

'He didn't hurt you, did he?'

'No, of course not . . . just – let's just say the whole experience is best forgotten. Can we leave it at that?'

'But you're OK now, aren't you?' She put her arm around me

and helped me sit up, patiently presenting me with water and mollifying tablets – again. I felt so sad and piteous, all I could do was smile at her feebly. She grinned back. 'Promise me you'll go easy on the drink from now on,' she said.

'Nade, please believe me when I tell you I never want to touch another drop of that stuff for as long as I live. Which isn't going to be that much longer at this rate anyway.'

'I suppose I'll leave it up to the imagination to guess what went on then.'

'Even the wildest and most disturbed of imaginations wouldn't come close.'

'You don't know how depraved I can get, matey.'

'I know you're probably not as innocent as you look.'

She shrugged and looked like she was about to say something, then changed her mind and averted her eyes.

'What's the time?' I asked eventually, breaking an inexplicable silence.

'Time I went to bed, my dear,' she sighed, standing up and stretching. With great physical exertion, I lifted my head to look over at my alarm clock, and saw the neon green illuminated digits change from 2:19 to 2:20 in a blink. I closed my eyes, flopped back down and uttered a heartfelt apology which was immediately dismissed.

'What are friends for, if not to help out in times of sexual disaster?' Nadine reached for the door and beamed at me comfortingly. 'At least I'm assuming that's what it was. Better luck next time, eh girl?'

I flapped my arms about and wailed miserably. 'I just want to have *proper* sex! I want it to be *grown-up* sex! Is that *really* too much to ask?'

Nadine's look answered my question. 'Do you mean, subdued lights and breathless anticipation and a sensitive lover who spends expert hours rather than amateurish microseconds on foreplay, and intelligent post-coital chat over chilled wine and endless smokes before doing it all over again except even better?'

'Er . . .'

'And then the delicious realisation that it wasn't just a

magnificent dream, or an alcoholic delusion? Just the sheer joy and liberation of waking up the next morning and not feeling grossed-out when you find yourself lying next to this fantastic Adonis rather than a bushy freak with halitosis that could kill at fifty paces?'

'Um . . . yeah. I suppose. That kind of thing.'

I gave her a quizzical look, which she didn't see, because she was gazing misty-eyed into the distance. She snapped out of it eventually, yanking the door open and winking at me before disappearing down the hall. 'Dream on, Abigail.'

The words rang in my head until I passed out a few seconds later.

Jasmine and her big black beautiful biker boyfriend came to visit me, unexpectedly, on the night of our residential Christmas party. I knew as soon as I laid eyes on her that she was on heroin again. She looked drawn and tired and stood before me, shivering in a man's biker jacket and a threadbare jumper before venturing forward to hug me with uncharacteristic sheepishness. The sight of the pair of them standing outside my bedroom door shocked me into flabbergasted silence. Honey towered above both of us – he was well over six feet tall, seven with his voluminous afro. It was a seasonally dismal day in early December but he was wearing large, dark shades and his stony expression certainly lacked any kind of Christmas cheer. Conversely, I was adorned in tinsel and a Santa hat, with baubles dangling off my ears and a synthetic white beard stuffed into my bra (don't ask). None of us said anything for a while; I simply let out a strangled cry of surprise, half-pleasure, half-dismay.

'Who is it?' Nadine called out from inside my room.

'It . . . it's Jasmine. My sister,' I answered hoarsely, barely loud enough for her to hear.

'And this is Honey.' Jasmine put her arm around Honey's waist and gazed up at him lovingly. Despite her obvious affection for this formidable Boney M reject, she was lacking her usual bounciness and self-confidence. She was trying to look happy, but her skin was pale and blotchy and she had obviously lost loads of weight. I frowned at her, then made an attempt to be polite.

'Pleased to meet you,' I stammered, holding out my hand. Because his eyes were obscured behind his obsolete sunglasses, I couldn't tell if he had heard me or even if he was looking at me – indeed I couldn't be sure if he was aware of anything going on around him at all. His waxwork expression didn't change, and he didn't move for what seemed a long time. Eventually, just as I was about dejectedly to retract my proffered hand, he dazzled me with a row of teeth – one gold one at the front – and held my hand in both his mighty paws. In a split second, he seemed to develop a character, albeit a questionable one.

'Enchanté Mademoiselle,' he said in an East London accent, curtseying at me clumsily and nearly falling over. From that point on it became clear that my sister's boyfriend alternated manically between bonhomie and barmy and that these two extremes constituted his entire personality. I would have expected nothing less of Jasmine's choice. He was absolutely fucked off his face.

I turned to Jasmine, lost for words, after Honey had released my hand and resumed his trance stance. Nadine came up behind me to investigate, peering over my shoulder. I prayed she was as broad-minded as she had made herself out to be. She was wearing a plastic hairband with gold stars on springs attached, and a fairy costume complete with wings.

'Er . . . we were just – getting ready for the Christmas party,' I explained weakly to Jasmine. 'This is Nadine, by the way. Remember I told you about her?'

Jasmine nodded and smiled as I made some brief and vague introductions, then I stepped back and reluctantly invited the two of them into my room. Honey slipped off his jacket, threw a crash helmet to the floor and took off his sunglasses, slipping them on to the top of his head where they nestled in the fuzzy mass of his hair. He marvelled at my room and was particularly transfixed by the lava lamp, the only colourful and remotely interesting thing there. In darkness everything is monochrome: my room was monochrome even in the daylight hours. Jasmine sprawled out on my bed and apologised for thrusting herself on me without prior warning.

'It was kind of a last-minute decision,' she explained lazily. 'Honey agreed to bring me here on his bike. *Kawasaki*, you know.' She whispered the last bit with conspiratorial awe, like a child after her first fairground ride. I was not impressed. I glared back at her.

'Oh, don't give me that bloody look like you're my mother or something,' she huffed. 'Don't worry, *of course* I wore a crash helmet and no, Honey has not been drinking. Anything else you want to earbash me about?'

'No, I see he's opted for the altogether safer tab of E,' I sneered, glancing over at him. He was staring at the swirling wax, eyes like saucers, mouth hanging open. Jasmine sighed wearily and sparked up a fag, not offering the packet around like she usually did. I didn't want to make a scene, especially not in front of Nadine, so I held back from confronting her at that moment. But my head was full of angry thoughts and questions: when, *why* had she gone back to H again, after all that effort? In any confrontational situation, it was hard to predict whether she would become aggressively defensive or remorseful and despondent – neither of which was pleasant to deal with, least of all when she was in that kind of a state.

Nadine seemed to sense the unease and made her excuses to leave. 'Er . . . I'll see you in the kitchen later then, all right Abi?' She turned to Jasmine. 'You and your . . . er, boyfriend are more than welcome to join in with the celebrations if you like. Plenty of booze to go round . . .' she trailed off and reciprocated my embarrassed look, then breezed out of the door in a dazzle of tinsel and a flap of gauzy wings.

'What celebrations?' Jasmine asked dozily after a long silence. She shrugged off her jacket and lay down on my bed.

'I told you, it's the Christmas party. Everyone's last opportunity to get their end away before going home to live on cold turkey for the next month.'

The implication was not deliberate, but she picked up on it

immediately and pouted sullenly. She blinked her sad, sunken eyes at me.

'You don't *mind* me and Honey kipping over do you?' she asked.

I didn't seem to have much choice. I shook my head so the baubles on my ears fell off and my Santa hat wobbled precariously. 'Jas, you know you're always welcome. You just took me by surprise. If you'd *told* me . . .'

'Yeah, yeah. Whatever. Just as long as we're not getting in your way. Got any draw?'

'A bit.'

'Lots of dealers round here?'

'Yeah, it's not bad.' I had been obtaining most of my supplies from a dealer I had met at a cheesier brand of nightclub in Brighton the second week I started uni. His name was Phil and he must have been about forty years old, and although not the most reliable or honourable of geezers, the stuff he sold me *was* proper skunk: aromatic and highly intoxicating. Worth every penny. The fact I was just about up to my overdraft limit was immaterial. I didn't think of it as a habit, more like a catharsis. An escape from the general shite of everyday life. It wasn't an addiction: Jasmine was the addict, not me.

Jasmine turned to her stupefied boyfriend. 'D'you wanna skin up?'

No response. A glob of red wax expanded and broke off inside the lava lump, floating for a second inside the purple liquid before sinking slowly back to the bottom to repeat the swell-rise-disperse-float-sink process all over again. Honey watched it all, absorbing every molten motion as if it was the most fascinating, life-changing event he had ever witnessed. Jasmine rolled on to her front and started rummaging around in my bedside cupboard, where she found some ropy-looking Rizlas and two empty boxes of matches. I wordlessly handed her my tobacco tin and she skinned up slowly and shakily, her face creased in concentration. Trembling hands, hollow eyes, sallow skin, frail frame, she was half the woman she had been when I left home only two months before.

Jasmine always used to say to me that she was looking for an impossible 'escape from escape', an abstract ideal of absolute freedom she masochistically believed in more strongly the more it eluded her.

It had been a crushing wake-up call for all of us when she overdosed on heroin in May 1994, a near-death experience that finally brought her down to earth with not so much a bump as a cataclysmic clatter. Her life up to that point had been the classic vicious cycle/downward spiral of so many other junkies and mental cases. But afterwards she seemed to gain some perspective and made a concerted effort to clean herself up once and for all. She attended the clinic every fortnight for three months, took her prescribed medication every day, saw her therapist and social worker regularly and even managed to hold down a part-time job. By the time I collected my disappointing A-level results in August, I was convinced I had my sister back for good, and for me this was a million times better than if I had got straight As and a scholarship at Oxford. Her schizophrenia over the years had been described as 'paranoid', 'catatonic' and 'residual', and she had displayed a perplexing and changeable assortment of positive and negative symptoms until none of us were sure whether she was schizophrenic at all any more, or if she ever had been. We thought it could have just been a convenient term bandied around by doctors who had no other way of classifying a confusing cluster of behaviours. The stimulant drugs Jasmine took in her teens – blues, speed, dexies – are known to trigger a psychosis very similar to schizophrenia, and the prolonged grief and feeling of isolation she had experienced since the age of nine must have just made the effects even worse.

It had taken her just two days to become a heroin addict. After every other drug she had smoked, ingested or snorted, it seemed to be a logical progression to her. It was a tragic counterexample to an increasingly disillusioned sister who was set on developing a mind of her own through education and conformity.

I cleared my throat. 'Jas, what's going on? Why have you . . .' my voice cracked before I could get the words out, and I fell back into dismayed silence, staring uselessly at my hands, the floor, anywhere but at Jasmine. She ignored me anyway, humming to herself as she stuck the papers together and messily heaped out tobacco. I decided to take a different approach.

'How's Dad? I haven't spoken to him since last weekend. He told me he hardly ever sees you these days.'

'He's OK.' She didn't look up; she just sniffed and wiped her nose with the back of her hand. 'Got a light?'

I reached into my pocket. 'When did you last see him?' I asked, handing her my lighter.

She shrugged. 'Couple of days ago, maybe. I'm living with Honey now. Had to get away from that place. I mean, that little shit Lewis was driving me up the wall. All he does is play Blur records and talk in that annoying sarcastic fucking voice all the time and invite his ugly fucking friends over to see who can piss me off the most. And Jane takes his side all the time, of course.' She altered her voice to do a passable, although slightly cruel impersonation of Jane. ' "Oh *Jas*mine darling, *try* not to let him get to you. He's just going through a difficult stage." You know, I was actually beginning to think I could get on with her as well.'

'If it's a difficult stage, it's one that's lasted for the past eighteen years.'

'Yeah. Well, you understand. I had to break out of there. Dad says . . .' she stopped mid-sentence and dropped the lighter to the floor. Her head fell forward and she started to cry, a quiet mewing noise at first and then louder, throaty sobs. 'Dad says he wants me there all the time, so he knows that . . .' Her weeping took control of her and I watched as she broke down, her face in her hands, rocking back and forth. I knelt down in front of her and pulled her towards me gently. 'How long have you been back on the H, Jas?' I whispered.

She shook her head, her entire body shook, her hands bunched into fists. 'I'm sorry, I'm so sorry . . .'

We sat on the floor together, and I let her get it out of her system, until tears started running down my own cheeks. 'I've tried. I've tried so hard. It's just useless.' She pulled away from me and rubbed her face with her sleeves, pulled down over her hands. 'I'm just fucking useless.'

I wanted to say something to her, anything, but the words wouldn't come out. I was choked up, angry and sickened. There was once a time when I had idolised and idealised Jasmine, now I just despaired for her.

She picked the lighter up and made some fumbled attempts to light the joint. She eventually succeeded, and took a couple of short, agitated puffs. Her ashen face was streaked with rivulets of tears, blackened with mascara. 'I've fucked up my arms good and proper,' she said, blowing a column of smoke into the air with a shaky exhalation, then lapsing into a coughing fit.

'Don't, Jasmine. Just don't.' I turned my head away.

She pulled up the sleeves of her jumper. 'Can't get a needle in these veins any more. Still not fully recovered from last time.'

She was holding out her arms to me as calmly as someone might show off their appendectomy scars. The insides were smashed up black and blue, the veins puckered and scarred. I looked quickly then turned away again, fresh hot tears springing to my eyes. My heart plummeted.

'Have to inject here now . . .' She rubbed distractedly at her groin, and rolled her sleeves back down.

I felt Jasmine's eyes on me for a long time, and I did my best to ignore her pleading gaze. 'Don't hate me.'

'Shut up,' I snapped, biting my lip to stop myself from crying again.

'Please.'

'Just leave it.'

There was a long silence. Jasmine handed me the joint and I stubbed it out angrily, although there was still three quarters of it left.

'I'm not going back to that place, Abi. I can take control of my life any time and I'd rather be dead than spend one more day of my life wasting away in there.'

'You think you're in *control*?' My fury came spilling out. I stood up and moved to the other side of the room. 'Jesus *Christ*, Jas, you lost control years ago, and you haven't even *tried* to get your life back. Look at yourself. Have you seen what you look like? You're just a . . .'

'A weak, selfish fuck-up,' Jasmine's voice rose above mine, no longer tearful and tremulous. 'I am a drug addict. I take drugs. So what? I'd rather be a drug addict than a paranoid schizophrenic or whatever the fuck they say I am. I know what I am, I've made choices in my life and OK, so they're the wrong ones, most of them. That's it. Big deal. I'm not mental. I'm not insane. Just weak and selfish. And stupid. I'm the same as everyone else inside where it counts. And whatever you might think, the desire to be different is nowhere near as strong as the desire to be the same. We *all* want to be accepted, all of us. Am I not making sense or something? Am I a social embarrassment because I sometimes lose control of myself? Tell me Abi, who *is* in control? What the fuck is this "normal" thing that everyone keeps talking about?'

'Don't you dare try to justify yourself.' I sat on the chair on the other side of the room and sparked up a Marlboro, one of Nadine's which she had left on my desk. 'Don't even think about making excuses.'

She sighed in exasperation. She had passed through all the emotions, from weepy to angry to defensive, and now she just looked drained. 'There is no excuse,' she conceded sadly.

'No, there isn't. I don't know how you could do this after everything Dad has done for you.'

'Please.' She looked at me imploringly. 'Don't go on. I've got a headache.'

I tried to steady my nerves, smoking the whole cigarette in half a dozen deep drags, eyeing her suspiciously through the grey haze. 'Well, I have a party to go to,' I said eventually, having no desire to further our discussion as I knew it would lead nowhere and solve nothing. I pulled the Santa beard out from my top and handed it to her. 'Here, just in case you feel in the party mood yourself later on.'

She shook her head. 'Don't think so, sis. I'm on a come-down. Feel pretty shit actually.'

She looked it. I said nothing. I flung the beard across the room and got to my feet. I was about to leave when she suddenly reached out and took my hand in hers and pressed her cold cheek against it. 'I've let you down.'

I pulled away irritably, opening the door with my other hand. 'Yeah, you have. You've let us all down, but yourself especially. You always do.'

The wide, sorrowful eyes fixed on me again; Jasmine knew how to make the most hardened of hearts forgive and pity her and it was infuriating. I sighed and crouched in front of her, trying to put some tenderness into my voice.

'Look, I'll sleep in Nadine's room tonight and you and Honey can have my bed. But . . . Jas . . . you know I'm going home for Christmas this weekend. It's not a good time . . .'

She lowered her gaze. 'I'm sorry. I just thought we could spend some time together.'

'There's no point when you're like this.'

She shrugged. 'No. I s'pose not.'

In the corner of the room, Honey stirred from his catatonic foetal position on the edge of my bed and finally managed to tear his eyes away from my lava lamp. Putting his sunglasses back on, he drawled, 'Hey, did I hear someone mention a P-A-R-T-Y?'

5
Eat the Conformists

In a large herd, it is very difficult to spot the odd mad cow.
New Scientist, July 2000

Jasmine's peers watched their weight and kept up with fashion fads and took their vitamins and plucked their eyebrows and used conditioner with herbal extracts and condoms with spermicide while she sold skunk and coke to sixth-form boys, slept on underground stations with fellow wasters and got herself arrested on a regular basis. It wasn't long before she was well known to the police who, with ever-increasing wariness and weariness, would cart her back home after finding her hitch-hiking on the hard shoulder in her underwear or very actively taking part in protests and riots on the streets or in trees or on privately owned land in the middle of nowhere. Dad was on first-name terms with most of our local police force before too long. After Jasmine's third and final ignominious appearance in the local paper – a picture depicting her at an illegal rave with only a plastic mac and a strategically placed umbrella to preserve her modesty – she became something of a local celebrity (at least within our parochial community anyway), nicknamed 'The Problem Page' and often recognised in our local high street.

The best memories I had of Jasmine were when I was too young to understand the seriousness of her condition – when having a sister who was 'different' was more of a thrill for me than an embarrassment and worry. One Monday morning at primary school, when I was ten, my teacher asked the whole class to write an account of the best day of their life. As far as I was concerned, I had just experienced the best day of my life that very weekend, with my wayward sister and her freakish friends. So while everyone else wrote touching essays about the birth of a sibling or the day their dog had puppies or a picnic in the park with their families or a particularly glittery Christmas, I filled five and a half pages of my exercise book with something altogether different:

> Saturday was my best day ever. Me and my sister Jasmine and her best friend Laurence went for a long walk in the country and it was sunny so we fished for tadpoles in the lake and climbed trees and picked magic mushrooms in a field and then took them back to Jasmine's boyfriend's house. His name is Justin and he said he would pierce my bellybutton for me if I didn't mind the pain. He has a pierced nipple and eyebrow and tongue and Jasmine says he even has a metal ring through his willy. I told him I don't like pain but I let him pierce my ears again because that doesn't hurt so much. I now have six earrings in my left ear and four in my right. He says next he will pierce my nose, but I don't think my dad would be happy about that. Jasmine made an omelette called trippy eggnog and put all the mushrooms in it. She says they are magic but they just looked like the ones in the supermarket to me. Laurence was with us and he is Jasmine's best friend but he didn't say very much. He is ill, he has something called aids. It means he has bad things in his blood and there are adverts on telly about it. I like Laurence a lot and we had a water fight in the garden and then a flour fight in Justin's kitchen. Justin has rats in his house but they are not pets. His house smells and it's really small and dirty, but sometimes Jasmine cleans it for him if she's not in a bad mood. We ate the trippy eggnog, and Jasmine and Justin went into the room upstairs and I watched a funny film with Laurence called the Goonies. Then my eyes went all weird and me and Laurence were laughing for ages and ages about something I can't remember until I couldn't breathe. Then Jasmine dressed me in her clothes and put makeup on me and gave me some of her cigarettes so I would look older. We all went

to a concert and it was so loud it made my ears go buzzy. Then we went to Laurence's house and Jasmine made some roll-ups called reefs. She said I was too young to have any but Laurence took me into the kitchen and made me a special fruit cocktail with no alcohol in it, just for me and him to share. He has a dog called Bacon who is really cute. Everyone fell asleep on the floor in front of a scary video called the exortis and I was scared so I slept in the bed with Bacon. And that was the best day of my life.

Not for the first or last time, Dad and Jane were summoned for an emergency parent-teacher meeting. Their parenting skills must have been stretched to the very limit: how could they possibly have separated two inseparable siblings without alienating themselves from both of us in the process? How could they have been expected to infiltrate and oversee a relationship that was so close and strong and yet potentially so dangerous? I trusted Jasmine and resented Dad and Jane for not being able to. I loved Dad and Jane and resented Jasmine for constantly causing them so much pain and hurt. And for a long time, I didn't know any better. I was stuck in the middle, getting the worst from both sides.

Jasmine and Honey left early the following morning, before everyone else was up. I brought them a bruised apple each, a pot of tea and two slices of stale dry toast, all of which remained untouched on my desk.

'I might see you over Christmas. I'll probably pop round, I'll see how it goes,' Jasmine said, pulling on her boots and zipping them up.

I gave her a steely look. 'Why should this Christmas be any different from any of the others you've managed to ruin?' I demanded, as Honey went ballistic trying to swat away a fly that didn't exist. 'Dad and Jane will do their best to make it a special family occasion, just like they did last year, and the year before . . . and you'll just sit in your room moaning about what a failure you are and not doing anything about it.' She lit up a fag and raised her eyebrows at me in an argumentative fashion, but I wasn't finished. 'And *that's* if you bother turning up at all. You'll probably spend most of the time with this . . . this . . .' I gestured at Honey, not being able to find quite the right noun to describe him. He had now apparently defeated the imaginary fly and was staring into midspace with a nondescript expression. 'And you won't give a second's thought to anyone else. *Jesus!* I'm just wasting my time talking to you, aren't I?' I threw some of my things – underwear, toothbrush, make-up – into a bag as I ranted at her. I had intended to go home the following day, but I was feeling so wound-up and frustrated and – I had to admit it – homesick, that I just wanted to get on a train and get out of that place as soon as possible.

'Give it a rest, Abi.'

I pulled off my jumper and threw it to the floor. 'You have no idea, do you?'

'Will you stop asking me crap rhetorical questions?'

I put a CD on – a popular chart band that I knew Jasmine didn't like, and sang along to the prosaic music in a deliberately tuneless and warbled voice. We glared at each other from opposite sides of the room. She finished her cigarette then got up to look at herself in the mirror. She stuck out her tongue and moved her head from side to side, then pulled down her lower eyelids to reveal livid tangles of blood vessels.

'I look terrible,' she said languidly.

'Correct.'

She turned her head slowly. 'I'll make it right again. I promise.'

'Of course you will.' I sat down at my desk and pretended to look through one of my textbooks. 'Now, unless you're coming home with me, would you please leave now? I have things to do.'

'What, really *important* things?' she retorted sarcastically.

'Just fuck off,' I snapped.

She sat back down again, not taking her eyes off me.

'Why have you become so cold?' she asked.

'I've just had enough. I'm not cold, I just give up on you. I'm sick of all this.' I put the textbook and a couple of notepads into my bag, sighing impatiently.

Jasmine shook her head solemnly. 'You think you're so fucking superior, don't you? Daddy's little girl. Gets her A-levels, goes to uni and pretends to be making something of herself. You're no better than me. You're just doing the same as the others and thinking it will get you somewhere different, somewhere better. If I fuck up at least I have the honour to blame myself for it.'

'How can you even say –' I felt my face flush with defiance and anger, and rose to my feet. She returned my stare with bold resistance, her dark eyes blazing.

'You have no right to lecture me. What gives you or anybody else the right to tell me what I can and can't do anyway?' She raised her voice to a screech and started coughing, a throaty, tickly cough which quickly progressed into a raucous hacking fit. Her bony body shook with effort as she doubled over, her hand covering her mouth, barking like a seal. Honey snapped back to life beside her for a few seconds and started to rub her back, almost affectionately (but largely ineffectually) as the coughing worsened. I waited patiently for her lungs to stage their protests, propping myself up in the doorway. She eventually recovered, and handed Honey his crash helmet after buttoning up her jacket and putting on her gloves. We tacitly reached a stalemate and hugged limply outside my door, with nothing left to say to each other. She lagged behind Honey as they walked down the corridor, not even giving a backwards glance before they vanished round the corner.

Desperate for someone to talk to, I went to Nadine's room, feeling a knot of tension tighten in my stomach.

She was wearing teddy bear pyjamas and a lilac dressing gown, packing her suitcase as she sang along to *Purple Rain* on the radio.

'Hello! I've only just got up, would you believe? Overslept again!' She pointed at the few articles in her suitcase. 'Just trying to get my stuff together before my dad gets here.'

I smiled weakly and looked at the floor.

'Jasmine gone already?'

'Yeah,' I mumbled, barely audibly. 'She's gone.'

I wondered if it was too early to burden her with my problems, whether I would be taking too much for granted if I unloaded everything on to her. It's always hard to know exactly how much you can trust someone. It's sometimes hard to stop yourself from just taking the risk and putting your trust in someone.

'Hey – are you OK?' She picked up a box of tissues by her bed and padded over to me. Her viridescent eyes scanned my face anxiously as I felt myself crumble and break down before her, tears spilling from my eyes. Unable to hold it back any more, I poured my heart out to her in one long uncontrollable babble. She put her arms around me and sat me down on the bed next to her, cooing soothing words and handing me tissues.

'Listen,' she whispered, putting her lips close to my ear and stroking my tangled hair back from my face, 'I know it looks bad right now, but maybe . . . well, she's got over these spells before, hasn't she? There's no need to make yourself ill with all this worrying. She's a strong person and she's got a strong family behind her . . .'

They were the same words I had used many times over the years to try to reassure my dad, and myself. But somehow it was a comfort to hear them from someone else, and even though Nadine didn't know Jasmine or anything about her condition, her natural incisiveness and sensitivity meant she knew when and how to say the right things. After about half an hour I was feeling much calmer. She fetched a bag of doughnuts and a carton of orange juice from the kitchen and we sat cross-legged on the floor and consumed our alternative breakfast in near silence. When she had finished, she licked her fingers and burped and clambered to her feet. 'Come on, you can give me a hand with my packing.' She stood on her bed and carefully took down the Indian tapestry from her wall. 'Here, help me fold this,' she said, handing me one end of it.

I obediently held two corners aloft, gazing at the rich colours woven into the beautiful brocade fabric until my eyes misted over. Nadine noticed me looking at it, and mistook my glazed expression for rapt admiration.

'I'll get you one if you like,' she offered.

'What?'

'While I'm in India . . . these things are two a penny out there. Do you want one?'

She took it out of my hands and rolled it up, then stuffed it into a side compartment in her suitcase.

'When are you going to India?'

She rolled her eyes. 'D'uh! Don't you listen to a word I say? I'm spending Christmas out there with my relatives. None of this come all ye faithful and goodwill to all men bollocks for me, matey.'

'Oh. I'm sorry, I forgot.'

'What are you up to, anyway?'

'I'll give you a clue. It starts with "bugger" and ends in "all".'

'Good for you.'

She smiled at me and I belied the sinking feeling of despair that still gnawed inside me and smiled back at her.

'Don't worry, Ab,' she said, 'Jasmine is going to be just fine. You'll see.'

The minute I walked through the door into the glorious domesticity of the hall I was greeted with the heady waft of edible cooking and the comforting sight of clean and hygienic surroundings. Nothing had changed, which I found pleasing and disconcerting at the same time. The house still had its unmistakably warm, welcoming aroma, Jane was making a valiant attempt at creating a wholesome pasta dish and Dad was still his wonderfully dappy and lovable self.

'Ah, here she is!' he exclaimed, pushing himself with some effort out of his seat and holding out his arms to me as I entered the hall, ruddy-cheeked and breathless from the wintry air outside.

'All right, folks?' I chirped, already conversant in the basic student vernacular. (Parents become your 'folks', and more specifically your Dad is your 'old man' and your mum is the 'little old lady'. Ingenious, really.)

'Welcome back,' he said, wrapping his arms around me and kissing my forehead. 'Blimey, you're cold, love. I'll make you a cuppa. Leave your things there and go into the lounge to warm up.'

I hung up my scarf and coat and kicked my shoes off. 'God, it's good to be back,' I said, padding to the lounge and collapsing on the sofa.

'How did the first term go then?'

'Oh, mostly OK,' I said vaguely, sinking back into the cushions and wishing to sleep for a very long time. I stretched and yawned. 'I mean, it's been a lot of fun.'

He frowned and pushed his glasses to the end of his nose.

'Hard work as well, of course,' I added hurriedly.

'Hmm, I'm sure. Tea or coffee?'

'Either, just make it bloody strong, please.'

Jane flitted in, florid and flustered, wiping her hands on her 'Sexiest Cook in the World' apron, clucking about how wonderful it was to have me back, was I hungry, had I met any nice boys, what was my course like. She bent over and hugged the breath out of me, ululating about how thin I looked. This was true. For the last two weeks of term I couldn't afford very much in the way of food, so I was forced to live on tap water and other people's charity and leftovers. Fortunately, I had kept aside just about enough money to buy some smoking gear to retain my sanity over the holiday.

'I hope you've been behaving yourself,' Jane remarked pointedly.

'You know me. A little angel.'

She decided, wisely, not to pursue that particular line of questioning. 'I hope you like Italian food. I've been going to cookery lessons at the local college.' She straightened up and patted at her hair, hastily scraped back into a tufted silvery bun at the back of her head. 'It's kind of my own recipe. A bit of a pasta concoction.' I smiled at her. 'It smells lovely. I love Italian food.'

'And Lewis has gone away for the weekend with his girlfriend, so all the more for us.'

'Lewis has a *girlfriend*?'

'Yes, did I not tell you when we called you last week? Helen. Lovely girl. Pretty.'

'Pretty desperate, more like it,' I muttered.

At the dinner table, things were silent for a while. I hurriedly stuffed my face, grateful for nutrition at last, while Dad and Jane nibbled and shifted quietly, casting me sidelong glances in the hope that I might open up to them and confess, 'I'm smoking too much, I'm utterly skint, this is my first hot meal for over a month, I failed to even have crap sex, I'm usually too stoned to know what the hell's going on in my lectures and that's only on the very rare occasions I actually bother attending, I passed out on a stranger's bed after vomiting over his most intimate parts, oh and by the way, Jasmine's a junkie again.'

No such admission was forthcoming, so they tried a different tactic.

'I remember when *I* was a student,' Jane mumbled dreamily, breaking the silence.

'You were a bit wild, weren't you?' Dad humoured her, waving his spoon and winking at me.

'Oh I *was* . . .' Jane chortled. 'I got up to all sorts of outrageous revelry back in those days.'

I looked up from my plate good-naturedly, showing just enough interest so as not to appear rude. Jane's idea of outrageous revelry was drinking a little too much punch, thrashing about to Jimi Hendrix and Led Zeppelin, sharing a joint with a mute meathead metaller called Thumper or Axel, and peeing in someone's fishpond.

'Of course, it was the bra-burning era, wasn't it?' She twisted some spaghetti on to her fork and let out a faint, lilting laugh. I raised a questioning eyebrow. 'Oh Abi, you girls take so much for granted these days,' she continued. 'It hasn't always been like this, you know. Back then, we were conscious of our liberation every single day, we basked in it, revelled in it.'

'Really?' I said, half-interested.

'Of course. You think we'd be shocked to hear about what you students get up to, but let me tell you – I bet I could have given you a run for your money. Your father too, I'm sure.' They grinned at each other knowingly across the table, as parents often do. I opened my mouth to say something, but then she settled back into her maternal routine, refilling my glass and offering me some more bread.

'The dinner table is not really the best place to talk about such things, anyway,' she said. She picked up the pepper mill and absently ground out a black blizzard over her already over-peppered pile of pasta. 'Student antics are not the most savoury of topics, as you well know.'

'But,' Dad interjected, coughing into his hand, 'do feel free to tell us anything. Any news, any problems you have had, anything you think we might be able to help you with, or –'

I sighed and let my cutlery clatter to my plate. 'Look, I appreciate your concern, but if you are trying to ask me if I got up to anything out of the ordinary over the last couple of months, let me set your minds at rest now by assuring you I have actually lived quite a boring life.'

They looked at me incredulously. For their benefit, and my own guilt, I counted out the boring facts and necessary lies on my fingers. 'No orgies, no late-night drug fest,' (true, and not so true) 'no skipping lectures due to alcohol-related malaise' (a bare-faced lie) 'and I am working hard, eating well and avoiding drugs.' (Lies, unashamed lies.) I swigged back some water, and banged my drained glass down on the table. 'Satisfied?' I asked the two blank faces opposite. Jane reached out bashfully for the parmesan cheese and Dad shuffled uncomfortably in his chair. 'I haven't even got laid yet!' I added, unnecessarily, regretting the admission at once.

'Oh Abigail, *must* you be so coarse?' Dad cleared his throat and gave Jane an apologetic look. This from a man who once owned a greenhouse full of marijuana, lived in sin with a minor, attended swinger parties in the early sixties and once drank his own urine for 'inner cleansing'.

I dipped a crust of bread in my spaghetti sauce, smeared it around the plate and munched on it thoughtfully.

'Father, need I remind you that you're not quite so –'

'Have you heard from Jasmine?' he interrupted, suddenly very serious.

A heavy silence descended. I wiped my mouth with a napkin and poured some more water into my glass.

'She's not well, is she?' Jane asked.

'No.' I looked down and sighed. 'She's not well at all.'

Dad put his elbows on the table and his head in his hands. 'I knew it. It's all gone wrong again.' He mumbled to the tablecloth, 'Why, *why* do we always find ourselves back at square one?' He looked up sadly and addressed Jane and me. 'Hanging out with the wrong crowd again. That new boyfriend of hers. I knew he was no good. She's so impressionable. So misguided. I should have *done* something.' He shook his head and dropped it in his hands again. 'She's just a baby really. Just a baby.'

Jane and I exchanged glances. Desperate for something to do, she started clearing the table. I pushed my plate away and moved my chair nearer to Dad, hesitantly reaching out to touch his arm.

'She's not a baby, Dad. She's a woman with a mind of her own, and you've got to stop blaming yourself for everything. You've done so much for her. What more could you do?'

He put his hand on mine and squeezed it. 'When did you see her?'

'She turned up out of the blue last night, with . . . Honey, whatever his name is. You could tell just by looking at them . . .' I trailed off and studied a stain on the tablecloth. Jane ruffled my hair as she walked past and out into the kitchen, shutting the door quietly behind her as she left.

Dad was staring into the distance as if in a daze. 'She was here last week, you know,' he said quietly. 'That's the last I heard of her. She looked – God, she looked dreadful.' He sighed deeply and furrowed his brow, his mouth set into a grim line. 'She came over to have a bath, pick up some clothes, ransack the cupboards and insult Lewis. She barely even acknowledged me. I don't know where she's staying, and I've been going out of my mind with worry.'

'She'll come back, you'll see.' I straightened up in the chair and tried to smile at him.

'I can't go on like this,' he said, not looking at me. His voice dropped to a whisper. 'I thought we were getting somewhere, you know? She hadn't taken her medication for at least a fortnight. She said she didn't need it. I'm back to normal now, Dad, that's what she said to me. *Back to normal.* A few days later I found her huddled on the doorstep at seven in the morning, delirious with drugs, semi-naked and freezing cold, dirty syringes in her pockets, *Jesus* . . .' He put an unsteady hand over his eyes, shaking his head in despair. 'She didn't even recognise me, Abi. Her own father.'

My heart sank. 'Dad, why didn't you tell me this –'

'Not even Jane knows about this,' he said, almost too quietly to hear. His eyes met mine. 'There's no point worrying her with all this. She knows *something* is wrong, but . . .'

'So what happened? What did you do?'

He sighed deeply, took his glasses off and polished them slowly on the edge of the tablecloth. 'What *could* I do? I took her in and cleaned her up, gave her some money. Forced some food into her. Lectured her. Told her to come home. She slept in her room all day and was gone again by the evening. Just got up and left. I thought about calling Rayneham . . .'

'What good will that do?'

'It beats doing *nothing*, for Christ's sake. The situation's not getting any better. It doesn't make it easier just because we've dealt with it before. It gets *harder*. You know it does. It just gets harder every time.'

'But nobody expects you to cope on your own . . .'

He fumbled his glasses back on and pushed them up the bridge of his nose, fixing me with a solemn stare through the smudged lenses. I felt overcome with pity and love for him, this poor, comical-looking man who had devotedly seen me through the most formative years of my life. He had aged so much in so little time; the creases of his laughter lines had deepened and sagged, no longer looking as if they had originated from half a lifetime of being happy. His kind, hazel eyes had lost most of their former sparkle over the years and now they just looked rather tired and droopy, although his eyebrows, bushy grey thickets of animated fuzz, made him look more like a mad professor than a care-worn father. I reached out to put my arm around his shoulder and buried my face into his shirt: Old Spice and Old Holborn.

He was silent for a long time, his expression blank.

'Dad? Did you hear what I said? Nobody expects you –'

'I know, darling. I know.'

'I mean, maybe . . .' I thought of a stupid idea and stopped myself from saying it.

Then I went ahead and said it anyway. 'Maybe she could come and stay with me at uni for a while. Just for a week or so. You never know, it might do us both good. We could keep each other out of trouble.'

The fuzzy eyebrows animated themselves into a flurry as he turned to face me in disbelief. 'Are you mad?' he demanded. 'She's not just some juvenile delinquent, Abigail. She's a drug addict with a severe psychosis. How do you think she'd possibly fit in with your university mates? How do you think it would make her any better? And how do you think *you'd* cope? She's like a bomb waiting to go off. You've seen for yourself what she can get like.'

'But she *listens* to me, Dad. Really. She needs to be given a chance to mix with people who share her lust for life but also have some kind of . . . *ambition.* She thinks she's lost all her potential, and that's part of the reason we keep finding ourselves back in this situation. She just doesn't see the point in trying any more.'

'That's exactly it. You are doing now what Jasmine should have done seven years ago – making the grade and working hard for a career and a good future. She had the ability, the intelligence, she had everything going for her. Instead she became a junkie. If she stayed with you it would be like a constant reminder to her of what a failure she is.' He grimaced and hastily corrected himself. 'I mean, what a failure she *thinks* she is.'

'You're making her sound like a lost cause,' I scolded.

'I just want her to get better, to be happy. I'll never give up on her. You know that.'

'Well, it was only a suggestion,' I mumbled. 'It will probably just be a case of going from one funny farm to another, I suppose.'

He didn't know whether to look alarmed or amused at this very weak joke. Finally, he smiled and said, 'I appreciate what you're saying, love. I'm not a pessimist or anything, but after so many years you do start thinking there really is no way out of this. Just . . . try to be Jasmine's *friend* – you know she thinks the world of you. Just be there for her as much as you can. I hate seeing her in that horrible place just as much as you do, but sometimes it's the only way. At least when she's in Rayneham I know she's getting the right treatment, and that she'll be cared for.'

'Drugged, analysed and labelled more like it,' I snapped, without thinking.

'You're so idealistic. It's not all black and white.'

We sat silently, Dad holding both my hands in his, but not looking at me.

'Would either of you like dessert?' Jane called out from the kitchen just as I was about to say something tangential and irrelevant.

Dad made a face. 'She's made a cake, bless her,' he whispered. 'It's impolite to refuse it but suicide to eat it. Just say you're full, OK?'

I nodded, remembering the cake Jane had baked for my school fête, many years before. Not so much 'Victoria sponge' as 'Victorian flannel'.

Jane stuck her head around the door and attempted to lift the gloomy mood.

'Anyone for fruitcake?'

Christmas was the usual uneventful event, dull and tolerable by turns and full of the predictable yuletide treats. The compulsory viewing of all the usual festive films – *Mary Poppins, A Christmas Carol, Texas Chainsaw Massacre* (Lewis's novel suggestion, from his own arcane video collection) – was punctuated with customary crap cracker jokes, over-indulgence (food, drink and sleep), and the phrase 'Next year we're getting a bloody *fake* tree.' The weight I had lost during the weeks at uni was piled back on again threefold, so my second New Year's Resolution was to join a gym – my first being to cut down smoking, which was equally unlikely. You know you're not a kid any more when you feel that all the sparkly magic has gone out of Christmas – and the pretence is hard to keep up after hearing 'Merry Christmas

Everyone' and 'I wish it could be Christmas every day' for the millionth time when all you can think about is the threatening letter your bank manager is about to send you.

But getting a card from the elusive ex-boyfriend did cheer me up considerably, especially as I hadn't even thought about sending him one. Admittedly it was a crap one with a picture of a candle and some holly on it, saying 'Season's Greetings' – the sort of card that's always left over from a bumper selection box. His mum had probably forced him into sending me one, but even so, it was still signed, 'Love, Nick'. Love. Not just 'from'. The boy still had feelings for me, albeit tiny leftovers.

To everyone's relief and apprehension, Jasmine split up with Honey and moved back in during the third week of December. She stayed in bed all day and moved furniture around, drank gallons of coffee and wailed like a banshee all night to prove she was well on the road to recovery. She barricaded herself in her room and didn't speak to any of us for a while, although on Christmas morning we were all pleasantly surprised to find presents for each of us under the tree, wrapped up in newspaper and tied with velvet ribbon, our names written on each small parcel in silver pen with a tag saying 'Luv J'. They were touching tokens: a recorded tape of sixties music for Dad, a Gameboy key ring for Lewis, a cookery book for Jane and a pencil case for me, complete with pencil, two novelty rubbers and a 6-inch plastic ruler. She'd certainly done better than me: all I'd managed was a hastily written card for everyone, taken from a bumper selection box.

Dad was on the phone to Rayneham every other day, but decided against committing Jasmine as an in-patient for a number of reasons, not least of which was the fact that it was already overrun with patients and desperately underrun with staff. Besides, she was determined to do it her own way or not at all.

It turned out that I didn't get the opportunity to properly see or speak to Jasmine until I returned home startled and sober from Ben and Sylvie's New Year's Eve Ball (apparently, the word 'party' becomes defunct and unfashionable when you leave school unless it is formally preceded by 'cheese and wine' or 'dinner'). I didn't celebrate the dawning of 1995 in quite the way I'd anticipated. For hours I had sat on a doorstep with Sylvie, holding her hair away from her face as she sobbed and puked her way through telling me what a bastard Ben was. They had had an argument over something or other a few days before, for which he had neglected to apologise and over which she had neglected to have a proper girly cry. So I mopped up the tears and dutifully ignored bastard Ben for the entire night, right up until I saw Sylvie eating the face off him as midnight was chimed in. Having apparently reconciled their differences, they then scampered upstairs in a torrent of frisky laughter and whisky kisses. This left me, the supposed best friend, downstairs in Ben's house with a bunch of people who found me just as uninteresting as I found them. Drinking held no appeal and when I discovered, to my utmost horror, that I was the only smoker there, I saw little point in sticking around. My premature departure became inevitable and all the more hastened after a spotty bloke with a mullet hairstyle and a withered sprig of mistletoe 'accidentally' spilled his shandy over my skirt.

I got home – miserably clear-headed and with all faculties in perfect working order – at just after two o'clock. It was pitch black outside and the only light on in the house was the one in the kitchen. I hung my coat up and wandered in to discover Dad and Jasmine playing Scrabble and sharing a bottle of Happy Shopper red wine. Dad was in his pyjamas and paisley robe, Jasmine looked quite stunning in a silver cocktail dress with her hair swept back and her eyes made up.

'Well, hello!' Dad said to me, glancing at the clock in surprise. 'Goodness, is that the time already? Did you have a good party?' He looked slightly drunk and very knackered.

'Not really,' I sighed. Jasmine gave me a plastic tumbler and silently poured some wine into it before I had a chance to object.

'You're looking really nice, Jas,' I told her.

She didn't respond. She just turned back to Dad and said curtly, 'Your turn.'

Dad's shiny, mottled face creased up as he studied the Scrabble board and his seven letter tiles.

'What are you doing?' I asked, my observational skills obviously not being particularly sharp, in spite of my sobriety.

'Drinking some disgusting wine, having a chat, playing some Scrabble, what does it look like we're doing?' Dad replied.

I sipped the wine. It was, indeed, disgusting. My tastebuds recoiled at the vinegary tang.

'So who's winning?'

'*He* is,' Jasmine sniffed, tapping an elongated column of ash from her cigarette into a nearby cup.

'Only because I had "ersatz" on the double-word score,' said Dad. 'That was just a bit of luck on my part, really.'

'I mean, what kind of word is that anyway?' Jasmine grumbled. I didn't know if she was talking to Dad or me or herself.

'Sounds like one of Dad's hippy words,' I said.

'Do you want to join in, love?' Dad offered, pulling up a stool beside him at the kitchen table.

'Well, gimme a look at your letters, then.'

I sat beside him and we all talked quietly together and finished the horrible wine, and then got through another (marginally less horrible) bottle. Jasmine nearly won the game in the end, by putting 'Y' on the end of 'PHONE' to make 'PHONEY', while Dad was stuck with the last three letter tiles: an unusable q, and two a's.

'Triple word score as well,' she claimed triumphantly.

'No it isn't!' Dad protested.

'Oh, let me win, Dad. Just this once,' she pleaded.

He chortled and reached for the bottle of scotch, snaffled from the drinks cabinet when the last of the Christmas wine and unpalatable perry had run out.

'Let's call it a draw then, shall we?' he said, filling our glasses and raising his own. 'Happy new year, girls,' he hiccuped. 'Here's to a bloody good one.'

Jasmine downed hers in one, then leaned in close and pulled both of us into her outstretched arms. 'Have I told you lately that

I think you're the bollocks?' she said, kissing the top of Dad's head.

'Steady on there, love, you'll give your old man a complex,' he chortled, blushing and looking happier than I'd seen him in a long time.

'And you, Abi,' Jasmine turned to me, her eyes dancing in the fitful flicker of the flashing coloured lights outside. 'You may be a shitty little student, but you're still my sister and . . . you're all right, you are.' She pressed her face against mine, her skin warm and soft and fragrant. She giggled and lit a cigarette, then tossed her head back and laughed at the ceiling for no apparent reason, her hair coming loose and falling around her shoulders as her laughter escalated into a manic cackle.

Dad and I beamed at each other knowingly, accustomed to Jasmine's private little jokes. She was with us again. Spirited, effervescent, wearying, incorrigible, irrepressible, weird, wonderful. My ersatz sister.

I entered the new term with a distinct air of optimism, spoiled only by marijuana withdrawal symptoms, a few tons of extra body mass, my failure to have completed (or even started) a required course essay, and fruitless attempts to push the niggling worries I still had about Jasmine to the back of my mind.

The obligatory 'Welcome Back to Student Hell' celebrations began with another hall party, which was already well under way when I arrived. Marbles was having simulated sex with a shrieking Juliet on the kitchen table, Alex was fondling another mystery blonde in the corner, and Rachel and Simon were coiled together in the corridor, drinking a bottle of Babycham. The feeling of being the only sober person in the vicinity struck me immediately and I slunk off to my room, stepping over the chirping, burping lovebirds and nodding at Alex, who gave me a cheeky wink and a thumbs-up sign while his playful platinum-haired cohort necked him hungrily and wriggled a hand inside his jeans.

Back inside my cold, grey room, I threw my bag to the floor, pushed the door shut, slipped off my coat and boots and flopped out on the bed, which looked even smaller than I remembered. I wrestled with the pillows and flung the sheets around until I had established a vaguely comfortable foetal position in a nest of crumpled linen. I took a few deep breaths and closed my eyes, with the full intention of falling into a deep sleep in spite of the frenzied fracas going on outside.

Trying to salvage a moment's peace in my dismal bedroom was, of course, a futile exercise. After just a few precious minutes of solitude, Catherine burst in without knocking, wearing an obviously brand new fur-trimmed ankle-length coat and not much else. She stood in my doorway and looked at me with a terrified expression.

'Do you know that twat Maurice is trying to get into my mate's knickers?' she blithered at me in alarm.

Wearily, I propped myself up on my elbow. 'What?' I blinked at her blearily.

'Oh, sorry, were you sleeping?'

'Fat fuckin' chance,' I grumbled. 'Don't you ever knock?'

She ignored me, leaning against the wall with her pelvis sticking out like a movie hustler, hands in pockets. 'Me and Nadine have just got here too. Come and join us downtown. It's only half-nine, you *can't* go to bed yet.'

'Now that's where you're wrong. Here I am and here I stay. Goodbye.' I turned my back on her and stared wide-eyed at the wall, hugging the flaccid pillow to my chest. Warm air frosted to a white mist in front of my face as I exhaled. A bit of central heating in the place was obviously too much to ask for. There was one small radiator in my room and all it ever did was clank occasionally and provide somewhere to hang my underwear.

'Oh come on, Abi. What's wrong with you?'

'It's called terminal apathy,' I retorted blandly. 'Or "being boring". Or just mental exhaustion. Call it what you like. Just bugger off and leave me to it.' I moved my head and smiled at her meekly over my shoulder. 'Sorry, Cath, but I ain't budging.'

She pouted her glossed lips at me. 'What a pathetic excuse for a student you are,' she said, not without vituperation.

'You know, you're so right. Nightie night then.'

Nadine's voice caterwauled from the kitchen: 'For fuck's sake, Marbles, you *abject cretin*, people have got to *eat* off that table, you know,' followed by the unmistakable peal of Juliet's laughter and the rapid scampering of two pairs of feet and the slamming of a door. Marbles's bedroom door.

'Ugh, yuk. Like, *really* yuk.' Catherine looked pained. 'What the hell is Jules playing at? Marbles is *such* a wanker.' She was very quiet for a while, a look of appalled concentration on her face as if she was waiting to detect other sounds to fuel her disgust: the rip of a condom wrapper perhaps, or the slap of flank on flesh and the guttural grunt of Marbles 'getting jiggy with Mr Biggy' and the feverish squeak of Juliet doing likewise.

Mercifully, all was silent outside, give or take the sporadic slurps and whisperings of Simon and Rachel and the odd flush of a toilet and subdued music from Garston's room ('Digging your scene').

Catherine's expression softened when she glanced over at me again. She took a cigarette from behind her ear and lit it with a match which she then blew out after watching it shrivel black down almost to her fingertips.

'Come on. It's shit here. Me and Nadine are on a quest to find a man. One who isn't a dickhead.'

'Ha! Good luck.'

'You coming then?'

I groaned. I just wanted a bit of peace.

'Oh, *all right* then, if I must,' I mumbled, well aware that I was fighting a losing battle. 'Just give me a moment.'

'Oh, did you have a good holiday by the way?'

I got up slowly and put my boots back on. 'Not bad. You?'

She scowled. Catherine put immense effort into ensuring every facial expression was executed in an elegant and stylish way, so that even a negative emotion was conveyed with the minimum of lines and creases and the maximum of sullen prettiness.

'I put on six bloody pounds,' she spat. 'Can you believe that? I mean, *look*!' She pulled up a barely-there skinny-fit top to reveal a concave, toned stomach, a flat terrain of tanned, smooth skin. Even her bellybutton was no more than a perfect crescent-shaped dimple, daintily punctured with an amethyst and silver belly ring. 'Look at the flab!' she demanded, pinching at her taut flesh and knowing very well that I had more fat on my little toe.

'AND . . .' she continued, obviously not realising that I had only made the enquiry out of politeness, 'I didn't get anything that I asked for. My excuse for a boyfriend bought me this awful French perfume, and I didn't even get enough money to buy that gorgeous dress I fell in love with. You know, the one I showed you in November's *Vogue*.'

'Cath,' I said gently, 'it was three hundred pounds.'

'Well, exactly. I've got a massive family. Only twenty quid from everyone and I should have had more than enough. Not much to ask really, is it? And my sister works in a fashion house, she gets *loads* of freebies.'

She looked as if she was going to go into a rant, so I chose to agree with her and change the direction of the conversation slightly, rather than pointing out that three hundred quid was considerably more than I had to live on for the entire term.

'Christmas sucks,' I agreed heartily. 'Nice coat though.'

She managed another line-free smile. 'It's not bad, is it?' She opened up the front and dropped it from her shoulders to reveal the lining, cerise and satiny. She stroked the collar and cuffs and made a purring noise, looking at me coyly through her elongated eyelashes. Detecting my involuntary flinch of disapproval, she hastily added, 'It's not *real* fur! God, no!'

'It suits you,' I said, meaning it. 'You look like a film star.'

'Cheers.' I always felt Catherine warmed to me the more I handed out empty compliments, comments about her appearance that she knew were true anyway and certainly didn't need telling. She was undeniably very pretty and quite a sweet person, but she was more boring and uninspiring than I ever thought it was possible for another human being to be. I sighed and stood up, stretching and stifling a yawn.

'Shall we go then?'

'Are you going like *that*?' She didn't even bother trying to hide her distaste. I shrugged, looking down indifferently at my grey leggings and scuffed DMs, laced with tartan ribbons.

'We're only going to a pub, aren't we?'

'Well, yes, I suppose so, but –' She looked at me quizzically, not wanting to overstep the line. She did anyway. 'Don't you want to put some make-up on? Jazz yourself up a bit?'

I gave her a look that I think more or less answered her question.

'Fine, fine. Please yourself.'

Nadine burst in, all gleaming smiles and shiny eyes, looking like she'd spent the last month on a health farm.

'Good to be back, innit?' she said, throwing her arms around me. 'How was yours then?' She kissed me on both cheeks with rapturous excitement, making a couple of casual aside comments about how nice my hair and skin looked (lies).

'What?'

'Christmas. Good one or what?'

'Hmmm . . .' I checked my bag for cigarettes, money (a tenner and some shrapnel), a condom (hope sprang eternal), door key and union card. 'It was OK. What about you?'

'Fab, sweetie. Absolutely wonderful.'

'Did you get everything you wanted?'

'Oh yes. Wasted and laid. Perfect.'

Catherine raised her eyebrows at me. 'All right for some, isn't it?'

'Where are we off to then?' I asked, as we walked out of my room into the corridor, now sinisterly dark and deserted.

'Anywhere away from this place. I mean, *Marbles and Jules*! Who'd have thunk it, eh?'

Catherine made a retching noise. 'She's on the rebound. She got dumped on Christmas Eve.'

'Maybe she just likes him,' I suggested, not unreasonably.

'Stranger things have happened,' Nadine nodded.

'Anyway,' said Catherine 'how about we go to that new posh wine bar near West Pier?'

'Didn't know there was one. How about just a local pub around Falmer? I can't be bothered to go all the way to . . .'

'Yeah, that sounds good, Cath,' Nadine chipped in, cutting me off. 'I'm up for that. Anything to avoid the union and cheap beer.'

'And the drooling imbeciles,' Catherine added.

'Off we go then.' Nadine grabbed my arm and dragged my reluctant bulk along as she chatted good-humouredly to Catherine about kitten heels versus wedge heels, and bottled beer versus pints.

It seemed I didn't have much of a choice. Two against one.

We arrived at our destination half an hour later, and Nadine and Catherine soon put paid to my childish protestations by plying me with Chardonnay.

'I can afford to treat you, mate. My dad got a generous Christmas bonus, and as his youngest and favourite, I get to reap some of the rewards,' Nadine explained as she presented me with the third glass. 'Or rather, I get to piss them up the wall.' I wibbled a final objection and then downed it, considerably less begrudgingly than the first two.

'Cheers, Nads.'

'Hey, don't mention it. Just don't call me Nads.'

Catherine had slunk off to chat to the barman, who merrily poured her one unidentifiable drink after another from two over-iced jugs containing bright blue or frosted pink liquid. He was well into his thirties and had a disturbing laugh but Catherine had insisted he would 'do for now'. The wine bar wasn't so much posh as faux-posh; plush upholstered seats in semi-private booths with framed black and white prints on the walls and polished laminate flooring; the clientele ranged from spiral-permed underage girls and their psyched-up, bellicose boyfriends to yapping yuppies with bite-sized mobile phones and needlessly loud voices. And there was the odd student as well, of course.

We watched Catherine flirt with the barman for a while, and then Nadine pushed her chair closer to mine and leaned towards me. 'Is everything OK with you now, mate? You've got a face like a wet weekend, and I know you're not really a grumpy old cow. I don't want to stick my beak in or anything, but . . . is it Jasmine? Is she still . . . er . . .'

I shook my head. 'Sorry. It's nothing really. I'm just . . . tired, I suppose. That's all.'

'Tired?' She gave me an incredulous stare. 'We've just come back from a four-week holiday Abi. You should be full of beans.'

'I know I *should* be, but I'm just . . . not.'

'Did you get your Chaucer essay done?'

'Nope.'

'Did you read that whatshisname book about war and madness?'

'No. *Catch-22* is still bookmarked at page five, I'm afraid. Anyway, who do you think you are? My personal tutor or something?'

'Did you do *anything* worthwhile?' she demanded.

I descended into humble silence, suddenly finding great interest in a congealed tomato ketchup stain on the table.

'I'll take that as a no, then.'

'I just never found the time,' I moaned.

'What are you like, eh? Anyway . . . *is* Jasmine better?'

I sighed and shrugged my shoulders despondently. 'She's a bit fucked up still. She'll pull through. She always does.'

'You two are really close aren't you?'

'Yeah, I suppose. Sometimes though . . . sometimes it's hard to love her as much as I should.'

'What do you mean?'

'No . . . that's wrong. Sometimes I wish I didn't love her as much as I do.'

'Oh dear. Sounds like you need to get blind drunk. Might help you start making sense.'

'I doubt it.'

Nadine finished her wine in three hearty gulps, and looked at me intently for a few seconds. 'Look, how about we move on? There's a great gay club ten minutes down the road from here. It will lift your spirits, I promise.'

'Gay club?'

'Jasmine wouldn't want you to sit around worrying about her and getting all depressed and boring, would she?'

I studied a faded lipstick stain on my drained wine glass, and twisted the stem around listlessly. Nadine's exuberance usually inspired me, but by now I was just finding it exhausting, and I made no attempt to look excited.

'I look a mess,' I whinged. 'My clothes are awful and I haven't washed my hair for three days.'

'So?'

'I'm not in the mood.'

'Look, I'll get you another drink, and then we'll be on our merry way, OK?'

'No.' I stood up quickly, determined not to drain Nadine's patience as well as her finances. 'Let me get this round. I owe you big time,' I insisted.

Nadine acquiesced. 'And tell Catherine to put her tits back in while you're up there. She's beginning to come across as a bit of a slapper.'

She nodded towards the bar, across which Catherine had now draped herself, seductively preening her baby-blonde bobbed hair, her eyes wide and enraptured and her bountiful chest pushing upwards and outwards from her skimpy top. The barman was mesmerised, ignoring the pleas of increasingly impatient note-waving punters who surrounded him in thirsty swarms.

'*And* she's wearing fuck-me boots,' Nadine sniffed, eyeing Catherine's zip-up leather thigh-highs with a reproachful sneer. 'Still, she can get away with it I suppose. And they *do* make her look fuckable. Sort of.' Nadine had a knack of being disdainful and insulting in a mild and rather charitable way.

I fought my way through the rabble and eventually purchased two cocktails, had a slight cardiac arrest when I received negligible change from my last solitary tenner, and carried them back carefully to the table, managing to spill at least a quid's worth on the way.

Ten minutes later, we trundled off to the club, more than a little tipsy, leaving Catherine to let her boots do the talking.

I wasn't expecting her and I certainly hadn't prepared myself for another impromptu visit, but for some reason I wasn't surprised at all when I opened my door the following Sunday morning and found Jasmine asleep outside in the corridor. Well – not so much asleep as out stone cold.

I stood over her and gently nudged her with my foot. No response. I knelt down beside her and shook her shoulders, repeating her name from a hissed whisper to an impatient hollering into her ear. She groaned and opened one eye, then closed it again. I was contemplating the cold water/Marbles's pants method of resuscitation when suddenly she opened both eyes and smiled at me. 'Me again,' she mumbled.

'For God's *sake* Jasmine, what the –'

'Page?' Marbles's voice rang down from the other end of the corridor. I straightened up and looked over at him in irritation. 'Oh *what now*?' I snapped. He gave me a quizzical look. 'Your dad's on the phone,' he said offhandedly, retreating back into his room in a flash of stripy pyjama.

'Shit,' I said to myself. Then, louder, '*Shit.*'

Alex emerged from the bathroom wearing nothing but a towel and his usual self-assured smirk, shower-fresh pert nipples and flexed muscles displayed for everyone to marvel at. 'Do you know her?' he asked me, pointing at Jasmine and raising his eyebrows.

'Unfortunately, yes. She's my sister.'

He stepped carefully over her, his head cocked to the side, assessing her as if she were a curious zoo exhibit. 'Looks like she's been on a bit of a bender,' he observed, his cackling laughter setting my teeth on edge. 'Ha! Ha! I'll have whatever she's havin'!'

'All you'll have is my fist in your face if you don't sod off,' I warned him, almost meaning it.

'Ooh, *handbags*,' he trilled in a falsetto voice, clutching his wash bag to his chest and mincing towards his room with a camp wiggle.

Nadine emerged into the corridor then, grumbling with the typical high dudgeon of a student awoken before midday.

'What's going on out here?' she whined, barely able to open her eyes.

I grabbed her without a second's hesitation. 'Jas has just turned up,' I explained, waving my hand at the oblivious heap of my sister, now unconscious again and making strange sibilant noises. 'I've got to take a phone call from my dad. Can you just try to . . . maybe get her into my bed, do you think? Kick, shove, threaten, do whatever it takes. Just get her out of the corridor.'

'Er, *excuse* me, but –'

'Cheers, mate. You're a star. I won't be long. I promise.'

Ignoring her bleating objections, I raced to the phone and was out of breath when I picked up the receiver and blurted out, 'Hello Dad. She's here.'

There was a small pause. 'Oh, I'm so sorry love.' Dad's voice sounded far away, muffled, like he was talking with his hand over the mouthpiece. 'I only just found the note in her room. It says, "I'm going to stay with sis for a while. Feeling better now. Just need some fun. See you soon." I would have stopped her. I know this must be very inconvenient for you.'

'Hey, don't worry about it. It's not a problem,' I assured him. 'I don't think she'll be here for very long anyway.'

'How does she look?'

'Oh, you know . . .'

'That bad?'

'It's OK, Dad. We'll be fine. Look, I have to go now. I'll call you when she leaves.'

'Look after her, won't you?'

'Of course. See you soon.'

I hung up and hurried back to my room. Nadine was still standing over Jasmine, looking perplexed. A bemused audience of Simon, Rachel and Catherine had gathered round, pointing and whispering as if they'd never seen a wasted human being before. As if they'd never been in a similar state dozens of times themselves.

'Can't shift her,' Nadine said. 'Look, I need a shower. I'll give you a hand once I'm dressed.'

'Yeah, cheers.' I took a hold of Jasmine's wrists and tried to drag her head first into my room. I stopped short when I heard the painful sound of a bone cracking, worried that I might end up pulling her elbows or her shoulders out of their sockets.

'Here, let me help,' Frank offered, appearing seemingly from out of nowhere and striding towards me.

'No, really, it's all right, I . . .'

'I'll pick her up this end, you take the other end,' he said, holding her floppy, inert legs, and taking a boot firmly in each hand. It was more of an order than a suggestion. I did as I was told. Within seconds, we had successfully deposited Jasmine on my bed, and, to my surprise, Frank carefully removed her boots and pulled the covers around her with a gentleness that was almost paternal.

'There,' he said, smiling at me. He looked weird with no make-up on. Weird as in 'almost normal'. Pleasant and rather sweet, really. 'She just needs to sleep it off for a while.'

'Well . . . er, thanks for your help,' I stammered.

'Don't mention it,' he mumbled, and backed humbly out of the room, shutting the door quietly behind him.

Ten minutes later, Nadine brought along a pot of coffee and a plate of jaffa cakes, and we put the radio on full blast in an attempt to stir Jasmine from her drugged dormancy. But she just snored sonorously while Nadine and I enjoyed a calorific and caffeine-loaded breakfast. I tried to get some black coffee into Jasmine, but all she did was gurgle it and spit and dribble it back out.

'Well, sorry to be a bore after so much excitement but I'm afraid I've got to tootle off to the library now to finish this crappy assignment thingy,' Nadine announced, cramming the last jaffa cake in her mouth. She got up from the floor and cast me a worried look. 'Will you be . . . all right?'

'Sure. Good luck with it,' I said, smiling up at her despite feeling suddenly and inexplicably apprehensive about being left alone with Jasmine.

She glanced over at my obliterated sister and said, 'Yeah, you too.'

Jasmine didn't properly come round until late afternoon, when I took her for a brisk walk around the university grounds to clear her head. In the evening we went to a vegetarian restaurant downtown and had a strangely stilted conversation over a selection of hippyish delicacies. She stuffed herself on tofu and organic carrot cake, while I made do with a vegan salad bowl, half a melon and a glass of crushed ice cubes laced with strawberry soda. Jasmine insisted on paying, which was just as well, since I barely had enough for the tip.

Once she had regained her strength, she looked up at me guiltily and said, 'I know I'm getting in your way again. I've got this annoying habit of popping up when you least need it.'

I didn't contradict her. 'I just wish you'd phone first,' I said.

'Well, I was hanging around Victoria station and there was a Brighton train just . . . waiting there for me. So I got on it.'

'It's a miracle you made it here at all. You were out of your box.'

'Heavy night,' she explained dismissively, and we said no more on the subject. She stared out of the window, her elbows resting on the table as she smoked a Marlboro, absently scratching at her thin, pale arms and humming quietly to herself.

'I feel sick,' she said, stubbing out the cigarette in my half-eaten melon after just two or three puffs.

I was going to tell her she only had herself to blame, but she knew that anyway. So I just sucked the last of the melted ice cubes through my straw and asked her how long she was intending to stay.

'Until your patience or my money runs out, whichever happens first,' she replied, not turning away from the window.

'I have lectures tomorrow,' I told her, as if I was a devout lecture attendee.

'That's OK. I could look around for a job or something. Thinking about moving down here permanently.'

I gave her a dubious stare. 'With who?'

'You?'

'I don't think so.'

'Why not? You'll have to find a place to rent around here later this year anyway, won't you?'

I fell silent.

'Do I embarrass you?' she asked me, after I had been evading her gaze for too long.

'Of course not.'

'You still love me, don't you?'

'*Jas*mine . . .'

'It's just that sometimes, y'know . . . sometimes I think we're kind of – disconnected. Things have changed. We were like best friends before, and now . . .'

'Shall I order coffee?' I piped up chirpily, reaching out for the menu and pretending to take an interest in the speciality brews.

She bowed her head. 'No thanks.'

'Tea?' I suggested, desperately.

She scraped her plastic fork on the table and shook her head. When the waitress came past she asked for the bill, then looked out of the window again.

'We could go for a walk on the pier if you like,' I offered.

'Maybe.'

'I'm meeting some course mates at a pub near here at eight.'

'But . . . I wanted us to go out together tonight. Just you and me. Then I'll leave. I promise I will. I just wanted the chance to . . .' She left the sentence hanging on a heavy sigh as she pulled her woolly bobble hat down over her ears. It flattened her hair down and somehow made her look twelve years old, framing her elfin facial features so they appeared more childlike. She wore no make-up; just Vaseline on her cracked lips and a touch of black mascara which had smudged slightly under her eyes. She looked like a beautiful actress pretending to be a junkie. A beautiful actress in a daft blue and white knitted bobble hat pretending to be a junkie.

'You're welcome to come along too, of course,' I added hurriedly, making it sound like an obligation on my part.

'Yeah, cheers.' She turned around and unwound my borrowed university scarf from the back of her chair and wrapped it round her neck. The waitress handed Jasmine the bill and she glanced at it, her eyebrows shooting to the top of her head.

'Looks like it's going to be a dead heat between your patience and my money,' she muttered.

We left the restaurant and wandered about aimlessly for a while before finally ending up in the pub, a bluesy little basement tavern which provided a free movie on a giant screen as well as numerous comfy sofas for loafing drinkers to pass out on. Two of my course mates were there, as they had been since noon, putting the finishing touches to a seminar presentation and a poetry appreciation. They urged me to attend Monday's lecture, insisting I absolutely *had* to go or else face the public humiliation of a right royal bollocking from the tutor. Although I did try to involve her in our admittedly dull student-centred conversations, Jasmine merely sat quietly in the corner out-drinking all of us and yet remaining on the exact same spaced-out plateau that she had occupied for the whole day. She barely said another word to me, even when we got back to campus; just a hug goodnight before settling down on my bedroom floor with a scratchy blanket and a spare pillow.

When I returned from the compulsory lecture the following morning she had already gone, leaving nothing behind but a few scattered fag ends and the redolent smell of her perfume.

After Jasmine left, I surprised everybody, myself included, by boldly attending another *two* lectures that same week. I was almost terrified into doing some serious coursework after one of the tutors cunningly slipped the word 'exam' into his spiel. This new-found academic motivation, although very much heartfelt at the time, was sadly short-lived. At least, it lasted until Marbles and Alex came up with the novel idea of a three-legged pub-crawl. This excitingly crass suggestion unfortunately came on the very night I was planning on settling down at my desk with a folder full of lecture notes and a brain full of enthusiasm for nineteenth-century English prose. Never mind, there's always tomorrow night, I thought, abandoning my bundle of papers and piles of novels and texts as I tied my right leg to Nadine's left and the pair of us hobbled behind Marbles and Alex, Simon and Rachel, Catherine and Juliet, Garston and Frank, all conjoined likewise. My New Year's Resolution to cut down on weed was going better than I had anticipated – I was learning to love alcohol and was slowly building up my tolerance level. (Of course, I was to discover the hard way that to cut back on one addiction to make room for another is not necessarily a wise policy.)

The ten of us were off our faces before we even had the basic sense or foresight to think about possible routes for the proposed pub-crawl. This was due, in large part, to the communal bottle of Bacardi which Garston had brought along with him, and the cans of cheap but potent lager we had consumed with cheerful complacency before our clumsy departure. We had all managed, with much intermediate pant-wetting, general hilarity and mobility problems, to stagger a couple of hundred yards down the road before first thinking about aborting the mission.

'I need a shit,' Marbles announced, trying to head into the bushes at the side of the road and thus nearly causing Alex, helplessly shackled to him, to topple over on to the pavement in a blunder of colourful language.

'Can't you wait until we at least get to a pub?' Simon implored.

'I've got to go *now*.'

'Well take this fuckin' thing off of us will you? I'm sick of being tied to you,' Alex grumbled, trying in vain to establish an upright position. 'Whose crap idea was this, anyway?'

'Yours,' everyone chorused.

'Look, we've come this far. We may as well go the distance.' Nadine, ever the optimist, clutched my shoulder and lifted her left leg to dodder forward clumsily. A few seconds behind her train of thought, I stumbled and tripped and finally regained my balance, then proceeded to make similar awkward robotic movements in roughly the opposite direction.

'Yeah, come on guys,' I yelled chirpily over my shoulder after we had gained an unsteady rhythm and boldly progressed several inches. We were alone in our enthusiasm, which was a shame, because I was feeling uncharacteristically euphoric. Eight blank faces looked at us grimly. Juliet started wailing about chipped nail polish and laddered tights, while Garston complained that he was too drunk to go any further, and did not relish being attached by an Arsenal football scarf to a 'depressive freak' who insisted that The Smiths were a mediocre band manufactured specifically for 'trainee wannabe Goths'. Marbles farted with great resonance and ill-deserved masculine pride, and Alex pushed him away disgustedly, causing him to overbalance into the brambles and bushes, taking Alex down with him in an impressive slapstick display.

Without too much further disagreement, it was eventually decided in a rare flash of collective wisdom that we should all untie ourselves from our partners and abandon the three-legged pub-crawl project for another time. Utilising what little motor-sensory control we still had between us, we followed an indirect and meandering route downtown, finally embarking on an altogether different kind of pub-crawl – a predictably static one that started and finished at the Leek and Winkle.

My drunken merriment gave way to a more reflective state of drunken depression towards the end of the evening, while I sat desolately on a clammy toilet seat contemplating my meagre existence. It's a fact of life: no matter how deeply the subconscious worries and fears are buried, alcohol has a knack of dredging them back up again. I had consumed well over my lightweight limit in order to become happy and sociable, and now the negative thoughts had come creeping back into my consciousness and I was back to being miserable and dull again.

My head spun as I focused on the graffiti on the back of the cubicle door in front of me. The polite message 'Please dispose of your feminine hygiene products in the sanitary bins provided' had been both defaced and flagrantly ignored – indeed, some rebellious or illiterate soul had gone to the trouble of sticking their own particularly unhygienic hygiene product on the u-bend for all to admire. Beneath this sign, someone had written 'Karen woz ere' in chunky black marker pen. Next to that, in the same pen and the same handwriting, was the proud declaration 'Kaz R loves Jimbo P'. I stared at the words, trying to glean some hidden meaning from them. Failing that, I attempted to make anagrams out of the letters. *Mole's job iz v. krap* was the best I could come up with, even after several minutes' deep concentration. I grew bored with that game before too long, unsurprisingly. I chewed the inside of my mouth until I could taste blood. My knee started shaking uncontrollably and I tried clamping it still with an equally shaky hand. I thought about my course, and how little proper work I had done. I thought about how disappointed Dad and Jane would be when I returned home with nothing to show for their parental aspirations but a new addiction and a scrap of paper from my course tutor saying 'Abigail Page? Who the fuck is she?'

I thought about my inherent inability to pull a bloke – any bloke really, never mind a nice one. My glaring lack of sexual success was beginning to have a malignant effect on my self-esteem. Maybe I wasn't trying hard enough. Maybe I was trying too hard.

I thought about the epically impecunious state of my bank account, and how I had reassured my hard-up father that I was 'nowhere near my overdraft limit'. The truth was, my overdraft limit was exceeded weeks ago, and in a ruthless and self-defeating method familiar to students everywhere, my bank had punished me accordingly by means of . . . further fines. Eagerly pouncing upon me at my most financially vulnerable like a lithesome lioness on a knackered gazelle, they had no qualms at all about threatening to charge me more interest on a mounting debt that they knew I couldn't possibly pay off this side of middle age. Letter after letter had warned me of my impending financial doom – 'Dear Miss Page, We would like to draw your attention to the fact that you are extremely poor and, as such, we would like to offer you an extra £1,000 on top of your current overdraft. You are already shamefully in debt to us so what difference can a few more zeros make? Please fill out the enclosed umpteenth pointless form, the small print of which stipulates a barely legal self-protecting clause which entitles us to plague you with demands for money until the day you die.' – and because I was a student and I needed my kicks, I gave little heed to the possible tragic long-term consequences of my short-term expensive hedonism.

And, more important and terrible than all these disastrous things rolled together, I thought about Jasmine. The very fabric of my existence seemed to be held together by these tenuous threads: the stress of my poverty, the poverty of my sex life, the madness and slow disintegration of my sister, the meaningless-ness and aimlessness of my day-to-day behaviour. What else was there?

My thoughts were interrupted when someone stampeded in and ran some water in a basin, blew their nose noisily and had a brief altercation with the tampon vending machine. I groaned inwardly, suddenly realising that I now needed a number two. I had neither the energy nor the inclination to empty my bowels, but the fact that I was conveniently placed on a public convenience seemed to get everything in motion. I braced myself for an embarrassing evacuation.

'Abi? Are you in here?' Catherine's voice, slightly slurred.

'Oh, go away,' I muttered, under my breath. 'Yeah, yeah, here I am,' I called back, trying in vain to put some perkiness into my own slurred tones.

'You OK?'

'Fine, fine, Cath. I'm just . . .'

'Been sick?'

'No, I think . . . I'm just paralysed.'

Not entirely true, my guts were getting very lively. I strained for a couple of seconds, which sapped my last remaining energy.

'Need a hand?'

'Er . . . not advisable, Cath.' For a horrible moment, I thought I was going to projectile vomit all over Kaz R's careful scrawling. Then the sickness feeling descended and last night's dinner made a rapid and noisy exit before I even had a chance to cough or flush to cover up the revolting sounds.

A heavy and mortifying silence followed. I felt my face burn.

'Er, like, *gross*, Abigail.'

'Sorry. I think there's more to come, I'm afraid.'

'You should get it on with Marbles, you're both disgusting,' she quipped, only half-joking. I managed a feeble laugh.

'At least I do mine in the proper place,' I argued in my defence. 'Marbles would rather go in the bushes.'

Basic bodily functions – unless under controlled conditions, stringently sterilised and as far removed from how nature intended as possible – were anathema to Catherine. As far as my admittedly very basic knowledge of human biology went, I was of the impression that all human beings do actually need to crap and fart every now and then, but Catherine seemed to flout this anatomical rule – her often bemoaned 'weak bladder' being the only evidence that she had any kind of waste disposal system going on at all in her perfectly packaged body.

'Yeah, I suppose,' came her eventual response.

I was surprised she hadn't beaten a hasty retreat *tout de suite*, especially now the air was pervaded with the inevitable and sickening aroma of an extremely unwell student. She sounded like she was concentrating on something else – probably gazing into the mirror and retouching her make-up, I reckoned, knowing what she was like. That was always her priority, come hell or high water or vile stenches. Never a hair out of place, whatever the situation.

The smell was enough to stop me passing out, at least. I slowly reached a weak arm behind me and yanked awkwardly at the flush, finally managing to get it to function on the fourth attempt after it made a few unpromising gurgling sounds.

'It's last orders at the bar,' Catherine informed me distractedly.

'Do I sound to you like a woman in need of more alcohol?' I grunted.

'Well, you certainly need something.'

I heard two more girls come in then, giggling and chatting vociferously as girls in pub toilets often do. With every intention of showing me up, Catherine said to them, 'Sorry about the smell. It's my mate. She's eaten something that's disagreed with her.'

To my relief and amusement, one of them responded, in a broad Scottish accent, 'That's aeright. We thought it was your perfume.' They giggled again (I could just picture Catherine's horrified expression and I let out a little chortle myself), and locked themselves into the cubicle next to me.

I heard Catherine grumble in defiance and root about in her bag and spray herself with Chanel Number 69, or whatever the latest trendy fragrance was.

'There. That's better,' she said, proudly, to herself.

I closed my eyes tight until pinpoint neon shimmers of red and little spermatozoa of light swam in the black.

Catherine's voice interrupted my private psychedelic reel. 'We'll be leaving in a minute. You'd better get yourself together, dear heart.'

I slowly opened my eyes again, and everything was swimming, like looking into a washing machine. No: I was *in* a washing machine, on turbo-speed spin cycle. I closed them again and moaned.

'Sounds like you've got the squits,' Catherine pointed out kindly. With the next rumble, I was disposed to agree.

Nadine came in at that point, and started to say something that sounded like, 'Oh my God you wouldn't *believe* what that shameless tosspot has done *now*,' before sniffing the air and heaving in disgust, leaving her sentence hanging. 'What the fuck is that stink?' she demanded instead.

''S Abi. She's not very well.' Catherine obviously started mouthing something silently at Nadine, because there followed a good deal of confused whispering, and Nadine eventually addressed me, sounding concerned.

'Let's go back now, mate. You've had a bit of a rough night. And what in the name of sweet baby Jesus have you eaten?'

I didn't answer. I was thinking about how crap life was, how despicable students are, how ill I was, how ill Jasmine was . . . *oh God*, poor Jasmine. I had been such a bitch to her, I hadn't even tried to understand. I was too busy being a despicable, ill student and thinking there was nothing else in life apart from this pitiful daily ritual of mine. I put my elbows on my knees and my head in my hands and felt an overwhelming surge of total despair. She had repeatedly warned me that this would happen, and I had vehemently denied it every time. She said I would find a new set of mates and give her less and less of my time, until I'd eventually become so preoccupied with my shallow lifestyle that I'd forget about her and all the things I'd learned from her.

And she was right.

She was dying. That was the truth I had to face. While the people around me were worried about things of little more consequence than the state of their hair, or how attractive and original they were, or where they were going for their next drink, or how many people they could get into bed, or how many drugs they could take before requiring hospitalisation, my own sister was killing herself slowly through no real fault of her own.

She was the one I looked up to, who cared about the things that mattered. All I wanted to do was have a good time, without thinking about the really important things. I was so selfish. I hated myself.

'I hate myself!' I croaked pathetically.

Nobody seemed to hear me; Nadine was zealously appraising Catherine's appearance with rapturous ramblings of admiration such as 'No, *really*, you look fine,' and '*Honestly*, Cath, you're so gorgeous it makes me sick,' and Catherine was accepting and prompting the flattery in her usual gratingly immodest way.

I fumbled for the greaseproof (and probably shitproof) toilet paper, scared that if I stayed stuck there for much longer my bum would sucker itself to the seat.

'Hey, do you think Abi's all right in there?' Nadine suddenly piped up.

Catherine ignored her. 'Are you *sure* these shoes don't clash with my dress?' she whined.

I sighed, slumping over awkwardly to my right and resting my forehead against the partition, cold and dank against my skin. The girls in the next cubicle were taking hits of cocaine and kissing each other and nattering excitedly. A body was suddenly slammed up against the flimsy partition on the other side, barely an inch from my head, and I heard a zipper and a rip of fabric and a couple of whimpers and moans.

I tore off some paper and looked at the back of the door again, my eyes drawn to some graffiti I hadn't noticed before; three simple and strangely evocative scribbled words that clenched at my insides and slowed my heart, bringing my drunkenness into a sudden dreadful clarity. Underneath 'Karen woz ere', etched in red marker pen, were the words '*ConformConsumeDie*'.

6

Us and the Lemmings

The strongest piece of advice I would give to any young woman is: Don't screw around, and don't smoke.

Edwina Currie, Sayings of the Week, *The Observer*, 3 April 1988

Freeze!

I stopped dead, seized by panic, and felt a shiver of fear course through me. I turned slowly to face the blinding rows of oscillating blue and white lights, the wind whipped up by helicopters overhead, the incessant, deafening thud-thud-thud of the whirring blades almost drowning out the piercing shriek of sirens. Flashlights shone straight into my eyes, scorching red stars into my retinas and I put my hands up to my face to block them out, while people shouted random words like strange codes into radios crackling with static. I pressed my back up against a dead-end metal and barbed-wire fence, quivering in terror as a voice boomed out:

You have no choice but to give yourself up.

Strapping men in uniform surrounded me like a formidable blue wall; this should really have been a fantasy of mine but instead it was horrific. I was like a fox surrounded by hounds, exhausted after the chase and with nowhere to go. There were thousands of them, and they had rifles and they were pointing at me, every single one of them. I felt my heart in my throat, a spontaneous cold sweat wetting my clothes and sticking my hair itchily to the nape of my neck as I quivered in terror, knowing there was no escape.

Face the wall and spread your legs with your hands up and palms against the wall.

The instructions were being blared at me through a loud-hailer by a strange little man in FBI uniform with a bored American drawl and an extremely large and unruly beard. He looked exactly like my father did in the seventies, except dressed incongruously in a uniform and jackboots rather than peace robes and Jesus sandals. His striking similarity to my dad made me momentarily forget about my fear, and I neglected to heed the hollered orders, which were barked out a second time, even louder and more severe:

This is your last warning, you are completely surrounded.

'Dad?' I said (rather stupidly), peering through the blinding haze of a hundred fluorescent lights. It wasn't his voice though, and now . . . it wasn't his face. The great blue wall had faded to a dense grey mist and now I was no longer against a wall; I was in a floodlit football stadium with just one helicopter hovering above me, and two policemen (I somehow knew they were policemen, even though one of them was my old Maths teacher from school and the other looked uncannily like Michael Caine) ambled towards me with handcuffs and truncheons at the ready. It was only at that point that the small rational part of my brain connected with the overused fantastical fantasy part, and I realised that this could – possibly – be a dream. But then, there had been so many experiences in my (alleged) waking life that I believed or hoped were only dreams. Sensations, phenomena, bodily awareness – such day-to-day, graspable, corporeal things that make up the very essence of what constitutes reality are often also eerily real and authentic in dreams too. Sometimes the feelings are even heightened, like an amazing drug trip, or a terrifyingly bad one.

The policemen – Mr Ferris (Maths teacher) and Mr Caine (it was *definitely* him – although he occasionally morphed into Woody Allen) – each grabbed one of my arms and pinned them roughly behind my back, snapping on the handcuffs and reading me my rights. Then, in a flash of inspiration, I realised what it was I had done.

'But I didn't mean to kill him!' I cried out, feeling the painful sharp tug of my shoulder blades as I was yanked in different directions. I felt the kickback of a gun, and only then heard the muffled crack of gunfire, dying to a ringing echo; a pain like whiplash throughout my whole body made me remember a similar noise – louder and more sinister – when I had shot Nick earlier on in my dream. In microseconds everything scrambled up, rearranging itself frenziedly into the present, the real, the physical, and I plunged back into consciousness with a start to find myself staring up at a familiar cracked ceiling. I was breathless with the adrenalin of deep REM sleep, of a dream that was already fading and fragmenting to vague wisps of nonsense in my memory. This time upon waking I didn't feel so scared. It was my third consecutive dream about murdering Nick, and they had increased in absurdity and incomprehensibility. The first one had been wildly erotic and deliciously sadistic – having secret, sordid sex with Nick in the opulent marbled hallway of a huge, mysterious and slightly creepy mansion, then suddenly pulling out a gun from nowhere and pointing it right at his head, enjoying his screams for mercy before squeezing the trigger. The second one was less erotic but more sadistic – perfect. And this third one – just plain weird. The dreams seemed to have come out of nowhere, and while they always seemed so *real* at the time, with the detached hindsight of consciousness, they became totally ludicrous. Dreams blow ordinary things up out of all proportion and the dreamer doesn't give it a second thought: it's just normal – mundane, even – if you find yourself sitting on the back of a blue whale in the Albert Hall getting serenaded by Pavarotti's disembodied head, or if the entire New York police department and the FBI (not to mention old Maths teachers and stalwart British movie stars) are threatening to shoot you just for 'accidentally' killing your ex-boyfriend.

Sadly, I didn't have the time or the inclination to analyse and extract meaning from these essentially meaningless visions, and besides, I had more important things to worry about than the deepest, darkest recesses of my mind.

Of course, it didn't take a psychoanalyst to tell me there was something missing in my life. It was Valentine's Day. I had been a student for almost five months and, notwithstanding the odd drunken snog with a variety of halitosis sufferers, I was still *sans amour.* Still a sad, snivelling resident of Singlesville. I wouldn't have minded, but I seemed to be constantly surrounded by hot-blooded, rampant couples shagging each other's brains out. It didn't help that my room was next to Simon's, which he shared with Rachel on the nights he wasn't sharing hers. For all their faults as a couple – and there were many – there was a lot to be said for their sex life. Or rather a lot to be screamed, moaned, shouted, babbled, grunted and groaned. They copulated like rabid animals – regularly, passionately, endlessly, noisily, revoltingly. The bedsprings would be going like the clappers, Rachel making a sound as if she had electrodes clamped to her nipples, Simon yelping with mounting urgency ('Baby! Baby! Yes! Yeeeesss!') as he approached the final showdown, until finally – my own relief surely being far greater than theirs at this point – the act was over for another night. Then the only audible sound was the odd giggle or whisper until they fell asleep, entwined, no doubt, in a loving embrace. Of course, I would often go to great pains to block out their sexual delirium – head wedged under my pillow, humming to myself, or even putting my walkman on and allowing the more soothing tones of Offspring or Hole to lull me into a deep and sexless sleep.

It was getting to me. So much so, I had started smoking again – vast quantities of brain-numbing homegrown, daily and nightly if not hourly. I figured that the more stoned I was, the less I would notice that I was one of the terminally unattached – not to mention a terminal slacker.

And then there were these Nick dreams. I hadn't thought about him for days on end – weeks, even. Then he comes creeping back to haunt me.

I first met Nick through Sylvie at an emotionally turbulent time in my life. It was contempt at first sight. I wore black and drank snakebite by the pint to make my point: *I am a teenager, what's your problem*? Nick responded to my obvious lack of *joie de vivre* by risking the line, 'Has anyone ever told you that you look like the brunette out of Bananarama?' and, not being a fan, I had answered, 'Has anyone told you that you look like the ugly big blue fuzzy one out of the *Banana Splits*?' He had chuckled and wiggled his eyebrows at me good-humouredly. 'Hey, I like your style,' he said, before attempting to warble the *Banana Splits* theme tune (very badly). At that point, I had leaned over to Sylvie and Ben, the evil perpetrators of this disastrous half-blind double-date fiasco, and simply said, 'That's it. I'm outta here.'

It was only by chance that I met Nick again at a party the following weekend and, after eyeing each other with steamy suspicion from different sides of a room, we ended up having a slightly more in-depth conversation. By some capricious twist of fate our mutual dislike blossomed into love and, more importantly for us as sexually curious sixteen-year-olds, raw lust. We did it everywhere, in every conceivable and inconceivable position, with no inhibitions or restraint. Our own front gardens, other people's front gardens, on the back seat of the bus and the front row of the cinema, in the library, on top of some poor sod's grave in a cemetery, a recently-sprayed crop field (embarrassing allergic reaction on arse cheeks followed), we even made it to a bed once or twice. Our hormones were on a rampage, bouncing energetically off each other like bingo balls, each of us delighting in the wanton desire of the other; this was The Real Thing, the Ultimate, the feeling of weak-kneed, butterfly-bellied, pant-saturating passion I had only ever encountered in Jilly Cooper novels and arty foreign films. The sex we had intoxicated every fibre and nerve-ending of my body, rendered me insensible, exhausted, obsessed. Licentious, dirty, wet, wonderful sex that made me breathless just thinking about it. Well, it was pretty good for a while, anyway.

I was jolted back to the present by a knock at the door. I didn't bother acknowledging it; I knew it was Nadine and I knew she'd come in anyway.

'Awright, how's our Abi?' she greeted me in a vaguely Yorkshire-ish accent, flitting across the room to fling back my curtains with her customary 'Isn't it great to be alive' cheeriness.

Weak yellow sunlight hit my face. I pulled the sheets over my head.

'I had another dream about my ex,' I told her blandly from my smelly linen alcove.

'What happened?'

'Same as before, more or less.'

'Recurring dreams? That's your mind trying to tell you something.'

'What? That I should shoot Nick?' Maybe if I could get away with it, I would.

'Look, you know what day it is, don't you?' Nadine sat on the end of the bed and started rifling through my CDs.

'Isn't it your day off?' I groaned.

'Eh?'

I propped myself up on my elbows. 'Your day off from being so damn happy all the time.'

'Oh, *you.*' She flapped her hands at me and gave a whimsical little laugh. Then, with a more serious expression, she faced me sternly and said, 'Abigail Page, we're getting you laid.'

'Oh for pity's sake, don't start all this again . . .' I flopped back on to my pillow and crossed my arm over my face in despair.

'It's Valentine's Day, you emotional cripple! A day for love, and . . . stuff.'

'Stuff?'

'Yeah, *stuff.* Hunting down a sexy, sophisticated man. A European mature student or postgrad perhaps. Cool, refined, romantic. Strong. Heart-stoppingly good-looking. Hung like a donkey –'

'Gay, in other words,' I interrupted.

'Christ, Abi, I'm only trying to cheer you up.'

'So you think all I need is a bloody good servicing and I won't be so miserable all the time?'

'Can't hurt, surely?'

'If only it was that simple, Nade.'

'It *is* that simple. Those johnnies in your top drawer are fast approaching their use-by date, you know.'

I knew she had a point, but I really didn't think that mindless, reckless sex with a stranger – whether Nadine's presumably non-existent well-hung fantasy figure or the blundering, inept arsehole stereotype that was so prolific among male students – was the answer.

Still, it was always worth a try.

'All right, all right,' I swung myself out of bed and held up my hands in defeat. 'I honestly have no idea why you're so interested in my sex life, or lack of it, but how about we check out that crappy little Valentine Disco going on downtown tonight. The one you got that flier about: *Fiver entry and a guaranteed free Screaming Orgasm with every Sex on the Beach*?'

'Oh. I threw that away.'

'Never mind. Are you up for it?'

'Well, yes. But –'

'I'll give it a go on one condition.' I shoved my feet into my battered slippers and pointed my finger at her accusingly. 'No, make that two. Firstly, *if* I find I *am* in the mood for some action, and that's a big "if" – I get to choose the bloke myself. I don't want you thrusting me on the first drooling pervert who happens to amble our way.'

'What do you take me for!'

'Secondly, I'm only going to pull if you do as well – I'm sick of you going on about my dry sheets when your own make the Gobi desert look like a tropical fuckin' rainforest.'

'Bloody cheek.'

'Agreed?'

'I have my reputation to think of, you know.'

'Get out of here, you brazen hussy.' I threw an old balled-up pair of socks in the general direction of her head.

'Here's a deal. Roll us a joint and I'll bring you a cup of tea,' she said, heading out of the door and giving me a gentle shove as she passed.

'Hey, that's such a fair deal.'

Five minutes later she returned to find me half-asleep again and put an Oasis CD on full blast to wake me up – or rather cause me to open one eye and grunt at her.

'Here's your tea,' she said, placing a vast ceramic mug next to my bed, 'now where oh where is my joint, Miss Page?'

'God, it's far too early for that,' I grumbled.

'What's this I hear from the resident pothead? Too *early*?'

'Give over.'

'So it's full steam ahead for tonight then?' She positioned herself on all fours on the floor and, for some reason known only to herself, began executing a random series of lower body exercises.

'Yes,' I said. 'What are you doing?'

'Tightening my buttocks, toning my inner thighs and beefing up my calf muscles,' she replied matter-of-factly. 'And now,' she shifted around to lie on her back and started on some sit-ups. '*Now* I'm working on the old abs.'

She became exhausted after about twenty or so, and lay there panting for a while, which was just as well because I was feeling knackered just watching her. *Why*? I wanted to ask, but with Nadine the answer to such a question was invariably *why not*?

'Right,' she said finally, catching her breath and turning her head to look at me, 'you've got to promise me you'll make an effort tonight and not just sit sulking at the bar snapping at every bloke who approaches you.'

I took a sip of tea and winced as it scorched my lips and throat. 'I'm not that bad, am I?'

'Yes, you are.' She sat up and crossed her legs, digging around in her pocket for her fags. 'All I'm saying is, just try putting a bit of enthusiasm into it. You're only young once, you know.'

I *was* trying to muster some enthusiasm, but I had a feeling that sexual frustration was only a small part of the problem, and I couldn't see how a convenient, fleeting encounter with an inebriated unknown would do much to buck me up. It was more likely to fuck me up.

I'd need a new dress for starters.

'Let's go shopping,' I said. 'We may as well go the whole hog.'

Living in Brighton was one perk of my university life. The myriad side streets twisted and turned around the sprawling outskirts of the vibrant centre, rammed with Aladdin's Caves of eclectic and wondrous gadgets and artefacts and antiques and retro clothing. The main drawback was that, as a student, I couldn't afford half the stuff I wanted – and I was *constantly* bombarded with things I wanted. This conker-brown suede miniskirt, that purple velvet shoulder bag, this inflatable cactus, that fibre optic lamp, this silver celtic ring, that rare Orbital album . . . irresistible objects of desire confronted me at every turn. (Always the erroneous thought spurring me on: *when I graduate, I'll walk straight into a well-paid executive job, and one day soon, all this will be mine.*)

Nadine and I trawled the shops and stalls, idly fawning over trinkets and various garments, sloping off into dingy changing rooms and trying on skirts and sari-trousers and gorgeous silk dresses and tie-dye flares and corset-type bustiers with varying degrees of enchantment. Nadine even tried on a pair of dominatrix boots – great shiny thigh-high objects with steel toecaps that said 'fuck off' rather than 'fuck me'. Nadine was quite taken with them, but the £115 price tag put her off a bit.

After fruitless bartering attempts we resigned ourselves to the fact that the only things worth buying were the things we couldn't afford (even daddy's girl Nadine was nearing her overdraft limit now) and glumly went for a cappuccino at a tiny bistro on the sea-front. Nadine devoured a toasted cheese sandwich and chocolate fudge brownie, but strangely I couldn't bring myself to eat anything.

We stopped off at a second-hand bookshop on our way back to campus. Determined not to write off the entire afternoon as a waste of my time when I could have been (*should* have been) studying for forthcoming tests, I made a concerted effort to look for a couple of the textbooks I needed for my degree. Texts that, admittedly, I should have bought, read and digested by the first week of the first term. I searched for five minutes and couldn't find them, so I spent a further half an hour looking for a novel to read instead – preferably one that was in no way connected to my degree. Nadine lingered around the erotic fiction and world history sections (strangely adjacent to each other) and was mistaken for a shop assistant by a lanky, bespectacled and shockingly ugly youth in a lime green cagoule who asked her where the Occult section was. True to form, she went along with his mistake and directed him towards the 'personal development' section with a wave of her hand and a sweet smile. The youth thanked her and lurched off behind a huge mahogany bookcase.

'Oi Nade!' I whisper-shouted at her from the other side of the shop. 'You've pulled!' I gave her the thumbs-up and she flicked me the V, and under the scornful scrutiny of the real shop assistant, we continued our silent browsing, occasionally grinning and giggling when we caught each other's gaze. An entire six-foot bookcase was devoted to insipid romance books, colour-coded Mills and Boon paperbacks and novels with gaudy pastel covers and conspicuously similar themes. I turned away and almost fell over a stack of old books piled high on the floor. I picked up the one on the top: a shabby old hardback emblazoned with the title *Sexual Techniques for the over 50s.* The cover image was about as disturbing as it could have got without erring towards illegality. Nadine was meanwhile looking at a book about lemmings, and seemed fairly engrossed. I moved away from what appeared to be the 'Warped Sexual Practices and Emetic Romances' section and continued my quest to find a novel as she started reading aloud.

'Hey, Abi, listen to this, you'll love this . . . Norway lemmings live in the mountain regions of northern Scandinavia in large matriarchal groups where the smaller, submissive males are often oppressed by the larger, more aggressive females . . . blahdiblah . . . and when the female is ready to breed, the male's function as sperm provider comes into play.' She chortled in glee. 'How about that then? Wouldn't you just love a world like that? It's like, "Oi, bloke, piss off and leave me alone . . . hey, actually, come here for a second, I'm on heat and I need to utilise your little organ. It won't take long. Do what you must, all right . . . *then* you can piss off." Class or what?'

I selected a Maeve Binchy hardback and studied the blurb on the inside cover. 'Didya hear that, Abi? Cool eh? I'm just surprised more people can't see men in that way. It seems so obvious to me. Men as nothing more than walking sperm incubators. Receptacles for genes, if you will.'

I frowned at her. 'That's not a very liberal thing to say.'

'Maybe not, but bloody sensible. The jackboot would be on the other foot then. Us girls would have the upper hand. We wouldn't have to be beautiful or clever or stylish or easy or slim or big-breasted to get a man interested. We would just need to have a womb and they'd be putty in our hands. So to speak.'

'You're weird.'

'I'm an alcoholic and I need a drink.'

'I think you need more than that. Anyway, I thought you *liked* men.'

'Oh, you know,' she continued flicking through the book with a wry little smile, 'I love them really, I just think that most of them need a bit of slapping down every now and then. Hey! Bet you didn't know this. Apparently lemmings don't actually commit suicide but sometimes when an overpopulated group migrate they fling themselves into the sea and loads of them drown, mostly immature males . . . huh! As if there were any other kind! . . . oh, so they don't go chucking themselves off cliffs after all . . .' Nadine sensed my lack of interest and meekly replaced the book back under 'Natural World and Wildlife'.

I decided to buy the Maeve Binchy, and also found a dog-eared copy of *Less Than Zero* by Bret Easton Ellis for 50p, so I got that as well. We traipsed back through the town centre, dressless, penniless and pensive, and Nadine was strangely silent for a long time.

'Looks like it's the frumpy look for me again tonight then,' I said eventually.

She gave me an exasperated look. 'Don't be daft.' We stopped outside Burger King and she handed me a fag and lit it for me, shielding the match from the wind with her hand. I inhaled deeply as she used the same match to light her own fag, then shook it out and let it fall to the ground. We linked arms and slowly trudged our way across the road. After a few moments she said, 'You can borrow one of my dresses if you like. I've got one or two that would look great on you.'

I choked with laughter, almost swallowing the cigarette. 'I

wouldn't get one of your dresses over my *head*! You're skinny and I'm . . . big-boned.'

I tried to walk on, but she stopped short, pulling me back and glaring at me. 'Why must you always be so self-deprecating?' she demanded.

'What?'

'Don't put yourself down so much. You're always doing it. You put yourself down and you put other people down to make yourself feel better. It's really sad.'

'*What?*' I searched her eyes for the incandescent glimmer of her usual humour, but she was deadly serious. I really didn't have a clue what she was talking about. 'Nade, all I said was that you are . . . slimmer than me, which is just an objective observation. I didn't say I was a huge fat mound of blubber, I merely said I was comparatively larger . . .'

'Well, fine. Only you were beginning to sound like Catherine just then.'

'*Excuse* me?'

'You know how she bangs on and on and on about does she look good in this or that, is her profile better from the left or the right, does her arse look saggy, is she pretty enough, are her eyelashes clumpy, has she got food stuck between her teeth, is her hair looking like a fucking Pantene advert, does her breath smell, God! It's enough to drive me round the bend!'

'I don't believe I'm hearing this, I'm nothing *like* Catherine. She just fishes for compliments because she knows she looks good.'

'Hmm. Sometimes, Abi, just *sometimes*, it's not just good looks that get you noticed.'

'Why are you being so weird today?'

She winked at me mysteriously as she blew out a final billow of smoke and stamped on her cigarette, seemingly back to her normal self once more. 'Ain't that just what you love about me?'

In Hell, it is Valentine's Day every day.

Correction: in Hell, it is Valentine's Day every day where you are the only person who is not one half of a smugly happy couple.

Later that night, while we were in Nadine's room getting ready for the disco, I was feeling my initial rush of excitement ebb away fast.

'Red or pink?' She held up two different shades of lipstick and looked at me expectantly.

'I didn't think you liked make-up.'

'This is a special occasion. Now, red or pink?'

I fiddled with my bra strap and checked my rear end in Nadine's full-length mirror.

'The pink,' I said, 'red's too tarty.'

'Red it is then,' she said defiantly, peering into her compact mirror and applying it liberally. 'Whaddaya think?' She smacked her lips together and gave me a dazzling ruby and pearl smile.

'Very nice,' I said absently, still preoccupied with the size of my rear end (although this was of course not something I wished to interrogate Nadine about). 'Brown' was apparently the 'new blonde', and the 'curvy' look was back 'in', and I kind of won on both counts, I suppose. However, I was reluctant to believe that 'mousey' and 'bottom heavy' were exactly what the all-seeing gurus of fashion and style had in mind when making these tenuous claims.

'You look absolutely stunning,' Nadine whispered, seemingly without sarcasm. I turned around and grimaced. 'It will have to do, I suppose.'

Nadine had loaned me one of her skirts – amazingly, it fitted me, although I had a struggle with the zip and it was certainly quite snug around my more 'fleshy' parts. She had also let me borrow a necklace of hers, which glinted alluringly in a glittered décolletage enhanced by a padded wonderbra, cunningly one size too small. My slovenly look was completed with a strappy, slutty low-cut top I had found buried in the back of one of my drawers. After giving it a quick once-over with an iron, it looked OK and, being a similar powder-blue colour, it complemented Nadine's skirt quite tastefully. She had tried to foist a pair of dainty high heel shoes on me as well, but I insisted on wearing my old Kickers – they didn't match the rest of my clobber at all, but at least my feet would be comfortable. Nadine had styled my hair for me –

brushed it vigorously until my scalp hurt, then piled it on top of my head in tufty bronze twists and curls and tiny plaits held together by miniature butterfly grips. I had to admit, she had done a pretty good job of revamping my image.

'Are you nearly ready then?' I asked, helping myself to Nadine's array of perfumes and spraying Eternity on my wrists and neck for the fourth time that night. I must have reeked of the stuff.

'When you've quite finished depleting my cat piss supplies,' she retorted, snapping her compact mirror closed and shrugging on a grey chenille cardigan.

'Let's go.'

We got a cab to the disco with Alex and Marbles (whose aftershave could have stripped wallpaper), and Simon, Frank and Rachel followed behind in Frank's car (a black beetle, naturally). When we arrived, I put my reservations to one side and entered into the spirit of things. The venue appeared to be a disused warehouse, converted into a second-rate meat market arranged over two levels. Four huge screens on the walls projected a variety of images: an England football match from the 1994 World Cup, looped MTV music videos, a bizarre black-and-white film and a psychedelic animation; random televisuals without sound. The tables and chairs were adorned with red paper hearts and silver streamers, and banners saying 'Be my Valentine' hung from the high ceilings. Every now and then a female member of the staff (dressed in fluffy bunny outfits) would shower an unsuspecting victim with pink confetti and dried petals. Less fortunate punters would be attacked with 'The Love Gun', cheap red plastic water pistols filled with sparkly liquid and toted by trigger-happy male members of staff dressed as porn stars. A dodgy tribute band played cover versions of mostly appalling love songs from a rickety makeshift stage on the ground floor. Everywhere screamed tack and tat, and we felt right at home in no time. Nadine and I managed to evade two over-excited fluffy bunnies and three porn stars ('However much they're getting paid, it's not enough'), and demolished three pints each at the first floor bar before the proper music started up. We redeemed our 'two cocktails for the price of one' vouchers and hit the dance floor, Nadine's eagerness and excitement rubbing off on me in sporadic bursts. We were shortly joined by Marbles and Alex (both of whom had rather alarmingly taken to dancing topless), and Simon and Frank – mercifully completely clothed. We all bopped and swayed to a selection of inane and incongruously mixed tunes, until the DJ thought it would be highly amusing to play blasts from the past such as 'Especially for You', at which point I decided to go to the bogs to skin up. As I ducked through the crowds, a horribly familiar voice boomed behind me, '*Annie, is that you*?'

It took my mashed brain one second to work out who it was.

Petrified, I hardly dared turn around to face him, and it was all I could manage to move my head a tiny fraction in acknowledgement to stutter a tremulous response. The Great Ejaculator spun me around to kiss me magnanimously on both cheeks. He looked a little flustered and was thinner than I remembered. I batted my eyelashes at him in faux-shyness, smiling through gritted teeth.

'I knew it was you,' he said, beaming at me moronically, 'I'd recognise that scrumptious arse anywhere.'

It was a line that was well deserving of a violent (or at least vitriolic) response, but instead I found myself wondering what he meant by 'scrumptious'. Big? *Too* big? Enormous? Flabby?

'Oh hello, Craig. How are you?'

'All the better for seeing you.' It was the voice of a third-year male student consumed by pitiful desperation. He looked as if his face was about to crack with pleasure. I wasn't sure what he was looking so chuffed about; last time he saw me I was comatose and dribbling spew and sperm.

'Fancy bumping into each other in a place like this!' I exclaimed with unconvincing jolliness, drawing away from him subtly so as to not make it too obvious that I relished his company about as much as a hefty kick in the fanny.

'Greetings and salutations, pretty maiden.' He held my hand and kissed it, all the while looking into my eyes like a lost puppy dog. He was wearing a mandarin orange shirt unbuttoned to reveal a stain-streaked T-shirt underneath. The T-shirt said: *Unstoppable Sex Machine.*

My brain said: *Get the hell out of here. Now.*

'Well, anyway, I was just off to . . .' I began, pointing at a conspicuous sign that said *PLAY IT SAFE. This way to the Johnnie Machines. And the Bogs.*

'Would you like a drink?'

'I, er . . .'

'I'm here with my housemates. Do you want to come and meet them?'

'Look, Craig, I'm . . . um, er . . . I'm sorry about, er . . . you know. Last time. I was very drunk. I'm sorry.'

I thought an apology was probably in order after all; and an untimely reminder of my alternative fellatio technique should surely lessen his ardour.

'Darling girl, think nothing of it.'

Perhaps not. I looked into his eyes: the pupils were dark and glassy and so large there was virtually no blue iris left. He had the shakes something chronic and he kept grinding his teeth and touching himself all over in a weird way, like pre-masturbation foreplay. I think he was off his tits. He noticed me looking at him strangely.

'I've dropped a couple of tabs,' he explained needlessly. 'Just to get me in the party mood, y'know.'

He pulled me to one side and perched himself on the edge of a beer-soaked table. 'Do you want one?'

I thought about it for a second. It wasn't a bad idea, really. I had nothing against Ecstasy at all, and I had tried it once when I went clubbing with Jasmine when I was sixteen. It had just meant a few extra hours on the dance floor, going at it like a manic Duracell toy and spraying everyone with sweat in some kind of quasi-Nirvana state.

I eventually decided to decline, then tried moving away, but Craig seemed particularly amorous and held on to me, moving his body closer. My mood fell a couple more notches on the positivity scale.

'Then why not at least let me get you a drink. If you think you can hold it this time.' He gave me a mischievous wink and started jigging about when the DJ incompetently changed the record from 'Love is All Around' to (appropriately enough) 'Things Can Only Get Better'.

'Hey, dance with me!' He stood up to his full six-foot-plus height, grabbed my arms and tried to animate me by pulling me this way and that while singing along flatly to the song. I hung my head in embarrassment as he jived away like a dad at a wedding party. A passing fluffy bunny thought this execrable exhibition was really quite romantic, and gaily threw a handful of confetti over us and told us we made a lovely couple. Craig beamed even wider and bought a red rose from her for a pound.

He presented me with it and I said, 'All right then, one drink.'

'Hey, that's the spirit. What will it be?'

'Oh, anything. A Bud? Stella? Whatever.'

'OK. Don't go away. Won't be a minute.'

As soon as his back was turned, I made a beeline for the loos, feeling for my tobacco and Rizlas in my pocket. I spent longer than usual preparing the joint, and packed a load of gear in, trembling with excitement. This was the night I had vowed to get laid and here I was getting a thrill from a cylindrical scrap of gummed paper with a bit of forbidden horticulture inside. A case of craving THC rather than TLC, I supposed. Standing at the basins and gazing blankly into the mirrors on the wall opposite with my arms crossed over my chest, I smoked the joint lovingly, savouring every puff. The bogs soon became over-crowded with chattering girls clamouring for their share of mirror space, so I extinguished the stub of the joint in a basin half-filled with filthy water, scummy soap slivers and dirty tissues, and I promptly left.

When I managed to track Nadine down, I was pleasantly surprised to see that she was in a compromising situation with a hirsute, tattooed bloke in drainpipe leather trousers, so I decided not to bother her. At a loss, I lingered in the silent hope that someone other than Craig would come and save me from my isolation. After a few self-conscious minutes, a cluster of my course mates sauntered over and acknowledged me and asked me if I had written this essay or read that book. I said no to both questions and consequently the conversation, such as it was, died. They moved on and I sat down at a vacant table, feeling foolish.

Garston, Frank, Simon and Rachel joined me just as I willed the ground to open up and swallow me, and I could have cried with relief.

'Hiya,' I said casually.

'Hey, Abi, what's up?' I had known Simon for five months and this was practically all he had ever said to me, apart from the odd 'Ya dawn't wanna be doin' that.'

Nevertheless, I almost felt like kissing him for talking to me.

'Oh, you know . . .'

'Why are you sitting here on your own?' Rachel asked.

I shrugged nonchalantly, feeling about one inch tall.

'Seen Nadine?' Garston chipped in, saving me from having to think up an unconvincing reason (e.g. 'I'm just taking a breather between men').

'Looks like she's getting well oiled,' Garston added. His 'bawdy wink' attempt looked more like a severe facial tic.

'Not quite how I'd phrase it, but yes . . .'

'Oi oi, I'm right pissed, me,' Frank stumbled forward, one spindly arm flung around Simon's shoulders while the other reached over to slap me heartily on the back. He was wearing what looked like a knitted black cobweb under a black shirt, which was unadvisedly unbuttoned and tucked into his spiked belt. His nipples (both pierced), pasty white chest and sparse chest hair were visible and horrible through the crochet mesh of his top, and his tight PVC trousers left precious little to the imagination. He let out a jovial and distinctly un-Goth chortle as he spilled his beer, lolling about like a teenager at his first party. Which, let's face it, he probably was. He and Simon had become good friends over the last few months, which I personally found quite weird as they appeared to have nothing in common apart from being scrawny and reticent. Simon's T-shirt said 'Acid on the floor so you walk on the ceiling'. Garston's T-shirt said 'Dead Kennedys'. (When I know exactly what is written on people's T-shirts, it is a tragic indication of how much I am really enjoying their company.)

'How about you?' Rachel said, 'How come you're not beating them off with a stick tonight then?'

'That's just the way the world turns,' I replied, not knowing what the hell I was talking about. We sank into an uncomfortable silence. Simon started playfully splashing Frank with beer, and Frank retaliated with the rest of his pint – i.e. most of it. The frolicsome exchange progressed into an all-out fisticuffs, ending with the pair of them locked together on the floor in a rather pitiful beery heap, chuckling away obliviously.

'Oh, *you two*,' Rachel sighed, sounding like a wearied mother. I smiled weakly and then froze in horror when Craig's spaced-out voice shrilled, '*There* you are! I've been looking all over for you!'

You'd have thought that in a crowded club, packed to the gills with a thousand gagging-for-it students, he might have grasped the fact that I wasn't interested in him, and seek out another victim. With split-second cunning, I thought of a last-ditch plan and pulled Garston towards me.

'Kiss me,' I hissed at him.

'You what?'

'Please, *please* . . . just do it. I'll *pay* you. *Please.*' I pushed my face towards him but he drew away from me as if I were toxic, glancing toward Rachel with a 'help me, she's crazy' expression. Then it was too late. I was presented with a bottle of beer, now lukewarm and pissy. Craig followed it up with a cursory kiss, inaccurately aimed at my cheek.

'Where did you scarper off to, you little minx?' He beamed expectantly at my bemused hallmates and ruffled my hair.

Weeping inside, I made some mumbled introductions. Not sensing my peril or at least not caring, Rachel and her squawking male harem quickly made their excuses and left me to deal with the situation. Craig sat on the chair next to me and pulled me on to his lap. I swigged the tepid beer and he put his hands all over me. I let him.

'This place is getting a little bit boring, don't you think?' he slurred in my ear, pulling at my bra strap and raising an impish eyebrow.

He was high as a kite. He *desired* me. He wasn't hideously ugly. I kind of knew him. He was not going to take no for an answer.

He was a man. He was, for all intents and purposes, better than nothing.

I went back to his place.

In the desolate, barren wilderness that was my sex life, all I asked for was an oasis – just the illusion of one would have sufficed, just a brief glimpse of sanctuary. Something to quench the arid desert, if only for a short time.

That night with Craig, a solitary tumbleweed billowed across the horizon and there was no oasis in sight.

Things started reasonably well and got progressively worse.

We got in a taxi and hurled ourselves at each other with unbridled passion, kissing and gasping and grasping and grabbing at each other's clothes. We slid and slithered together noisily on the back seat and I caught the cab driver's eye in the rear view mirror as Craig put his hand between my legs and nibbled my earlobe. The driver simply stared straight ahead and said, 'Don't you kids leave any fucking stains on my seats.'

Then it was back to the student bachelor pad, back to the stinky bedroom, back to the spine-killing bed. Back on my back, with Craig choosing to woo me with Pulp and Porno for Pyros ballads and his crap coordinating dance routines.

'Do you mind if I roll a fag?' I asked, sitting up on his bed and straining my eyes in the dim light of the room. I threw my jacket to the floor after retrieving my tobacco tin from the pocket, and unearthed my last grain of resin, wrapped in a tattered scrap of cling film amongst my Golden Virginia.

Craig was preoccupied with gyrating his body in approximate time to the tunes blaring from his stereo. To my indignation, I was being ignored.

'Hello?' I shouted over the din. 'I'm going to make a joint. D'you want some?'

His reply consisted of a series of hip rotations, a cocked leg, a wild gesticulation of arms, a pelvic thrust or two in my direction and finally he collapsed on top of me, causing me to drop the tin, my lighter, and most precious of all, the last of my gear. 'I want you,' he murmured, heedless of my disgruntled yelps.

The music still roared on; heavy rock at ear-splitting volume. But Craig didn't want to dance any more.

Two minutes later we were naked and I was just about warming up. Without bothering to linger on other body parts, which may have unleashed the Sex Goddess within, Craig spread my legs and tried to rev me up manually. He didn't beat about the bush. Or rather, he *did.* He wiggled his hand about energetically as if I was some kind of finger puppet and he was trying to provoke an animated response.

He got one.

'Slow down, will you?'

He apologised, muttering something about not being able to help himself, then changed to the even less comfortable 'whisking' motion. Once a bloke has reached his late teens, it's not unreasonable to assume that he will have accumulated just about enough experience to know that a finger or two poked up the holiest of holes does not a satisfied woman make. I made frustrated tutting noises.

'I think you'll enjoy this even more if you took a tab. I'm whizzing my nuts off here,' he offered, pausing his fumbled fingering and textbook tongue-to-nipple foreplay.

'No, it's OK,' I said, wishing he was literally whizzing his nuts off. I moved my head to the side and was confronted with a larger than life colour photo of Craig and a sulky-looking blonde who was obviously his girlfriend. I shuddered and turned to look at a damp patch on the wall to my left. A fat brown spider, suspended by a barely discernible silvery thread, bungeed down from the ceiling, its legs furiously treading air. Outside I heard a car screech and a bunch of drunks coming home from the pub.

Craig continued whizzing, whisking and licking.

All those months, I had been waiting for the Sexual Breakthrough: a wonderful, uplifting, transcendentally pleasurable carnal encounter with a wild but sensitive stallion of a man who would linger over each erogenous zone with tantalising expertise, drawing out the most earth-shattering orgasm possible. I thought the longer I waited for this fantasy to be actualised, the more my hopes were justified, the more I *deserved* for it to happen.

Craig was not that man.

Although my expectations weren't high, 'Let me skewer you with my womb broom, baby' did somehow lack the romantic lilt I had been secretly hoping for after six long, celibate months. To add insult to extreme injury, the condom glowed in the dark. While we were getting down to business, I thought distractedly to myself, 'Oh whoops I'm mid-cycle,' and for some reason I remembered what Nadine had said about the lemmings.

'Can you check that the condom's intact?' I asked him as he pummelled away like a mad thing. You can never be too careful, after all.

'Of course it's bloody intact,' he grunted back breathlessly, not bothering to check. Every now and then he'd go limp, but he managed to regain momentum by sliding his hand under my body, grabbing my buttocks and lifting my hips from the mattress to watch my face contort in expressions which ranged from bemusement (for the first few minutes) to boredom (after ten minutes or so) to horrified agony (not long after that). This range of facial expressions was perceived by him to represent the ascending stages of sexual ecstasy. Throughout the ordeal, there was no real variation in position or tempo or technique; it was bang bang bang with the same kind of monotonous determination and detachment as if he was trying to break down a door with a battering pole. Even when I ran out of lubrication half-way through and had given up even pretending to enjoy it, he still persisted, stopping only once or twice to grin down at me and whisper, 'This is fantastic, isn't it?'

He finally let out a primal scream and heaved and convulsed as if constipated, his face flushing with exertion. My relief was indescribable. I kissed him. He collapsed across me and wheezed contentedly. It was over. He rolled off and lay beside me, removing the condom with a loud snap. He inspected the bedraggled thing close to his face and cooed proudly about his copious manly fluids. So proud he was that he took a drawing pin from the cork notice board on his wall and pinned it up, a grotesque trophy among his various smiley family pictures and lecture timetables.

I would have been out of there like a shot, but I was overcome with exhaustion. We lay down with our arms around each other, both of us pretending that we'd shared a special moment together. We sealed it with a cigarette, which we passed between us while talking dozily about whatever it is that young people who know nothing about each other talk about after sex.

'How many people have you slept with?' he enquired dreamily, stretching back with his head in the crook of his arm.

Now he asks me.

'Do you really care?' I asked, snuggling up to him. (I had little choice; the bed was tiny and we *had* just shared an intimate experience of sorts.)

'No . . . well, I just wondered. I was curious. You know.'

'You want to know if I'm a raddled old tart?'

'No, I didn't mean it like that.'

I decided to put his mind at rest. 'You're the fourth,' I said, honestly. (In between Tom and Nick there had been a very brief and unfortunate encounter with Lewis's much better-looking best friend, which I was still trying to live down.)

'Is that all?' He gave a strangled cry of surprise.

I sighed in exasperation. What the hell do men want? What's the right number? Is there a magic number? Is there a range? No fewer than half a dozen, maybe? And no more than ten? Do they want experienced virgins or innocent whores? Or a bit of both?

'Well give me a chance, I'm only a first year.' I blew a stream of smoke in his face and flicked some ash on to his repulsively filthy sheets. 'Anyway, I don't really go for all this casual sex malarkey. Not really my scene.'

He smiled at me in an odious, self-satisfied way. 'I bet I can make you change your mind.'

'Hmmm. Possibly.' I decided not to disillusion him and looked around for my various items of clothing.

'Oh, don't go . . .' he whined as I pulled my knickers back on. 'I thought you might at least stay the night.'

Ignoring my constrictive bra, which lay abandoned on the floor amongst the usual detritus of a male student's bedroom, I slipped my top over my head and said, 'No thanks. Best be getting back.'

'Oh *come on* . . . then I'll run you back to campus in the morning.' He patted the crumpled space beside him and whipped back the quilt to reveal his magnificent flaccid nakedness.

This was not quite the incentive I needed. I gathered up the rest of my clothes and Craig tugged pathetically at each item as I put it back on.

'It's not even midnight yet!' He traced his fingers up and down my back and started kissing my thighs, pushing my skirt up and nuzzling into my flesh. 'We can stay up all night together, just you and me,' he suggested, glancing up at me furtively through narrowed eyes. 'I've still got two neon johnnies left, you know.'

I didn't even bother responding to this. I stood up, straightened my skirt and draped my jacket over my shoulders. I retrieved my tobacco tin and picked the brown shreds from the carpet (along with God knows what else), found my hash remnant and put the lot back in my pocket. Finally, I bent down and kissed him on the cheek, more a motherly peck than the impassioned gesture of a ravished woman. 'Can I use your phone to ring a cab?'

'But . . . but you're my twentieth! Surely it deserves some kind of celebration?'

This was to be Craig's final and least successful attempt to inveigle me back into his bed. I was beginning to realise why female spiders eat their partners after mating.

'Phone?' I demanded. 'May I?'

He flumped back on to his pillows dispiritedly. The drug effects were wearing off, at last. Charlie Chaplin style, I waddled to the door.

'I'll call you,' he murmured.

I opened the door and glanced back at him. Please don't, I thought.

'Fine,' I said.

I spent most of the next morning in a bow-legged posture, wincing in pain at every toilet trip, and stubbornly refusing to respond to Nadine's interrogative questions about my hellish night of genital torture. She eventually gave up her line of questioning and persuaded me to go swimming with her in the evening. I agreed it was probably about time I subjected my unconditioned body to some proper physical exercise.

I was alone in my room shoehorning myself into a skimpy Speedo swimsuit for the first time in over two years, when something under my bed caught my eye. It was only a small, spiral-bound old notebook with the front page ripped and covered all over with stickers and biro graffiti and drawings; altogether a rather sad-looking pad of crumpled paper. I don't know why I was particularly drawn to it, but for some reason it stood out among all the other dusty arcane artefacts that dwelled under my bed. I ignored it at first – after all, it was only a notebook, and I had plenty of them lying about in my room, half-filled with meaningless scribbles when they should have been completely filled with meaningful lecture notes and essay plans.

I turned back to the mirror and regarded my bulbous, lycra-clad figure again; I slapped and prodded my thighs and poked at my cellulite and protruding stomach and the ample, rounded globes of my buttocks until I was fully convinced that there was no way I would be wearing my swimsuit in public until I looked much less like a splat of pasty, wobbling flesh and much more like a slim, foxy little sex kitten. I resolved to actively do something there and then about my wayward curves and bulges. And I had an hour to work on them until Nadine came knocking at my door with her sports bag and mineral water, doubtless looking feline, fresh and lithe in her flattering little cossie and jogging pants. So I got down on all fours and peered under my bed in search of my waist trimmer, my ankle and wrist weights, my skipping rope and my (as yet unused) 'thigh-master' contraption. I knew they were hidden somewhere in there with all the superfluous jumble. At length, I unearthed a collection of useless objects: a single tennis shoe, an old edition of the university newspaper, a cotton reel, a Body Shop gift set, eyelash curlers, a crossword puzzle book, a stapler, an elastic band or two, a PC disk . . . but nothing that was likely to assist any kind of keep fit regime. I stayed crouched on all fours and thought I may as well take a leaf out of Nadine's book while I was thus primed for action – so I tried a few donkey kicks and a couple of press-ups, then collapsed out on to my front, feeling weak and pathetic.

I then thought about taking an afternoon nap. Even sleeping was supposed to burn a certain amount of calories. I turned my head and glimpsed the intriguing little notebook just by my outstretched hand. Curiosity got the better of me and I propped myself up on my elbows and pulled it towards me.

I realised on closer inspection why it looked so familiar. It was Jasmine's old notebook – the same one she had used ten years before to explain the birds and the bees to me. She must have accidentally left it behind when she came down to see me. I had no idea she had kept it after all these years. It brought the memories flooding back and I laughed out loud as I flicked through the first few pages. Various detailed pictures and doodles were scrawled on the front and back pages in blue and black pen, and on the very first page, a particularly disturbing and badly proportioned diagram of a naked man grinned out at me, his various biro-blotched body parts labelled with exclamation marks (beard!, tongue!, nipples!, cock!, happy sacks!) in Jasmine's exuberant handwriting.

Several pages from the middle were torn out, and those that remained were dog-eared and full of inkblots. But the pictures she had drawn for me were all still there, preserved. I was going to close the notebook and put it in my drawer to give it back to Jasmine the next time I saw her, but then I turned to a page that said *JASMINE'S PRIVATE THOUGHTS. KEEP OUT* in bright red felt-tip pen and bold capitals. The innocent-looking notebook suddenly took on a more ominous meaning. Should I read on? This was my first thought. Surely there can't be anything written here that would really shock or surprise me? This was my second thought. Just the first few words, then I'll put it down. Third thought.

The struggle with my conscience was only a brief one. I didn't think I would be doing anything unforgivably bad by reading my sister's diary. I had good reason to want to read her 'private thoughts'. I never even knew she kept a diary. What harm could it have done? Surely it would only have allowed me a little more insight, maybe more understanding. That can't be a bad thing. I turned to the next page.

19 July 1984
Went down the park with Lisa and Darren. Few beers, few smokes. The usual. Took bus to ice rink. Woman on bus looked just like mum. Couldn't stop crying the rest of the day. Told Darren I was pre-menstrual. Just ignore me, I said.

It was nothing out of the ordinary. I knew that Jasmine would probably have had no qualms about reading my diary if she'd found it lying about. This is what I told myself as I read on. The diary entries were inconsistent and sporadic, full of spelling and grammatical errors and the odd incomprehensible word or sentence. Many had been ripped or scribbled out. Some didn't seem to be diary entries at all, just random scrawled thoughts or whole pages filled with surreal pictures and angry poetry and song lyrics.

2 October 1984
Bunked off school. Rain chucking it down all day, my favourite kind of weather. I risk my sanity for temporary flashes of enlightenment. Met Jamie up west end again. Gave me some maryjane, for free this time. Offered to take me back to his place. I said no this time. Saw Lisa and her boyfriend in the pub. Got home late again and dad was pissed off at me. Again.

14 February 1985
Haven't been to school since the 'mishap' with Mr O'Sullivan. I think he's been fired. Poor bloke. Didn't have any friends there really. They won't miss me. I don't miss them. What's the problem then? Dad thinks I'm on drugs. He's right. Poor bloke.

That appeared to be all there was. I couldn't help feeling disappointed. I had wrestled with my admittedly questionable sense of morality, all for three rather uninformative and out-of-date diary entries. I flicked forward to the last pages, until I found some more writing that looked like it could have been interesting. A whole page was filled over and over with the repeated words '*Free Spirits*', and a couple of pages on, Jasmine had written a poem called 'God the Director', dated December 1986, which I found deeply unsettling. I shivered as I came to another set of diary entries, and this time I had a sense of trepidation about reading them, like a cold tentacle of dread was holding me back. It was no longer an ethical dilemma about whether or not I should read them so much as whether or not I could bring myself to read them. I felt compelled to continue, even though this fearful hesitancy made me sickened to do so. Half-way through reading, I wanted to tear my eyes away but couldn't, even when they were awash with tears, even when I began sobbing and could barely see through the watery blur.

20 February 1989
Just found this diary after all this time! What has happened in all those years? Fuck knows. Think I'll put this in the bin.

22 February 1989
OK, so I didn't put it in the bin. Reckon with recent developments this could maybe end up as something of a curiosity in the medical world. How about this. I am mentally ill apparently. Schizo. That's interesting I thought, when a shit for brains doctor told me I had a narcotic-induced psychosis. Like I'm a social leper, I'm put away where I can't embarrass my family and these fuckers can do their tests on me to make sure I feel nothing. Over the rainbow . . . Drug-induced psychosis. Nobody to blame but me. I felt crap long before I took drugs. Why else would I take them if not to feel better? We all choose who we become but we don't choose how we end up. You do it their way or you're mad. Guess what.

1 August 1989
Why do I go on? What am I doing here? So many q's, so bloody few a's. I have already been locked up, drugged up, fucked up enough to last me a lifetime. I'm twenty and my life is over.

Jan 1990. Monday. (Here I am in wonderful Rayneham again, loony bin to the unrich and infamous.) Someone's trying to convince me that my family aren't really related to me at all. Tell me something I don't know. They make me laugh sometimes. Too many voices. I just want some peace. More drugs please vicar.

Feb 1990. Saturday. I think someone's been reading this. I know for sure they have been in my room. I'm looking around for cameras and microphones as I write this. I will definitely throw this away now. Maybe I'm being paranoid. Ha! There's the rub. If I admit I'm mad, does that make me unmad I wonder? Dr Morgan said something interesting to me. Insight is a symptom of sound-mindedness, he said. My learned friend. And so say all of us.

April 1991.
Dreamed that mum was alive. Woke up crying. I want to die.

Friday.
Oh my God my little sister is sexually active! Was looking for her doobie stash in her room and only found a packet of durex (open!) Sly little cow. Will have to give Tom a piece of my mind when I next see him. I will kill him if he hurts her.

November 1991. I think it's Sunday.
Coming down . . . my lovely hair gone. Shaved it off. I can still be beautiful. One more fix. Just one E and this sad junkie will be the heroin of her own story.

September 1992. I couldn't find this for ages. I had it hidden away. Somewhere so safe not even I knew where. I have been seeing someone. Not a man, unfortunately. Well, yes, a man, but not A man. It's to do with my psychological assessment. They want to check if I'm still mad. Can't work out what would be most fun – proving them right or proving them wrong. Watch this space.

January 1993. I play dead and sometimes it works. Sometimes I even convince myself. The side effects are still worse than whatever it is they are trying to cure. It won't be long now. I won't be long. I won't belong. This is getting boring. I will never write in this diary again.

June 1994. Tuesday or Wednesday. I am so lonely, it's like I'm banging my head against a brick wall over and over again and no one can hear me or at least they're not listening. I'm back in rehab because Chris took me back to the good days again. I thought one more wouldn't hurt. I was wrong. I feel so fucking lonely, so empty. I have to know have I been guilty this time.

November 1994. Would be nice to think my own family gave a shit. Called Abi but she was out and she didn't call back. I'm better off dead. Stopped taking my medication.
One more
. . . think I need a change of scenery. Sure Abi won't mind me calling in next week. Reckon she's just about all I've got left as far as friends go. How sad is that.

It ended there.

I was inconsolable by the time Nadine knocked on my door.

After almost a month of hearing nothing from her, Jasmine phoned me from Scotland. She had been staying with our grandparents while she 'tried to get her head together'. I decided not to tell her about the diary, although I was still reeling from the discovery. I was also understandably quite ashamed of myself for reading it.

'I'm so sorry,' she began, 'I've been such a shit. To you, to Dad, to everyone. Please forgive me.'

I didn't know how to respond. I breathed heavily down the phone, trying to think of something to say.

'Abi, I need you to trust me, if you think you can. I'm going to turn my life around. I'm going to get my life *back*, for a start.'

'How?' I asked.

Now it was Jasmine's turn for some heavy breathing.

'I don't know,' she said eventually. 'But I'm back on the new neuroleptics, and I'm not taking methadone any more.'

'You do sound much better.'

'Oh God, I *am*. Much, much better. Gran and Granddad have been so good to me. They send their love, by the way.'

'And me to them,' I said, guiltily realising I hadn't written or spoken to them since Christmas. 'Tell them I'll come and visit soon, maybe over summer.'

'And I'm back with Seth for good, we'll be moving in together in April.'

'You don't hang about, do you?'

'Jesus, sis, how much fucking time have I wasted already? I'm twenty-six this year and what have I achieved? It's just been one long series of fuck-ups. Not any more. Things have changed for good now.'

'I'm glad to hear it.' I tried to ease some of my guilt; ever since I had practically evicted Jasmine from my room, and especially since reading her diary, I had been plagued with a torrid sense of shame about the way I had treated her. 'Look Jas, I know you probably think I've been neglecting you recently, but you really are welcome to stay whenever you like. I behaved pretty badly towards you, and you didn't deserve it. I've been just as much of a shit as you have, and I am sorry if I made you think I didn't care. I really miss you and –'

'I'm pregnant.'

I stopped my sentence abruptly and felt my heart jump in terror and disbelief.

'You're *what*?' I thought perhaps I had misheard.

I hadn't.

'I'm having the baby,' she stated, as if it was the end of the matter. 'It might be my only chance. It's the best reason in the world to pull myself together and make something of my life.'

'B-but how? I mean . . .'

'Don't worry, it's not Honey's baby, it's definitely Seth's. And he's been off H for years now. He helped me with the junk withdrawal this time round, he's been a diamond.'

'Are you sure it's his?' My head was spinning.

'I'm almost one hundred per cent sure. I've got my dates all confused though. My periods were totally up the wall, you know. I didn't even think I could have babies.'

'But it's such a huge commitment, it's just so . . . . It's a *kid*, Jasmine. You *hate* kids.'

'Don't try talking me out of it, I'm not listening.'

'Have you really thought it through?'

'I'm *having* it, Abi. There's nothing anyone can say to change my mind.'

There was a long silence as I tried to let the announcement sink into my brain.

'Does Dad know?' I eventually managed to squeak.

'Only you and me and Seth know. I'll give it a few more weeks before telling anyone else, just in case . . . you know . . . I've done two home tests and Seth is making me see his local doctor, but it's definite. I can *feel* it.'

'But . . . but you've only just got over heroin withdrawal, surely that can't be good for the –'

'Yeah right, and I'm telling you, morning sickness is a breeze in comparison.'

'And what about the medication you're taking?'

'For fuck's sake, I suppose it's too much to ask for you to be happy for me?'

I sighed. 'I am happy for you Jasmine, if that's what you want.'

'It is. I know what I'm doing. Just let me get on with my own thing, OK?'

'Will I see you soon?'

'Maybe. You run along now, sweetie, get back to your wanky new friends and do whatever it is you students do. I'll call you again when I'm back at Dad's.'

And she hung up. I stared at the receiver in my clammy hand, and it droned back a dead signal at me.

Stunned, I wandered back to my room, opened up a textbook and started a 5,000-word essay. And nearly finished it.

'ShitfuckbollockswankshitshitFUCK!' Nadine screeched into the kitchen and flung herself dramatically at the table, knocking a box of Coco Pops to the floor and Catherine's plastic cup of vanilla Slim Fast, which toppled over and spilled out its nutritious liquid nothingness on to the floor, splashing my nightie in its trajectory.

I looked up nonchalantly from the March edition of *Vogue*, Catherine's bible. 'What's up?'

Nadine looked at me with wild panic in her eyes. 'I have a test on property law in ten minutes and I know bugger all about it. And my *bloody* alarm didn't go off! I've only just got out of bed, look at the state of me!'

'Calm down. Go and get dressed and I'll sling a coat on and walk there with you.'

'There's no time! I might as well just give up now, fake my own death or something.'

'You're talking crap again, Nade. Sit down, I'll make you a cuppa.'

'A cuppa! Why is that supposed to be the solution to everything? I don't want a bloody cuppa, I want a Valium and a bloody good reason why I'm bothering with this stupid bloody degree.' She flounced towards the fridge with a sigh and a moan. 'I mean, why, *why* do we put ourselves through all this? Do any of us honestly believe that some poor misguided bastard will actually employ us at the end of it all?' She grabbed an apple and bit into it aggressively.

Yoshi, whom I had barely noticed to my left, was nibbling a slice of toast and scanning through the stock exchange pages of the *FT* with the same avid interest that any normal bloke of his age would reserve for the 'Shaven Haven' pages of *Fiesta.* He looked up momentarily and said, 'I've already had a job offer, from Barings, actually.'

Nadine almost choked on her apple. I think it was the first time either of us had heard him speak since the first night. He calmly pushed his glasses up his nose and continued reading.

'Yeah, well, bully for you,' Nadine blurted out. 'But we can't all be spoddy smarty-pants, you know.'

Yoshi glanced up again and his face broke into a *lesser-spotted smile.* I did a double take. It was definitely a smile.

'That's very true,' he said sagely.

Nadine and I exchanged looks of bafflement and she took a pint of milk from the fridge and left the kitchen in a flurry, shouting a greeting of 'Get out of my way you malignant toe-rag' to Alex as he tried passing her in the hall.

'All right, Page?' Alex made his grandiose entrance and nodded in my direction, crossing over to the cupboards and searching optimistically for some clean utensils. He had taken to addressing everyone by their surname, simply because Marbles had suddenly decided this was the 'in' thing to do. I made an agitated noise at him.

'What's wrong with your girlfriend?' he enquired, flickering his feminine lashes at me and pulling provocatively at the waistband of his pyjamas.

'The same thing that's wrong with your boyfriend. She's bonkers.' I eyed him disdainfully, which was an easy disguise for the attraction that I and practically every other red-blooded woman secretly or obviously had for him.

'That would explain a lot. 'Ere, budge up, mate.' He pulled up a chair next to Yoshi and poured out a glass of orange juice. Yoshi cleared his throat self-consciously, finished his toast, folded up his newspaper and left for another all-important lecture.

'Friendly bloke,' Alex mused, staring at the scattered crumbs on the table.

He offered me some of his juice and started blathering about a forthcoming party in Bognor Regis with some first class local DJ. All the while I was trying to scrape together enough momentum and motivation to move my lazy arse down to my own lecture. I loved my course, I really did, but there were always so many other things to do – sleep, lounge about, go to parties, nurse hangovers, sleep . . .

'Hello Annie! I *thought* I might find you here!'

My one solitary 'successful' conquest exploded unexpectedly on to the scene just as I had lifted my bum a couple of inches from the seat, finally resolved to take a more proactive approach to my lecture attendance. Alex shot me his characteristic smirk and departed in a waft of Lynx deodorant and male pheromones.

I looked up in astonishment to see Craig's gormless face beam down at me. He stood before me, vacant and Brylcreemed and almost charming, a wilting apology in his right hand – this time a cluster of moribund flowers rather than a rapidly detumescing penis.

'What . . . why . . . what are you doing here?' I faltered.

With dramatic deliberation, he slipped into the chair opposite me and held the flowers under my nose. 'I thought I'd just pop in and see you. Do my boyfriendly duties.'

'*Excuse* me?' I looked at a particularly dead-looking daffodil and related to it. 'I'm sorry Craig, I was under the impression that the other night was just a one-off.'

He gave me a dolorous, pie-eyed look and groped for my hand across the table. 'I thought it might be a bit more serious than that.'

I was lost for words. This was like *Fatal Attraction* inverted, except with crap sex rather than steamy, abandoned romping. 'Whatever gave you that idea?' I asked.

'Oh. I thought . . . after Valentine's and everything . . . I mean . . . don't you want to go out with me?'

I tried to be kind. 'But . . . you told me you were only interested in meaningless flings.' I suppressed the urge to pick up the wilted bouquet and clobber him round the head with it.

'Well, yeah . . .' he sat back in the chair and preened himself as I gulped back some orange juice, glaring at him over the rim of the glass. 'Yeah, you know, I've been around . . .' he fondled a spiky tuft of rigidly styled hair and rubbed his unshaven chin. 'But you're different,' he added, leaning forward again and widening his eyes. 'You're special. I really like you.'

I detected a faint whiff of bullshit, and it wasn't just his aftershave. 'You can't even get my name right,' I said gently. 'And what's the point anyway when you're in your final year and we have nothing in common?'

He sighed, a deep, histrionic intake of breath, and shook his head sadly as if I had just turned down the offer of a lifetime. 'So, am I right in assuming you don't want to see me again?'

'To be brutally honest, no I don't. And I thought you felt the same.'

'Never? Not even once? Just for sex?'

This bloke had one hell of a complex. I shook my head. 'Thanks, but no thanks.'

'Oh well.' He pushed the dying stems towards me. 'Keep the flowers anyway.'

'Cheers.' It was the first time a bloke had given me flowers since I was sixteen and Nick had broken into his neighbour's back yard and ruthlessly (but very romantically, I thought at the time) violated entire flowerbeds of narcissi and tulips. This time round, the gesture somehow didn't have quite the same significance.

'Well, things to do, you know how it is!' I scraped my chair back and sprang up.

'Maybe I'll see you around . . . ? Just around campus I mean? Or downtown?'

'Yeah, maybe.' *Not if I see you first, mate.*

Craig got up and hovered in the doorway uncomfortably as if expecting an affectionate farewell embrace. Nadine burst in and saved me.

'You gonna walk me to my exam then?' she asked breathlessly. She held a stack of books under one arm and a bulging lever arch file under the other. A few pages of notes dropped to the floor, and she swore as she bent to pick them up. Her hair was all over the place, her eyes were bleary and unfocused and she had a little white moustache of milk.

'Yeah, of course. I'll just get my coat and shoes. Hold on.' I turned to Craig, who was still loitering. 'Er . . . bye then.'

'I'll be in The Hobgoblin down London Road next Saturday, if you're interested . . .' he said.

I waved my hand at him. 'Fine. Goodbye.'

He finally sloped off, and I breathed a sigh of relief. Nadine raised her eyebrows and glanced at the flowers on the table. 'I see he comes bearing gifts,' she drawled sardonically.

'He appointed himself as my boyfriend,' I said glumly, putting them in the kitchen sink where they would be shortly put out of their misery once and for all.

'Well, sounds like you put him straight. Come on, move your arse, I'm already late.'

We lurched towards the law department, Nadine studying a huge tome of a book all the way and every now and then uttering exclamations of woe and despair. I kept my own personal woes to myself, knowing that Nadine had enough on her plate without a whingeing mate to contend with. My sister was unstable, possibly insane and definitely pregnant, my impoverished state was worsening by the day, I had recently had disastrous sex with a weirdo stalker type, I had missed nearly every seminar and lecture for the last two weeks (apart from one, and the bloody lecturer hadn't even bothered turning up – very slack of him), I slept too much and, despite my determination to stick to my New Year's Resolution, I still smoked too much. My health was going downhill, while my scholarly progress was a constant uphill struggle. And yet again I found myself wallowing in shamelessly indulgent self-pity.

I had to face facts. I had become a student. Jasmine had been right all along. University is for tossers. And even *students* think that students are tossers. I was surrounded by them, I had become as one with them. We were all the same, and underneath it all we despised each other and resented the unification of our collective inadequacies because we wanted to be better. Every contemptible tosser we encountered was merely a sad reflection of what each of us had become.

I thought how nice and comforting it would be to take a long, leisurely walk on a very short pier.

7

Love Is the Drug

March was a very strange month.

It all started with the seventies night at a local student haunt, which began as an ordinary piss-up with karaoke crooning and vintage clothing, and ended up as something much more surreal. I was dubious at first, but the sight of Nadine, Marbles and Alex dressed as three-quarters of Abba was all it took to persuade me to don the flares, electric-blue eyeshadow and pink lip gloss to complete the tribute. Reliving the seventies psychedelia was usually Jasmine's scene. Whereas my dad tended to float off into his own sixties haze, the Beatles, the Stones, the stoned, the peace and love parade, Jasmine had painted her bedroom a jolting combination of Deep Purple, Black Sabbath and Tangerine Dream. She showed her deep appreciation of David Bowie by means of a small shrine in the corner: a life-size Ziggy Stardust poster, a framed concert ticket, a rare LP collection worth over two hundred pounds, and candles arranged like an altar around a signed photograph of the man himself.

Meanwhile my fashionably fey and gauche hallmate Garston believed that Duran Duran and Dexy's Midnight Runners represented the pinnacle of a beautiful, decadent decade. He did look a little odd that night, dressed implausibly as John Travolta in *Saturday Night Fever*. (You can take the boy out of the eighties, but you can't take the eighties out of the boy.) I didn't know which decade I felt the most affinity with, but I didn't particularly think much of the nineties so far.

So I threw myself into the nostalgic celebrations with great cheerfulness and even greater drunkenness. Against my better judgement, I had done a succession of tequila slammers with Nadine and Catherine, and was feeling slightly the worse for wear. I wasn't the only one.

After a colourful evening of the usual imbecilic behaviour (Nadine and I executed stirring renditions of 'Gimme Gimme Gimme (A Man after Midnight)' and 'Dancing Queen'), most of us ended up in Marbles's bedroom, which was soon filled with the smoky pungency of hash fumes. We all put our arms around each other and wailed like alley cats, belting out seventies medleys with great passion and very little tunefulness. We certainly put the 'odious' in 'melodious'.

Marbles sat on his bed, caressing and playing his beloved acoustic guitar, while the rest of us squashed up together on the tiny floor space surrounding him, a spellbound and intoxicated audience of nine. To the surprise of us all, Marbles put the 'mellow' in melodious, giving a euphonious rendition of 'Riders on the Storm', his slightly slurred voice blending well with his blithe strumming. He closed his eyes and sang *sotto voce* while I watched and listened in awe.

'Stop dribbling,' Nadine whispered in my ear. 'It's not *that* impressive.'

I blinked – possibly for the first time in a while – and told her to shut up. But then Alex put on a Pearl Jam CD and the pleasantly stoned tranquillity was shattered while he bored us all rigid with his Eddie Vedder impression. The time had arrived for the first (and by its very nature, the last) en masse soul-baring opportunity for all of us as hallmates and potential future housemates and/or lifelong friends. Surprisingly, Frank was first to speak, chewing dreamily on Juicy Fruit and tugging at the frayed sleeve of his black woollen jumper.

'Don't you think Marilyn Manson is just so . . . superb?' His eyes glazed over as he took another swig of beer and winced with the effort of pretending to like it.

'Get a life, Frank,' said Marbles, placing his guitar on the bed next to him and accepting a communal joint from Catherine, who refused to smoke cannabis any more because she had heard it makes you age quicker. Nobody actually called Frank 'Frank' to his face, except Marbles. But then, on the rare occasions when Frank actually talked to Marbles, he always called him 'Maurice', which really wound him up.

'Marilyn Manson? Who's she?' Nadine asked.

The subject was quickly changed.

I leaned against Nadine, exhausted and inebriated and contributing very little to the ensuing conversation apart from the occasional yawn.

'Fuck this, I need a wank,' Alex suddenly declared.

'Don't you mean you need a shag?' Juliet purred, putting her manicured mitt on his leg, a seductive smile creeping on to her face in a not entirely subtle way.

'No.' He pushed her hand away and looked at her sternly, slightly boss-eyed. '*No.* I need a *wank.* I am desirous of personal masturbation.'

'But . . . wouldn't you rather have a shag?' Catherine chipped in, making her suggestion only slightly less screamingly obvious than Juliet's.

Alex began to get impatient. 'No.' He stood up, uneasily, like a new-born foal, and slammed his beer bottle down on Marbles's desk with an emphatic bang. Spastic from drink, he glared around at nobody in particular and said, 'I am having a wank. On my bloody own.'

'Oh for God's sake just *go* then. Piss off and toss off, we're not stopping you. I've got some tweezers if you like.' Nadine winked at him as she drank in large gulps from a can of Scrumpy.

Alex leaned down toward her, drooling inanely, and whispered something in her ear. She slapped him across the face and told him to take a cold shower. Unfazed, Alex straightened, staggered about for a bit, and then bellowed, 'Would anyone like to join me for some hand-to-gland action?'

'Get the fuck out of my room, you dirty bastard,' Marbles yelled, throwing a pillow at him. Alex obeyed, noisily and clumsily, and was shortly followed by Juliet and Catherine, who were giggling furtively about whipped cream, or something. The conversation was resumed after a brief silence, unfortunately along the same vein.

'The difference between male and female masturbation is that usually a man wouldn't mind a woman there helping him out,' Rachel remarked.

She felt our eyes on her and she became a little embarrassed. 'I mean, men do it as a poor substitute for sex. When they can't get a woman, they've always got their right hand, haven't they?'

'Or left,' Garston, a self-confessed lefty, pointed out.

'Or both if their cock is really big,' Marbles added, a self-confessed liar rather than ambidextrous stallion.

'But women,' Rachel continued, 'they usually do it because men don't know *how* to. And they'd rather be left alone to do it, than have a man there with them to ruin their concentration and cock it up.'

Simon's hand was cavorting skittishly under her top. She pulled him towards her and kissed him and said, 'I think you've just got to get to *really* know another person's body. That's why me and Simon never have to . . . you know . . .'

Nadine pretended to sneeze, cunningly incorporating the word '*Bollocks!*' in her feigned nasal explosion. Simon and Rachel meanwhile just snogged unashamedly while we all exchanged looks of disgust.

'It's interesting, don't you think, that if you're a bloke who bashes the bishop . . . so any bloke, really . . . you're a wanker, purely by definition. If a woman masturbates, she's liberated, or something.' This was Garston's philosophical take on the subject.

'Yeah, but blokes don't mind admitting they do it while girls would never confess to it,' Marbles agreed, passing the joint on to him and blowing slow smoke streams from the corner of his mouth as he spoke. 'I mean, Jules didn't admit to it, and believe me, I was grilling her for a pretty long time.'

'I bet you were,' Nadine said.

'Catherine also denied it flatly,' Marbles added with a belch.

'Rachel's here trying to convince us that Simon sees to her every need. My sister pretends she doesn't even know what it is . . .'

'You asked your *sister*?' Garston spluttered in astonishment.

'Page?' Marbles then turned to me. 'I suppose you'll deny it too?'

Before I could blush or elicit any kind of appropriate response, Nadine spoke.

'I have a vibrator.'

Simple as that, straight upfront.

Twelve round, amazed eyes fixed on her as she smoked calmly, ignoring our astounded expressions. After a long silence, she looked back defiantly at the blank faces and demanded, 'And is that really such a big fucking deal?' She turned to me with mild annoyance. 'I thought you of all people would be OK with talking about something so natural and obvious?'

I didn't know where or how she got that idea. I smiled weakly and she let out an exasperated sigh. 'God, you lot are so uptight and anal.'

Marbles cackled like an evil cartoon villain after committing a dastardly crime. 'I think maybe all of us should reveal something embarrassing about ourselves now that Ferrell has dropped that little bombshell,' he suggested.

'I'm not embarrassed at all,' Nadine insisted.

'*We* are, though,' Garston said.

'I was once obsessed with Boy George,' Frank confessed, as if he had been dying to share it with us for ages. God, he must have been really pissed. This got everyone else on a roll.

'I have a tattoo on my bum,' said Rachel.

'She does, you know,' Simon confirmed proudly.

'What's it of?' I asked, not really wanting to know.

'It's a butterfly and a rosebud . . . with Simon's initials underneath,' she cooed rapturously. 'Here, I'll show you.' She shifted around and unzipped her skirt but I stopped her just in time.

'No, no – it's OK. I believe you.'

'I once made a girl faint from giving her too many orgasms,' Marbles told us.

Nadine snorted dismissively. 'You're such a prick, Maurice. The poor girl probably passed out with boredom.'

'I don't suppose you'll ever know, will you, sweetheart?' he grinned, leering forward and pulling up his shirt to reveal a glimpse of toned torso.

She ignored him pointedly. 'Well, I'm cream-crackered,' she said, yawning widely. 'And unless there are any other illuminating confessions, and preferably true and interesting ones, I'm off to bed.'

Nobody was willing to share any more secrets, and certainly no true and interesting exposés were likely to be revealed. Even Garston's admission that he ate frogspawn when he was seven and that his fiancée had left him because he asked her if he could do her 'up the gary' failed to captivate anyone (although Marbles was suitably amused and impressed). One by one, everybody made their excuses and retired to their respective boudoirs and it was gone three in the morning when I suddenly – to my surprise – found myself alone with Maurice Venables, his eclectic music collection, his seemingly endless supply of duty-free fags and his 'Topless Babes 1995' calendar. I'd been alone with him several times before during the day and had felt mostly indifferent to his presence. Now though, with the lights down low and my spirits up high, I felt weird and uncomfortable and subliminally excited. And I didn't know why.

'Got any blow?' he asked finally, breaking a silence which felt a lot longer than it probably was.

I fidgeted and groped around in my pocket.

'Er, no. I don't really do it any more. I mean, I try not to buy. It was beginning to affect me, you know?' I made a vague, 'I'm really losing it' gesture, which he didn't seem to notice.

Instead he smiled dopily and opened up a new packet of full-strength American cigarettes, and threw the plastic wrapping to the floor. 'You skank skunk off other poor bastards now, do you?'

'No. Yes. Sometimes. If necessary.'

My throat was sore and my eyes felt dry and droopy. I started biting my nails as I watched him put two fags in his mouth and light them both up. The flame and glowing orange tips cast lambent light and shadow on his features. I noticed for the first time that he had a tiny dimple in his left cheek and a scar by his right eyebrow. 'I suppose it's time we both crashed,' he murmured, passing me one of the cigarettes. I didn't want it but accepted it anyway. 'It's been a pretty good night, hasn't it?'

I nodded in agreement, smoking silently as he got up and started searching through his CDs. He swapped Pearl Jam for Red Hot Chilli Peppers then changed his mind and put Nirvana on. He wriggled about rhythmically to 'Smells Like Teen Spirit' at a very loud volume until a rudely awoken and bad-tempered Yoshi knocked on the door and told him to turn it down.

'Not all of us live a nocturnal life, you know,' I heard him say crossly.

'Sorry mate,' Marbles said.

He closed the door and gave me a bemused look. 'I thought moles *were* nocturnal,' he japed, smiling his insouciant smile again.

I giggled nervously. 'Don't be mean. He's just not cut out for student life.'

'You can say that again.' Marbles turned the music down and flopped back on to his bed. 'Shit, it's nearly a year since Kurt Cobain topped himself,' he mused, staring at me through an unkempt fringe. He was usually as vain as Alex, especially when it came to his hair – it was nearly always gelled back into a tidy middle parting, with barely a strand out of place. I personally thought he looked better when he was pissed up and scruffy and dishevelled, like tonight, with his hair uncombed and crumpled shirtsleeves rolled up above his elbows. Like Alex, he was grossly scurrilous and prided himself on the consistent way in which he presented himself as such: he walked with the kind of swagger that suggested he should be returning to his cave with a dead animal slung over his shoulder, and had an inexplicable penchant for speaking and dressing in the style of a white rap artist with delusions of being black. He was the type of bloke who would even ask the local prostitutes if they'd give him a 10 per cent student discount. There was something appealingly uncouth about Marbles though, a kind of churlish masculinity that was most obvious when he wasn't even trying to be laddish and loutish.

'Yeah, it was a shame, that. They were a really good band,' I mumbled absently, drawing hard on the filter tip and inhaling too deeply.

'Hey, are you OK?' Marbles asked as I proceeded to hack my lungs out. I nodded, spluttering and embarrassed.

'These ciggies are pretty fucking potent, probably too strong for you,' he patronised, blowing out a vast stream of smoke as if to demonstrate what an accomplished smoker he was.

I felt ridiculous and girly. 'I think I should go to bed now,' I decided after another eerie silence, stubbing out the half-smoked fag in one of the many ashtrays Marbles had lying around his room, all of them stolen from pubs. He also collected beer mats, pint glasses and snooker cue chalks. I didn't know why – maybe he was just a kleptomaniac.

I looked down at my hands. They were trembling. My surprise at seeing them tremble made them tremble even more. I was rapidly degenerating into a gibbering wreck, a bundle of frayed nerves. I gave Marbles a desperate look, expecting him to say something like, 'Hey I didn't know you were epileptic', but he just shrugged neutrally and said, 'Goodnight then, Abigail.'

He had never called me Abigail before. He rarely even called me 'Abi'. It was always 'Page', or 'bird' if he was feeling particularly argumentative. This new and unexpected turn of phrase unnerved me even more. I was convinced I was going to go into spasms right there, in the middle of the room.

I tried to gain some composure, taking silent deep breaths and trying to gather my jumbled, rattling thoughts into some semblance of order. 'Goodnight, Maurice,' I managed to stutter.

'Hey. You're the only one I'd let get away with that,' he said, his enigmatic grin doing nothing to ease my attack of the shakes. I got to my feet and hesitated by the door, my hand hovering over the handle, convinced that my knees would buckle beneath me at any moment. If only I hadn't had that last shot. If only I had gone to the kitchen with Nadine to share a pot of strong coffee (or a coffer of strong pot) and eat lots of toast and take a hiccuped vow of teetotalism from henceforth. If only I had walked back to campus via the kebab van and vomited up the evening's merriment at the first whiff of dodgy spit-roast carcass. If only . . .

'Is something the matter?' Marbles asked, not moving, not blinking.

He looked at me. I looked back at him. He ran his hand through his hair and let out a low, shaky laugh. I ran my hand through my hair and let out a silly high-pitched giggle.

'No, everything's just dandy sweetheart,' I replied, barely audibly.

'See you in the morning then,' he said, under his breath, his gaze steady and fixed. He bent down and dropped his fag stub into a discarded beer can on the floor. I heard it fizzle out in the last dregs at the bottom.

I tried to grip and turn the door handle to get the hell out of there, but due to drink and euphoria and something else, I just couldn't quite reach out for it. There I stood pathetically grabbing at mid-air, laughing at my unbelievable crapness and ineptitude. The more I tried to stop looking like a fool, the more my sensibilities eluded me.

I was vaguely aware of Marbles saying my name, quietly and patiently and repeatedly, almost like a mantra. It sounded like it was coming from a long way off. Eventually I turned to him, unfocused, uncoordinated and rabbiting unintelligibly. 'Could you open the door for me please . . . ? I can't . . .' I collapsed against the wall, my hysteria escalating by the second. 'I'm sorry, I'm not usually quite this . . .' I dissolved into further giggles, too drunk to feel the embarrassment that would no doubt come back to me tenfold the next morning.

'Abi . . .' he said my name again, louder, and the husky sound of his voice shut me up this time. I stopped giggling and we stared at each other again, purposefully, sultrily, silently. I found I was working hard to catch my breath.

Do these things happen because of drunkenness or in spite of it? Is it always better when it's unplanned and least expected?

A cocktail of adrenalin and endorphins and hormones seethed and fizzed together, coursing through my veins with dynamite force. Something phenomenal between us surged and crackled to life, culminating in an ineluctable force that crushed what tiny fragment of restraint, or sobriety, or whatever, I may have had. He got up and crossed the room towards me in one stride, grabbed me by the shoulders and pushed me against the wall and, as if I was expecting it, my hands went to the back of his head, my fingers through his hair, and I pulled his face towards mine. The chemistry was instant, electrifying, unbearable. As first kisses go, it was not particularly graceful or sensuous by any standards. Our lips and teeth clashed almost on target and as he pushed his tongue deeper into my mouth, I felt a rush of awesome exhilaration, like I was someone else. We were both making animalistic noises by the time he ripped my shirt open, and I was only too glad to reciprocate the gesture. He smelt of tobacco and faded aftershave and sweat and Carlsberg. I buried my face into the warmth of his chest and inhaled the manly smell, became dizzy from it. Months of sexual frustration came pouring out, with such overpowering ferocity I thought I would pass out with lust.

My flares fell crumpled at my ankles before I even felt the zipper go, and I trampled out of them and kicked them aside as Marbles tugged my bra straps down my shoulders. It wasn't one of my best items of lingerie, but I could have been wearing one of my gran's baggy old grey brassieres and I don't think he'd have noticed, or I'd have cared. My fingers fumbled at his belt buckle but it was already undone and I undid his fly with one hand while he gripped my other hand and guided it firmly down the front of my knickers, urging me to feel myself. He moved his lips from mine and began voraciously kissing my neck, my throat, my face, my breasts, shoving me harder against the wall as he rubbed at my crotch, encouraging the movement of my hand beneath the white cotton.

I was on fire. I was aware of nothing but libido, colossal and insatiable, every part of me throbbed with it, was consumed by it, enslaved by it.

Marbles now had his trousers and trusty Calvins half-mast around his thighs. With slow, deliberate movements, he took my hand out of my knickers and sucked my fingers one by one, looking at me lustily through his hair with a smutty smile. His lips parted slightly as his face came towards mine again to kiss me, alternately softly and passionately until I thought I would go mad, then he reached behind me to slide his hands down the back of my knickers, squeezing my buttocks in his palms and hauling my pelvis upwards and towards him. I took short gasps of air as he ripped aside my gusset, slipping a finger or two inside me before stretching and snapping the elastic and pushing up into me in one swift and effortless manoeuvre. I was practically there already, crying out after the first few thrusts, hot tears springing to my eyes as I felt the blissful waves shudder through my body. I had almost forgotten what it felt like, and had to consciously stop myself from screaming out something ridiculous in my moment of abandonment. Instead I whimpered and sobbed with relief, digging my fingernails into his shoulders as the sinews of his body stiffened with the final strokes. His jaw clenched and he made a strange noise in the back of his throat, finally falling forward with a gasp and blaspheming vociferously into the hollow of my armpit. I ran my hands over him and felt his buttocks tense and relax and held him there for a few seconds as we basked in the sweaty afterglow, panting like dogs. He held me close for a second and then pulled away slightly and held my face in both hands and kissed me tenderly.

Just as I felt the heady after-effects ripple away, he withdrew and wiped his dick on my thigh surreptitiously (not so that I didn't notice though). Then he pulled his pants and trousers back around his hips and zipped up his fly, leaving his belt loose and his shirt hanging off his shoulders.

'Mmm, I think we both needed that,' he murmured, raking his hair back from his eyes and stretching his arms above his head with a stifled yawn.

I found it disconcerting how he could be so damn casual about it, like he'd just had a little jog around the block or a warm-up session at the gym. I was dumbstruck. I think it was probably the best sex I'd ever had in my life. I pulled my shirt around me and tried to do up a couple of buttons, realising they had all but one been ripped off. Adjusting my pants and stepping back into my trousers, I felt myself flush with a strange mixture of emotions.

'Are you going to join me then?' Marbles asked, springing back on to his bed and placing his guitar over his crossed legs. 'I'll play you whatever song you like.'

'You mean . . . stay the night? In bed? With you?'

He laughed, a short, dulcet chortle. 'Is that such a revolting thought?' He caressed the strings and began softly playing a few simple chords.

I was suddenly overcome with self-consciousness. 'No . . .'

'Don't worry,' he said, looking up from his deft musical fingering, 'you don't have to if you don't want to.'

'It's not that.' I touched my face gingerly, wondering what I looked like. My lips felt swollen and my whole body tingled with a sensational post-coital buzz, but now reality had set in. I had just had unprotected sex with someone who calls himself Marbles. Waking up next to him in the morning would have just made it all too real, too flawed. If I left while I was still feeling this good, this alive, it would surely be easier to pretend it had never happened and we could carry on as normal for the rest of term. Put it down as a one-off, and it wouldn't have to change anything. No regrets.

'S'pose I'll see you tomorrow then?' He lit up another fag and regarded me through narrowed eyes. I was disconcerted to find myself wanting to leap on him and do it again. Again and again.

'Yeah, I suppose.' My hand managed to find its way to the door handle this time. I opened it just a crack.

'Page?'

I closed it again. 'Yes?'

He shook his head and sighed, tapping the front of the guitar with his knuckles.

'Nothin'. Goodnight.'

While I was busy having unsafe sex with fellow student layabouts, my sister took an unexpected turn for the worse and was sectioned for streaking across Wimbledon Common in broad daylight. Well, she *was* the insane one. I was obviously of sound mind. I didn't like alcohol and I got drunk nearly every night. I knew smoking was making me ill and lethargic and I made no real effort to stop. I had gone to university to enhance my appreciation and knowledge of English Literature and I had barely read a single book. I abhorred conformity and constantly allowed myself to be lured by student organisations which invited me to 'come in and relax with a pressure group of your choice'. I tried to make friends by being someone I wasn't.

Little did I know my Marbles sex encounter was to be one of the less weird incidents of that mad month of March.

March the eleventh was Rachel's birthday. She had never been to London and had always wanted to go clubbing there, so we decided to all chip in for her travel and entrance expenses and go up as a big group for the whole weekend. It was all us girls, plus Marbles, Alex and Garston. Frank had submerged himself in another bout of depression and Yoshi had gone home for the weekend yet again (not that he ever came out with us anyway). Simon was unfortunately 'coming down with something' and so was sent to bed with a hot-water bottle and a vat of steaming Lemsip by Aunty Rachel. Simon's untimely illness was particularly unfortunate because he had donated the largest sum of money towards ensuring that his girlfriend's birthday weekend went swingingly well.

Rachel somehow managed to tear herself from his side and allowed us to help her develop an instant Simon-free personality with a new hairstyle and makeover (courtesy of a clucking Juliet), and a miniature magnum of champagne (courtesy of an over-generous Nadine).

Simon had naturally been consumed with guilt for being too incapacitated to join us for his girlfriend's birthday jaunt, and so had bought her an especially lovely present to make up for it. Rachel was wearing it round her neck when she finally emerged from her room after spending half the day getting ready, blushing at the wolf whistles from Marbles and Alex.

Juliet exclaimed, 'What a pretty necklace! It really sets off the colour of your eyes!'

'Jules, it's a *ruby*,' Nadine pointed out. 'Rachel does not have red eyes.'

'I meant the diamondy bits around the outside. They really sparkle.'

'Tell me, dear heart, have you ever considered a career on the cosmetics counter at Selfridges?'

'Ummm . . .'

'She *is* right though,' I said, wisely intercepting the Juliet/ Nadine exchange before it progressed into a bit of a bitch fight, 'it is a lovely necklace, Rachel. It's just such a shame Si can't make it.'

'Yeah, but who needs a boyfriend to have fun anyway?' She looked sad as she said it, but there was no time for mawkishness as we all had a train to catch. We loitered impatiently outside while Rachel said goodbye to Simon for about the thousandth time, and then we were finally on our way. We had only just arrived at the train station when Rachel realised she had forgotten her handbag.

'How did you manage to forget *that*?' Catherine whined, 'You take it everywhere with you!'

'It was all the excitement . . . and you were rushing me. I'm sorry, I can't go without it. We'll have to go back.'

'For fuck's fucking sake!' was Alex's restrained response to this latest setback. 'Are we *ever* going to get there?'

'Look, you can borrow money off me,' Nadine offered, breaking the dismayed silence. 'It is your birthday after all and I don't mind buying your drinks and whatever.'

Rachel gave her a grateful smile and shook her head. 'It's not just the money. I don't feel right without it.'

'Well you've felt fucking right enough for the last half a bloody hour, haven't you?' Marbles snapped at her. 'Look birds, our train will be here any minute. I'm going with or without you. And so is Cheadle. And my main man Garsty here.'

'Oh how noble of you, Maurice,' said Catherine, hands on hips, with the demeanour of a vexed schoolmistress. Marbles shrugged and slouched towards the ticket office, the hood of his sweatshirt pulled up over his 'Yankees' baseball cap, loose change jangling in the pockets of his voluminous jeans. He was closely followed by his loyal disciples, his 'main man' looking more like a wan woman in his effeminate glam-rock eighties clobber.

'Oh, what am I going to do?' Rachel moaned, looking around at all of us with wide, imploring eyes.

I spoke without thinking. 'Hey, don't worry. You wait here with Cath and Jules, and me and Nade will go back and get it for you. We can get the next train can't we, there's no real hurry.' My offer was made in a fleeting moment of mad munificence, and was met by a scornful look from Nadine and an appreciative hug from Rachel.

'Oh *thank* you, that is just *so* sweet of you! I'm sorry to be such a pain. Tell you what, we'll get you something from the coffee shop over there for when you get back. And the first round will be on me tonight.'

I heard Nadine mutter something under her breath. Rachel beamed at her and she deftly concealed her scowl with a rictus of a forced smile.

'Here's my room key. We'll wait right here for you,' she said, handing me a weighty collection of about twenty key rings with two keys hiding somewhere among the clattering jumble.

'And don't be too long,' Catherine ordered.

We turned and started walking away and Nadine yanked me towards her sharply by my sleeve. 'What did you have to go and say *that* for?' she hissed in my ear. 'I mean, what's wrong with *her* legs? Why do *we* have to go?'

'I was only trying to be nice. It's not like you to be so uncharitable.'

'I have my limits you know.'

'It's not far back anyway.'

'All the more reason for her to go herself.'

'It *is* her birthday, Nadine.'

'Big fat deal. No one noticed when it was *my* birthday.'

'Oh God – when was your birthday?'

'Christmas Eve.'

'Why didn't you tell me?'

'It's a horrible time to have a birthday.'

'Yeah, I suppose it is. Well, how about we have a very belated celebration of your birthday next weekend then?'

She put her arm around me. 'You're very sweet, you know.'

'Yeah, I know. So, what would you like to do?'

'Oh, I don't know. We'll see, yeah?'

We dragged our feet lethargically, smoking half my packet of cigarettes on the way, and eventually reached our block back at campus, which eerily stood in total darkness and silence. We went straight to Rachel's room and feverishly began our urgent handbag-recovering mission. Our search came up with nothing, even after looking under her bed and in her wardrobe and rifling through her drawers and under piles of strewn clothes.

'Jammy little cow, she's getting it right regular,' Nadine remarked, after discovering a staggeringly soppy Valentine card, three or four half empty condom boxes and some strawberry massage oil in Rachel's bedside cabinet.

'Yeah, but it is Simon we're talking about here,' I pointed out. 'And let's face it, he's a bit weird at the best of times.'

'True, true.' She looked around the room at the many displayed photographs, mounted in prettily impractical frames on all available surfaces or stuck to the wall in scattered mosaics of glossy faces, nearly all of them being Simon's and Rachel's, snapped together in some slushy lovestruck pose or other. 'But they really *love* each other. I mean, it's *real* love, innit. You don't get that much these days. I know it makes you sick to look at them together, but secretly wouldn't you love something like that? You know, a solid relationship with your equal, your soulmate, someone who doesn't care when you look like death in the morning and puts up with your PMT and makes you melt just thinking about them . . .' She picked up a teddy bear from Rachel's pillow and fondled it wistfully.

'To be honest, I haven't given it much thought,' I lied. 'Oh sod this, I don't think her bloody handbag's in here.'

'It must be in Simon's room,' Nadine said.

I tripped over Rachel's Winnie the Pooh slippers in a flurry of colourful language. '*I'm* not bloody disturbing him. He might be asleep, or dying, or something.'

'Oh good Lord, there's nothing wrong with the boy. You know the real reason he's not coming tonight, don't you?' She dropped her voice to a whisper and grinned at me impishly.

'What are you talking about?'

'Well, Rachel thought he was going to propose to her and buy her a zonking great engagement ring, you know the way some girls get when they've been going out with some poor bastard for longer than five minutes?'

I nodded slowly, remembering my own hopes not so long ago that Nick would get down on one knee and bestow me with an obscenely huge diamond and a dazzlingly romantic proposal. The nearest I got to it was a shite plastic ring from a cracker one Boxing Day, a cheeky wink and 'Let's go upstairs for some frenzied intercourse.'

'Anyway,' Nadine continued, 'Si didn't quite come up with the goods as Rachel had hoped and they've had an argument about it, end of story.'

'Hmmm . . . it's a bit of a crap thing to have an argument about, innit?'

'Well, there you go. Singletons one, couples nil.' She found a packet of Polos on Rachel's bedside table and helped herself to one. 'Well, we're just wasting time now, I suppose we had better check in Simon's room.'

I sighed, scanning the room one last time. 'Yeah, maybe you're right.'

We locked Rachel's door behind us and walked the half-step distance to the adjacent room. On it, above an unoriginal 'Warning: Hazardous Zone' poster, was a sign saying 'Simon's Room'. Nadine pointed at it and huffed in contempt. She was about to open the door but I grabbed her arm and whispered, 'Shouldn't we knock first? I mean, it's very quiet in there.'

She tutted at me impatiently. 'What if he's asleep?' she hissed. 'No point waking him up, is there?'

'But he's not even ill, you said so yourself. And he's hardly going to remain in a peaceful slumber with two heffalumps like us scrabbling around, even if he *is* asleep.'

My logical argument was flagrantly disregarded, and Nadine

pushed the door open, cautiously and just a little at first, then flinging it wide. The two of us stood in the doorway together as the jaundiced light from the corridor seeped into the darkened room, illuminating a scene of unimaginable surrealism, of gruesome discovery. 'Karma Chameleon' played at a subdued volume on Simon's CD player, but for several awestruck seconds I was aware of no other stimulus but the bizarre visual one in front of my disbelieving eyes. Nadine and I just stood, staring, amazed, trying to absorb the scene, trying to ascertain whether or not we were simply dreaming a terrible, freakish dream. All we could do was look on dumbly, open-mouthed. Simon, kneeling on the floor in the middle of his room, was also open-mouthed, but for an entirely different reason. Frank the Goth was standing upright with his back half-turned to us, presenting a whole new edge to the phrase 'homo erectus', while Simon appeared to be more orally gifted than we had originally given him credit for.

But we were only subjected to this homoerotic display for the briefest of seconds, mercifully. In the blur of confusion that followed our dramatic entrance, Frank yelped with shock and hastily zipped up his black jeans, and Simon recoiled in horror, staggering backwards to cower in the corner of the room. A frisson of shock coursed through me as the four of us were frozen in suspended animation for what felt like an eternity.

Simon started crying; a weird, pained sound like a child who had just been slapped. Frank mumbled 'bugger, bugger, bugger,' over and over again, shaking his black lacquered hair in mortified despair. The silence was protracted and agonising. I held on to the doorframe to keep myself from toppling over.

Eventually, Nadine spoke, in a shaky and slightly vitriolic voice. 'Abi and me were just remarking on what a good couple you and Rachel make.'

Simon continued sobbing, squirming under our scornful scrutiny. I didn't really know what to think of this unprecedented and extremely unsavoury discovery, but I did think that they deserved to be caught out. Just . . . not by us.

'We've just popped back to collect your girlfriend's handbag,'

Nadine continued. 'Just as well she didn't come back for it herself, isn't it?'

She turned to Frank, who was blushing beetroot through his white make-up. His humiliation was almost tangible. 'Please, do feel free to wop it back out. I'd hate to think I was breaking up something beautiful.'

I found my voice, a barely audible croak in the back of my throat. 'I don't think we should be here . . .'

'Too bloody right,' Nadine agreed.

Another awful silence.

'Aha! There it is!' She spotted Rachel's handbag under the chair and swooped on it. I thought – hoped – that would be the end of it. Perhaps we should have left promptly and convinced each other that we had just experienced the same weird hallucination, a glimpse into a silly parallel universe. But Nadine had a few things to say first.

'You are a pathetic little fuckwit,' she told Simon. 'And *you* . . .' she swivelled toward Frank, 'you are just . . . just . . .' She searched for the right word but it didn't quite come to her.

From my standpoint – a shocked but generally opinionless observer standing on the threshold of this absurd scene – the lunacy of the situation struck me harder than its potential or actual seriousness. I saw Simon, skinny closet poofter from Leeds, erstwhile trusted boyfriend of the sweet and simpering Rachel – traumatised, head down, quaking in shame. I saw Frank, *Goth extraordinaire*, caught with his pants down in the wrong place at the wrong time with the most very wrong person. I saw Nadine reprimanding the pair of them like a strident, morally outraged mother.

And I saw the funny side.

I clapped my hand to my mouth but it was too late to suppress an evil-sounding snicker. When all three of them looked sharply around at me, the humourlessness on their faces just made me laugh more. I bellowed out loud, doubling over and cackling uncontrollably.

Nadine already had one hand on her hip, now both hands were placed firmly on her haunches as she turned to me incredulously.

'And what, pray tell, is so damn funny?' she snapped. I looked up at her helplessly, but as soon as we made eye contact I saw a smile creep on to her face and then we were both off, holding on to one another and snorting with mirth.

'It's not funny!' she insisted, through her laughter.

'I know it isn't, but . . . it *is*!' I waved my hand helplessly at the unlikely couple, whose expressions of dread and shame were now replaced with looks of bewilderment.

Frank coughed and shuffled and looked at his feet. Simon furrowed his brow in confusion and mild indignation. Both of them looked pale and scared and somehow much smaller. I couldn't help feeling sorry for them.

Frank stared at Nadine and me, the expression on his face far too earnest considering the farcical circumstances. 'Listen, you two, this is my fault. Don't have a go at Simon. And don't make light of the situation.' He sat down heavily on the chair beside Simon's desk and sighed deeply. 'I love him,' he said, plainly. This was obviously news to Simon as well as to Nadine and me, and Simon looked up curiously from his huddled position in the corner.

'You what?' all three of us chorused together.

'I love you, Simon,' Frank said, turning to him with a sincere tenderness I had never seen before, let alone from a Goth. Before Simon could respond, Nadine piped up: 'Er, hello? Like, excuse me? I hate to intrude on this romantic interlude, but are you not forgetting something?' She had finished seeing the funny side now and had switched back to her chastising mother routine.

'Rachel,' Simon said tremulously, almost too quietly to hear.

'Do you love her?' Nadine demanded, except gentler this time. Frank started to say something, but Nadine cut him off. 'You can keep it zipped, matey, you've made your feelings perfectly clear.'

'Of course I love her,' Simon replied, looking offended.

'Are you gay?' she asked casually, sitting herself down on Simon's bed and lighting a cigarette. I was tempted to inform her that it wasn't really any of our business and that we should just return to the station to meet the others, catch our train and get on with the weekend as if nothing had happened.

Simon paled and his lower lip started to quiver. 'I . . . I don't know.' He shook his head and gave Frank an apologetic look. Then, glancing sheepishly at Nadine and then at me, he said it again, even more quietly. 'I really don't know.'

Nadine offered her cigarettes around and everyone took one except Simon, who was too distraught to do anything but quake in the corner. Although I felt a twinge of sympathy for him, I wondered how I'd feel if I found out that my boyfriend had been seeing another *man* behind my back. It had shaken me up enough to discover that I was a consolation prize in a male-orchestrated competition in which the ultimate trophy is the one with the prettiest face, biggest tits, slimmest waist and longest legs. But to be second best to someone who has a penis – well, you can't really compete can you? You're more or less disqualified at the first hurdle.

The nicotine calmed me down. Leaning against the wall, I exhaled a stream of smoke before asking, 'How long has this been going on?'

A clandestine homosexual affair was not the sort of thing that was easy to keep secret, especially in a hall such as ours.

'Nothing's been going on,' Frank said wearily, a little tetchily. 'I've always liked him, but it wasn't until tonight that . . .'

'Yes, well, quite. When the cat's away,' Nadine quipped.

'It's not . . . like that. It's not some sordid affair,' Simon stuttered.

'No, I'm sure it's all very sweet and innocent,' Nadine sniffed. She stood up suddenly and announced, 'Well, I suppose we should be going now. We've got what we came for. Shame we got a little bit more than we bargained for, but never mind.' She gave the pair of them a sarcastic smile. 'It's been so nice chatting with you two, but I'm afraid us girls have an exciting night of dancing, drinking and fornicating ahead of us. And don't worry, Si, I'll make sure Rachel behaves herself.' She flung Rachel's handbag over her shoulder and sashayed out of the room. I gave them a last glance and followed her.

We had barely reached the front door when Simon came stampeding down the hall towards us, calling out in desperation.

When he caught up with us, there were still tears in his eyes and he implored us breathlessly, 'Please don't tell her. Please.' We looked blankly at him, unsure of how to feel. He continued his entreaty, fresh tears rolling down his cheeks as he sobbed his way through an apology and a half-baked explanation that was touching in its inanity.

'It's not us you should be apologising to,' Nadine said, finishing her fag and stubbing it out on the wall. 'I have nothing against you being queer, in fact I think it's pretty cool you've admitted it to yourself, but –'

'I'm not . . .'

'*But*,' Nadine interrupted, 'the sooner Rachel knows the better. She thought you were going to ask her to marry you for God's sake!' She shook off Simon's hand, which had clamped itself on her shoulder throughout his tearful tirade. He hung his head and mumbled something.

'We won't tell her,' I assured him, reaching out to touch his arm. '*You* have to, though.'

'It's just that . . .' Simon rubbed at his tear-splotched face with his sleeve and gazed at us sadly. 'It's just there's never been anyone but Rachel. All my life . . .'

Nadine stopped him again. 'Exactly. And if you want . . . something else, you're going the wrong way about it. *Tell* her. And soon.'

'I can't . . .'

'Yes you fucking can. It just takes a bit of guts.'

'But you two won't say anything?' he squeaked. 'I don't want to hurt Rachel, I can't break up with her.'

'Well, you can't have it both ways,' Nadine sighed impatiently. 'You'd better have a good think about things. But me and Ab aren't the sort to go shooting our mouths off, so don't worry about that.'

'Promise?'

'We promise, Simon. Just pull yourself together, and decide what side of your bread you want buttering, all right?' Nadine was good at making complicated things sound simple. Simon made a small, peevish sound but then smiled weakly at us.

'I'm glad it was you two and not anyone else. I mean, Marbles or Alex . . . God knows what they'd have done.'

I shuddered to think what they'd have done.

Nadine looked at her watch. 'Shit, we've really got to go now, OK? We're going to miss the second train. We'll leave you to . . . whatever.'

I gave him a commiserative pat on the back and then we left him to mull over his AC/DC dilemma, or perhaps to resume what had been so rudely interrupted.

'What kept you? You've been *ages*,' Catherine moaned when we finally got back to the station, panting and knackered.

Nadine thrust the accursed handbag at Rachel, and grunted a reply. 'Let's just get out of here.'

Meanwhile, Jasmine's rehab process was going badly. After her Wimbledon Common episode, she was committed with no chance of repeal for the immediate future. Dad phoned me in a panic on the morning of Mother's Day.

'I think you might want to come up, Abi. I'm sorry, but things are going badly up here. Jane has left me,' he said, his voice quaking with emotion.

'What?!'

'She . . . she had to go, really. I don't blame her. Jasmine went totally out of control last week, she had one of her turns and chased Lewis around the house with a hammer, calling him every name under the sun. They could hear the commotion all the way down the end of the road. The next minute Jasmine's all sweet and calm again, chain-smoking in the lounge, stroking the cat and watching telly, wondering why we're all looking so terrified of her.'

'But –' My heart plunged and I blinked back spontaneous tears. 'But how –'

'Jane moved the last of her stuff out last night. She says she still loves me but she just can't . . . take any more. I'm here all alone and Jasmine's relapsed. The voices have come back and she's stuck in a room at that awful place and there's nothing I can do. I'm going out of my mind.' He broke down, and all I could hear on the other end of the line was distant snuffling and sobbing. I closed my eyes and breathed deeply.

'Dad, I don't know what to say. I'm so . . . sorry.'

He blew his nose and gulped for air. 'I have to keep myself together for Jas, but I don't know how much longer I can be supportive. I feel like I'm watching her drown and I'm powerless to help.'

What should I have said to him? Anything but what I did blurt out: 'You know she's pregnant, don't you?'

There was a short silence.

'Is this your way of saying things could always be worse?' he asked.

'Oh, Dad . . . things *are* worse. Jas phoned me from West Lothian a few weeks ago. She told me she was having Seth's baby. But . . . she sounded so much better then, like she was really getting her life back together . . .'

There was a longer silence. 'She's been asking for you,' he said eventually, quietly.

'I'll be there in three hours. I'm leaving now.'

I was there in two hours and forty minutes. I went straight to the chronics ward (it was called the Freehaven wing, ironically), and met Dad in the canteen – a huge, echoing room filled with gnarled tables and chairs like an old-fashioned classroom, with a chessboard floor and a serving bar at the far end staffed at intervals by a pair of crabby old ladies in pinnies and frilled caps. Vending machines stood around blinking 'exact money only' and 'sold out'. Several small semi-opaque windows on each side let in minimal light and so the place was dark and gloomy except for the humming sodium lights overhead. It smelled of mashed potato and cold gravy, and reminded me of the time I had thrown up on a dinner lady when I was seven after being force-fed ravioli.

Dad hugged and kissed me and held me close. 'Jane will be here soon. She wants this to be over just as much as we do. She does love Jasmine, you know.'

I sat down opposite him with a sigh. 'I know she does.'

'I think we're seeing Dr Morgan later on. About the . . . situation. Do you want to come along?'

Dr Morgan had been Jasmine's consultant ever since she was first diagnosed as schizophrenic. He wasn't exactly an objectively objectionable person, but ever since I had overheard him describe my sister as a 'waste of a beautiful young woman', I had harboured a certain amount of childish resentment against him and was never able to shake off my perception of him as a florid, flabby, flatulent fool.

'Yes, I think that would be a good idea,' I said.

'Do you want a drink?' he asked.

'I want to see Jasmine. Where is she?'

He pointed at the door and swallowed the last of his tea. There were six empty plastic cups on the table in front of him already, and the foil ashtray was brimming with cigarette stubs. 'Turn right out of here and she's the third room on your right.'

I got up slowly but then sat down again. 'Are you OK Dad?'

'Oh, you know,' he stacked the empty cups up listlessly, one inside of the other, and gave a one-shouldered shrug. 'Surviving.' His smile was absolutely sad. He faltered, struggling to keep up the pretence of being strong. 'I'm sorry to drag you away like this, but . . .'

'We're in this *together*. All of us.'

'The baby's due in October, by the way.'

'What?'

'Jasmine's baby. Your niece or nephew. My first grandchild. First week of October, they reckon.'

'Oh.'

'That's if . . .' he trailed off and looked down at his hands, clasping them together to stop them from shaking. 'Well, anyway. I'll come and get you in about a quarter of an hour. See if you can get through to her, Abi. You're the one she talks to. You know what to say. I can't even bear to . . .'

'It's all right. I'll see you in a bit.'

I squeezed his arm and plodded towards the door, the sound of my footsteps bouncing and reverberating off the high walls.

After several unanswered knocks, I entered the room and was

at once overcome with a sickening and familiar feeling. There is a sense other than smell and taste and sight and hearing and touch, a sense dependent on but separate and distinct from those simple sensations – spurred by memory and recollections, by the atmosphere of a place, by nuances and a gut feeling. A déjà vu sense, except it isn't transitory and vague, it stays with you and it's potent. This is what I was feeling when I entered and the door swung shut behind me: an instinctive apprehension, a permeating dread. A feeling I had had so many times before in this same place over the years.

The room was – if possible – pokier and bleaker than my room at university, thick with smoke and a palpable claustrophobia. The curtains were drawn as if someone had died and the floor was laid with plain carpet tiles, threadbare and dirty. I could only make out shadowy shapes in the semi-darkness and The Pixies playing on Jasmine's cassette player was the only sound.

I pulled back one curtain and light strained through the bars of the window, throwing irregular stripes of light on to the bed, the walls, the floor.

On the bed under a mound of blankets, Jasmine groaned and threw an arm across her eyes, trying to block it out. Her extraordinarily hyper-surreal collection of oil paintings covered the walls, along with a Sid Vicious poster and a Keith Moon poster, and there were ashtrays, cushions, drapes, rugs and various family photographs strewn around randomly in an attempt to make it more homely. Jasmine was drugged and kept drifting in and out of consciousness. I pulled up a chair and sat looking at her. She was mumbling something under her breath: 'All my thoughts . . . all I am are my thoughts . . . what I'm not . . .'

It took me a while to realise she was singing along to the song playing in the background. I remained quiet, and just watched her.

Fashion features at that time were being run out about 'heroin chic' and how the grunge look had given way to a stylish emaciated 'drug-raddled waif' look. Looking like a heroin addict was apparently the ultimate fashion statement. I had read something about it in one of Catherine's magazines and I hadn't known whether to laugh or cry. A grainy picture had depicted a sallow girl with blank eyes smudged with grey and purple shadow, lips and cheeks left pale, whose entire body probably weighed the same as my head. She was caught in an angular pose, all torsion and taut skin, bony limbs like pipe cleaners draped with printed gossamer fabric which had been sliced and sewn into a snappy little number made to order from a Paris fashion house. Two thousand pounds for that look. A more authentic but distinctly less glamorous look was right in front of me. Of course, the dress Jasmine was wearing was only a pink polyester nightie, but she had otherwise captured the look frighteningly well.

'I set my alarm for half-eight,' Jasmine whispered eventually. 'That's when they come in to give me the first lot of stuff.' She turned on to her stomach and sank her face into the pillows. Then she looked over at me and said, 'So then I think about getting dressed and having something to eat, but I realise I just feel too shit and what's the point.'

I moved the chair closer to the side of the bed. She held out her hand, limp, inert, and I held on to it weakly.

'So I just lie back in bed and put a tape on auto-reverse so I can just listen and let the drugs do their thing, whatever . . .' Her voice was monotone, characterless. She lifted her head slightly and stared at me as if she didn't recognise me. 'It was good of you to come, sis,' she murmured eventually, pulling her hand away and turning around to face the wall. She curled herself up into a ball and put her hands over her ears.

I took advantage of the fact that she had her back to me, and quietly took her diary out of my bag and put it in a side drawer under a pile of notes and pictures. I sat down again and thought about lighting up. My knee started shaking uncontrollably. I crossed one leg over the other and clamped it down with my elbow, resting my chin in my palm as my eyes flickered around the room for something mundane to concentrate on.

'Got any fags?' she asked me, after I had studied the fire procedure on the back of her door about a hundred times.

'Er . . .' I felt for the packet in my pocket, knowing I had two left and that I shouldn't offer one to her.

'It's all right, I've got my own secret stash somewhere. Unless they've found it and taken away the only damn pleasure I have in this hell-hole.'

I searched my brain for a possible conversation starter.

'How are you feeling?' I asked, knowing as soon as the words came out of my mouth that it was the most stupid thing I could have said.

She turned her body back round and her eyes momentarily flashed with her characteristic humour. 'Just ticketyboo, sis, can't you tell?'

'I'm sorry, I just . . .'

'No, really. Thought I'd check in at Hotel Rayneham for a while, catch up with a few old friends, utilise the five-star facilities, great views . . .' she nodded towards the barred window, '. . . friendly staff, obligatory daily pill-popping, my own spectacularly crap room, and my very own set of mental health notes penned by my very own consultant who thinks he can sum me up in a few words and keep me here until his clever old drugs have sufficiently fucked up my thought processes.'

'*Jasmine . . .*'

'Of course, they're clever *new* drugs now, aren't they?' She started to laugh, a low, throaty chuckle which then escalated into raucous howling. Then she became exhausted and was silent again for a while, staring up at the dangling unlit bulb in the middle of the ceiling. She held her arms out in front of her and waved them about as if conducting an imaginary orchestra, then let them flop back down by her sides and sighed, 'Can you pass me those pills on the sideboard, please?' She propped herself up on a heap of pillows and rubbed her eyes. 'These days I can't even get out of bed without amphetamine in the morning.'

'It's two p.m., Jas.'

'See what I mean?' She smiled guiltily as I passed her the pills and poured her a glass of water from the plastic jug by her bed. 'Things have gone bad again, haven't they?'

I shrugged. I didn't know what to say to her.

'Dad's here?'

'Yes. He's waiting for Jane in the canteen. I wanted . . . to be alone with you for a little while.'

She reached under her mattress and pulled out a packet of Marlboro. ''Fraid I'm not much company right now,' she said.

'We'll be seeing Dr Morgan later.'

'What, to discuss how fucking loopy I am?'

'We just want to get you *out* of here.'

She lit up a fag and took a big drag into her lungs. 'The doctors tell me I'm not fit to be a mother,' she said. 'Apparently.'

'Shouldn't you try to give up?' I asked hesitantly, watching the smoke curl from her lips.

She gave me a mildly scornful look. 'I *have* given up. I gave up a long time ago.' She pulled on the filter again and let out a long stream of smoke from her mouth and nose, gazing dreamily into the distance.

'It's not good for the baby,' I chided. 'Why can't you try –'

'Shh!' She held up her hand and sat upright as if listening for something.

After a moment, I tried to continue: 'I thought that you –'

'*Shhh*! Can't you hear that?' She leaned forward, suddenly alert, the untapped column of ash on her cigarette breaking off and dropping into fragments on the floor.

'What is it?' The room was silent except for the music and the distant hum of a lawnmower outside in the gardens.

'Oh,' she resumed her slouched position, taking another deep puff, 'it doesn't matter.'

There was a small knock at the door.

'Fuck off if you've got a patronising air and a clipboard,' Jasmine quipped.

Dad poked his head around the door and flashed both of us a tentative grin. 'Hello girls. Do you fancy a bit of lunch?'

Jasmine grimaced. 'Not in the canteen here. The food's shit. But Dad –'

'Hmm?'

'You could get me some coffee, if you don't mind. Black,

strong, three sugars. There's a proper coffee machine in the day-room, just ask one of the assistants.'

'Anything else?'

'Not really hungry right now. Just gotta wait for my upper to kick in then I can drag my bones out of bed.'

I saw Dad's face fall and I saw the effort he put into forcing a smile as he walked over to her and sat on the edge of the bed. He stroked back her hair and kissed her forehead. 'Don't worry, love – you'll be home with us soon.'

Jasmine turned her head away and her voice wavered when she spoke. 'I won't be coming home this time. I've ruined things enough already. I'm big and ugly enough to take care of myself now.'

Dad kept his hand on her head and said nothing, just looked at her with heart-breaking affection and despair. 'Are you ready to go then, Abi?' he whispered, not moving.

I stood up uneasily. 'I suppose so.'

'I'll bring you a coffee in a moment, OK Jas?' He gave her another kiss and left the room. There were tears in his eyes.

I loitered by Jasmine's bed, still stuck for words.

'It's OK. I know you don't know what to say to me. Thanks for coming. I appreciate it.' She coughed tremulously as I bent down to hug her. 'I love you, Abi,' she said, out of the blue, leaving me stunned and dumbstruck. 'You know that, don't you?'

I just nodded, biting my lip. I felt like I couldn't breathe.

'I'll come and see you when I'm feeling better. It will be just like the old times.'

I lowered my head and mumbled, 'Yeah.'

We looked at each other and she smiled, a tired but seemingly genuine smile. Then she fell back on to her bed and covered herself up so just her head was sticking out, black hair and anaemic skin and dark whirlpool eyes. 'Don't worry about us. We'll be fine,' she whispered.

'I'll see you again soon,' I promised.

'You can count on it,' she yawned, stretching out and putting a pillow over her face. 'Give Dr Shithead my kindest regards, won't you?'

'Now, Jasmine is an unusual case.' Dr Morgan adjusted his wire-rimmed specs and scratched his sideburns contemplatively. 'Sanity is not a simple and definable concept, as you all know, but while I'm convinced that Jasmine is not . . . strictly *sane*, for want of a better word, I don't believe she is . . . totally out of touch with reality. Not to the extent that she can be described as *in*sane.'

His omnipresent clipboard wobbled precariously on his tweed lap as we eyed him curiously.

'We've been over this before,' my dad said wearily. 'It's been the same old story for almost ten years. If she just stayed away from drugs . . .'

'Drug abuse can of course only make things worse, but – it's just hard to know with Jasmine.'

'What do you mean?' I demanded.

He turned to me, fixing me with his piggy eyes. 'I mean . . . if she had avoided drugs, I'm not entirely sure it would ever have had to come to this. Schizophrenia is, physiologically, a chemical imbalance in the brain. And looking at Jasmine's notes . . .' he flicked through the scribbled pages on his clipboard while Dad, Jane and I exchanged looks of bafflement and unease. 'Well, her condition runs deeper than drug dependence, obviously. There's no miracle cure for schizophrenia. It doesn't have to be the end of the world, but some people may never recover. And those who do may relapse at the slightest trigger.'

'How about telling us something we don't know?' Jane snapped. She was uncharacteristically irritable, and took large gulps of watery coffee from a paper cup as she eyed Dr Morgan in a most unchristian way.

'Yes, of course. Let's get straight to the point. We need to discuss the latest . . . er, situation.'

'Situation?' Dad coughed hesitantly and moved forward in his seat.

'She's ten weeks' pregnant. She's only just got over another heroin withdrawal, which has left her body in one hell of a state. I don't think . . .'

'We'll be here for her, no matter what. We'll give her all the help she needs. She'll be fine,' Dad insisted.

'Thomas . . .' Dr Morgan sighed, tweaking off his glasses and rubbing the dented red marks on the bridge of his nose.

'Mr Page,' Dad corrected. He liked to keep things formal when discussing his elder daughter's mental frailty.

'. . . Mr Page,' Dr Morgan continued, suitably snubbed, 'I'm not sure you realise what a strain this is going to be. It is vital that Jasmine is monitored and supported throughout.' He sat back in his leather chair and flung one leg over the other. A glimpse of white sock was all I needed to convince me he still lived with his mum. 'She seems to be in a state of dysphoria at the moment – lethargic, uncooperative, often hostile . . .'

'Isn't that because of the drugs you keep giving her?' I asked, trying to keep my voice under control.

He appeared to ignore me. 'Pregnancy is only likely to exacerbate these negative symptoms. Any drug we *do* give her –' he looked over at me, 'has to be very carefully prescribed, because we have to think about the possible effects on the foetus. We don't want to take any risks, but there is a fine line between ensuring the safety of Jasmine and the health of her baby.'

'Why can't she just come home with us?' Dad asked. 'We'd take good care of her . . .'

'This must be very frustrating for you, I do understand, but please be assured she is in the best place at the moment. We are doing all we can for her. Like most schizophrenics, Jasmine unfortunately cannot recognise that she is seriously ill, and therefore believes that she doesn't need the treatment. She has already started accusing the staff here of trying deliberately to abort her baby . . .'

We all looked at each other uncomfortably.

'And as you are aware, she is experiencing auditory hallucinations again. I have had to prescribe a new antipsychotic and mood stabiliser . . . just a small and controlled dosage, to see how things go. She should hopefully start gaining some weight soon, and her first antenatal scan is in a couple of weeks . . .'

'She will . . . be all right, won't she?' I found myself asking him, in a small, pathetic voice. I knew he would probably only say what he knew I wanted to hear, but I needed all the assurance I could get.

He smiled in a restrained and professional way, a sympathetic twitching of the lips. 'It's very hard to be sure with Jasmine, Abigail. She goes through these phases, you see . . .' he regarded each of us in turn as he cleaned his glasses with his tie and then slipped them back on, blinking frenziedly. 'Schizophrenia is not a simple term referring to a single, treatable illness. It is a very complex personality disorder, and we can only do our best when it comes to diagnosis and efficacious drug administration. We're working in the dark a bit, really. There's so much we don't know and I'm sorry that so many of your questions cannot be answered with any degree of certainty.' He sucked on his pen for a while, staring hard at his notes as if the answer to his professional quandaries would suddenly leap out from the page. He leaned forward and whispered in consolatory tones, 'I know this is terrible for all of you, but you must be prepared to make some drastic changes in your lives. She needs constant care and attention. And the baby is going to need someone to look after it when it arrives.'

I was incensed. 'What makes you think Jasmine is not capable of looking after the baby herself?'

He shook his head, as if the idea was ludicrous. Even Dad and Jane looked at me in that 'too young to know any better' way which I used to get when I was at primary. 'Jasmine will be a *brilliant* mother,' I protested, feeling silly and insignificant as I said it. 'She'll prove it to all of you, just wait and see.'

Dad took both my hands in his. 'Sweetheart, I know you have faith in your sister, but we have to face facts.' He glanced over at Jane, who lowered her eyes and scrunched her empty cup in her hand. 'Jasmine can't look after *herself* at the moment. It's a miracle she's alive.'

'But . . . but . . .' I felt my lower lip wobble, and I turned my head away. Dr Morgan took a piece of paper from his clipboard and handed it to Jane. She and Dad pored over it as I sulked despondently.

'Jasmine's health report,' Dr Morgan announced. 'From last

time, you will remember. I made it clear that any more illegal drugs would only find her back here. She does have this habit of . . .'

'We can't look out for her all the time, she's nearly twenty-six years old,' Dad cried out. 'We've done our best, God knows.'

'Please be assured, I'm not blaming you, any of you,' Dr Morgan responded, his voice annoyingly calm and even. 'I think the solidarity you have shown is remarkable. But for now, she must stay here where we can keep an eye on her and make sure she's fully rehabilitated. She is particularly vulnerable at the moment, so we all just need a little bit of patience.'

My patience had run out. The walls of Dr Morgan's clean and uncluttered office seemed to be closing in on me.

'I need some air,' I announced. I got up quickly, knocking over my chair, and slammed the door behind me.

Outside in the corridor, the bleach and tea and launderette smell hit my nostrils as starkly as the bleak whiteness of the floor and walls hit my eyes. In-patients milled around and wandered past in a long straggling line, like a comatose conga, swallowing their pills with enervated synchronicity before sidling back to their hermetic rooms. In the large day-room opposite, more patients sat around in their nightwear watching, or more precisely not watching, an afternoon soap on the antiquated television set.

I observed them with a strange mixture of compassion, confusion, wariness and gladness that I wasn't one of them. A man in a wheelchair sped towards me, laughing dementedly. I dodged out of his path just in time and he missed me by millimetres, entering the day-room and parking his wheelchair next to a tattered armchair, in which sat a man of similar age and mental constitution. This one merely chose to sit in the same place, in the same position for hours on end, just staring and dribbling and every now and then shouting 'Fuck off!' at irregular intervals. I recognised both of them from previous visits. I think they were permanent residents. They had scared me when I was younger; now my heart went out to them.

I was in Cuckoo-Land, surrounded by a gallimaufry of lunatics, a collection of people from all walks of life who were clinically mad and blissfully unaware of it. They went about their daily business, taking drugs and doing whatever they liked and ignoring the sane people employed to control them, and thinking every day was normal – which of course, it was for them.

I returned to university the next day. Back to my cramped, boxy room in the imbecilic environment to which I had become happily accustomed. Back to normal.

'I have another theory,' Nadine said, the following Saturday, while we were confabulating drunkenly in one of the union bars. 'Nobody is actually *mad*, they are just . . . conditioned to behave in an unconventional way when they are stuck with a label and put in an asylum with other maniacs. Mad is what people are when they can't be explained in any other way.'

We had both become bored with discussing Simon and Frank's love affair, especially since we were loath to share the revelation with anyone else. Instead we talked about my latest visit to Rayneham, as it was all I had on my mind anyway. I had promised to very belatedly celebrate Nadine's twentieth birthday that night, but so far it had been more of a slurred philosophical debate over constantly refilled glasses of wine, dredging up whatever random factoids and statistics and theories we had learned from our respective sociology and psychology A-levels.

'I don't think it's quite that simple, Nade,' I said. 'Anyway, shall we go back to your room to watch those videos now? I'm fed up with talking about serious stuff. Let's just pig out on chocolate and gossip the night away.'

'OK, why not?' She shrugged and ordered another bottle of white wine from the bar.

Everyone else on the hall had gone to a party or back home, so when Nadine and I returned, tittering and tottering about on ungainly and uncoordinated limbs, the place was deserted. We went into her room and gorged on Pringles and Galaxy bars throughout *Thelma and Louise*, barely saying a word to each other. That is, until the Brad Pitt scene started, and I suddenly felt an overwhelming urge to confess something.

'I had sex with Marbles,' I blurted out.

'Oh yeah?' She didn't seem surprised in the slightest, she just gave me a wink and turned back to the film, crunching noisily on crisps.

Her reaction was not what I expected. 'Aren't you going to hit me and demand an explanation?'

'Oh my dear girl, it's hardly up to me what you do with your body, is it?' she said, not tearing her eyes away from the screen. 'This was the seventies night, right?'

'Er . . . yeah. How do you know?'

She smiled and was quiet for a while. 'You two couldn't keep your eyes off each other all night,' she finally muttered.

'Hardly,' I said, feeling curiously consoled by this statement.

'Well, he's not my personal cup of tea, but anyway . . . it passed the time, I suppose?'

I looked down at the half-melted slab of chocolate in my sweaty palm. 'It was rather good, actually,' I admitted bashfully.

Nadine coughed and sprayed out semi-chewed crisp fragments. 'Maurice slipped you one and it was *good*?' she spluttered, her perfectly arched eyebrows disappearing into her fringe. 'Are we talking about the same Maurice "please form an orderly queue, laydeez" Venables here? The same "first served, first come" Marbles that we all sadly know and love?'

'He's not *that* bad,' I objected.

'Darling, he's a slag.'

'Well, whatever. We haven't talked about it since, and he's just acting like it never happened,' I mumbled. 'I get the feeling he's regretting it.'

'For God's sake Abi, would you rather he'd *told* everyone about it? Do *you* regret it?' She looked at me with her wide, demantoid eyes, stuffing her face with another fistful of crisps. My silence disturbed her. 'Oh my God Abigail, you're not . . . *in love* with him are you?'

'Oh don't be ridiculous!' I scoffed, cramming chocolate in my mouth and staring back at the screen. 'He's a prat. He's not my type.'

Nadine wasn't completely satisfied with my response. 'What's the point of having a *type*? It only restricts an already restricted market of potential partners,' she said.

Then, with a sigh, she added, 'But yes, I have to agree with you that he's a prat. Shall we change the subject?'

'Yes, please.'

We descended into silence. In fact, we didn't speak at all until the film ended and the credits rolled.

'Well, that was a very entertaining film,' Nadine said.

'I can't believe you hadn't seen it already. It's the ultimate chick flick.'

'I've led a sheltered life, obviously.'

'There's another two vids in there to choose from,' I said, pointing to the bag I had brought back from the video shop earlier that afternoon, which also contained what was left of the blissfully fattening snacks: popcorn, crisps, chocolate and two bags of pick 'n' mix.

'Both of them rated eighteen, I'm afraid,' I added.

'Ooh, my mummy and daddy would smack your botty if they knew what kind of influence you were having on me.'

'That's a joke!' I huffed. 'You're the filthiest little cow I've ever met.'

She pretended to be offended and turned her back on me as she studied the back of the video cases. 'Hmmmm . . .' she pondered aloud, 'they both look pretty shite to me, if truth be told.'

'That's what you get for hurrying me.'

'Oh, this one will do,' she said, holding up *Basic Instinct.*

'You sure? Bit of a racy one. Michael Douglas *au naturel.*'

She grimaced. 'Not an overly pleasant thought, but I think I can just about handle it if you can.' She ripped the top off a second Pringles tube and seized upon a bag of sweets as if she hadn't eaten for weeks. I opened up two cans of ginger beer, feeling like a mischievous twelve-year-old and liking it. It made a change from the constant obligation of becoming pissed and offensive. The company wasn't bad either. It felt like a midnight feast round at a mate's house. I suppose it was in a way. I didn't even mind that I was rapidly sobering up.

I put the tape into Nadine's VCR and we sat glumly through the trailers before finding ourselves resuming our discussion about Marbles and madness.

'I just don't seem to know what I want,' I moaned, biting the head off a jelly baby, 'Or where I'm going. My family is falling apart, my sister's been knocked up and institutionalised, my love life is non-existent, my period is more than three weeks late . . .'

Nadine choked on a marshmallow puff. 'God, Abi, you're not . . . as well, are you?'

'Oh, it's just stress or something. When I, er, you know . . . with Marbles, I was already a couple of days late, so I think it's OK . . .'

'You *did* use something, didn't you?'

I swallowed audibly and fixed my eyes on the film with feigned fascination.

'*Abi*!' She reprimanded me with a slap on the wrist. 'You mean to tell me you could have a mini Marbles gestating inside you like some kind of . . . demon seed?'

'Don't be stupid.'

'Or he could have given you some horrible fungal infection. STDs are rife among students you know.'

I frowned. 'It was just a one-off. And I *don't* regret it, by the way.'

'It only takes one. Looks like the clap clinic for you, my love.'

'Please don't wind me up about this. I thought that as my friend one of your primary functions was to cheer me up.'

'Hey, as *my* friend you're not supposed to make me feel physically sick by telling me about your sexual perversions.'

'One brief encounter with Marbles hardly counts as a perversion.'

She gave me a doubtful look.

I conceded. 'OK, so maybe it's not necessarily within the normal range of human sexual activity.'

'Don't worry. You're a student, sweetie. It's forgivable. Define what's normal around here anyway.'

I sucked ruminatively on a citrus gobstopper. 'Normal is striving towards a worthy goal rather than smoking and drinking your life away, normal is not having casual sex when there is a terrifying variety of diseases knocking about, normal is . . .'

'Fucking boring.'

We smiled at each other and watched the film for a while. Sharon Stone relieved herself of her clothes and propositioned a drooling Michael Douglas.

I lay back on the floor, stretched out and sighed heavily. 'Oh why can't I have a body like that?' I grumbled vacuously.

'Don't start,' Nadine pleaded, 'or I'm turning the damn thing off.'

'I mean, how *fair* is that?' I continued, ignoring her. 'Perfect legs, tiny bum, flat stomach, absolutely amazing tits.' I appraised every one of Ms Stone's obvious good physical features, in ascending anatomical order. 'I mean, she's an entirely different league, isn't she? My tits are just . . . well, pendulous *udders*, really. They just . . . hang there. No real shape or aesthetic, just mediocre mounds of fat with nipples on the end.' I looked down at my inferior chest with fond discontent. Nadine made a petulant noise. She reached over and calmly slid her hand inside my shirt and touched my left breast beneath my bra, feeling it briefly before giving me her own opinion.

'You've got great tits. Shut up,' she said, matter-of-factly, without even blinking. Then, with just as much deliberation, she took her hand away and put it straight back into the rapidly depleting pick 'n' mix bag. I gawped in astonishment, not so much shocked at her audacity but at the fact I was considerably less offended and repulsed than I perhaps should have been.

'Er – thanks,' I eventually managed. I dumbly watched her scoff more sweets, then another fistful of Pringles, then a mouthful of ginger beer. She felt my eyes on her and turned to me with a suspicious half-smile.

'What?' She wiped her mouth with the back of her hand and gave me a curious look.

'Nothing.' I shifted my body and my gaze, playing with the top button of my shirt and wondering whether to do it up. I left it and let my hands drop to my lap.

'Do you not want to watch the film?'

'Er, I – yeah, sure. Well, I've seen it before.'

'Why did you get films you've seen before?'

'I thought you might like them . . .'

'Well this one's a bag of poo, mate. No offence, but I know what I'd rather be doing.'

'Er – what?'

'For starters, roll us a joint if it's not too much trouble. I know you bought some gear the other night, so don't give me that "I don't do it any more" bollocks. Here, you can roach this if you like,' she said, handing me her dad's business card. Grateful for something to do, I obliged, fumbling clumsily with Rizlas and resin to produce a crappy spliff, torn at one end, bent in the middle, with the skins unstuck along one edge and the roach hanging out.

'Hmm. This isn't up to your normal expert standard,' she complained, holding it up and squinting at it with disdain. 'Now, did you get any chewing gum? I've got breath like a ho's gusset.'

'Pleasant image, Nade.' I found a slightly fluffed stick of peppermint Orbit in my purse and tore it in half. 'Here you go.'

'Cheers, nice one.'

She took it out of the foil and chewed on it noisily as she searched for a lighter. I wondered why it was always the heaviest smokers who were never able to find a lighter. I had bought at least twenty since starting university and they had all mysteriously vanished without trace. Nadine got up and turned her lamp off and lit the joint with the flame on her candle.

'Turn the film off,' she ordered.

'It's not that bad, is it?'

'Yes.'

I pressed the stop button and fuzzy grey interference crackled on to the set. She stood over me and turned the set off with her foot. The room was submerged into silence and semi-darkness. Nadine sat down opposite me, cross-legged, and passed me the joint. A strange sensation washed over me, sparking the synapses like an intense drug rush, like a strange feeling of vertigo.

'Still has the same effect,' she whispered, the gleam in her eyes animated by candlelight through an ethereal cloud of smoke.

I suddenly felt quite faint. My heart was ricocheting against my ribcage and my head was swimming. I thought about excusing myself. I felt sick with delirium. Or delirious with sickness.

My voice came out as a squeak. 'How about the other film then?'

She moved closer so our knees were touching. 'How about something completely different?'

'Umm . . . we could always go back down the pub –'

'You're not even warm, Abi.'

I tried taking a toke of the joint but found I was incapable of inhaling it. Something was slowly dawning on me. I had never prided myself on being the sharpest tool in the box, but that was more to do with extreme naïvety than a lack of gumption. Not that I had ever been blessed with abundant common sense, of course. My internal thoughts were babbling away to distraction so I didn't know how long it was until Nadine spoke again.

'You can go now if you want to,' she was saying. 'I won't be offended.' Her fingertips were just touching my leg. I didn't flinch or move.

'Why would I want to leave?' I asked, staring straight back at her.

'How long have you known?' she murmured.

My insides knotted as she edged towards me, closer and closer, her hands moving up my legs, to the insides of my thighs.

'Known?' I repeated, stupidly.

She pulled her T-shirt over her head and put her hands back where they had been, except a little higher. This was like a game of spin the bottle or truth or dare gone very wrong. Or very right. I couldn't quite decide. All I could hear was the sound of my heart thumping wildly in my chest as my breathing became shallow and rasping.

'I worked it out,' I said, not knowing what else to say.

'Oh, you worked it out, did you?' Her bra looked very white and her skin looked very brown in the flickering glow of the solitary candle. It occurred to me that I was in a rather bizarre situation and I wasn't scared and I didn't want to get out of it. Like a lucid dream. I was almost in control. 'When did you work it out?' She began to undo my shirt, one button at a time, very slowly.

'Er ... I ... about thirty seconds ago.'

She laughed. 'Maybe I'll have to shave my head or something,' she mused.

'Don't you dare.'

'Is that a threat?' Her face moved towards mine but stopped when we were about six inches apart.

I gulped, trying to control my breathing. 'You'd better believe it,' I stammered.

'I love it when you're like this.'

'Like what?'

'Like this.' Her breath warmed on my cheek and her hand fluttered back on to my bare skin, which prickled hot and cold at her touch. I felt like I was melting. She smelled of freshly washed clothes and clean hair and cocoa butter body lotion and subtle perfume. I started to say something else, but she stopped me. It wasn't like the kisses I was used to, the kisses from boys that are hard and determined; rough kisses that will predictably lead to rougher sex, or quick, hungry kisses that will rapidly lead to rushed, passionate sex. It was different, better, strange, more sensual, phenomenal. We undressed each other slowly and softly, exploring every single inch as each new part was exposed.

By next morning, I was convinced in no uncertain terms that the existence of the vibrator really does render men redundant.

8

Seeking Asylum

Madness need not all be breakdown. It may also be break-through. It is potential liberation and renewal as well as enslavement and existential death.

R. D. Laing, *The Politics of Experience*, 1967

We woke up at the same time, side by side and face to face, and just stared at each other. What do you say to your best friend when you wake up naked next to her in bed? 'Mornin', love, how was it for you?' maybe, or 'We didn't really just . . . you know . . . did we?'

What was I even supposed to *think*?

So I merely lay there and looked at her – at the flickering shadows of her eyelashes on her cheeks, at the big black circles of her pupils, at the plump curve of her upper lip, at the tiny mole on the side of her face, at the slope of her shoulder and the tone of her skin. I wanted to touch her but I didn't dare. I wanted to speak but I couldn't think of anything appropriate.

She broke the silence before too long. 'I need a cigarette.'

I responded, too quickly: 'Yeah, me too.'

Then we started giggling, ridiculously, inexplicably.

'I'm sorry I seduced you,' Nadine said eventually. 'It was bad of me.'

I felt like I wanted to rinse my brain under a cold tap. I just smiled back at her, giddied and bashful.

'Now, fags!' she exclaimed, turning over and sitting up slightly so the sheets slid off her body. She opened her drawer and found an unopened packet of Marlboro Lights. 'These should do us until breakfast,' she said, tearing the wrapper off. We smoked almost the entire packet between us in stilted silence before I eventually plucked up enough courage to ask her: 'Are you . . . um . . . a lesbian, Nade?'

Smoke poured out through her nostrils as she spluttered with laughter. 'Have you been lying there all that time wanting to ask me *that*?'

'Well, I . . .'

'You make me laugh,' she said, making it sound like both a compliment and an insult. She stubbed out her last cigarette in an overbrimming ashtray and turned to me purposefully. 'OK, what do you *really* want to know?'

'Er . . .' Where did I start? My head was reeling.

'Look, tell you what, how about I just tell you everything? Number one, yes I am a lesbian, no I'm not AC/DC but I do sometimes sleep with men just to remind myself how fucking lucky I am to be a dyke. Number two, I haven't officially told my parents but they're pretty laid-back and they'd have to be blithering idiots not to have guessed by now. Number three, I don't expect you to become my girlfriend because I realise you are heterosexual and more than a little dazed and confused. Number four, yes I fancy you like mad but I reckon I can keep it under control if it makes you uncomfortable. Number five, just because you've slept with me doesn't make you a raging dyke, it just means your taste is finally improving. And number six, I don't believe in casual sex but . . . oh God, I'm going to regret confessing to this, aren't I? Well, I, er . . . I slept with Alex early on in the first term.'

'I knew it!' I exclaimed. 'I just *knew* there was something going on between you two.'

She made a face. 'There's nothing going on, as such,' she said. 'But, sadly, he claims to be in love with me. Claimed, I should say.'

I was taken aback. 'Shit, Nade . . . you've slept with the best-looking bloke here and you don't even . . .'

'Er, let me stop you there. Alex is a pretty boy but he doesn't know a fucking thing about how to pleasure a woman, I can tell you. It was like playing Scrabble with a dyslexic.'

'But . . . but if you're a lesbian surely you should be repulsed by men? And men don't get much manlier than Alex Cheadle, for God's sake!'

'Oh what can I say? I was bored,' she said dismissively. 'And anyway, I wouldn't say men repulse me *per se.* They . . . amuse me.'

'I think that you being a lesbian is a bit of a waste,' I opined without thinking.

She made a dismissive noise. 'Good Lord, why should it be a waste?'

'I mean . . . well, I don't suppose you have any plans to . . . er, marry, and have babies and stuff?'

'Too bloody right! Why would I want to do that? I have a life and I intend to live it, mate. Right up until I'm a wrinkly bag of husbandless, childless bones.'

There were still so many things I couldn't get my head around, but I didn't want to keep asking questions. Instead I just said, 'I had a good time last night.'

She took me by surprise by grabbing the back of my neck and pulling me towards her to kiss me full on the mouth. 'No regrets?' she murmured.

'No . . . None at all.'

'Good.' She pulled the covers off me and idly trailed a hand over my thighs with lackadaisical desire.

'But . . .'

'But what?'

'How do you think everyone else is going to react to this?'

She shrugged. 'Who cares?'

'This hall is so bloody incestuous,' I realised, counting out the various pairings on my fingers, 'There's Simon and Rachel of course, and Simon and Frank which we don't *actually* know about, Marbles and Juliet, Marbles and me, you and Alex, me and you . . .'

'Garston and Catherine,' Nadine added.

'You *are* joking.'

'I'm afraid not. They were taking a shower together last week, and Cath made a big show of having to go to the doctor's for the morning after pill.'

'Jesus.'

'It's all gone a bit mad, really. Then of course, there's Juliet and Yoshi . . .'

'Fuck *right* off!'

'OK, so I lied about that one. But it's only a matter of time. And it will be Marbles and Alex getting on with a bit of pillow-biting next.'

'Ha! Not in this lifetime.'

'Abi, believe me, those two are far too pally and homophobic not to at *least* have thought about shagging each other.'

'What an unpleasant concept.'

'Hmm, I don't know. I think they'd make quite a sexy couple actually.'

I looked over at her alarm clock and realised I needed to be somewhere else. 'I have a seminar in about twenty seconds,' I said.

'Are you going to it?' she whispered, drizzling the last of the baby oil from my chest to my bellybutton.

There was no competition.

'Only in spirit,' I replied, feeling myself mellow and melt once again.

An hour later, I ventured out of her room to collect some clothes and cigarettes. Dressed only in her royal blue satin kimono, I dumbly watched Alex and Marbles approach me from the other end of the corridor, kicking a football between them.

Alex nearly choked on his banana when he saw me. For some reason, I always found it difficult to take a man seriously when he was eating a banana, and Alex was no exception.

'Fuck me Page, you look like you've gone a couple of rounds with Mike Tyson,' he sputtered.

'Thank you,' I said. 'I've actually been up all night having sex with Nadine.'

They both made incredulous noises and looked at each other until their expressions matched, then faced me again and chimed together, 'Good one, Page,' before sidling past me and going outside for a kickabout.

I was growing increasingly concerned about the absence of my period. A few days later, after some more Sapphic frolicking with Nadine, I ransacked the kitchen cupboards in a search for something pickled in vinegar. To my joy, I found a half-empty jar of gherkins in the fridge with a label on it saying 'RACHEL'.

'Oh she won't mind,' I said aloud to myself, grabbing it eagerly and searching for a fork. The hunt for a clean fork in the shabby confines of a student kitchen is even more hopelessly unrealistic than a hunt for a jar of pickled gherkins. Our washing-up rota worked primarily on a 'pass the buck' basis, resulting in the ruination of perfectly good cutlery and crockery. Items were left to stagnate on the sideboard, while any leftover food became crusty and mouldy long before anyone had the sense to throw it out. The smells were often hard to bear. Civilisations of bacteria, as yet undiscovered by medical science, bred and flourished in the sink and at the bottom of our communal fridge, and fungus sprouted from between the filthy, cracked floor tiles. Creepy-crawlies multiplied to infinity and beyond in the crevices in the skirting boards. Grime coated all surfaces and there was a small plastic Kinder Egg toy stuck in the toaster, so preparing the staple student diet of baked beans on toast was a hazardous culinary venture. Alex had a strange and rather perturbing habit of skewering insects and cooking them over the hob, so there were various bits of bug – a dismembered thorax, a wing, a segmented leg – dotted around the top of the oven, along with spilt sauce and other stains.

I found a distinctly unhygienic dessert spoon and settled down with my vinegary craving.

Marbles walked in dreamily just as I munched into my fifth gherkin. He beamed at me with far too much vivification for such an ungodly hour.

'Awright Page?' he mumbled, yawning and pulling the cord around his dressing gown. 'What you up to, in here by yourself?'

'Eating,' I garbled, spitting out fragments of gherkin.

'It's nearly four in the morning,' he said, casting me a quizzical sidelong glance.

'So?' I watched him wash up two cups and switch the kettle on. 'Got company have you?' I asked, knowing that it was the only explanation for his flushed features and blissed-out demeanour.

He leaned against the slime-infested counter and flapped his arms indifferently. 'Got lucky with some nympho I met down that shite Paradox place. Three times already and I only brought her back a couple of hours ago . . . I tell you, she's *insatiable.* My cock is *burning.*'

'Too much information, Maurice.'

'Anyway, whatcha eating?'

'Pickled gherkins,' I replied.

'Oh.' He sighed and shuffled over to the fridge. He opened it and stared for a few moments at the manky contents before a thought occurred to him and he spun around and looked at me, his eyes suddenly wide and round with panic.

'*Gherkins*?' he spluttered, holding on to the fridge door for support as he reached a logical conclusion.

'Er . . . yes. Do you have a problem with that?'

'Gherkins,' he repeated, studying the jar in front of me as if to confirm his fears. 'It's just . . . it's not the kind of thing . . . I mean . . . you're not . . . ? Er . . .'

I screwed the lid back on the jar and smiled at him reassuringly. 'Calm down. I just felt peckish, and I fancied gherkins rather than something normal, like a sandwich . . .'

'You sure?'

'Positive.'

He smiled back at me uncertainly, and poured boiling water into the cups. 'So,' he began, clearing his throat and pausing before continuing, 'er, you and Nadine then . . .' He spilt some milk and swore quietly.

The news of the relationship between Nadine and I had naturally spread like wildfire through the hall, and was met with surprising tolerance, ranging from disappointment/delight in Alex's case ('two lesbos, one Cheadle, *many* possibilities'), to mild disconcertion in Juliet and Catherine's case ('But they *can't* be lesbians, they've got nice hair and they're quite pretty and wear vaguely nice clothes.') I was personally still in a state of pleasant shock, and although I knew I wasn't gay, I also knew that Nadine made me feel better than any of the men I had ever been involved with.

'It's not something I expected . . .' I faltered as his eyes locked on mine, and looked away shyly. 'Marbles, I wanted to talk to you about . . .'

I fell silent when he sat astride the chair opposite me and took out a packet of B & H. 'What?' he said, passing one to me across the table.

'Oh, sod it. Never mind. Forget it.' I shook my head, ignoring the proffered cigarette, then stood up, crossing over to the fridge to replace Rachel's gherkins (there were now only two left in there, floating in a sad dribble of bitty yellow vinegar, so there was no way she wouldn't notice).

'Hey, wait a minute,' Marbles said, getting to his feet hurriedly and blocking the doorway just as I was about to leave. 'I thought that . . . well, do you mind if I ask you a personal question?'

'The answer's no, Maurice. Can I get past, please?'

'Is that no I can't ask you, or no being the answer to the question I was going to ask you?'

'I don't know. Both.' The sight and smell of him and the sound of his voice was making me light-headed, like a charge of pure amyl nitrite to my brain.

'Good.' He put his face very near to mine and whispered in my ear, 'That's the answer I was hoping for.'

'Is that it? Can I go now?'

He let his arm fall to his side, moved back and shrugged. 'Off you go then.' His gaze fell and he walked away, collecting his two cups and sloping back to his room without even a glance or a gesture in my direction.

I watched him and contemplated the possibility that the gherkins were indeed a bad omen. I was bursting out of most of my bras and zippers, and I had started to feel nauseous most mornings and grumpy most evenings. Instead of sensibly putting either of these factors down to water retention, PMT and over-consumption of drink and junk food, I resolved to buy a pregnancy test the next morning.

'Oh ... my ... God. That's it, my life is over.'

I watched Rachel's face turn white as the line in the test-strip window turned blue. We were both huddled together in one of the toilet cubicles on a Friday afternoon. It was the last day of the second term and Rachel, like me, had been missing a few spokes in her cycle of late. But unlike me, she was a genuine *duffee.*

Having initially convinced myself that I did indeed have one in the oven, I had attended the last lecture of term wearing my unsightly but nevertheless comfy white cotton culottes. This transpired to be a great mistake, and not just in terms of fashion. As another tired tutor wibbled on about iambic pentameter, I moaned on and on to my course mate (a sweet and clean-living girl Hannah; a devout Christian who avoided boys and alcohol, unless she was drunk or randy), sounding off tirelessly about what a raw deal us girls have when it comes to sexual disasters, et cetera. I was so busy moaning, I failed to notice until much later on that the lower part of my body had come to resemble the Japanese flag.

Upon returning to my hall, the scrubbing up process involved an hour of standing in tepid bathwater, wrestling with the stained culottes and a bar of soap, cursing aloud my lack of menstrual punctuality. It was while I was moaning in agony with another violent grip of abdominal cramps that Rachel rushed in, holding aloft a Boots bag and ironically proclaiming her own pregnancy angst.

'Oh, Abi, it's you. Oh, thank God. I'm so glad you're here,' she panted, in obvious distress.

I was not in the mood to be faced with the possibility that someone was as pissed off as I was feeling at that particular moment, so I shot her a look that said, *Don't mess with me, I've got the painters in and I'm having a very bad day.* She didn't notice my livid glare and slipped into one of the toilet cubicles, pulling a rectangular box out of the bag and sitting down on the closed toilet seat with a sigh.

'Be honest now. How much of a disaster would it be if I was . . . in the club?' She studied the instructions on the back of the box, biting her lips nervously.

'What?' The Lifebuoy soap slipped out of my hand and plopped into the murky bathwater. I looked over at her from my awkward position; ankle-deep in water, sullied culottes in hand, wearing only a baggy T-shirt, a scowl and a super-plus tampon – surely not the ideal ally for Rachel in her hour of need.

'I don't even need to do this. I just know. I *know*.' She ripped the box open and studied the test stick inside for some seconds. 'Right, I'm gonna piss on this, then I'll need you to help me come to terms with the result. Female solidarity and all that.'

'Shouldn't Simon be here?' I asked, as she pushed the cubicle door closed and locked it.

'He's done enough,' her muffled voice drifted over, amidst sounds of rustling and various muttered expletives.

So I rinsed out the culottes, drained and rinsed the bathtub, and slipped into my robe as Rachel weed on to the stick. Two minutes later, the double blue line in the little window confirmed her fears and she was weeping on to my shoulder, cursing Simon and lamenting her fecundity.

'I don't understand, we're always so *careful* . . .' she snuffled.

Since discovering her boyfriend with Frank, I hadn't really spoken much to Rachel. Stuck with her in this unenviable situation, I decided it was best to do the concerned friend routine with as much care and tact as possible.

'Hey, it's not the end of the world,' I soothed. 'Don't worry, everything will be all right.'

'That's fine for you to say, you're a lesbo. I wish I was!' she wailed melodramatically.

I was more offended by this than I ought to have been.

'I'm not a lesbo, Rach. In fact, I thought I was pregnant too, up till about an hour ago.'

She looked at me cautiously. 'But –'

'But nothing. I like Nadine. I *love* her, as a person. I think she's beautiful and very special. But . . . I fancy *men*. I am *attracted* to men.' I didn't know why I felt such a sense of pride at this admission of my heterosexuality, but at least I had it clear in my mind at last.

Rachel made no pretence at being interested in my sex life. 'Well, anyway,' she said, tearing off a handful of toilet paper, 'how do I tell Simon about this?' She waved the test stick in the air before stuffing it into her pocket with a sigh.

'Sorry, mate, I really can't help you there.'

'Just between you and me, Abi, he's been acting really . . . funny lately, you know? You don't think he's going off me, do you?'

'If the nocturnal sounds I still regularly hear coming from his room are anything to go by, no.'

She blushed and tried to smile. 'That's not the problem. It's just that . . . he goes into these quiet moods. He won't say anything to me at all. And he's started listening to this really weird, fucked-up music. But then sometimes he'll be so nice to me, buying me flowers, giving me compliments and stuff.'

'You're lucky,' I said, 'most blokes are cagey bastards all the time.'

'No, but it's just not like him. We've always got on so well in the past. All the time. He doesn't really talk to me any more.'

'Well, you've certainly got something to talk about now, haven't you?'

She looked at me with her watery blue eyes and her face crumpled into another sob.

I hugged her and offered to make her a cup of tea.

'Lace it with brandy,' she said. 'I'm going to need it.'

When I went home for the Easter break, there were many things on my mind. Jasmine was still in rehab and seemingly not going anywhere fast, Dad and Jane were still trying to patch things up between them, and I was scared of losing Nadine's friendship. On top of all this, I had some important exams to study for. I was well aware that I couldn't afford to fail these exams. My method of studying for my degree usually relied on borrowing a course mate's lecture notes and copying essays and perhaps every now and then turning up for a seminar and trying to win the tutor's praise with a carefully chosen assortment of polysyllabic words to describe texts which I had barely even bothered to browse over. Bluffing my way through potentially awkward situations came as second nature to me, and it was just as well. I lacked any kind of motivation.

And I lacked money. My penniless state was such that I resorted to begging the manager of my local supermarket for a little bit of holiday work. Or if possible, a lot of holiday work. I was lucky enough to get some – only fifteen hours a week scanning barcodes through the tills and replenishing shelves, but better than nothing. The thought of payment was enough impetus to get me out of bed in the morning – a very rare feat.

In between stacking shelves and telling little old ladies where the cat food was, I reinvented myself as An Intellectual (part-time) and a devoted sister and daughter (more or less full-time). When I next visited Jasmine she still appeared to be morose and indolent, although the doctors insisted she was slowly stabilising and would be able to come home by the end of April.

'How's uni going then?' she asked me, sipping from a can of Coke and looking out of the window at the gardens, where a small group of supervised loons were playing leapfrog and tag and rolling about on the grass.

'Fine. Everything's going OK. What about you?'

We were standing in the day-room, and the catatonic fuck-off man was in his usual seat, staring out lifelessly into the distance, while another in-patient was engaged in an animated, if slightly one-sided, argument with the fish tank in the corner. I thought Jasmine was looking much healthier – although still tired and depressed, a great improvement on the skinny, haggard scrap she had been when I visited her the month before.

'Oh, I can't complain,' she sighed, slumping back into a battered old sofa and patting the space beside her. 'Well, I could, but who's listening?'

I sat down in the indicated space and took her hand. 'Have you stopped smoking now?'

She shrugged her shoulders and made a tetchy noise. 'I've cut down, all right?' she said glibly. 'What about you?'

'Herbal tea is supposed to help if you want to give up,' I offered, not knowing if it was true. 'I tried some camomile and was nearly sick. Mind you, at least it took my mind off my cigarette craving for a while.'

'Bollocks to that. Give me nicotine and alcohol any day.'

I decided not to nag her about her delicate condition and the importance of a healthy lifestyle. What a pathetic hypocrite I would have been if I'd even tried.

A frail, stooped old lady shambled in just as the *Neighbours* theme tune began blaring from the television set. She had a walking-stick in one hand and a bundle of wool in the other and she sat in the chair opposite us to continue knitting what appeared to be a ridiculously long scarf.

'That's Emily,' Jasmine told me, nodding towards the old woman. 'She's going senile.' She lifted her hand and waved, yelling, 'All right Em, how did it go with George Formby?'

The old woman didn't respond for a while. She peered at Jasmine over a pair of half-moon spectacle frames and her wrinkled face broke into a crooked, toothless smile.

'Jathmine!' she lisped. 'Me an' George have set a date. Will you come?'

'Sure will!' she yelled back. 'You knitting him a scarf are you?'

'Eh?'

'*Is that scarf for him?*'

'Fuck that my darling, I'm knitting me a home in the country.'

'Nice one, Em. Keep it up,' Jasmine shouted back. She noticed my bewildered expression, and smiled good-naturedly. 'We all speak the universal language of mad here. It comes naturally after a while.'

'Oh.' Not a lot I could say to that, really.

'Anyway, that old girl's eighty-five,' Jasmine said. 'She married the only man she ever slept with, she's got three children and six grandchildren, she's never touched any drug, not even alcohol – I kid you not. She went to church every Sunday and she never even swore before she came here.' She finished off her Coke, crushed the can and threw it in the general direction of the bin. It hit the foot of the fuming man by the fish tank, who was in the middle of verbally abusing a bored-looking koi carp. For some reason, he thought the propelled can was a hand grenade and started to have some kind of hysterical seizure. Jasmine ignored him and continued telling me about Emily. 'But then her husband died and she went ga-ga. Just suddenly . . . snapped. Her eldest daughter put her in here about a year ago, I think. And she's settled in quite well, really, *haven't you, Em*?' She shouted the last bit, but Emily was absorbed with her needlework and didn't hear.

'She's a bit deaf,' Jasmine explained. 'But anyway, they're merrily pumping her dilapidated, octogenarian body with all sorts of shit to stop her from becoming a total embarrassment.' She pulled out a packet of low-tar cigarettes and offered me one.

I glared at her sternly. 'I thought –'

'Leave it out, it's my first one of the day for fuck's sake.' She smoked thoughtfully for a while, and then got up and crossed over to the fuck-off man's chair and waved her hand in front of his face. He didn't move or blink.

'This one's called John,' she muttered, gazing at him sadly. 'He was on heroin for twenty years. *Twenty years.* A suicide attempt back in eighty-eight left him like this. Look at him. Lost in a faraway world of his own. Poor bastard.' She glowered at me, blowing smoke angrily out of her mouth and nostrils. 'Promise me you'll put me out of my misery if I ever get like that.'

'Oh for God's sake Jas, don't even *think* like that. You're having a baby. You've got loads to live for.'

'You really think so?'

'I know so. Where did all this self-pity come from?'

'Not much else left,' she muttered, sucking the last drag down to the filter, then throwing the stub on to the rough brown carpet and stamping on it. 'I just can't help myself any more, Abi. I feel like I'm constantly getting moved along by a tidal wave, and I don't know if it's going to wash me ashore or further out to sea. I take this pill and that pill because it's s'posed to help me, and when it doesn't help I take some medication of my own so I can at least feel *something*.' She moved back to the window, pressing her forehead against the glass. 'They've put me on some new tranny now. Another chloro-something I can't even remember the name of. Jesus, I could set up my own pharmacy with the load of shite they've got me taking.' I got up and stood next to her, watching her breath steaming on the cold glass and the dark reflection of her eyes blinking sadly back at her. 'They've got a cure for everything these days, haven't they?' she said, quietly. 'Even a broken spirit.'

'Give over, Jas.'

'Well what would you know? You're just as bad as me, just as lost and stupid. You're too busy getting drunk and sleeping around to even notice your fucking colossal attitude problem . . . I mean, *you* of all people.'

'W-what do you mean? What are you talking about?'

She tapped her fingers on the window and sighed. I noticed she had a ring on her middle finger. 'I'm sorry,' she said eventually. 'I'm taking it out on you when it's not your fault. I get like that sometimes. Ignore me.'

'That's a lovely ring,' I remarked, an attempt to divert the subject.

She looked at it and smiled wryly, twisting it around on her finger so it caught the light. 'It's from Seth.' She blushed a little and balled her hand into a fist and put it in her pocket. 'Soppy sod,' she whispered, glancing at me with dewy eyes.

'It's an *engagement* ring?'

'It's a token of affection. No wedding bells I'm afraid, sis. Seth couldn't organise a piss-up in a brewery. And can you imagine me as a *wife*? I wouldn't wish that on anyone.'

I put my arms around her but she didn't respond. 'I can't wait for you to come home,' I mumbled.

'My scan next week,' she said. 'Do you want to come?'

'Yes. I'd like that.'

She touched my head and kissed my hair, then pulled away. 'See you then.'

'You want me to go now?'

'I'm tired. It's the drugs. They drain me.'

Her voice drifted off as she shuffled back to her room, leaving me with the sounds of a dumbed-down dialogue on a television that nobody was watching, the clicking of Emily's knitting needles and the distant screeches of in-patients playing outside. From the tatty old chair in the middle of the room, John the fuck-off man made a barely discernible movement. This was a sure sign of an imminent verbal explosion. In a shower of spit, he yelled out aggressively at nobody and nothing.

'Fuck off!' he said, leaning forward in his seat, his face contorting with rage. Then he calmed down and resumed his normal posture, back to his silent staring.

My ex-boyfriend's new girlfriend gave birth to twin boys on Good Friday. Sylvie heralded the news via the telephone, waking me up, interrupting a potentially erotic dream and pissing me off in one fell swoop.

There was nothing particularly good about Good Friday, actually. Nadine called me later that afternoon just as I was about to sink myself into a bubble bath and subject my rubber duck to a diatribe of self-pity.

'I'm missing you,' she said. 'Can we meet up?'

'Umm . . . I'm not sure. This whole week's been a bit of a shitty one.'

'All the more reason, surely? Look, I'm staying at my cousin's in Watford for the weekend – she's got more drugs than you can shake a pipe at. Northern lights, purple haze, some really evil fucking shit here. Why don't you come over?'

'Nade, I –'

'It's OK. No pressure. Just thought it would be nice. Seeing as I'm only down the road from you.'

'I'm sorry. I miss you too. It's a great idea.'

'But . . . ?'

'But. Don't think I can do this weekend. Family stuff.'

'Would you mind being a bit more vague?'

'You know what it's like.'

'Yeah. Sure.'

'Tell you what, give me your address and number there, and I might pop over tomorrow. See if I can get away.'

'All right. Got a pen?'

Later that evening, once I had bathed and dressed and listened to a Prodigy album from beginning to end and smoked the last of my fags, it occurred to me that spending some time with Nadine was just what I needed. So I phoned her back and we met up that night at an overcrowded pub in Watford High Street.

'You look lovely,' she said, presenting me with a gin and tonic and pulling me towards her. 'It's so good to see you again.'

'You too.' I searched around the throbbing masses of people for somewhere to sit. Nadine took my arm. 'It's OK – my cousin and a couple of her mates have got some seats over there. I'm sure they won't mind us imposing.' She nodded over to a table of four or five girls, all done up to the nines and squeaking with laughter.

She introduced me to everyone and I was disconcerted to receive a couple of knowing nods and furtive glances. Nadine's cousin seemed particularly charmed to meet me, casting me frequent loaded smiles and gazes from over the rim of her pint glass. She was called Sava, and was the image of Nadine, except slightly larger and louder. Similarly, she wasn't backward about coming forward.

'So how long have you and Nadine been together then?' she asked me, shouting over the din of the jukebox.

'Er . . .' I looked nervously over at Nadine. She had her hand on my knee but had turned away from me, deep in conversation with someone at the other end of the table. 'It – it's not really like that . . .' I stuttered.

Sava shook her head, her smile putting me on edge. 'She's not the sort of person you can say no to, is she?'

'What – er . . . does she . . . um . . .'

'Chill. Just enjoy it. She knows the score.'

I was chain-smoking Superkings and rapidly losing my voice. I listened quietly as Sava told me about Nadine's history, skirting around the issue of any past boy- and/or girlfriends and instead divulging childhood escapades, her love of travel and her 'impressive natural intelligence', which was apparently unique to Nadine as the rest of the family were generally 'a little bit lacking in the brains department'.

'Lovely bunch of people though. Very accommodating,' she

added with a wink. By the time we staggered to Sava's flat, we had all overdone the ethanolic refreshment and it was time to settle down and mellow out with the legendary skunk supplies. The last thing I remember was taking one toke from a reefer of the smelliest and most potent skunk I had ever inhaled in all my life, and then it was lights out for me until I was shaken conscious at three o'clock the following afternoon and dragged down to the local.

I had only intended to stay with Sava and Nadine until Saturday night, since Easter Sunday had been reserved as a sacred family day and I was obligated to make an appearance or else for ever be held in contempt. However, while I was there, time seemed to flow in a warped, fluid blur of getting stoned and passing out and waking up and getting stoned until I lost track of what time it was, what day it was, and even where and who the hell I was.

'What time is it?' I mumbled, emerging from interminable hibernation at last, my mouth feeling like it was full of cotton wool. I was lying on the floor of the lounge with my head in the waste-paper basket, clutching someone's shoe.

'It's alive!' Nadine's voice shrilled.

I tried turning my head but was paralysed from the hairline down. 'Is it Sunday?' This was met by a hearty chortle.

'Oi Sav, she thinks it's Sunday!' Nadine called out. I felt a pair of hands on my back, pressing down between my shoulder blades, and then Nadine's face came into my line of vision. 'Hello stranger,' she said. 'I must say, you are the most boring company we've had so far this century.'

I groaned and looked at the shoe in my hand. 'Am I still in your cousin's flat?' I croaked.

'You might want to phone your parents. They called a couple of days ago.'

A piece of my brain was violently jogged back into its rightful place. 'What?!' I became animated all of a sudden, scrabbling into a sitting position far too quickly. Each movement rubbed a cheese grater against the inside of my head. 'Oh my God, oh my God, what day is it?'

'Tuesday.'

'Fuck me, no! No, it can't be!' I put my head in my hands and wailed in despair, '*Please* tell me you're joking.'

'Would I lie to you?'

My neck was unable to support my head. It kept rocking back and forth spasmodically, like a new-born baby. I tried to focus on Nadine, but there seemed to be several of her, all merging together, haloed with light and weird fuzzy colours. 'I . . . am . . . utterly . . . fucked,' I said.

'Really? And you look so well,' Nadine retorted sarcastically. Then she obviously took pity on me, fetching me a pint of water and some extra-strength headache tablets and stroking back my hair as I grumbled and whined and waited for the painkillers to kick in. When I was feeling marginally less like I'd just been hit by a truck, she winched me up, gripping me under my arms and pulling me upright. I sagged like a rag doll in her arms, every muscle of my body collapsing.

'It's all right, it's still early morning. Jasmine's scan isn't until this afternoon, is it?'

'Oh shit, the scan! How could I be so *stupid*?'

'Shhh . . . calm down. I explained everything to your dad on the phone. Very nice man, by the way. Not best pleased with you right now though.'

'What the hell have I been smoking?'

'More to the point would be to ask what you *haven't* been smoking.'

'Why didn't you stop me?'

'Sweetie, I may be your best mate and your part-time sex toy and your nurse, but I'm not your mother.'

She pulled my clothes off and stuck me under the shower, washing my hair and soaping me down with jaunty efficiency as I gradually gained full consciousness, each sense coming back to me slowly, my memory drip-feeding frame by frame. She finished off with a cold rinse, which woke me up completely. I sat blinking and dripping and solemn in Sava's spare bedroom, wrapped up in a fluffy towel, while Nadine dug out some clean clothes for me to wear. She combed and blow-dried my hair and left me to get dressed, then cajoled me into phoning Dad and Jane to apologise profusely. Later that morning, she drove me to the station and told me to say hi to Jasmine from her.

'Let me know how it all goes. I'll see you back at uni in a couple of weeks. Call me before then if you like.' She kissed me on both cheeks and then said, 'You know how much I care about you, don't you?'

I nodded dumbly.

'Let's not spoil it. Just friends from now on?' She held out her hand and I just fell into her, wrapping my arms around her neck and mumbling 'I'm so sorry' over and over again.

She finally pushed me away and turned the key in the ignition. 'Get out of here before I do something I won't regret.'

I opened the car door and practically fell out on to the kerb, and she leaned over and slammed it and sped away without another word.

I arrived just in time and met Dad, Jane and Seth in the waiting area at the maternity ward. Dad was still rightfully irate with me.

'Good of you to join us,' he huffed.

'She's already apologised, love,' Jane said. She turned to me with a suspicious look.

'I suppose you're feeling better now, dear?'

'I'm sorry I missed your Easter dinner, Jane. It will never happen again.'

She didn't want to dwell further on my selfish misdeed and swept the issue under the carpet with a wave of her hand. She then turned to the tall and moderately attractive man who was lurking beside her.

'You remember Seth, don't you?' she said.

He looked remarkably clean-cut for someone who used to believe he was the devil incarnate. He was wearing a *suit* with a *tie*, and although he still had his eyebrow pierced and his shirt hanging out, it was a far cry from the scruffy, extravagantly tattooed Hell's Angel I remembered from a few years before.

'Hiya, how's it going?' he said. 'Long time no see.'

'Good to see you again,' I replied. 'You look . . . well.'

Dad straightened up and put his hand on my shoulder. 'Jane and I are going back home now, Abigail. We've already seen Jasmine today and she said she just wants you two in for the scan. So . . .' he gave me a cautionary stare before continuing, '. . . if I can rely on you to make your own way home afterwards, dinner will be at five-thirty.'

'I'll be there, I promise.' I beamed at him through the last throbs of my migraine, feeling like my face would crack.

After they left, Seth and I drank two tasteless teas each before being summoned into a room at the far end of a bright, shiny corridor. Jasmine was already in there, lying on a couch with her belly exposed. She held out her arms and accepted a cuddle from Seth and a kiss on the forehead from me. I couldn't be sure of Seth's feelings about my sister and the baby – to be fair, there was no cast-iron guarantee that the baby was his, of course. But he did seem appropriately misty-eyed when the grainy image of Jasmine's foetus appeared on a black and white screen and the nurse poignantly announced, 'There's the baby – that blob right there.'

To my surprise, Jasmine started crying – not just a few little tears of rapturous joy and maternal gooeyness, but real, hearty sobs. 'Look at that,' she stuttered, pointing at the screen, 'you can even see her little heart beating.' The nurse pointed out various other parts: head, legs, arms, hands, an eye and a foot, and Jasmine got more and more emotional with each perfectly formed anatomical wonder.

'It's very small but everything seems to be OK,' the nurse said, with aloof professionalism. She rubbed the scanner instrument over Jasmine's abdomen one last time, lecturing her mechanically about the evils of smoking and 'other indulgencies' while pregnant.

'How do you know it's a her?' Seth asked Jasmine, interrupting the nurse mid-spiel.

'I can just *feel* it. Angel Page. My Angel.' Jasmine couldn't take her eyes away from the image on the screen, which looked more like some kind of deformed muppet to me, rather than a potential human being.

'I hope it's a boy,' Seth said. 'I want to call him Darius and teach him all about arthropods, Harleys and heavy metal, and play football with him down the park.'

'Darius my arse,' Jasmine sneered.

Seth grinned at me. I think he was winding us up.

The nurse shot them both a withering look, flicked the screen off and wiped away the jelly stuff from Jasmine's stomach with a paper towel.

'I don't think I need to tell you how important the next six months are,' she said, turning to Jasmine and handing her a pamphlet. 'If you take good care of yourself and get yourself checked up regularly, there shouldn't be any problems.'

Jasmine thanked her and sat up awkwardly, groaning about back pain. Seth helped her to her feet and told me to go back home, as he would take her back to the Freehaven ward.

'We've got some things to talk about,' he explained, as if to a five-year-old.

'I understand.' I looked over at Jasmine.

'It's OK,' she said. 'I'll see you again soon, sis.'

So I left them to it.

On the way home on the train that evening I was absorbed in my own thoughts and concerns about Jasmine and the baby when a jubilant, flamboyant evangelist boarded the train. She began proclaiming the praises of the Lord at the top of her voice, for all to hear: 'Jesus loves you if you are black or white, rich or poor, young or old. The only way to Heaven is through Jesus, and you can make him your Saviour *today*. Accept the Lord Jesus Christ into your life and your sins will be washed away, alleluia.' She stood in the gangway hanging on to a support with one hand, a couple of carrier bags in the other hand, addressing everybody and nobody in particular. Dressed like an ordinary, middle-aged woman in sensible shoes, long black coat and a plain dress, her faith in her Lord was absolute and she wasn't ashamed to prove it. As she continued her own belated Easter sermon on the Metropolitan Line, other passengers looked at each other in embarrassment, or avoided eye contact and shuffled and coughed uncomfortably or ignored her completely. I wasn't religious at all – far from it – but her joyous outburst captivated me. She put her heart and soul into it, eyes closed in reverential rapture, silver crucifix clutched to the breast, bible quotes uttered with awe and conviction. I looked around at the other people on the train: glancing at each other in bemused embarrassment, munching on sandwiches or foul-smelling burgers, ruffling newspapers and hiding behind the day's depressing news, calling their spouses on their mobiles to say they'd be two minutes late for dinner, gazing out of the windows at the gathering darkness outside, nodding their heads rhythmically to the music on their walkmans. Some even changed carriages. Despite the obvious disinterestedness of her congregation, the woman continued her praises, unerring, triumphant.

Opposite me, a man was sitting with his daughter. She was about six or seven and was messily polishing off an Easter egg. There was chocolate all over her face, in her blonde curls and on her hands and dress, and she sucked it from her fingers and wiped it on the seat. The man leaned down toward the little girl and said, 'Ignore the silly woman, darling. She's mad.' He said it deliberately loudly, so others could hear and nod their agreement. All the while, the woman was standing obliviously in the midst of this scorn and indifference, singing for joy.

'Thank you God for giving us Jesus, who died upon the cross so we might be saved . . .'

I couldn't take my eyes off this amazing woman. She didn't pause once. It was almost enough to convert me. I watched her for five, ten minutes or longer. And I watched the reactions of the 'unmad', the disdain and the discomfort and the smirks.

'That old nigger's radio rental,' I heard an Essex boy sneer to his mate. I was astonished to feel tears pouring down my face.

All too soon, it was back to university again, where academic matters had reached an exigent do-or-die plateau. I thought that perhaps Sava's skunk had killed off a crucial part of my brain – ever since my long and fuzzy Easter weekend, my memory had packed up completely and it seemed my powers of reasoning were fast following suit.

But with some crucial exams around the corner, it was time for me to grow up and do something worthwhile and constructive. I had been procrastinating for far too long. On my first night back after the Easter holiday, I sat in my room reading the same page over and over again, wondering why nothing seemed to be sinking in. Singing along with appropriate identification to 'Loser' by Beck, it suddenly dawned on me that I wasn't nearly as intelligent as I had given myself credit for. Since starting university, my IQ level had plummeted. I was doing something wrong. Or, more to the point, I was doing nothing right.

Marbles's friend came to visit later that week, with dire consequences. His name was Andy and he was – if possible – a hundred times worse than both Marbles and Alex put together. Obnoxious, oversexed and under-educated, his three-day sojourn managed to wreak havoc on our hall. The night before my first exam, I retired to bed at half past nine with a folder of notes and a highlighter pen, and the very best intentions to cram my brain with some useful facts. I was disturbed at nine thirty-three by Marbles, Alex and Andy banging persistently on my door and shouting all manner of obscenities. I tried ignoring them, but they wouldn't give up until I had agreed to join them and the others in an exceptionally puerile game of 'Truth or Dare' in the kitchen.

So I dragged my reluctant, pyjamaed body out of bed and took a seat at the table between Juliet and Nadine. Working around the ten of us assembled, we were each required to answer a very personal question or else obliged to complete a 'dare' – the nature of which seemed to increase in absurdity and potential for lifelong embarrassment as the game progressed. Predictably perhaps, it didn't take too long for the game to escalate out of control into Truth *and* Dare, so nobody had a choice but to humiliate themselves in every possible way in the name of student honour. When it came to Nadine's turn, there was much muttering between the boys before Alex turned to her with a nefarious smile, pulling at his new nipple ring through the fabric of his lime green Ben Sherman shirt.

'We want to know extensive details about what you and Page do to each other. Or else you will be required to demonstrate it here, in front of us.'

Top marks for originality there.

'Oh Alex, you're *such* a baboon,' Catherine whined. (Her own question, '*Would you do it with a farmyard animal to save your entire family from certain death*?' had been turned down in favour of a dare. She was therefore wearing a pair of Alex's unwashed pants on her head, and was required to leave them there for the duration of the game.)

Nadine did not respond; she just smoked calmly and glared back at Alex until he couldn't keep up the steely eye contact any longer.

'You really are a sad little man, aren't you?' she said eventually, making it sound more like a fact than an opinion.

'Come on, it's not exactly a difficult or taxing question,' Marbles piped up. 'Just give us something to keep us all going through those long lonely nights.'

'And you must get plenty of them, after all,' she retorted, tapping ash into his lager can.

'You bitch, I'd only just opened that.'

She extended her middle finger and smiled sweetly. 'Swivel, shithead.'

'So are you two, like, *real* clam-noshers, then?' Andy, obviously fresh out of the same charm school as Marbles, goggled at us with intrigue.

'Darling, if you weren't so hideously ugly, there really wouldn't be anything funny about you at all,' Nadine quipped.

'Hold on a minute ...' Andy looked at me and pointed a podgy finger. 'You're Abi, right?'

Wearily, I nodded.

'But you're ... wait a sec,' he dropped his voice to a whisper and turned to Marbles and said, 'Hey, I thought you said –'

He was cut short when Marbles kicked him under the table and announced, in a loud voice, 'OK Nade, don't worry about it. We'll let it slide.'

'Hey, that's not fair!' Juliet screeched. 'You've got to give her a dare. A *proper* one.' Her dare had been to shave off one eyebrow, which, to our extreme shock, she had done – willingly, laughingly, with her pink plastic razor. She had consumed enough alcohol to knock out an elephant, so I had the distinct feeling she would live to regret it the next morning.

'She's right, boys. Go on then, dare away,' Nadine challenged, blowing smoke in Alex's face.

'All right, I've got one,' Marbles said. 'Go and knock on Yoshi's door and beg him to ravish you.'

Nadine snorted in contempt. 'What kind of pissy dare is that?'

'Aha, but there's a catch . . .' Marbles caught my eye fleetingly across the table with an evanescent smile, '. . . you have to do it *topless.*'

Juliet and Catherine exploded into fits of giggles and Nadine merely poured herself out a whisky, swigged it back and said, 'All right then, let the dog see the rabbit.' I stared at her in horror. 'Oh, Nade, don't do it. You'll scare the poor little thing shitless. He's probably never seen a naked woman in his life.'

Marbles corrected me. 'Er, *wrong,* sweetheart, he has *definitely* never seen a naked woman in his life.'

'But . . . it's wrong to persecute him just because he's shy. He's not doing anyone any harm.'

'Hey, since when was revealing my breasts to someone considered persecution?' Nadine demanded. '*You* didn't seem to have any problem with it, if I recall rightly.'

That put me in my place. I promptly shut up and sank into a sulk.

Never one to renege on a dare or risk seeming inhibited, Nadine took her T-shirt off and tucked it into the waist of her jeans. 'Don't wait around,' she said. 'I may be some time.'

We all leapt up and jostled to get a view as she slunk off down the hall to Yoshi's room, which was instantly recognisable by the 'Table of Elements' chart he had stuck on his door, under a rather sweet cartoon picture of a computer emblazoned with the words 'Love me, Love my PC'. When she had reached the door, she reached behind her to unhook her bra but then changed her mind and stared at us all in exasperation. 'How do you expect me to do this when you're all standing there ogling me?' she whispered at us. 'This is a delicate operation, you know.'

'We have to make sure you complete the dare to our satisfaction,' Marbles explained.

'Well, must you make it so bloody obvious? Sod off, will you?' She waved her hand at us impatiently and then knocked on the door, a couple of quiet raps at first, followed up with three loud thumps. The boys chattered and squawked excitedly together like demented budgies. We all suppressed evil laughter when we heard Yoshi's scared little voice call out, 'Who is it?'

Nadine put her face close to the door and said, 'It's me. Nadine. Can I come in?'

'W-what do you want?'

'Just a little chat, if you don't mind.'

'Er . . . I – I'm in the middle of an accountancy project at the moment.'

'If it's OK, I'd like to take your mind off it for a little while,' Nadine said, flicking a wink at us.

There was a pause while we all felt fit to burst with mirth. Laughter escaped in uncontrollable snorts as we doubled over with our fists jammed into our mouths. Then we heard Yoshi say, 'All right then. The door's unlocked. It will have to be quick though.'

Nadine shrugged and opened the door and disappeared inside, leaving us all in stunned silence.

Andy was the first to say something. 'Your turn, Abi.'

Dazed, I returned to my seat and poured myself out a hefty measure, diluting it with a splash of Coke.

'I think you'll find it's Marbles next,' I said.

'Cheers, Page.' I glanced up at him and he mouthed something at me that I couldn't make out. He sat in the chair next to me and reached across the table for the vodka and his fags.

Frank came in at that point, soaking wet from the rain outside, and marched purposefully to the fridge, took out a can, opened it and downed it in about ten seconds.

'Wanna join in, Frankie?' Marbles offered.

'What's going on?'

'Truth and Dare,' Alex said.

I detected a shifty exchange of glances between Frank and the brooding Simon, who had been sitting quietly in the corner with Rachel in his lap. Frank hesitated before answering. 'Yeah, count me in.'

And so the night continued – challenges and interrogations, flirting and lewdness, until Nadine finally emerged from Yoshi's room at about midnight, beaming broadly.

'Well, what a pleasant little man he is,' she declared.

'What the *fuck* have you been up to in there?' Alex asked.

She ignored him. 'I'm off to bed now,' she said. 'Very knackered.'

I raised my eyebrows at her and she gave me a mysterious smile. 'See you all tomorrow.'

Alex was persistent. He grabbed her arm as she turned to leave. 'What took you so long?'

Nadine shook him off and said, 'I've just had some very pleasant social intercourse with Yoshi. And I can tell you, it beats sexual intercourse with you, hands down.'

I silently applauded her as she turned on her heel and slammed her bedroom door behind her, leaving Alex looking flummoxed and sheepish. Catherine chose that moment to fall off her chair and pass out in a heap on the floor.

'Er, I'd like to make an announcement now if I may, everyone,' Simon piped up suddenly, banging a spoon against his glass to attract our attention. His dare had been to strip naked and wear only a pair of Rachel's knickers for the rest of the night; a challenge which he had risen to and fulfilled with a frightening lack of reluctance or self-consciousness. 'I just want you all to know that Rachel and me . . .' he paused for dramatic effect and looked around at the row of expectant faces, squeezing her hand protectively in his. 'We're having a baby.'

Rachel looked at me with a bashful smile, but I lowered my eyes and shook my head as a chorus of voices around the table chimed their surprise.

'But . . . hold on, that means you'll have to leave uni, Rach,' Juliet pointed out sagaciously. 'And you'll get *fat*.'

'She's really on the ball that one, in't she?' Marbles whispered in my ear.

'It's a sacrifice I'm prepared to make,' Rachel stated bravely, as if she was the only thin woman in the world to have become pregnant.

Frank made a dyspeptic noise, coughing his excuses and scraping his chair back before flouncing to his room with apparent urgency. Then it was Simon's turn to glance at me bashfully.

'So what are you going to do then?' I asked them. 'Have you got somewhere to live?'

'Well . . . kind of. My mum says she'll help. I can live at home for a while, and maybe restart my degree next year, or something.'

'But I'm sticking by her, no matter what. If necessary, I'll drop out and get a job. We'll manage. It will be great.' Simon kissed Rachel with deferential tenderness while everyone marvelled at his devotion, with exclamations ranging from 'Oh that's so sweet!' to 'Bloody stupid bastard!'

After the Simon and Rachel revelation, we all continued drinking until feelings of nausea overpowered feelings of euphoria. Any niggling thoughts I may have had about my looming exam were soon drowned out. Marbles, Alex and Andy eventually disappeared to have a 'milk race' over a picture of a pretty vacant American celebrity, and without their ebullient influence over the proceedings, the rest of us finally decided to retire.

The next morning, splats of puke of assorted colours and textures had congealed all over the walls and floor of the hall, and there was a blockage in one of the toilets and a strange sticky substance in my hair.

Needless to say, I failed my first important exam in spectacular fashion, but at least I had just about survived a particularly arduous student initiation test. This was small consolation, however, when I was summoned for a serious and non-negotiable non-progress meeting with my tutor.

9

Living it Down

There are many unpleasant consequences to getting drunk on a regular basis, aside from the inadequacies and deformities you would normally expect.

For example: RDAs. Otherwise known as Random Drinking Accidents.

Since starting university, I had been inflicted with a bewildering assortment of scars and bruises, all of them unexplainable, and their various causes blotted from my memory. A stern admonition from my tutor, coupled with the discovery of my latest, and most perplexing RDA – a large, purple (almost hand-shaped) bruise above my left buttock – convinced me that no alcohol would ever pass my lips again, for damn *sure* this time. I resolutely primed myself not to be swayed by the pressures of my student status, promising myself and my exasperated tutor that if academic success meant complete social failure, then so be it – I would devote whatever was left of my brain to more creative and intellectual matters.

And I did everything in my diminished power to stick to my promise. I sat in my room for hours on end, refusing to succumb to the gorgeous oblivion of alcoholic stupor or dope-induced indolence. It did of course help that most of the others on my hall were also confined to their rooms, similarly cramming their grey matters with necessary knowledge. The hall descended into studious serenity for a while, like the calm before a storm.

One night, I even found the motivation to pick up a pen and start writing. It was a letter to Jasmine, so not directly relevant to my degree, but it was a start, at least.

Hi Jas,
Things are going bad at uni. Looks like I might get chucked out – although I can't say I'm surprised. My own stupid fault. You were right though, students really are worthless wankers, we have absolutely no function in society apart from wasting taxpayers' money and spreading around new strains of VD.

Spoke to Dad the other day. He told me you're coming home next Thursday. And that you've given up smoking! Advice please. I'm still doing badly on that front. It's our birthdays soon, so I'll come down for a day or two and maybe we can go out somewhere together to celebrate, just you and me.

Anyway, I'll have to get down to some serious work if I want to convince anyone I still have some kind of functional organ knocking about inside my head. I can't afford dope, and I would give anything – anything! – for just one joint . . . Still haven't got a boyfriend, by the way. It doesn't bother me, but it would be nice I suppose

A knock at the door interrupted my train of thought and I threw down my pen in frustration.

'Who is it?' I called out.

'Er . . . me. Simon.'

'Simon?' He was the last person I'd expect. 'What do you want?'

'Can I come in please?'

'Just a minute.' I bundled my notepad under a pile of bookmarked texts and opened the door. Simon looked at me with his big, puppy-dog eyes and smiled shyly.

'Sorry to bother you, but can I have a word . . . if you're not too busy?'

I took a step back and waved my arm at my bed in an invitation for him to come in and make himself comfortable. Or as comfortable as is possible in a poky, smelly student boudoir. 'Take a seat,' I said. 'What's up?'

Simon perched his tiny bottom timidly on the edge of my bed and sighed excessively. 'I think ... you know what's been troubling me for the last couple of months. I just – wanted us to clear the air.'

I sat back at my desk and feigned ignorance. 'You and Rachel seem to be still going strong as ever. Congratulations by the way.'

The image of Simon fellating Frank was still alarmingly vivid in my memory, so I may not have been able to keep the sarcasm out of my voice.

'Don't make this any harder than it already is, Abi.' Simon pouted at me and looked down at his hands. I had no intention of making it easy for him, so I just sat looking at him expectantly while he blushed and stuttered.

'I just wanted to tell you ...' he hesitated and fumbled in his pocket. 'Er ... um, I don't suppose you've got a fag, have you?'

'Only roll-ups.'

'Oh. Never mind.' He sighed again, obviously having a certain amount of trouble articulating his feelings.

I tried prompting him. 'I take it this is about you and Frank.'

A look of consternation flashed across his face. He stammered something incoherent then cleared his throat and managed to simper, 'Th-that's what I wanted to clear up ...'

I regarded him expectantly. 'Yes? What?'

'That Murph an' me are like, not on together or anything. We never were. We're just friends. I'm not gay. I love Rachel, and I really want to make a go of it now that she's ... you know.'

Murph?

I held up my hands. 'This is none of my business, Si.'

He fidgeted and gave me a pleading look. 'I know it isn't, but ... I just wanted to make sure you don't think badly of me.'

'Of course I don't. But I don't think it's right for you to just pretend it never happened.'

'Abi, with all respect, I don't think you're in a position to judge.' He blurted this out and then seemed to regret it when he saw my indignant expression. I reacted before he had a chance to correct or justify himself.

'What the *fuck* is that supposed to mean?'

'Er . . . well, you and Nadine,' he said weakly, looking at the floor, reddening to the tips of his ears. 'You experimented yourself, didn't you, even though you're not . . . a lesbian.'

Now I was *really* annoyed. I got annoyed at the accusation that I *was* a lesbian, and now I was getting annoyed at the accusation that I *wasn't.*

'And how would you know?' I demanded, my voice wavering with defiance.

'Never mind how I know. You're not denying it, are you?' He had become bolder now, returning my stare and raising his voice a pitch. 'All I'm saying is that I don't really think it's appropriate that you judge me just because of one mistake I made.'

My anger rose momentarily and then subsided as I realised he had a point. 'OK, OK,' I conceded, 'let's just forget about it, yeah?'

'And you do believe me, don't you?'

'Why should you care what I think? What about Frank?'

Simon frowned. 'I don't really know what to do . . . he gets really depressed, you see, and I'm the only person he talks to. I only wish there was some way I could . . .' he trailed off and put his head in his hands. 'You lot don't see what a great person he is. He really is. He just feels so alone. I do really care about him, just not in the way . . .'

'OK, the message is clear,' I said. 'I suppose he knows where he stands?'

'I – think so.'

He avoided my dubious gaze, looking down at his hands again and inspecting his fingernails.

'You'd better talk things over with him, Si. Unrequited love can't be a pleasant thing to deal with if you're already depressed.'

'What would you know about depression?' he asked, firing me a fierce glance through his long blond eyelashes.

'A lot more than you think,' I replied hotly, remembering Dad's regular courses of anti-depressants in the years following my mum's death, and Jasmine's intensive period of depression during her early teens.

'Well, anyway,' he stood up and attempted a smile. 'I hope we can call it water under the bridge. I'm with Rachel, and that's the end of the matter.'

'Fine.' I held out my hand and he accepted it readily. 'Rachel's a lovely girl, Simon. You two really do make a great couple. I hope it works out, I really do.'

'Cheers.' He looked down at his feet and then suddenly said, 'What about Nadine?'

'What *about* Nadine?'

'Well . . . she won't say anything, will she?'

'Believe me, she has more important things to worry about.'

He gave me a strange look. 'Yes, I suppose she does.' He left after an uncomfortable silence, shutting the door soundlessly behind him. I was about to resume my letter to Jasmine, but to my irritation, there was another interruption. Marbles bundled in unannounced without knocking, oozing with salubrious charm.

'Page,' he said breathlessly, 'can we talk?'

'Don't you ever knock?' I scolded, feeling my heart rate spontaneously increase, just a little. 'I mean, it's *basic manners*, for Christ's sake.'

'Sorry, I need to talk to you.'

'What, *now*? What's so important?'

'Can we go down the beach? You're not busy are you?'

'Well,' I looked at the scattered files and books and handwritten notes and typed pages covering my desk and floor and felt an overwhelming urge to burn the lot. 'No, not really, but –' Our eyes locked momentarily and his lopsided smile was enough to convince me that my studies could maybe be put off for a little while longer.

'Just one hour of your time. That's all I ask,' he whispered.

'W-what's all this about?'

'*Please.*'

I was thrown by his serious tone. 'What's the matter?'

'Please?'

My curiosity got the better of me. I pulled on my jacket and followed him outside.

'This had better be good,' I warned him, after we had been walking in stilted silence for several minutes. 'I was trying to get down to finally doing some serious –'

'Wait till we get downtown,' Marbles interrupted me, 'I just needed to get out and . . .' he gave me a sidelong glance which was almost *romantic*. I put it down to a trick of the light. 'And I wanted some company,' he continued, 'er . . . *your* company, really.'

I did a fish-out-of-water impression. 'I must be dreaming,' I finally faltered, finding my voice, 'I could have sworn you just said something complimentary.' To bring an element of realism into my dream, he chortled derisively and quickened his pace. I trotted to keep up with him. 'Look, Marbles, it's just that you've barely said a word to me this term and now you're acting like . . . like –'

'Ice cream?' He indicated an ice-cream van at the side of the road and grinned engagingly. 'My shout.'

Not waiting for my response, he swaggered towards the van, rummaging around in his pocket for his wallet. I stood and watched dumbly, not knowing what to think, while he purchased two cones and walked back clutching them both in one hand as he pocketed the change.

'Cheers,' I whispered hoarsely as he thrust one at me.

'No problem,' he said, licking off a melted vanilla dribble from his hand.

We hopped on a bus and barely exchanged another word until we reached town. I gave him strange looks all the way, he evaded them by staring out of the window, his forehead pressed against the grubby glass. We got out by the Royal Pavilion and the welcome sea air filled my haggard lungs. Marbles handed me one of his famously strong cigarettes and lit it for me, staring intently into my eyes as I pulled on the filter and triumphantly sucked back the carcinogens without choking or coughing. I ambled onwards in any old direction, aimless and bewildered, and he followed at my side.

'Abi,' he said finally, lighting up a cigarette for himself, 'I've been talking to Nadine.'

I stopped in my tracks. He turned me around to face him.

'She said . . . she said that you . . . that you – er . . .' he chuckled under his breath and shook his head slowly, now avoiding my quizzical gaze, as if he was incapable of saying any more.

'Jesus, Maurice, I'm not a bloody mind-reader,' I grumbled.

'Sorry. This isn't easy.' He placed his hand on my back and guided me through a flock of warbling pigeons, which flapped and dispersed as we negotiated a route towards the pier. The smell of candyfloss and hot dogs wafted from the stalls. It was already starting to get dark and although it was surprisingly warm and still for early May, the chill sea breeze sent the strangest shiver through me.

'So – er, what *did* she say to you then?' I asked. Panic rose in me fleetingly as I tried to remember all the private things I had said to Nadine which she may have repeated in a state of drunken thoughtlessness. But that just wasn't her style, and I couldn't think of anything really incriminating or embarrassing I had told her anyway, at least nothing that would have interested Marbles.

'Let's go and sit over there,' he suggested. We walked along the seafront, and after some shy, tentative touches and a conspicuous avoidance of eye contact, he took my hand in his and held it. I did my best to keep myself under control, but I felt like I was soaring. He eventually pulled me towards a bench and sat me down next to him. There followed a lot of 'umming' and 'ahhing' on his part, and a lot of amused and confused eyebrow-raising on my part as I waited in anticipation for him to spit it out, whatever it was.

'Abi, I . . . I really like you. And Nadine said that you . . . that you like me too.' For the first time ever, I saw him blush. He fell silent after this outburst and concentrated on the scene in front of us. The beach was milling with tourists and squealing students, high on pints and pills before the clubs opened. The sea spewed its feculent foam in languid waves on to the shore and in the distance the sunset bled orange into deep azure blue. It was about as idyllic as Brighton could have got. My mind was racing and my heart was going even faster. I felt overawed, dizzy. If I hadn't been sitting down, I would almost certainly have keeled over backwards. I took a deep breath before responding. 'I really don't know where she got that idea from,' I confessed.

Did I like him? Did I? Was I *attracted* to him?

His blush deepened. I rushed to put him at ease. 'I mean, of course I do like you, but I just don't know why Nadine would tell you that. It's not like I'm *obsessed* or anything. Oh God what am I saying? What I mean is . . .'

Incoherence seemed to be catching. I decided to stop babbling before I dug myself into an even deeper hole.

'Hey, it's all right,' Marbles said. 'I just wanted to let you know . . . that night – you and me – it meant more to me than you think.'

I was astonished by the immensely gratifying effect these words had on me. 'Watch it,' I said, 'you're in serious danger of me taking you seriously for once.'

'I am serious. I like you. I . . . like you.'

'OK, so we've established that. And you dragged me all the way here just to tell me that?'

'No. Not just that. Nadine also told me that your mum died.'

'*What?*' Now I was *really* confused. 'Why did she tell you *that*?'

He shrugged. 'I suppose she thought it was something you and me had in common.'

'W-what?'

'My mum died of cancer just over two years ago.'

'Oh, God . . . I'm so sorry.'

'How did yours die?'

He saw my expression fall and he immediately added, 'Sorry, if you don't like talking about this . . .'

'No – no, it's OK. She overdosed on a drug cocktail. It was ages ago. I was very young. Much too young to remember. I can't say it's really affected me personally. I've only ever known my stepmum, and she's wonderful.'

We both turned towards each other, slowly and hesitantly, and he shyly touched my hair and my face and looked into my eyes with a sedate solemnity that I never thought he could ever have possessed, under any circumstances. Maurice Venables had suddenly become a Very Serious Bloke.

'You can't honestly say your mum's death hasn't affected you,' he said, tucking strands of my hair behind my ear and shifting closer towards me until I became more than vaguely aware of a burgeoning desire to do something rash and reckless in the heat of the moment. 'She's like, *half* your genetics. Your identity,' he murmured, moving his face within kissing distance.

'I . . . I really can't remember anything about her. I have a picture, that's all.'

'Can I see it?'

'Er . . . yeah, sure.'

I put a quivering hand into my coat pocket and pulled out my purse. I didn't know why Marbles, of all people, was suddenly taking an interest in my life and in *me*, but I was enjoying his company and was even enjoying the conversation, however weird it seemed. I was seeing a side of him I never knew existed, and I liked it. It was a bizarre feeling, having a civilised conversation with a bloke who I had previously perceived as all mouth and no trousers.

I pulled out a crumpled collection of photos from my purse. There was one of Jasmine and me taken in 1977, a year before our mother's death. I had just cut my first teeth – two stubby little milk teeth at the front – and Jasmine, aged eight, had just lost hers. My dad had had this photo enlarged and mounted in a special frame on his bedroom wall. It was probably the happiest, most natural and innocent photo ever taken of me and my sister. I also had two photo-booth pictures of me and Sylvie from four years ago, still in our school uniforms and cackling together like typical schoolgirls. And, to my disgust, I still had a photo of Nick, too – a long-since-forgotten, depressingly gorgeous picture taken when he still allegedly loved me. I immediately screwed this one up and stuffed it back into the bottom of my purse, wedging it under my maligned debit card.

'Here – this is my mum. She was nineteen when this was taken. Five years before I was born. Her name was Angel. The little girl she's holding is my sister.' I handed Marbles a faded, dog-eared picture of a dark-haired woman in a long, flowing dress, with two-year-old Jasmine tucked under her arm, smiling straight into the camera.

He held it and looked at it for a long time. 'My God . . .' he whispered, 'she was really beautiful.'

'Yeah,' I sighed, suddenly feeling quite emotional, 'yeah, she was.'

He handed the picture back to me and gazed rapturously into my eyes in such a way that for a terrible moment I thought he'd say something crass and insincere like, 'so are you', but thankfully he didn't. Instead, he moved around to face the beach again, and there was a long but not discomfiting silence.

'Were you close to your mum?' I eventually asked, sensing that he probably needed to talk about it, or he would never have been so upfront with me in the first place. He must have had to swallow a considerable amount of male pride to open up to me so honestly – and it was common knowledge that Marbles consisted almost entirely of male pride. Male pride and testosterone. I was only just beginning to realise there was a lot more substance to him. I was beginning to really, really fancy him.

He nodded, and didn't look at me. When he spoke, he sounded all choked up, like he was crying. He turned his face away when he spoke. 'You start thinking that . . . that you're the only person in the world who lost their mum when they were still young, and you're so wrapped up in your loss you can't see that it happens to other people as well. You feel hard-done-by, you know?'

'Oh God, Marbles, I'd never have guessed that you suffered such an awful thing. Have you not talked to anyone about this before?'

He shrugged and kicked an apple core on the ground with the toe of his trainer.

'Not really. I s'pose it's because everyone had been kind of expecting her to die. Like we had mentally prepared ourselves for it. But you're never ready for your mum to die, are you?' He glanced over at me and a tear slid down his cheek. He wiped it away and put his head in his hands, trying to hold back sobs and almost succeeding. All barriers came crashing down in an instant. I put my arms around him and drew him towards me. At first he was tense, a little embarrassed, self-conscious of his grief.

'I'm so flattered,' I whispered into his hair, as he reciprocated the embrace, clinging to me with a sudden childlike neediness.

'Why?' he mumbled into my jacket hood.

'That you've told me this. It means a lot. It's not every day that someone confides in you.' I felt him relax in my arms, and I wrapped myself around him, sank into him blissfully, curling up against his body with my head against his chest.

'I'd like to say I know how you feel, Marbles, but I don't,' I said. 'My mum died before I even got to know her. Before I even grew to love her. It's kind of hard to love someone you never knew.'

This prompted further tears, more restrained this time but just as heartfelt. He pulled me closer and kissed the top of my head, my hair muffling his sobs.

'I'm sorry,' he sighed, after he'd calmed down. 'You don't think I'm a sad wanker, do you?'

I looked up at him in awe. 'I think you're fantastic,' I said gushingly.

We stayed on the bench holding each other, immobilised and astounded by the emotions we had just shared. I never wanted the moment to end.

'Will you be my girlfriend, Page?' he finally said, his voice strong and deep again.

My heart fluttered into orbit. 'I thought you'd never ask, Venables.'

Frank the Goth was on Prozac.

He prowled the corridor in the twilight hours, looking cadaverous and mournful, and locked himself away during the day, refusing to talk to anyone. He stopped eating and instead lived on irreligious music, listening to bands like Christian Death and Cannibal Corpse with fanatical regularity. I think I knew part of the reason behind his depression, and it wasn't just his apocalyptically saturnine music collection.

Conversely, I needed a drug which would increase my brain-power and motivation to work, while simultaneously suppressing my libido, which had now reached dizzying heights. Dope managed to do the latter to a certain extent, but alcohol failed on both counts. A combination of the two rendered me utterly useless. Although Marbles served as a very pleasurable distraction for a while, I couldn't ignore the fact that the end of the final term was fast approaching. I vowed to myself that after my birthday, I would go to the library, find myself a quiet seat and set up camp there until I had managed to retain some information useful to my degree. After a frolicsome fortnight of shag and skag, hump and hemp, that time came around far too quickly.

My nineteenth birthday – 15 May 1995 – started badly. For one thing, it was a Monday.

My first thought when I woke up was that I had just one year left of being a teenager. I wasn't sure whether this thought was comforting or not. Marbles, breathing heavily beside me, broke wind with thunderous force and flung a leg over my body, pinning me to the mattress – or at least what tiny share of his bed I had been apportioned. I blinked up at the ceiling, remembering what had happened on my last birthday, my eighteenth. Official adulthood was not something I had been particularly looking forward to. Unfortunately, my family took a different view and went to the trouble of throwing me a huge, elaborate party, which I had not appreciated nearly as much as I should have done.

My strop was partly due to Nick's badly timed, inauspicious dumping of me the week before. He had done it with all the grace and sensitivity of a charging rhinoceros, thus: 'I really like you but you're probably going away to university in a few months so there's not much point in staying together, is there?' I had initially responded to this unprovoked statement by kissing him laughingly, throwing my head back and shrieking, 'Oh Nicholas, you *are* a joker!' It was impossible to take him seriously because at the time I was lying spread-eagled on his bed, completely naked except for his leather jacket, and he had only just finished performing some particularly pacifying oral sex on me. Nick had glared at me gravely until my smile was replaced by an expression of terrified disbelief, and then he had said, 'No, Abi – I'm serious.'

And so I listened to my life fall down around me as he tried, and failed, to explain why he wanted to end our relationship. And ultimately, of course, begin another one. With someone else.

My eighteenth was therefore not quite the merry event it should have been, and I was far too involved with feeling sorry for myself to bother even pretending that Dad and Jane's family 'n' friends birthday bash was doing anything to cheer me up. It was of course outrageously selfish of me, but in the prime of my adolescent pig-headedness, I saw no way of getting through such a black time other than by causing everyone around me similar misery.

Jasmine, at her own birthday celebrations three days later, gave me something infinitely more important to worry about, however. Her regular dealer, a bloke with the appropriate name of Chris Heron, gave her the birthday present she really wanted and didn't need, which she cooked up in a teaspoon and squirted eagerly into her arm, collapsing almost immediately as it seeped into her bloodstream. She overdosed on pure heroin and nearly died.

That put things into perspective for me, the self-absorbed sister in her own micro world of broken relationships and A-level stress.

'Happy birthday,' Marbles mumbled, opening one eye and peering at me dozily.

'Why do people always say that?' I snapped huffily. The memory of the year before had made me over-sensitive and fractious. I slithered down the bed and then hastily slithered back up again when a mephitic waft of stale fart, previously held captive beneath the sheets, breezed up my nose. 'God, you stink,' I grumbled.

'Bloody hell, Abi, what's rattled your cage?' He rubbed his eyes, stretched, scratched his bollocks and yawned widely. I put my arm around him and lazily flicked a random lock of hair out of my face.

'I'm sorry. I was just thinking.'

'God, what do you want to do something like that for?' He turned on his side and ran his fingers down the front of my body. 'Thinking is boring,' he said.

'I know, but I've really got to get my act together, Marbles. I've done fuck-all this entire year.'

'Not true.' He moved forward and kissed me hard on the lips. 'I'd say you've achieved quite a lot, actually.'

'I'm *serious.*'

'So am I. Let's shag.'

'*Please.* Please, can we just . . . you know, *talk*?'

'I'm all ears. Shoot.'

'Can you take your hand away from there, please?'

'Sorry. Go ahead. Let's talk.' He rolled on to his stomach and sighed.

'I've got a lot of things on my mind right now,' I explained. 'My tutor wants my head on a stick, I haven't read any of the books I was supposed to read, I'm living on borrowed time and borrowed cash, and . . .'

'It's your sister, right? Isn't that what's really bugging you?'

'H-how do you know that?'

'I just know.'

I glared at him sceptically. 'Nadine's got a big mouth,' I remarked.

'No, it's not that. I – er . . . overheard you two talking once . . .' he trailed off and gave me a guilty smile. 'I didn't mean to . . .'

'Yeah right.'

'But, really,' he whispered, 'I'd like to think you can tell me stuff now. Now that I'm your . . . boyfriend.' He turned on his back and guided my hand down to his 'tummy banana' (his phrase, not mine), which tumesced at my touch with a spontaneity I still found disarming. He then lit a cigarette and stretched one arm above his head, smoking casually as I played about with it desultorily, my mind occupied with other things.

'Go on then,' he said.

'Go on then what?'

'Talk to me.'

He handed me his fag and I took one puff and then gave it

back to him. Marbles smoked a lot. He not only had a post-coital fag, he had a pre-coital, and even a *during*-coital fag sometimes.

I remained silent, stuck for words.

'You finding it hard to talk to me?' Marbles asked.

'No, I just . . .'

'Tell you what, it's too early for a serious discussion anyway. Let's just shag and then I'll give you your birthday present.' He pushed his fringe out of his eyes and looked at me lustily through his eyelashes.

'That's your answer to everything, isn't it?'

'Works for me.'

I sighed and took the cigarette from him again, finishing it off in two deep drags. 'I have a seminar at ten, and if I miss it, I'll be flayed alive.'

'But we've only been together a few days, we should be enjoying each other's bodies every opportunity we get.'

'It's been two weeks, Maurice, and Durex could have *sponsored* us.'

He flashed me his fail-safe smile and said, 'It's your *birthday* though. I was going to take you somewhere nice . . .'

'Oh yeah?'

'Heaven and back for starters.'

'I'm touched, really I am. But can't it wait until after my seminar? I've got to lead this crappy group discussion on Shakespearean tragedy.'

'Listen, if you don't let me shake my spear at you, *that* will be a tragedy.'

'Fair enough,' I acquiesced, snuggling down under the stinky covers and splaying my thighs. 'Just five minutes though,' I warned, holding out my arms to him. 'I'm not going to let you make me miss this one.'

'I'll do my best,' he murmured, taking another cigarette from behind his ear and moving on top of me as he fumbled with his lighter.

I went home that Thursday, partly for Jasmine's birthday, and partly to get away from the disheartening build-up of revision that had accumulated on my desk. Marbles's ruthless libidinal zeal was beginning to tire me, and my lack of will-power meant I was easily persuaded to partake in activities which did little to increase my chances of eventually obtaining a BA honours degree.

I was shocked at how much Jasmine had changed since I last saw her, just a month before. She had put on a lot of weight – not just her stomach, but all over. She had also dyed her hair bright red and was wearing some new clothes – clean and smart and not at all like the clothes she usually wore. I hardly recognised her when I returned home to find her slumped on the couch, laughing like a drain at a commercial on the TV. Her new course of medication was working – provided she stuck to it – and regular visits by a new social worker and a reassuringly clucky midwife meant Jasmine could now live at home permanently. She smiled up at me as I walked in through the front door.

'All right, sis, how's tricks?'

'Hiya. *God*, Jas, you look . . . pregnant.'

'Yeah, cheers. Knew I could rely on you for an ego boost.'

'What's with the hair?'

'Don't you like it?'

'No, it's nice. Happy birthday, by the way. Hold on a minute . . .' I rummaged in my bag and pulled out a very badly wrapped present: my limited finances had just about stretched to a box of chocolates (unimaginative) and a David Bowie video (unoriginal). 'Hope you like it. Sorry it's not much.'

'Oh, you didn't have to get me anything . . .'

'I wanted to. Besides, I only did it to make you feel guilty for not getting me anything.'

'*Au contraire*, impatient one.' She handed me a plastic bag, filled with a variety of random, unwrapped gifts: a velvet box containing a silver necklace and earrings set, a book called *Stop Smoking Now*, some incense sticks in jasmine and sandalwood, strawberry bath pearls and a trance CD. 'Not much either, but it's the thought that counts,' she yawned.

'Thanks. Where's Dad?'

'Upstairs.' She pulled me down towards her and whispered in my ear, '*He's smoking a reefer.*'

'Still not patched things up with Jane?'

She crossed her arms and sighed. 'I feel so sorry for him, Abi. He just slouches about all day looking like he's about to burst into tears.'

'He's been under a lot of stress lately. He'll be all right,' I said.

'We're all supposed to be going out for dinner together tonight – Jane and Lewis will be here at seven. I just hope it works out OK, you know? I hate it when Dad is miserable . . . he's not the same without Jane around.' She heaved herself out of her seat and waddled to the door. 'Anyway, do you want a tea or something?'

'Yeah, good idea.'

I followed her out to the kitchen and watched her run water into the kettle and open a packet of herbal tea. Denzil slipped in through the cat flap with insouciant grace and mewed at my feet until I picked him up and cuddled him.

'That bloody cat, he's such a softie.' Jasmine bent down and nuzzled into the tufty grey fur on Denzil's head, purring along with him. 'Killed a poor little sparrow the other day though, didn't you, naughty boy?' Denzil blinked his big yellow eyes blamelessly back at her, his expression both bored and adoring as only pampered family cats know how.

Jasmine straightened up and smiled at me. 'Tea or coffee or herbal crap?'

'Oh, tea. The proper stuff please.'

She groaned and rubbed at her back. 'Have you *seen* what I'm supposed to be eating these days?'

'Pork pies and ice cream, by the looks of it.'

'Cheeky bitch.' She opened the fridge and took out tubs of bio yoghurt, organic vegetables in seal-fresh bags, pasta salad bowls, apples and freshly squeezed orange juice and cartons of skimmed milk. '*These* are examples of the more *tasty* things I've got in my prenatal diet. I ask you!'

'And you're still not smoking?'

She nodded, humble rather than self-satisfied. 'Thought it was probably about time I made an effort. Now I've got this poor little bugger to think about . . .' she stroked her stomach and gave me a wistful look. 'I feel like I'd kill for a fag sometimes, of course, but . . . small price to pay, isn't it?'

'I'm proud of you, Jas.'

'Really?'

'Really.'

She poured the boiling water into the cups: an Earl Grey for me, and a camomile and fennel for her. She poked listlessly at her teabag as it brewed, filling the air with its steamy astringent scent.

'Your big exams soon, innit?' she said.

'Don't remind me.'

'You'll be fine. You're the clever one, remember.'

'Yeah, right. So clever that my tutor wants me to repeat the year.'

'All you need to pass exams is the ability to waffle and bullshit. Both of which you have never had any problems with.'

'Oh thanks very much,' I said, knowing she had a point.

She handed me my cup and then sat down at the breakfast bar, munching her way through a packet of jammy dodgers.

'I have a boyfriend,' I confessed after a brief pause, offering an alternative slant to the conversation.

'Oh yeah? Bet I can guess who it is.'

'Bet you can't.'

'That one in your digs who loves himself, with the poncey hair and the aftershave.'

'What?' It didn't take much brain-racking to work out she was referring to Alex.

'Oh, no, not him. The other one. The slightly less poncey one with the big nose and the comedy trousers.'

Marbles was not a classic good-looker, but he certainly had a few striking features. There were so many things about him that were not *inherently* sexy, but the more I had got to know him, the more these things had made him captivating and fanciable. For example, he was good at chess. A *genius* at chess. I had always found chess dull, but with Marbles it suddenly became wildly attractive and exciting. He could breakdance like a demon, roll a perfect joint with his hands behind his back, knew how to say 'fuck you' in eight languages, played pool like a pro, occasionally wore glasses that he didn't really need, and was the only bloke I'd ever met who didn't look totally preposterous in a back-to-front baseball cap. One of his eyes was never fully open, giving him a permanently sly, sleepy look, and I found that amazingly, *gob-smackingly* attractive. I had it bad.

'Hmm. Interesting choice,' Jasmine mumbled, her mouth full of crumbs. 'So how long has this been going on then?'

'Couple of weeks or so. His name is Marbles.'

Her lips twitched with bemusement as she offered me the last biscuit. 'Trust you, Abi. So I suppose you could say that my loss is your gain, then?'

'Huh?'

'Never mind. So you're getting a regular dose now are you? No wonder you're looking more sprightly. Bit of colour in your cheeks at last.'

'Do you think so?' I sat down next to her and sipped my tea. 'I really like him,' I murmured, feeling myself blush.

'Well, good for you. And anything's an improvement on that dipshit you went out with before. Just don't go getting yourself in this predicament, will you?' She patted her bump and winked at me. 'Dad will end up losing what little is left of his hair.'

We giggled and then she hugged me close and whispered, 'It's good to have you back home for my birthday. This summer we'll spend some proper time together, yeah?'

'Yeah, I'd really like that.'

She took a gulp of her tea and then left the rest to go cold, claiming it tasted of 'putrefied hamster wee', and I finished off my substantially more satisfying brew and opened another packet of biscuits.

We both tucked in voraciously and after a while Jasmine stood up and gazed blankly out of the kitchen window, turning Seth's ring on her finger and biting her lip absently. After a long silence, she suddenly announced, 'There's so much shit in the world.'

She carried on staring then looked down at her bump and ran her hand over it again, sighing deeply. 'Sometimes living just seems like more trouble than it's worth, Abi. I never thought I'd be cruel enough to bring someone else into this shitty world.'

I looked at her warily. She caught my eye and managed a weak smile. 'Oh, ignore me.' She rinsed her cup in the sink and watched the water spiral down the plughole. 'It's just my hormones.'

Dad very kindly treated us all to a slap-up meal at an over-priced Thai restaurant ordering us to 'make the most of this rare display of foolish generosity'. I therefore gorged myself, knowing it was likely to be the only substantial meal I would have until I returned again for the summer holiday. Following many long weeks of 'talking it over' with Dad, Jane finally moved her things back in on Saturday. On Sunday I left my newly united family and went back to university, feeling almost on top of the world.

Almost.

I resided for forty-eight hours almost non-stop in the university library, laboriously ploughing my way through books that should have long since been read, analysed and written about in extensive detail. I couldn't even call it revision, because that would have suggested I was merely refreshing my memory. What worried me most was that everyone on my hall was acting as if the exams were merely a tedious necessity rather than a nerve-racking source of stress. Marbles, who was doing the most boring and impossibly complicated science-and-statistics-type course imaginable, always achieved consistently good grades with minimal effort. He drank more, shagged more and studied less than anybody else, and claimed his first exam was a 'piece of piss'.

The evening before my last exam I returned from a hard day's slog at the library, my mind still reeling from information overload, to find a naked lunatic tearing up and down the hall, frenziedly babbling something incomprehensible in Japanese. Marbles pulled me into Alex's room, grinning like a Cheshire cat.

Alex was lolling languidly on the floor with two roll-ups stuck up his nose. 'What's going on?' I hissed at the pair of them.

'I think congratulations are in order,' Marbles said, staggering forwards and trying to put his arm around me, but missing and collapsing next to his crapulent comrade in a blithering heap.

'We've achieved the impossible!' Alex exclaimed triumphantly, pulling one of the roll-ups out of his nostril and offering it to me. At that moment, Yoshi burst through the door and squealed at us, before streaking off again.

'*What have you done to him?*' I demanded, staring at them in disbelief.

'He's off his tits!' Alex chortled.

Drooling, Marbles crawled towards me and winched himself up my leg, clinging to my hip as he made a largely unintelligible attempt at explaining how he and Alex had managed to turn the hall bookworm into a stark bollock naked, stark raving mad imbecile. I only managed to decipher the ominous words 'spiked', 'slapped', 'wedged right in the crack', and 'fortunately elasticated'.

'At last!' Alex cried, 'Yoshi is one of us!'

Now reaching the end of my first university year, I was discovering for myself that the never-ending pursuance of self-gratification that is student life can rapidly become a jejune, tedious humdrum. The novelty wears off, the blur of lost time quickly comes to represent an entire wasted year, and what was once grandiosely viewed as the quest for self-discovery and personal development on the rocky road to adulthood is finally seen for what it really is: the quest for prime absurdity. And so this is what student life is all about: 10 per cent discounts on all the things you could never want; half-hearted fumblings and mechanical kisses with strangers in the back of seedy nightclubs; gallons of watered-down dregs to turn you into someone you are not and do not want to be; disastrous sex with people your mother would disapprove of, a split second of youthful hormone-propelled insanity exchanged for a lifetime of cringing regret. Membership of social cliques which dictate what you should believe in, only to contradict it all by taking so many second-rate drugs you no longer care about anything. Wasting away in a previously unvisited library after multiple lecture evasions; desperately cramming the tiny, drug-riddled vegetable of your brain in the few days leading up to the exams ensconced in a grotty little room that smells of masturbation and feet. Pissing away your grant and squandering your loan and moaning that it was never enough in the first place. Recycled clothes and hairdye and pretensions and 'outrageous' japes that have been seen, done and made predictable and dull by countless others before you. Spontaneous adoption of a faded, jaded humour which relies wholly on sarcasm and ridicule of others who are highly unlikely to be any more worthy of ridicule than you are yourself. Infinite debts, liver failure, organ shrinkage and microscopically improved job prospects which start and probably finish at the dole queue when you realise you are so out of touch with reality that the very thought of gainful employment is enough to confine you to bed in sheer terror. Having nothing to show for any of it as you reach your final year but a scrap of personalised paper with some posh writing on it, but justifying it to yourself by passing them off as 'the best years of your life'.

Now a third of the way through the best years of my life, I was beginning to realise how little I had actually accomplished. After the exams had finished for everyone, and the local chemists were frantically replenishing their depleted stocks of *Pro Plus*, we had two blissful weeks of doing bugger all – and this time, without any boring academic obligations hanging over us, it really *was* bugger all.

No longer fuelled solely by caffeine and chemicals, we spent our lazy, early June days eating grease-soaked chips out of paper cones, buying second-hand CDs with what little cash we had left, getting drunk and disorderly and lounging around and larking about.

In the lead-up to results day I barely gave a second thought to the very real possibility that I had failed. I had managed to convince myself that I wasn't really bothered one way or the other, and for as long as I continued losing myself in the traditional rituals of misspent youth, this self-deception came all too easily.

10
Let's Jump

A miracle took place.

Everyone on my hall passed their exams: Yoshi and Marbles and Nadine with flying colours across the board, everyone else with slightly less emphatic confidence, and me bringing up the rear with a scraped pass in each module. But it was good enough – just.

The last night of our first university year was planned to be a big one – our final opportunity to go out together as a dysfunctional student family before returning home for the summer. It meant saying goodbye for ever to being a naïve fresher, goodbye to the incestuous group of campus hallmates, goodbye to the poky little rooms we had tried to make home. Of course, this also meant accepting a new identity as a slightly less naïve second year, and living with a more exclusive group of incestuous housemates in a clapped-out student shack. Against my better judgement, I had agreed – happily, I'll admit – to share a house in Lewes with Marbles, Alex and Nadine. Together we formed a bizarre 'love quadrangle' – Marbles and I were still in the honeymoon throes of our relationship, Alex fancied Nadine (I would go so far as to say he was probably in love with her, as much as it is possible for Alex to love someone other than himself), Marbles and Alex shared a suspiciously close lad–lad alliance, and I sometimes still felt awkward and self-conscious around Nadine. It was to be the four of us. In one small house. With one bathroom. Surely this was asking for trouble.

Emotions and spirits were high that last night. I was astounded and disheartened by how quickly the first year had gone by. In the morning I woke up early – not just before midday, but before *nine* (a veritable phenomenon for an idler like me) – and I actually *felt* awake. I sprang out of Marbles's bed with sprightly buoyancy (as opposed to being pushed out by his snoozing bulk), and went to my room to finish packing my things. I then spent two hours in the university bookshop with my extensive second-year reading list clutched in my hand. It was only when I came out of the shop with a bulging bagful of core texts in my hand that I realised I had just done something alarmingly sensible. And, as it was a sunny day and I was in a very odd frame of mind, I went down to the beach and started reading one of the books. With interest. I became so engrossed that I lost track of time. But then a seagull crapped on me and I decided it was probably best that I headed back.

By early evening, my mood had lapsed back into normality after my third joint and my second glass of wine. Four of us congregated in Catherine's room, a pastel haven of vapid girlitude filled with frilly accessories, dozens of out-of-date glossies, empty Evian bottles, cosmetic superfluities, and plastic bags from just about every high street fashion store in Brighton. Juliet, Nadine and I listened in pie-eyed awe, boredom and amusement respectively as Catherine subjected us to a lengthy harangue about the evils of men and alcohol.

'I've had it with men, you know,' she was saying as she unravelled heated rollers from her hair and gazed into one of her many mirrors. 'Starting from tonight, no more alcohol and definitely no more men for me. Celibacy and sobriety. That's the way forward.'

She raised a perfectly sculpted eyebrow at us as she applied her third coat of lip gloss. She had been getting ready since breakfast time, but she still hadn't decided what to wear. She shook her new curls out, running her bejewelled fingers through them as she pumped her hair all over with fixing spray, until the room was filled with its throat-burning reek.

'But . . . but there'll be nothing left, Cath,' Juliet said. 'Your life will be a void.'

'Anyway,' I piped up, 'you've already had half a bottle of wine tonight.'

She pointed her blusher brush at me and made a tetchy noise. 'I most certainly have not,' she protested.

'Er – evidence,' said Nadine, finding the empty green bottle beneath a pile of tried-on and rejected bustier tops and holding it up above her head.

'Hmph.' Catherine hoisted her breasts up and squashed them together inside her tight zip-up wet-look dress, so they spilled over the top like bald Siamese twins trying to escape from a rubber glove. '*That* was just a bit of party fuel for while I was getting ready. Tonight I'm just going to be me. I'm going to be nice to everyone, and to do that I don't need drink and I don't need to flirt. I'm just going to be *me*.'

Nadine rolled her eyes and groaned. Catherine was adamant. 'I'm serious. After last night, I'm off the male species for good. I mean, who did that creepy shit think he *was*?'

At a previously undiscovered nightclub the night before, Catherine had unwittingly managed to attract the attention of a notably hideous man wearing khaki slacks, a smirk and a bumfluff beard. His T-shirt had said: 'I like the Pope. The Pope smokes Dope.' He had accosted Catherine and attempted to drag her into the disabled toilets for what he allegedly described as 'disabling sex'. Catherine, being perilously pixilated and therefore pretty much open to suggestion, had gone along with it quite willingly at first. Her delayed reaction did not take effect until she found herself pressed up against the wall with her legs dangling over the support bars each side of the toilet and her head wedged between the seat and the loo roll dispenser. The horrific reality of her situation finally dawned on her when she knocked her funny bone on the cistern and inadvertently powered the flush mechanism, soaking her hair. With his khakis crumpled round his ankles and his organ primed, her would-be paramour was less than amused when Catherine's size six Saxone made firm contact with his prone ball bag.

'But it's our last night tonight,' Juliet mumbled, her words slightly slurred, 'I think we should make the most of it, don't you?'

She beamed at us beatifically, resting her head against Catherine's shoulder as she dragged on a Marlboro. She had spent much of the previous night and the first few hours of that day freebasing cocaine in between having raucous intercourse with a fellow sociology student called – if her orgasmic cries were anything to go by – 'Douggie'. So she was more mellow than usual. In fact, she was almost comatose.

'Well, I'm ready to go *now*,' Nadine said, knocking back the last of her Hooch and letting out a burp of great volume and reverberation. 'No point hanging about. Let's grab the boys and fuck off out of here.'

'Hold on, I still need to choose what dress to wear!' Catherine whinnied. 'And . . . how does my hair look, by the way?' She fluffed it up, piling the wavy strands loosely on top of her head and pouting at us.

'Like you've spent all day trying to make it look as if you've only just got out of bed,' Nadine said, yawning and not bothering to look at her. She picked up an old copy of *Cosmo* and read the content features advertised on the airbrushed cover with a look of disgust. 'Incidentally Cath, do you really need a magazine to tell you what weight you should be, where your G-spot is and how to make a man fall in love with you?'

Catherine squinted at her. 'Actually, there's a lot of very insightful stuff in there.'

'Yes, I'm sure there is.' Nadine didn't bother to find out, and instead threw it back on the floor.

'Hey,' Juliet whispered, opening one eye and peering at Nadine through a veil of silky brown hair, 'can I ask you something a bit . . . well, rude? A bit kind of . . . personal?'

Nadine shrugged. 'The worst I can do is refuse to answer.'

Juliet glanced at me before venturing her question. 'What do lesbians actually . . . you know . . . *do*?'

Nadine plucked my joint out of my fingers and took a couple of tokes before responding. She tilted her head back and exhaled a cloud of smoke at Catherine's pink lampshade and said, in a neutral voice, 'Imagine the best sex you've ever had with a bloke. Times the pleasure by a thousand. Take away the heavy-handed foreplay, the flatulence and the facial hair.' She took another puff before handing the joint back to me. 'And then times the pleasure by a thousand again, just for good measure.'

Catherine's ice-blue eyes widened. She looked as if she couldn't decide whether to be impressed or appalled. 'But . . . at the end of the day, women need *men.* We've been biologically designed to – er – *accommodate* them.'

Nadine smiled. 'Darling, we're biologically designed for many purposes. Having sex with men is certainly not one design function we should feel obliged to utilise.'

'Maybe you just haven't met the right man,' Juliet mused.

'Oh please. Spare me that one.'

'All right, so men can be complete shitbags, but I could *never* be a lesbian. It's unnatural.' Catherine squeezed her feet into her dainty little sandals and popped a miniature hairbrush and a few items of make-up into her bag. 'There's just something a bit . . . icky about it.'

'Don't knock it till you've tried it,' Nadine said, standing up briskly and shoving her fag packet in the back pocket of her jeans. 'And before you ask, that's not an offer, I don't fancy either of you two.'

Juliet suddenly sat bolt upright and stared at her in surprise.

'Right, everyone, I'm off. Last one under the table is a homosexual,' Nadine announced, pulling the door open.

'You're so impatient!' Catherine scolded, looking back into her mirror. 'Just give me two more minutes.'

Nadine sighed and looked at me, knowing that those two minutes would probably amount to another hour.

Juliet continued staring at Nadine. 'Why don't you fancy me?' she asked, with apparent seriousness and umbrage.

We returned to our hall en masse after many blurred hours of unadulterated buffoonery which began at a cheap and cheerful pub/club and finished at a cheap and cheerless curry house. There were spontaneous sentimental group hugs all round, and even Frank and Yoshi joined in with the various crass valedictory rituals. Juliet and Catherine left us for an 'exclusive' party at midnight and Simon and Rachel retired a bit earlier than the rest of us because they were both feeling a little bit 'peaky'. After a particularly feisty group feast of vegetable biryani, two 'extra-hot' vindaloos, one sensibly tame korma, two chicken jalfrezis, three bowls of greyish rice, one bowl of saffron rice, gallons of gassy beer and plate after plate of poppadums and naans, we limped, belched and vomited our way back to campus. Marbles promptly took Nadine, Alex and me to his room where he forced us to sit through a cheesy porn film called 'Three Goes into One'. Nadine fell asleep half-way through, shortly after volunteering the remark, 'That's *never* gonna fit up there surely.'

Alex, bloated from Indian food and beer, fell asleep not long afterwards, spread-eagled on the floor with his fly undone and his mouth hanging open.

I was finding it pretty hard to stay awake myself by then. I had, after all, been awake and moderately active for nearly twenty hours. Marbles glanced over at me and reached across to rub my thigh. 'Is this not doing anything for you?' he asked, increasing the pressure of his hands by my groin.

I studied the visuals on the set in front of me and stifled a yawn. A flabby bloke with a handlebar moustache was thrusting away with great profligacy and drawling obscenities in a dubbed-on pseudo-American accent. Meanwhile, the 'actress' with whom he was locked *in extremis* was poised to do something predictable with an aubergine and a bondaged blonde.

'Er . . . it's doing *something* for me. It's leaving me stone cold.'

He smiled crookedly and shuffled over to kneel behind me. 'Well, we can't have that, can we?' he whispered, stroking my hair away as he bent to kiss my neck. He started to massage my shoulders with an all-too-familiar male urgency that suggested it was not for relaxation purposes, but a determined prelude to something altogether more sinister. His breath warmed the back of my neck as he continued with his usual routine: yes, Marbles really did believe that oral sex meant talking about what he planned to do to me.

'You look so gorgeous tonight . . .' he said softly, flicking his tongue around my earlobe.

This was a blatant lie. I was so pissed I could hardly stand, I had chronic wind, my clothes were rancid with stale perspiration and my hair had that fuzzy, frizz-dried look that I often got after a hard night's drinking and dancing. I turned my head to accept a kiss from him which started as a tender and rather sexy exploration of my lips and mouth and quickly progressed into a vigorous, wet and rather uncomfortable snog. Just as I thought lockjaw was about to set in, he stopped, pulled away and got up.

'Did you see where I put my fags?' he asked me distractedly, slapping the back pockets of his trousers and scanning the floor.

'No. Can I please stop this video now?'

'Yeah, whatever.' He switched on the light by his bed and took off his T-shirt. With some relief, I stopped and ejected the video, and the TV set blinked back to a weird documentary on Channel Four. A distraught woman was explaining to a sympathetic female interviewer about how her son was turned into a fish finger by aliens. I swiftly changed channels.

Marbles eventually seized upon his ciggies – his second pack of the evening – and tried lighting one with a dud lighter. He tried about ten times and then irritably threw the lighter in the bin and searched for another.

'Here,' I said, offering him mine.

'Ta.'

I aimed the remote control at the television and fired it off, enjoying the silence as a shrieking celebrity faded to black. But then, from his splayed stance on the carpet, Alex started to snore – a warthoggish, nasal rumbling which provided a stark contrast to the light, breathy sounds coming from the slumbering Nadine. This snoring symphony continued until I caved in and threw a pillow at Alex's head, which shut him up for all of three seconds. Marbles sat down opposite me and eyed me as he smoked. After a while, he said,

'Page?'

'Hmm?'

'Can we go to your room?'

'Now? Why?'

'Well,' he glanced over at Alex and prodded his leg. Alex made a gurgling noise and rolled over on to his side, a dribble of saliva creeping from the corner of his mouth. 'Al and Nade aren't exactly scintillating company right now, are they?' Marbles remarked.

'That's very true.' I was about to say something else, but he suddenly pulled me towards him and unzipped the back of my dress, running his fingers down my spine, nuzzling into my hair and my neck as he mumbled about how I smelt good enough to eat.

'What planet are you on, Marbles? I smell disgusting,' I giggled, drawing away and smiling at him. He dropped his gaze and listlessly flicked the filter of his cigarette, crumbling ash on to the floor. Finally he said, 'I've got to tell you, I'm afraid this will probably be our last night together for a while.'

'W-what?'

'I'm going to America with my brother and JD in a couple of days, and after that . . . well, I'm not sure but I'll either find some work with JD in California, or else my dad wants me to come back to England and get some experience at his company, and the money's not bad . . .' he trailed off when his eyes met with my incredulous stare. I had been secretly (and not unreasonably) looking forward to a fabulous summer of sun, sloth and sex with my new boyfriend, but now it appeared that my plans had been foiled.

'I thought you said . . .'

'Yeah, I'm sorry.' He grabbed me by the shoulders and tried to make me look into his eyes, but I petulantly avoided his gaze. 'I know I said we should see each other every weekend, blah blah, but that's before I knew my entire bloody summer had already been more or less planned out for me.' He took a last, aggravated pull on his fag and exhaled audibly, querulously, blowing out a stream of smoke and squashing the stub out on the carpet.

Noticing my disgruntled expression, he made an unimaginative and very male attempt at placating me. Marbles's 'how to get round a pissed off girlfriend' repertoire can be summed up as follows:

1. Look adoringly at girlfriend with glazed expression of lust/lunacy.
2. Switch on your sexiest, most irresistible 'cheeky little monkey' smile.
3. Press groin (erect, naturally) into soft part of girlfriend's body. Any part will do so long as she gets the idea that you're hot for her.
4. Fondle nearest available erogenous zone (a breast, perhaps) with minimal concern for girlfriend's personal comfort.
5. Keep telling her she's beautiful and turning you on so much you can hardly stand it.
6. Await reaction. Anything other than a slap or a knee in the bollocks means you're well in. So continue groping until she falls for your manly charms.
7. Keep waiting. Hang in there. You'll get a result eventually.

Marbles was getting well into stage three of the appeasement process, when suddenly two very, very drunk girls burst into the room, adorned with paper streamers, helium balloons and silly string. Light from the hall flooded in and temporarily blinded us.

'Whoops, sorry . . . are we interrupting something?' one of them slurred, stumbling forwards and landing dangerously close to Alex's outstretched feet. It was Juliet, quite literally off her tits on just about every mind-altering substance in the world.

'Yes, you are actually,' Marbles snapped, putting his arm around me, protectively rather than amorously. 'Me and Page were about to shag.'

'We *were*?' I spluttered.

'Oh, I'm *really* sorry,' said the other girl, who at first I thought was Catherine, but was actually one of Juliet's course mates, a hairy Australian neo-feminist whose name I couldn't remember.

Juliet staggered to her feet, spread her legs apart and declared her love for everyone in the room. Alex woke up at that point, and from his low-level horizontal vantage point the first thing he saw when he opened his eyes was a direct view up Juliet's buttock-skimming skirt. He seemed quite happy with this aspect, and lay flat and motionless on his back, arms folded across his chest and a sleepy, stupid grin spreading across his face.

'Ooooh!' Juliet's friend squeaked suddenly, swooping down and crouching next to Alex's head. 'Aren't you that really fit one that Jules keeps banging on about?' She peered at him admiringly through the steamed-up lenses of her glasses.

'God, give me strength!' Marbles muttered, collapsing back on to his bed next to Nadine and putting his hands over his face. 'Can you all just fuck off, please?'

'They're all really weird, this lot,' Juliet explained matter-of-factly to her Antipodean comrade, who was still preoccupied with fawning over Alex. 'Alex is fit and straight but doesn't want to shag me, Maurice is straight – I had him once – but is now sleeping with an ex-lesbian, Abi. That's Abi,' she pontificated, waving her hand at me. 'And Nadine – the one asleep on the bed – she *is* a lesbian, a *real* one, and she won't sleep with Alex even though he's kind of been after her and he's like, *really* nice.'

'Oh, poor Alex . . .' The Australian simpered, caressing his face and cooing maternally. 'Me and Jules aren't doing anything right now, you know . . .'

'Apart from pissing me off,' Marbles grumbled quietly, his hands still covering his face.

'Come to Jules's room with us, Alex,' the Australian gushed. 'We're looking for some company . . . some sexy male company.'

Alex hiccuped and put his hand down the front of his trousers. He moved his head slightly to the side and squinted at her to assess whether or not she was worthy of the Cheadle charm. Noting the bushy armpits, the reek of pure ethanol, the clusters of acne on the forehead and chin, the crooked and slightly protruding teeth, all viewed through powerful beer goggles, he shrugged and said, 'Why not?'

Juliet staggered about on vertiginous heels and handed me a

Malibu bottle which she told me I could finish off. I thanked her with a nod and a mumble. It was empty.

The Australian was meanwhile gleefully trying to winch Alex up by his belt. I watched passively as, after much flapping and fussing, he was forcibly dragged out of the room, down the corridor and into Juliet's bedroom.

Once the sounds of their giggling and the odd mercy plea from Alex had faded away down the hall, Marbles reached under his mattress and pulled out a small plastic bag of white tablets.

'Well, that's got rid of them,' he said, turning to me and smiling lustily. I had a feeling he was going to resume his appeasement process. 'Don't know about you, but I'm looking forward to seeing what kind of sad, regretful, shambolic state Al's gonna be in tomorrow.'

I didn't return his smile. 'I'm exhausted. I want to go to bed now,' I said stiffly, turning my head away when he moved across to kiss me.

He made an impatient noise. 'Don't be arsey with me, Ab. Don't you think I *want* to spend time with you this summer?'

I didn't answer.

'Hey,' he whispered, taking a tablet out of the bag and placing it on his tongue, 'how about we stay up all night and do it like wild rabbits?'

'Well,' I replied tetchily, 'if I'm not going to have the pleasure of your company for the next two months, I suppose I'd better make the most of this last opportunity . . .'

He didn't pick up on the bitter sarcasm in my voice and he winked at me dozily, grabbing the back of my dress and pulling me towards him. 'That's the spirit,' he said, flashing me his winning grin as he kissed me, transferring the tiny white pill from his tongue to mine.

Sacrificing their usual religious ritual at St Michael's, Dad and Jane picked me up on Sunday morning, arriving in an explosion of parental adoration just as my millionth self-inflicted migraine was beginning to subside.

'Is Jasmine around?' I asked them as soon as we got in through the front door, noticing an ominous silence about the place.

'Er . . . no,' Dad said hesitantly, 'she's er . . . she's not here right now.'

'You know how restless she gets, dear,' Jane piped up. 'Oh, by the way, you've got some mail on the hall table.'

I picked up the depressingly small and unpromising bundle and glanced through it: catalogue offers, a new paying-in book from the bank (ha! Like I'd need it!), and an appointment reminder from the optician. And an envelope with what looked like Sylvie's writing on the front. I threw the post back on the table and sighed. 'I'll open it later,' I said. 'Where is she then?'

'Who?' Jane seemed very distracted all of a sudden, and Dad had already disappeared into the lounge to switch on the *EastEnders* omnibus.

'Jasmine,' I said. 'Where's she gone?'

'Will you make the drinks while I do the lunch?' Jane asked, 'I'm making you something really delicious. My special recipe chilli con carne.'

I followed her into the kitchen. 'Jane, you know I'm vegetarian,' I reminded her gently.

'That's why the recipe is so special,' she chirped. 'I got you some of that meat substitute. Soya protein . . . stuff. You know. The girl in the shop told me it tastes just like meat, too.' She produced a packet from the fridge and whacked it down on the kitchen table, beaming proudly.

'Thanks, that's a really sweet thought.' I smiled at her warmly, flicking the kettle on. 'You didn't have to go to any trouble though.'

'No trouble at all. We're hoping your sister might make an appearance later on tonight as well.' She noticed my concerned glance. 'She's gone on a marching protest somewhere up north,' she explained. 'Legalising cannabis, I think. Or a demonstration against live exports. Some worthy cause or other.' She let out a nervous laugh. 'In her condition, too! There's no stopping her. Stubborn as a mule, that girl.'

'She knows I'm coming home today, doesn't she?'

'We've told her enough times. But you see, she tends to . . . well,' Jane's voice softened to a whisper, 'she forgets things. Pregnancy does that to you. You don't know whether you're coming or going half the time.'

'She's all right though, isn't she?'

'You know Jasmine. She's a survivor.'

'You and Dad are worried sick about her. I can tell.'

Jane leaned back against the breakfast bar and sighed. 'She's not taking any medication at all any more,' she said. 'And she's started to confide in me now, Abi. For the first time, she's really opening up to me. But after so many years of all that terrible tension between us, I just . . . don't know what to say to her. How to help her. She's so fragile. I'm so scared for her.'

'Why did she stop taking her medication? Didn't the doctors warn her . . .'

'That's the whole problem, love. She thinks they're trying to kill her baby by drugging her. I mean, how do you get through to someone like that? She must know how much we care about her. How are we supposed to make her feel safe? What more can we do?'

I didn't have an answer to that; it was a question I had been asking myself for years. Instead I said, 'Is it OK if I go upstairs and unpack my stuff?'

Jane forced a smile. 'Lunch will be ready in about half an hour,' she whispered absently, busying herself with emptying the dishwasher and sorting cutlery into the drawer. 'Maybe we can all have a proper chat together at the table. You can tell us all about uni. And this new boyfriend of yours, Marvin isn't it?'

'Something like that, yeah.' I turned and trudged towards the stairs and picked up my suitcase, my head reeling with a strange ambivalent mixture of relief and dread.

Sylvie didn't take long to catch up and throw all the latest gossip at me. She took Monday afternoon off work and dragged me into McDonald's, where perplexed parents plied their cantankerous offspring with 'Happy Meals' and sullen gangs of school-leavers in Kappa and Adidas chain-smoked through cheeseburgers. We sat at a sauce-smeared formica table and rambled at each other, ignoring a lecherous gang of pre-pubescents behind us and the screaming toddler beside us who refused to eat his chicken nuggets.

Through mouthfuls of burger, Sylvie informed me that Nick's babies were called Chris and Carl, and that he and Sarah were going through a 'bit of a bad patch'. She gushed about how she and Ben were going on holiday together to Majorca, and likewise I gushed about how I had a new boyfriend who was funny and clever and sexy and all the things that boyfriends are supposed to be but rarely are. I just about managed to stop myself from going into a verbose encomium, but only because Sylvie's stifled yawn signalled to me that I was beginning to ramble. She then told me that Nick was having his twenty-first party at the end of July and that I was most certainly invited by virtue of being her friend, rather than by vice of being Nick's embittered ex. I told her that Jasmine was having a baby in October. She offered me the last of her fries and invited me clothes shopping with her the following weekend.

I joined a temping agency during my first week back, and was assigned various menial jobs ranging from packing tin foil to transferring telephone calls to stuffing envelopes. By July I had scraped together enough paltry pence to just about afford some kind of a social life.

It occurred to me that I was experiencing a bad case of wanderlust. I got two or three postcards from Marbles every week, chronicling his escapades around the United States from Miami ('cool') to New Orleans ('wicked') to Phoenix ('awesome'), and finally to Los Angeles and then San Francisco, where he was staying with his brother and his native Californian mate JD in a 'beautiful fucking great apartment' overlooking the beach. The 'Yank babes' were apparently 'hot but fake', and gratifyingly (although maybe not completely sincerely) 'not a patch' on me.

I was missing him even more than I thought I would. Not only that, but I was envious of him. I desperately wanted to travel, to explore the big, wide world, sampling the different cultures and learning the languages, taking hundreds of pictures, revelling in the diverse beauty of human nature. I wanted to get on a plane and do something interesting and important. A poor student's hopeless fantasy. So I ended up going to Glastonbury festival with Jasmine and Nadine.

It turned out to be one of the most enjoyable, if slightly hazy and silly, weekends of my life. Despite her usual reckless manner of flinging caution to the wind for the sake of a new venture, Jasmine was initially hesitant about going. And for a number of understandable reasons, Dad and Jane were not happy about letting her go. But it was for two days only, we had an ample four-(wo)man tent (Jasmine, now heavy with child, easily counted as two people), and I knew the change of scenery and the traditional idiocy that goes with Glastonbury would probably do her good. It was brilliant to see Nadine again. I was cheered to see that she and Jasmine got on famously, and the pair of them nattered together heartily about David Bowie (Nadine's aunt apparently went to school with his wife), male inadequacies, Germaine Greer, chart music and the evils of vivisection.

While they talked, I merely listened and smoked joint after joint. Reinstating my habitual porridge-brain state, after an entire drug-free month, was absolute bliss. Huddled in a tent for two days and nights proved to be the ultimate bonding experience for all three of us. On our second and last night, after checking out a couple of live performances and dance marquees, lolling about on the grass, getting tacky henna tattoos and suffering several revolting experiences in the portaloos, we congregated together in our sleeping bags, lying side by side outside our tent on a groundsheet. It was a warm, close night and the sky was indigo black scattered with stars, luminous through gauze drifts of cloud.

'Looks like it might rain,' Nadine murmured.

'I hope it does,' Jasmine said. 'I love rain. Thunderstorms are best. Afterwards the air feels so clean. So breathable.'

It was about two or three in the morning, and most of the other festival goers were either coming down or reaching the peak of their highs, screeching at each other in a cacophony of distant cat-calling.

After a brief spell of crying and laughing and mumbling to herself, Jasmine finally dozed off while Nadine held her hand and sang to her (Bowie's 'Quicksand' and, rather strangely, Dr and the Medics' one hit wonder 'Spirit in the Sky'). I just watched them, overawed by Nadine's compassion and insight. Once Jasmine was asleep, Nadine turned her head and looked at me squarely, the whites of her eyes glistening and her raven hair catching celestial silver rays in the moonlight.

'Your sister is the most amazing person I have ever met,' she said, plainly, honestly. The words were more complimentary and meaningful to me than if she had said something flattering about me specifically, and when I heard them I was nudged into a higher state of consciousness.

I stared back at her and said, 'You don't know how much it means to me, to hear you say that.'

She propped herself up on one elbow and lit a menthol cigarette. 'You're really lucky. You two are really close. I think that's lovely.'

I put my hands behind my head and studied the moon, full and lucid, my warped, doped vision picking out frenetic shapes and blue faces and craters that probably didn't exist. 'Yeah. I suppose. We've always had each other, but . . . it's not really enough for Jasmine. I know she's permanently suffering in some way and I know that I can never understand in the way she needs me to understand.'

'Well, for what it's worth, she seems a damn sight more with it than most of the freaks I've met at university. And she's so excited about the baby. It will be a whole new start for her, you know, and she's making such an effort. Aren't you looking forward to it?'

'The baby?' I looked over at Jasmine and smiled. 'Yeah, in a way I suppose. But . . .' I softened my voice and turned to face her, 'I just have this awful feeling that it won't be as positive as everyone thinks it will. I can't explain it. I just feel terrified for her.'

'How do you mean?'

I sighed and lit up my final joint, breathing in the mollifying fumes before answering. 'She makes out she's so independent and brave, but the truth is just too horrible for me to even think about. I can't understand it no matter how hard I try, and I've read every bloody book in the world about schizophrenia. I mean, I don't even know what it is, what it's supposed to stand for.'

'The old "what is normal" question again?'

'The tragedy is that you're alienated from society, and you're alienated from your*self*. Written off as mad. I mean, how would you feel if mental health experts pronounced you mad? How would you prove them wrong?'

'Do *you* think Jasmine is insane?' Nadine asked.

The question startled me; I had never been asked this before, by anyone, because it was always implicitly assumed that I just went along with the opinions of everyone else. Jasmine was a recovering addict, and the addiction had made the chemicals in her brain go wrong, so she was also clinically insane. The pills the doctors gave her were called antipsychotics and there were many different types, mostly designed to block these things called dopamine receptors in her brain and reduce both the positive and negative symptoms of this thing called schizophrenia. Schizophrenia was a severe mental illness which, unchecked and untreated, would have rendered her too dysfunctional and deviant for a normal society. This was everything I'd been told, it was all that I knew, and it was true – of course it was true. I'd never questioned its truth.

'Abi?' Nadine whispered, reaching out and stroking my arm.

I eventually attempted an answer. 'I think she is very lonely and scared. And needy. My dad says she's still his baby.' I paused, blowing smoke circles and watching them waft and fade into the air above my head. 'She's demanding and infuriating and uncontrollable. She has no inhibitions and she sometimes doesn't make any sense. But how many times have I not made sense? Or you for that matter? No, I don't think she's insane. No more than anyone else. We all instinctively react to what our hearts and minds tell us, don't we?'

Nadine smiled at me in agreement, and I felt a sense of relief, like an unburdening, as she took my hand and held it in hers.

A rowdy group of three blokes shattered our private silence when they returned to their semi-erected tent next door to ours.

'All right girls?' one of them hiccuped, falling over the laces of his boots and ending up in a puddle of ominous-looking liquid. The atmosphere clanged with a familiar drunken vibe, and Nadine and I rolled our eyes at each other and retreated deeper into our sleeping bags.

'Fancy a smoke?' enquired another, a dumpy Brummie with orange hair and an impressive beer gut that made Jasmine's six-month pregnancy look positively lissom. He grinned over at us, not looking where he was going, and fell over his crumpled friend, who had not had the energy or the inclination to pick himself up off the ground.

'It's OK. We're just off to sleep now,' Nadine said.

'You're not staying outside are you?' asked the third, in a Welsh accent. 'It's gonna be pissing it down soon. Don't want you girls getting all wet in your skimpy little T-shirts. That would never do.'

'He's got a point,' I said. 'We'd better go inside.'

'Yeah, in a minute,' Nadine sighed.

'Give us a knock if you change your mind,' said Brummie, staggering to his feet, 'plenty of gear to go round.'

'We'll bear that in mind,' Nadine promised him. We watched and listened stoically as the three of them struggled clumsily into their fast-collapsing tent, amid cries of 'Watch it you bastard, that's my nob,' the clattering of glass, the fizzing crack of a can being opened, the strike of a match, the occasional soft thud of body on canvas, the rustle of clothing, the zipping of the entrance flap and finally, of sleeping bags. I woke Jasmine and we crawled on all fours into our tent, which was like an oven inside, thick with the smell of hot plastic and Pot Noodle. We lay on top of our sleeping bags and fanned ourselves, too sticky to sleep. Jasmine declared she had a craving for rhubarb and custard, but instead had to make do with an overripe banana salvaged from her backpack. She then wrote something in her notebook by torchlight, kissed us both goodnight and turned over to go back to sleep.

Things were relatively silent for a while, give or take the odd brief commotion from the boys' tent next door and the euphoric whistles and shrieks of distant revellers. Before long, as predicted, it started to rain, and the hypnotic smattering of the raindrops on the canvas above sent me into a trance. This was until I turned on my side and tried zipping up the sleeping bag beneath me, somehow managing to get my pubic hair caught in the zipper.

'Buggery bollocks!' I exclaimed in agony, for want of a better imprecation.

This pained cry prompted a bizarre game of 'swear-word tennis' with our drunken neighbours, who seized upon my involuntary outburst and elaborated with their own unique profanities. As I tried to extricate my pubes from the zipper, Brummie bloke bellowed out 'Beef curtains,' loud and proud. His mate was gripped by a fit of uncontrollable giggling before he managed to stammer, 'Hairy pie!'

The rain started beating down heavier. Dark shadowy splats dropped and drizzled down the side of the tent, thrumming hard against the fabric.

'Velvet love glove,' called out the Welsh bloke.

'Stench trench,' Brummie added.

'Bushy bicycle stand.' Welsh.

'Fabulous furry fuzzbox.' Giggly bloke.

I was about to tell them to shut up, when Nadine, who I had assumed was sleeping, added her own little donation: 'One-eyed trouser snake.'

And so the strange exchanges between our two camps continued, progressing quite naturally on to slang terms for various other body parts and functions. Even after the boys' tent collapsed and they had to stumble about blindly in the darkness with a wooden mallet and a handful of tent pegs, they still managed to come up with interesting and imaginative words and phrases, hollered back at us through the driving downpour. The last thing I remember before finally dozing off was Nadine wailing, 'Please can we stop this stupid bloody game?' in one ear and the sound of Jasmine's maniacal chuckling in the other.

I only decided the day before Nick's party that I would go to it – just because I wanted to prove that I wasn't afraid to see him again, and that I was well and truly over him. When I had finally prepared myself to go, I was as jittery and tense as I had once been in my young, starry-eyed early teens in a prelude to a first date. It was truly pathetic.

Nick's parents had gone away, so the party was held at their house in Radlett. The home bar was fully equipped, the DJ was enshrined at his decks with his headphones half-on, mixing away like a thing possessed, and the impetus to get bladdered was at an all-time high.

I spent the first hour or so latched on to Sylvie and Ben, not caring that I was acting the gooseberry so long as I maintained my evasion of Nick. I hid behind punch bowls and various soft furnishings, trying to blend myself into babbling crowds of people I had never met and keeping my head down and covering my face with my hair in a laughable attempt to conceal my true identity. I caught a tantalising glimpse of him every now and then before eventually pulling myself together and plucking up enough courage to approach him. It was an accident, really. I was outside in the garden ostensibly admiring Nick's parents' new crazy paving when suddenly I heard his voice behind me, talking loudly to someone about the latest Charlatans album and the extortionate price of disposable nappies. Or maybe it was disposable contact lenses. I inched slowly in his direction until I 'accidentally' bumped into him and he took a step backwards and said, 'Hey, watch it.' I turned round and his eyes looked me up and down as if he didn't recognise me, but of course, he did recognise me. 'Hey Abi, I didn't think you'd come.'

I tried to act aloof. 'I didn't think I would either,' I said. 'It would have been nice to get a formal invite rather than hearing about it from Sylvie.'

He gave me an odd look, as if he was trying to work me out.

Eventually he said, 'Well, it's good to see you again. It's been a while.'

'Yes,' I agreed, unable to think of anything sufficiently flippant or nonchalant to say. Instead I tried to hold his gaze as I took a delicate sip of wine from my glass. However, my hand was a little unsteady, so the 'delicate sip' was therefore more of a sloshy slurp, and Nick's typically absent gaze was diverted over my shoulder at someone or something far more interesting than an ex-girlfriend trying to look sophisticated and seductive.

'Wait there a second, will you,' Nick mumbled at me, touching my shoulder gently and walking away. I obeyed dumbly, and stood fixed to the spot watching three of Nick's friends and his brother dealing drugs under the dining table. A freshly coupled couple giggled their way up the stairs, people milled around smoking and laughing and talking loudly above the music, the curtains at the French windows flapped in the breeze, and I stood in the middle of it, an outsider on the inside. It suddenly occurred to me how pointless it all was. What was I doing there? Who did I think I was? The past year of my life had already slid away into obscurity, and I hadn't changed one little bit since splitting up with Nick. I thought I had been growing up, learning about life, but all I had been doing was throwing up and learning which drink and drug combinations gave the best highs and the worst hangovers. I resolved to leave the party there and then. I knew virtually nobody there, and the only reason I had gone in the first place was to settle a score that didn't even need settling. It was just to heal my stupid wounded pride.

'Thought you might like some of this,' Nick said, appearing again suddenly, and snapping me out of my ruminative mood just as I was about to put my glass on the table, fetch my coat and get lost. He waved a bag of white powder and wiggled his eyebrows at me in a way that he knew drove me crazy. No – that *used* to drive me crazy.

I found myself talking to him, clearly and sensibly, even though I could feel my face flush deeper with every word I spoke. 'I thought the only powder you were into these days was baby powder, Nicholas,' I said. 'Where is Sarah tonight, by the way? At home with your little darlings I suppose?'

His face fell. 'Sarah couldn't make it,' he snapped. He looked around, then snatched my arm and pulled me into the corner of the room. 'Look, my private life is none of your fucking business. I thought you'd be over all this by now.'

I gave him a wide-eyed look. 'Over what? Over *you*? Ha! Don't flatter yourself, I was over you before you even dumped me.'

'Look, this is my party and I can kick you out if I don't want you here, you know.'

'Oh, I'm *so* scared by that threat.'

He pushed me, just a gentle shove, and I pushed him back, harder. We glared at each other and neither of us said anything until Nick came out with this little gem:

'Do you want to go upstairs?'

'Ex*cuse* me?'

'Just for a chat, y'know.'

I blinked at him, trying to prevent a barrage of emotions from bubbling to the surface. *Why upstairs? What's wrong with down here?*

'Um . . . well, er . . . I don't know if . . . oh, all right then, just for a little while,' I mumbled, demonstrating not for the first time the triumph of hormones over rationality.

Nick's room was exactly how I remembered it, if a little emptier. He didn't live with his parents any more of course (he had set up home with Sarah and the twins in a semi in Milton Keynes apparently), but the place still smelled of him – a faint whiff of deodorant, hair gel, clean and dirty socks and wanky tissues, all these smells mixed together to make the aroma of Nick. I know it sounds vile, but to me it was aphrodisiacal. I felt my self-control disintegrate slowly, along with my pride, principles and promises to myself that I would never even entertain the idea of being unfaithful to Marbles. Especially not with the scum of the earth.

'How's university life then?' Nick asked, his mellifluous tones lulling me into reminiscent rapture. He sat on his bed and indicated that I should sit next to him, which I did, willingly, foolishly.

'University life is just peachy,' I told him, smoothing down the hem of my new dress. 'Thanks for asking.'

'So, have you met someone . . . else? Someone special?'

Yes, yes yes! He's wonderful and I'm missing him like crazy.

'Well, kind of. Not really.'

What the hell was I saying?

'Sylvie mentioned that you were going out with someone . . .'

'Yeah, I am really. Nothing serious.'

I had to face it, I was no longer in control of any logical or reasonable part of my brain. There was an impassioned battle going on between my conscience, my rationality and my loins. My loins were winning. Nick edged closer to me, just a little bit. My conscience was struck a fatal blow by the ample arsenal of my hormones. I edged closer to him, just a little bit. He kicked the door shut with his foot.

I am a silly tart. I am a stupid, stupid tart.

'You don't want any of my brother's coke, then?' Nick enquired, licking his finger and dipping it into the bag of powder with a demented grin. 'It's class stuff. You can't get much better than this.' He put his finger in his mouth and sucked on it slowly, eyeing me with an unsubtle horniness, a ravenous look which I did my best to ignore. It took all my effort, all my strength, to study the design of the carpet and mentally count backwards in threes from ninety-nine.

'No thanks. I'm quite happy just with wine,' I said, tipping my glass at him before taking another swig, and nearly choking on it. Sex appeal was radiating from Nick with a fierceness that was hard to bear, like standing too close to a fire. Eighty-seven, eighty-four, eighty-one, seventy-eight . . .

He put his hand near my leg. I felt his eyes on me. 'Do you want to know why I split up with you, Abi?' he asked.

Seventy-two, sixty-nine . . . sixty-six, sixty-nine, sixty-five, sixty . . . brilliant, now the mathematical part of my brain had also decided to pack up.

'No, I don't care,' I replied weakly.

'You've got so much emotional baggage. You're always so uptight about something or other. When I tried to get close to you . . .'

I turned to glare at him in disbelief. '*Emotional baggage?*' I echoed incredulously. 'Where's this emotional baggage bollocks come from?' I moved away from him and folded my arms in defiance and outrage. '*You're* the one with a girlfriend who you treat like shit and two kids who you should be with tonight. *That's* baggage, Nick. That's what I call *real* baggage.'

I had obviously struck a chord. He retracted his hand and lowered his eyes. 'You're right,' he mumbled. 'I never meant for things to turn out this way. I never meant to hurt you.'

The cliché alone was enough to hurt me. I took the opportunity to get out of the room while I still had the chance. Nick had fallen silent and humbled, so I put my empty wine glass on the floor and tried to gain some composure. Nanoseconds before I was about to stand up and bid him a polite but suitably cold farewell, Nick made a sudden movement and, to my shock, my horror, my delight, he pushed me down on the bed and kissed me roughly, his hands finding bare flesh at once as he slid them up the inside of my dress. All hopes of keeping my fidelity intact wilted as he pressed himself against me, the familiar taste and physical feeling of him on me firing my entire body into a tailspin of lust.

'God . . . God, I hate you,' I murmured. My sheer tights crackled with static as he expertly pulled them off and then slipped my knickers down over my knees, pressing his face in at the divergence of my thighs.

'I hate you too,' he assured me, undressing swiftly and pulling me on top of him. When you cheat on someone you really care about, no matter how good the sex is, you will inevitably feel like shit afterwards. At that precise time, the voice of my conscience was merely a dying gasp, and my hormones were having the mother of victory parties. But afterwards, *afterwards*, the inanity, the awful stupidity of my actions hit me hard. The guilt I felt after sex with Nick was made worse by the fact that the sex was, in the event, a complete let-down. Buzzing with the well-preserved memories of the way things used to be between us, I had accepted and reciprocated his advances with a great sense of eagerness, expectation, and . . . relief, I suppose. Relief that he still found me attractive. It sounds piteous when it's analysed so simply, after the event, but that was the plain truth. But Nick had plunged into proceedings with ill-deserved aplomb and five minutes later, after a literal anti-climax, we fell asleep. Or rather, he was asleep and snoring like a traction engine and I was staring blankly at the ceiling in terror, searching for one small reason why I had just let him have sex with me. When it became obvious that this reason was neither evident nor forthcoming, I removed his deadweight arm from across my chest and got the hell out of there.

My nephew was born on 19 August, almost two months early but otherwise fighting fit. The birth was nerve-racking and yet magical, fraught with stress and raw emotion from beginning to end.

Jasmine surprised us all. After initial, frenzied demands for morphine, 'and fucking loads of the stuff', she handled her labour in a composed and courageous manner, even asking for Jane as her birthing partner rather than Dad, me, or the hyper-vexed Seth, who remained in a state of oblivious panic for the entire sixteen hours.

'What if it isn't mine?'

'Shut up, Seth.'

'What if there's something wrong with it?'

'Shut up, Seth.'

'What if . . .'

'SHUT UP, Seth.'

Eventually, at half past four in the afternoon, Jane swung triumphantly through the doors of the maternity ward into the waiting room where we had been going out of our minds for what felt like days. Her expression was one of absolute euphoria.

'She . . . she's done it,' she gushed. 'She's . . . had a baby.'

Seth strode over to her, his leather boots squeaking on the shiny floor. As the likely father, his first question was probably going to be 'Is it a boy or a girl?' But his query was a bit different.

'What colour is it?'

Jane was far too emotional to notice that this was quite an offensive question, so she just blurted out, 'Pink. It's a beautiful pink baby boy, Seth. Four pounds two ounces. Congratulations. He's perfect.'

And with that, Seth flung his arms around Jane and wept aloud.

And a lot more crying went on after that, not least from the new addition to the Page family, who Jasmine named Floyd Angel despite opposition from Dad and Jane.

'How about James? That's a nice name,' Jane had suggested optimistically.

'There's already enough "J" names in this house,' Jasmine said. 'I'm calling him Floyd.'

'Or what about David?' Dad piped up. 'There's a good English name. David Bowie, David Gilmour . . . they're two of your heroes, aren't they?'

Jasmine was quick to point out that there were also a lot of tossers around with the name David. 'I'm calling him Floyd, and that's the end of it. Mum would have loved it.'

So, Floyd it was. He had to be kept in the Special Care Baby Unit for a while, but apart from his small size and a touch of jaundice he was healthy and strong and, as far as I was concerned, a nephew to feel proud of.

I expected the arrival of the baby to change Jasmine drastically, but the change was only very subtle. She did become noticeably subdued and temperate, devoting herself completely and with apparent ease to her maternal responsibilities. It seemed to me that motherhood was the ultimate accomplishment to her; it had given her a new perspective. Finally, after so many years of uncertainty, she felt she had something to call her own, a sense of true identity, of belonging and purpose. My niggling problems – the clandestine indiscretion with my bastard ex-boyfriend being an overriding one – were pushed to the back of my mind as I helped Dad and Jane rally round with weekly Mothercare excursions and occasional night duties.

'It's just awesome,' Jasmine said to me one evening, exhausted but upbeat and smiling despite the fact she was in the middle of changing Floyd's nappy. 'I can't believe he's mine. I feel humble. I feel . . . amazed. I just can't believe it.'

'Well, *I* believe it,' I moaned. 'I got bugger all sleep last night thanks to your sprog and his incessant squawking.'

'He just hasn't got his sleeping patterns sorted out yet, have you?' She tied up the nappy bag and leaned over Floyd's writhing little curled-up body, making cooing and clucking noises at him. He gurgled and whacked her on the nose with his fist.

'Jasmine, babies have no concept of sleeping patterns. They just wake up and make a noise if they want feeding or changing.'

'Or if they want a cuddle,' she said, picking him up and holding him against her. 'Babies smell so lovely,' she enthused, sniffing the top of his baldish head with a rapturous look on her face. 'I could smell Floyd's head all day. It's like fuzzy peach.'

'Whatever, Jas.'

The day before Marbles was due to arrive back from America – a week or so before the start of my second university year – I took Jasmine out to our local and we spent some quality time alone together for the first time in what felt like ages. It was a long-overdue opportunity for a sisterly heart-to-heart.

'You think I'm coping, don't you?' Jasmine said quietly, as I brought the drinks over from the bar – an orange juice for her, and the same for me, with a double vodka shot in it.

'You *are* coping,' I replied, sitting down opposite her. 'You've been brilliant.' She sighed and looked down at her hands. 'I'm useless without you lot. Thanks for all your help. I know I act like an ungrateful cow most of the time, but you and Dad have been brilliant. And Jane is just . . . well, I don't know what I'd do without her.'

'Yeah, she's great. She really cares about you, you know that?'

'I know.' I was surprised to see her eyes well up with tears. 'I owe you all so much.'

'Don't be silly.'

She reached both her hands across the table and gripped my arms, the tears falling from her eyes as her voice wavered with emotion. 'I'm . . . I'm still me though, even after all this,' she stuttered. 'My priorities have changed, but I'm still *me*.'

'Of course you're still you, Jas. We wouldn't want you any other way.'

She bowed her head and sighed, taking deep breaths before continuing. 'It's only a matter of time,' she said, 'before I let everyone down again. Floyd deserves the best and I can't give him that. I can't even give him second best. What chance has he got with a loser ex-junkie psychotic for a mother?'

'Hey, don't you *dare* say that. You're a wonderful mother to that baby. You've surprised all the doctors, you've even exceeded all our expectations of you. I am so, *so* proud of you. We all are. You're amazing.'

She shook her head, not looking at me. 'I am shit,' she said, spitting out each word. Her eyes flickered back up and she stared at me, her bitten nails digging into my arms as she pulled me firmly towards her. 'And I'm *scared*, sis,' she sobbed, her eyes swimming with more tears. 'I'm just so bloody scared.'

'Listen to me,' I whispered, moving my chair around to sit next to her. 'I don't want you talking like this. It's just this post-natal depression thing. You don't mean all this, I know you don't. So many people care about you and now you've got a baby who is relying on you to hold yourself together. Look at me, Jasmine. *Look at me.* Everyone who knows you – who *really* knows you – thinks you are so strong, so . . . incredible. Can't you see that?'

Her hair, now rust-coloured and limp, hung over her shoulders as she hunched forward and wiped her cheeks with the back of her hand. 'I'm such a burden to everyone,' she muttered. 'I feel like I can't talk to anyone about how I feel because they'll only take my baby away from me. They'll say I'm not fit to be a mother, and they'd be right.'

I sipped my drink and wondered how I could comfort her. 'Didn't your midwife talk to you about this? Didn't she say you'd probably feel a bit down for a while after the birth?' I put my arm around her and said, 'We're all here to help you, Jas. We'll help you get through it.'

She fixed me with her doleful doe eyes. 'I know you mean well,

Abi. You can't understand that I will never be free for as long as I'm *me.* It's not going to go away, and I can't keep up the pretence any longer. And now I've lumbered a poor innocent baby with my problems as well as you, Dad, Jane and everyone else whose time I have wasted over so many futile fucking years.'

'But . . . you're well again, Jas. You've more than proved yourself. We love Floyd and we love you, and there's nothing for you to worry about. I promise. We're here for you.'

Of course I meant what I said, but it felt like I was reading from a script, that I was just saying what I knew she wanted me to say, repeating well-rehearsed lines. She sighed sadly. I knew there was more she wanted to share with me, but instead she held up her full glass to my nearly empty one and tried to smile. 'A toast,' she mumbled quietly, sitting back in her chair and pausing for effect. 'To sanity, freedom and my beautiful son.'

I clinked my glass against hers and said, 'Hold the sanity.'

We drained our glasses and she turned to me, now bright and smiling again as she leaned across to kiss me. 'You're the best sister in the world,' she said. 'The absolute best.'

I was comforted rather than unsettled by this emotional conversation with Jasmine; gratified that she felt she could still rely on me as a confidante whenever she felt depressed or frightened, and confident that I had provided the reassurance she needed. I was convinced that eventually Jasmine would settle down with Floyd (and possibly even Seth) to lead the life she'd always wanted, and in the mean time she knew she could rely on us, her old erstwhile family, to support her every step of the way.

The thing that was really troubling me was seeing Marbles again – my growing excitement at finally being reunited with him was marred by the guilt I felt over my treacherous shenanigans, guilt which only seemed to get worse by the day. He returned from America on Sunday morning and called me on his mobile immediately, even before sleeping off his jet lag. Even before collecting his luggage from the carousel at Heathrow.

'Been up to much then?' he asked, after we had got the usual gushy, romantic pleasantries out of the way.

'Oh, this and that,' I sighed vaguely.

'How about staying round mine for a few days before uni starts? I've really got to see you before my nads implode.'

Marbles was not well known for his gentlemanly tact and charm. After considering an array of possible responses to this proposition, I said, 'I've got a nephew.'

'Oh nice one, Abi. Congrats to your sis. Anyway, what do you say? My place tomorrow maybe?'

'I'd love to.'

'I'll pick you up in my dad's convertible at about midday. If that doesn't get you frothing at the gusset, wait till you see my bedroom.'

'You're such a poser, Maurice.'

'True, but a damned sexy one. You'll get to meet my family I'm afraid. I warn you now, my dad's a bit . . . er . . . a bit kind of "care in the community", if you get my drift.'

'What do you mean?'

'You'll see. So, tomorrow yeah?'

'Sounds good to me. Looking forward to it.'

'Not half as much as me.'

When I hung up I realised that I was possibly falling in love with him. I also realised that I had every reason to hate myself.

That night I couldn't sleep so instead I showered and washed my hair then slunk off to the kitchen to drink endless filter coffee until three minutes before noon, when Marbles heralded his arrival with a screech of brakes and a noisy novelty klaxon.

The Venables family lived in an absolutely stunning house in Surrey, more or less midway between my own home and the university. Straight after I was briefly introduced to his 'embarrassingly unhip' dad ('Please, call me Nigel. It's not my name but I think it rather suits me, don't you?'), his brother Ollie (a taller, more chiselled but less sexy version of Marbles) and his sister Steph (a wannabe actress who was saving up for breast implants), Marbles impatiently dragged me up to his bedroom where I was held as a willing sex hostage for forty-eight hours.

It was only after two days of ravenous, frantic fornication that I finally plucked up enough courage to confess. We were sprawled across his bed and I was stuffing my face with Maltesers and grapes at a ratio of ten to one while he dozily watched a violent film on his TV, his arm draped around my shoulder, fingers stroking my back. I tipped my face up to kiss him and he held me close as he kissed me back, and I was suddenly so overcome with guilt that when we pulled apart I blurted out: 'Marbles . . . I think there's something you should know.'

'Oh yeah, what's that?' he grinned down at me and looked as if he was about to say something facetious, but then he saw the seriousness on my face and his smile faded. 'What?' he demanded, sitting up and clutching my shoulders, staring into my eyes for some clue when I didn't respond. 'What is it?'

I thought about the worst-case scenario – Marbles would go totally apeshit, cut my tits off and boot me out of the window, then hunt Nick down and torture him slowly with the aid of a vat of boiling oil, a blunt army knife and a roll of barbed wire. The best-case scenario, I supposed, would be for him to just shrug his shoulders and say, 'Never mind. We're all only human. I met some Pamela Anderson look-alike on Miami beach, so I guess we're even.'

But somehow that wasn't the reaction I wanted either.

I knew I *had* to tell him, but I just didn't know how to get the words out. My mind sluggishly mulled over the best – or least dreadful – way to break it to him.

'I'm so sorry,' I mumbled eventually, 'I didn't want it to happen . . .'

Marbles reached the obvious conclusion and pulled away from me, instantly repelled. There was a terrible silence.

'Who was it?' he asked eventually, his voice subdued, menacingly so.

I lowered my eyes and willed the shag pile to swallow me up. 'My ex,' I whispered, face burning, heart sinking.

'Oh, great. Just fantastic.' He got out of the bed with lightning speed, pushing me aside as he grabbed his shorts from the floor.

Self-loathing surged up inside me. My tears did nothing to recede Marbles's anger.

'You fucking bitch,' he yelled, pulling his shorts on, shaking with rage. 'You fucking *bitch*.'

'Marbles, please . . . I'm so sorry . . . it was a mistake . . .' I stammered, trying to focus on him through a blur of tears. 'I'm so sorry . . .'

'What good is fucking *sorry*? Three months I was faithful to you. I didn't even *think* about anyone else.' He turned to me, his eyes blazing as he did his trousers up and tightened his belt. His movements were brisk, furious – I had never seen him this angry before, he was like a different person.

'So. Was he good? Was it worth it?' he demanded, after a dreadful silence.

I bit my lip, my cheeks stinging hot with tears. I couldn't look at him, I couldn't speak, I felt too ashamed.

'How many times?' he shouted. 'How many times did you fuck him?'

I was struck dumb; pathetic tears poured incessantly as he stood over me.

'Once? Twice? Ten times?'

'Please don't . . .'

'And why did you have to go and tell me *now*? After sleeping with me again? Making me believe that . . .' He trailed off and turned away as he unwrapped a packet of B & H, now sounding upset more than angry. I glanced up at him sheepishly, knowing another apology would be insultingly inadequate. He eyed me darkly as he smoked. 'Do you love him?'

I put my head in my hands and sighed. 'No. I hate him,' I said, semi-honestly.

'That's supposed to make me feel better is it?' he spat contemptuously. 'My girlfriend shags someone behind my back and she doesn't even have the decency or the self-respect to even *like* the cunt.'

'*Please* . . . I only told you because . . . because I don't want to lie to you. Our relationship means a lot to me. Please forgive me. I don't want to break up with you.'

'Well it's a bit bloody late for that, isn't it?' He took several deep puffs on the cigarette in quick succession, then used the stub to light a second fag, which he smoked with just as much agitation.

'But . . . I care about you,' I said, genuinely meaning it, but the words came out sounding weedy and hollow. 'I *really* care about you.'

'Yeah, right. God, you make me feel sick. I can't bear to even look at you. You were the only girl I ever . . .' he turned away, blinking back tears. He ran his hand through his hair and sighed, setting his jaw and glancing back to me with a stern expression. I knew he was as upset as I was, but his rage added strength to his resolve. 'S'pose I'd better take you home then,' he sighed, bending down to pick up my clothes from the floor and the foot of his bed, throwing them at me without looking.

'Marbles . . .' I pleaded with him, knowing it would achieve nothing but nevertheless sacrificing my last shred of dignity as I dropped to my knees on the floor and literally grovelled for forgiveness.

'Get dressed,' he snapped, pulling a shirt out of his wardrobe and purposely turning his back to me as he buttoned it up and tucked it loosely into his belt. I was just pulling on my Levi's, cringing under Marbles's frosty glances, when there was a sudden shrill noise from the other end of the room. It rang out several times before Marbles walked over to his desk and picked up his mobile, looking at it curiously before taking a deep breath and holding it to his ear, greeting the caller with a gruffly laconic '*Yes?*'

I sloped off into the bathroom with my bag to clean up my blotchy face.

I splashed some cold water on my cheeks then sat on the closed toilet seat and held a towel to my face, trying hard to stop myself from having another outburst. I was sick to the core with regret and unhappiness.

'Abi?' Suddenly Marbles appeared in the doorway, his expression of rage and revulsion now replaced by one of bewilderment. He held out his mobile and said, 'It's for you.' His voice sounded weird, strained.

My heart, already in a palpitant state, made a terrible lurch as I accepted the phone and tentatively pressed it to my ear. Dad and

Jane were under strict instructions to only call Marbles's mobile in case of a dire emergency.

'Hello?' A heavy, awful sense of foreboding made my voice tremble. This sense of foreboding turned to total terror when all I heard on the other end of the line was barely audible snuffling and confused whisperings. 'Hello?' I repeated, more forcefully, trying to control myself from yelling, screaming, wailing. 'Dad? Jane? Is that you?'

Hysteria rose in me. Something was wrong, something was very, very wrong. '*Hello?*'

Marbles mumbled something and started stroking my hair, a gesture of concern that I barely noticed.

'I can't hear you,' I gibbered frantically, feeling as if something was blocking my windpipe, feeling like I was sinking in quicksand. I held the phone away from me and blinked up at Marbles desperately. 'I can't hear anything . . .' I told him feebly.

'Abigail?' A distant, shaky voice – Jane's – crackled out of the phone and I quickly put it back to my ear and blurted out, 'Yes? Jane? What's wrong? What is it?'

'Oh, Abi . . .' she said, her voice trailing off to a whimper. 'Oh my God, Abi, I'm so sorry, oh my God I'm so sorry, so sorry . . . '

Jane never blasphemed. I listened to her weeping, choking, and suddenly I knew – I just *knew.* The realisation fell down on me, crushed me, knocked the breath out of me.

'No . . .' I whispered, trembling all over, suddenly dizzy and nauseous, 'No . . . please . . . no . . .'

'Darling, she's . . . dead. She's dead, darling. Jasmine. Jasmine. Oh my God, Jasmine is dead. Oh my God, I don't believe it, she's k-killed herself and she was only here with us yesterday and she seemed so happy and oh my God, now she's *dead.*' Her voice rose and rose to a soprano pitch, culminating in a fit of crying and howling. The words smashed into my consciousness like massive boulders into a tiny pond, sending out huge waves of monumental sorrow and shock through my entire body. I said nothing. I did nothing. I was numb. Marbles knelt down in front of me and put his arms around me, drawing me to him, but I didn't, *couldn't* react, because that would have meant accepting it.

The room started spinning, everything around me sliding in and out of focus as the mobile fell from my hand and I squeaked out three tremulous words: 'I'm coming home.'

11

The Long Way Home

Schizophrenia cannot be understood without understanding despair.
R. D. Laing, *The Divided Self*, 1960

Marbles drove fast and hard, one hand on the steering wheel while the other lit and held and flicked cigarettes, one after another. The rain was chucking it down, sheets of it sloughed from the front and rear windows by rapidly vacillating wipers. The lights of oncoming cars rose and dipped as they sloshed past, the wind-whipped rain drumming continuously while the wipers squeaked and thudded to keep up with the deluge. Neither of us spoke. I stared straight ahead, and Marbles didn't look over at me once.

We arrived back at my house and Marbles deftly swung the car into the drive, the vibrations of the chassis shuddering away beneath us as he killed the lights and the ignition. Together we sat in silence, looking out into the darkness at nothing. The rain had eased but the sky was tar-black and sporadic droplets still splattered the glass of the windscreen. I concentrated on the sounds of the dying storm outside until I became aware of nothing else.

The only light on in the house was the porch light. Marbles took his seatbelt off then leant across to unfasten mine. I didn't move an inch.

'Do you want to tell me what's happened?' he asked eventually, twisting around in his seat to look at me. His tone was direct but gentle, and yet I couldn't respond because I didn't even want to tell myself what had happened.

'Is there anything I can do?' He reached out and touched my hand and all I could do was shake my head, every fibre of my body screaming out for him to take me in his arms and let me howl myself hoarse. After a slight pause, he clicked his door open and walked around the car to open the door at my side. He crouched down and looked up at me anxiously, not caring that the rain was spitting down on his glasses. 'Abi?' His hand on mine again and he held my fingers to his lips and kissed them, all the while watching me intently for any flicker of response.

Jane appeared at the front door. Our eyes met and I felt the blood drain from my face. Marbles took my arm and levered me carefully from the seat. As we stood facing each other, he put his hands on my shoulders and said, 'Just call me if you need me, OK?'

I remained motionless while he got back into the car, slammed the door and turned the ignition. The tyres crunched over gravel as he moved slowly out of the drive, tail lights throwing back bright white beams then vanishing around the corner in an instant, every sound remote and echoic in my ears, like being underwater.

As with all devastating news, the news of Jasmine's suicide took a long time to sink in. The shock was more tremendous than anything I'd ever known, but slowly the dream-like daze of disbelief gave way to a natural mourning, a mourning that I thought would never end, that made me ache from crying.

In the early hours of Wednesday 27 September 1995, while everyone else was sleeping, Jasmine wrote five suicide notes, moved Floyd's crib from her room into Dad and Jane's, went downstairs and drank half a bottle of spirits, dropped some acid, threw up repeatedly in our front garden, took Seth's motorbike from the garage and then, still dressed in her nightie and with no leathers or helmet, crashed it explosively off a deserted road ten miles or so from the house. This time she had been determined that there would be no chance of revival, no possibility of being brought back to life. No ambulance men, no doctors, no stomach pumps, no antidote, no scars, no slow recovery, just two sombre policemen on the doorstep at midday and a death certificate confirming 'death by misadventure'.

She left a note for each of us: me, Dad, Jane, our grandparents and even Lewis. Dad locked himself away for the week leading up to the funeral and sobbed incessantly, day and night. He wouldn't talk to anyone, he wouldn't see anyone, he wouldn't eat or sleep. With suicide, there is always the issue of blame, and he blamed himself completely – and of course, wrongly – for Jasmine's death. We were all utterly beside ourselves with grief and for ages just walked around the house in shattered silence, shell-shocked and dumb, not answering the phone (which more or less rang continuously), not acknowledging anything.

The start of the second university year came and went, and the week after Jasmine's death – two days before the funeral – Nadine took leave and visited me to offer her support. This was a particularly touching gesture as not only was I the most miserable company anyone could inflict on themselves, but because she was the only one of my friends who could offer me any real comfort – and more importantly, the only one who was genuinely prepared to make an effort to do so. The house was slowly filling up with various friends and relatives in the lead-up to the funeral, so Nadine and I slept downstairs on the couch together. Or, more accurately, she whispered soothing words in my ear until she finally lost consciousness, and I stared sleeplessly night after night as memories of Jasmine flashed relentlessly through my mind at a rate of a thousand per millisecond, like a disjointed film, a dream being rewound and played back. It was suddenly as if my life had no meaning – it had been inane enough when Jasmine was alive, but with her gone, an important part of me just seemed no longer to exist. Or at least no longer to function. I felt empty, hollow, totally absorbed in a new, cheerless, alien world that I couldn't – and didn't want to – escape from.

It was Nadine who persuaded me to read Jasmine's suicide note, which for a long time remained scrunched up in its unopened envelope in the pocket of my dressing gown.

'Whatever she wrote,' she said, 'she wrote it especially for you. It might actually help you.' She reached into my pocket and tried to thrust the small white envelope into my hands, but just the sight of Jasmine's childishly scrawled words *To my sister* on the front was enough to make me sick with sorrow.

I pushed it away and croaked, 'No, I can't. I just can't.'

'Well ... how about I read it to you, then?' she offered hesitantly. 'Do you want me to do that for you . . . ?'

I shook my head.

'Are you sure?'

I nodded.

She held out her hand. 'Here, come with me,' she said.

'Where?'

'Follow me.'

I took her hand and she led me up the stairs, stopping outside Jasmine's room. I held back and stared at her in wide-eyed disbelief, horrified at what she was suggesting.

'No. No way,' I said. 'I can't go in there.'

'Yes you can.' She opened the door and stepped inside, but I wrenched my hand out of hers and backed away.

'You don't understand,' I whispered.

We looked at each other for a moment, the only sound being the background blip-blip of Lewis's computer game across the hall and alternate male and female voices from the kitchen downstairs, talking in hushed tones.

'It just takes a bit of courage,' Nadine said softly, opening the door a little wider so I could see Jasmine's bed, patchy autumn sunshine from the veiled window dappling light on to the creased sheets.

I hung my head and sighed deeply. 'Courage that I haven't got,' I confessed.

'You know that's not true. You're Jasmine's *sister*. Surely you must have a little bit of what she had?'

'She had my share,' I said.

Nadine smiled at me sadly. 'I'm sorry. I thought it might have been a nice idea. I mean . . .'

'You know, you're right. You *are* right.' I stepped forward and hesitated, then took a deep breath before moving inside. Nadine stood silently by the door as I wandered around the room as if in a daze, feeling overwhelmed by Jasmine's presence. Her few belongings – old books, mostly unread, favourite teddy bears sitting in a row under her window, posters, drawings, pictures and cards from old friends stuck to the wall, hundreds of seventies vinyl records and cassettes, mostly sleeveless or boxless, photo frames, mostly framing nothing but a blank space – everything was just how I remembered it, just exactly how she had left it. And it all felt so eerie – the duvet on the bed was thrown back and crumpled just as she had left it and there was a stone cold cup of coffee sitting on her bedside table, as if still waiting for her to return. The floor was littered with screwed-up balls of paper, tear-soaked tissues filled the waste paper basket, snapshots removed from the family album and scattered around. A picture of Floyd on the day he returned from hospital. A picture of Jasmine and Mum from twenty years ago, flying a kite on Hampstead Heath. A grainy picture of Dad with his old trademark beard and bell-bottoms, holding me under one arm and Jasmine upside-down under the other, the pair of us squealing in excitement and fear as he leered into the camera with a barmy look of fatherly derangement. And the only family portrait taken of all four of us, taken just a year before our mum died.

Nadine watched me as I sat down on Jasmine's bed, on the patchwork quilt she had made herself, and held some of her favourite clothes to my face, breathing in her aroma deeply, letting it wash over me. It was Jasmine, jasmine, indescribably evoking smells, everything was redolent of her, saturated with her. The spirit of her was ambient; a discernible feeling of peace, of calm, of final resolution. I wasn't afraid any more. I held out my hand for the letter and Nadine handed it to me wordlessly, tears streaming from her own eyes as she tried to smile at me.

I tore open the envelope and tried to focus on the scrap of paper inside.

Make something of your life.

Do it for me.
I love you.
J.

Marbles and Alex travelled up together on the day of the funeral and provided shoulders and tissues throughout the ceremony. Dad, emaciated and ghostly, sat at the front clinging to Jane with his head bowed. Floyd was fractious throughout the funeral, but Lewis bawled louder and for longer. His note had simply said, *When there's too many snakes and not enough ladders, the game isn't fun any more. Love Jasmine x*

Dad's note had been heart-breaking. Jasmine had written *I love you* over and over again in her spidery handwriting, and finally *I'm so sorry, Dad, please forgive me* in squashed capitals at the bottom of the page when she had run out of room.

Jane, who somehow managed to maintain the family through the ordeal, devotedly gave Floyd the love and care he needed and that the rest of us were too preoccupied and grief-stricken to give him. Her note explained more than any of the others: *I just can't pretend any more. Floyd was more than I ever deserved, and I know you will be good to him like you were to us for all those years. Sorry isn't enough and I can't think of what to write that will justify what I'm about to do. Nothing can. J x*

I asked Nadine if she would read out one of Jasmine's poems at the funeral, and she did so – loudly, clearly, and with absolute feeling. The poem was called 'Sanity Fair' and Jasmine had written it when she was first committed to Rayneham, in 1988. By the time Nadine had finished reciting it, nearly everyone in the congregation – even the vicar – was in floods of tears. At the end of the service, Jane had insisted that Pink Floyd's 'Comfortably Numb' played everyone out.

By the time the funeral was over, I did feel that I had gone some way to accepting her death. At least, I came to realise that looking for a rational explanation was pointless – there wasn't one – and that trying to attribute blame was equally pointless. Her epitaph message read, 'Jasmine Liberty Page 1969–1995. You were loved by everyone who knew you', and it struck me how ironic it was that only now, after her death, her middle name for the first time had some kind of congruence. And that nobody had ever really *known* her. Some people might have said it was a wasted life, some may have described her as selfish and cowardly for killing herself, and I think they were the people who knew her least of all.

After the 'party' (a celebration of Jasmine's life held at Seth's house, which involved being approached by countless old friends and distant relatives and past social workers, all of whom were eager to remind me that my sister was 'extraordinary' and 'gifted' and 'unique'), Marbles took Nadine and Alex and me back to Brighton in his car. He let me fiddle about with Jasmine's tapes in the cassette player, and nobody complained even once when I replayed the same songs over and over, turning the volume up and down and up again and weeping as I whispered the lyrics under my breath.

Even back at university, even after trying to settle back into the old student routine, I could not take my mind off Jasmine. I thought I would never come to terms with it. Time after time I found myself writing letters to her, picking up the phone to talk to her, hearing sounds in the night and thinking, *hoping* it was her, seeing people in the street who bore little or no resemblance to her and running up to them joyfully before realising my mistake and apologising, more disappointed and sad than embarrassed.

Nadine suggested I should see a counsellor, but I insisted that I just needed to be left alone for a while.

So everyone kept out of my way. Or rather, I kept out of their way, confining myself to the upstairs room I was supposed to be sharing with Marbles (had we not split up), while he transformed the shabby front room into a makeshift bedroom for himself. Everyone else also kept their distance until I realised I was starting to feel lonely and isolated and it wasn't really helping me at all. I was just languishing uselessly in my own self-pity.

But life went on, regardless.

Rachel and Simon got married on 5 November, just a week before their baby was due, giving a whole new slant to the tradition of fireworks night. As if to counterbalance the tragedy of Jasmine's funeral, the comical farce that was their wedding was enough to lift me out of my gloom for an entire day. The service was held at a tiny little Methodist church near Rachel's parents' house in Leeds, and the reception was in a massive marquee in Simon's parents' garden. By some ironic twist, Simon had chosen Frank the Goth to be his best man, and the pair of them looked earnest and nervous in their matching top hats and tails as they waited outside the church for Rachel to turn up in a silver limo with her dad and her chief bridesmaid. A catalogue of minor disasters ensued: Rachel's dad, already pissed out of his skull, toppled over as soon as he got out of the car, hitting his head on the stone steps leading up to the entrance of the church, and getting blood on his hired suit. Rachel had a small fit and declared that she was starting to have contractions and that the whole thing would have to be called off. Her bridesmaid tucked her nebulous skirt into her knickers and tried to hijack the limo to take Rachel straight to the hospital. Then Rachel changed her mind and said she wasn't going to let her dad's alcoholism and her impending firstborn get in the way of her marriage to Simon. After a few frantic moments, she decided it was a false alarm anyway and the three of them boldly made their way up the aisle. Rachel floated expectantly, the bridesmaid toddled awkwardly, forgetful of the fact her skirt was still hitched up at the back, and Rachel's father hobbled, clinging on for dear life to his daughter's arm and beaming away proudly in spite of the fresh claret that had started to trickle from his head wound.

It was in the middle of an undeniably touching ceremony as 'I do's' were being bandied about with much sincerity that Nadine leaned over towards me and whispered in my ear. 'Did you ever tell Marbles about you-know-what?'

I stared at her vacantly. 'What's that?'

She tutted, nudging me in the ribs. 'You know what *you-know-what* is,' she muttered, 'Simon and Frankie. The "affair that never was".'

'Oh.' I smiled faintly and turned to the front as Simon fumbled a ring on to Rachel's finger and several wails of sentimental joy arose from the front of the church. 'No. Best forgotten really, I think.'

'Yeah, maybe you're right.'

'I think those two have got it sorted really,' I said. 'Look at them. Getting married, kid on the way, a weird best mate each . . . ' I watched as the bridesmaid flicked Frank a seductive wink and he turned away, blushing to the roots of his hair and smiling shyly.

Nadine snorted with laughter. 'Bless them. Good luck to them I say.'

Rachel had dropped Simon's ring on the floor and Frank and the bridesmaid were scrambling about trying to find it. Meanwhile Rachel's dad had started to sway from side to side with his hands in his pockets, threatening to burst into song at any moment.

'And while we're on the subject of weird best mates . . .' Nadine continued, ignoring the pantomime at the altar, 'when the hell are you and Marbles going to get yourselves sorted out?'

Not knowing quite how to react to this, I gazed blankly ahead and said nothing. Nadine was persistent. 'As your friend and housemate, I am duty-bound to set you straight about a few things, just for the sake of a little bit of household harmony.'

I glanced at her out of the corner of my eye and made an exasperated noise. 'Leave it out, will you,' I sighed.

She ignored me, jabbing her thumb over her shoulder where Alex sat with Marbles and Garston, chortling away like schoolboys in assembly. 'As if having a room next to His *Wankiness* wasn't enough,' she went on, 'I mean, you should *hear* some of the noises Alex makes at night, Christ, it's enough to make me *hurl*.'

The ring was quickly found and presented, and meanwhile Frank was discovering that his best man duties were about to be tested further. He had already fulfilled the 'wear a silly suit' obligation, and the 'make sure the groom turns up and doesn't act like an arse' responsibility, as well as the obvious duty of 'ring master'. Now he found himself faced with the undesirable task of trying to prevent the father of the bride from bellowing out all verses of 'Hi Ho Silver Lining' and 'Mr Tambourine Man'.

Nadine was still going on at me, not taking the slightest interest in the family fiasco unfolding in front of us. 'But let me tell you – worse, much worse than living with Alex – who incidentally is still intent on his utterly pitiful quest to 'cure' me, would you believe – is having to live with two miserable fuckers like you and Marbles, who are obviously crazy about each other but too damn stupid and stubborn to do anything about it.'

'Nade, we're at a *wedding*. I don't think this is the time or the place –'

'Sorry mate, but I have to tell you this. I can't take much more. I'm going to have to move out unless Alex finally gets himself some poor deluded soul to call his girlfriend and you and Marbles stop this crap act you've got going. Maybe then I can get on with my own life at last.'

I scowled at her and denied knowing what the hell she was talking about.

Rachel's dad was escorted out of the church by Simon's dad, and the muffled laughter around the church stifled to polite coughs. Simon, looking flustered, whispered something at Frank, and Frank shrugged and whispered something to Rachel. Rachel shook her head and said, loud enough for everyone to hear, 'I don't care. He can fuck off for ever as far as I'm concerned.'

Then things went back to normal for a while, and they continued exchanging vows, with no further distractions.

Nadine put her hand on mine and squeezed it gently, her tone mellowing. 'You've had a shitty time of it, mate, I know. We've all been so worried about you. I know you're finding it hard to get over it, but you don't have to shut us all out.'

'I'm not . . .'

'You *have been*, Abi. I just hate to see you like this. I want things to go back to how they were, like when we were all . . .'

'Oh I suppose you think I'm happy with how things have turned out, do you?' I snapped back at her.

'Would Jasmine want to see you like this?' Nadine demanded,

getting impatient. 'She'd be ashamed if she could see that droopy, self-pitying expression on your mug – she'd be *ashamed*.'

This was more than ample provocation to jar me into defensive mode. I opened my mouth to protest in the strongest possible terms, but was silenced by Nadine bashing me on the head gently but firmly with the *Book of Psalms*.

'*Ow!* What the f –'

'Will you *listen* to me,' she hissed at me, raising her voice. A few of the older people sitting in the pews in front of us turned around in annoyance, their fingers pressed to their lips and shushing us in a much louder and more irritating way than we had been conducting our conversation.

'Can we talk about this later, please?' I implored her under my breath after we had been adequately chastened and obediently resumed our subdued, ladylike seating postures, facing the front with legs and arms crossed.

Nadine didn't answer. The whole congregation fell silent as Simon and Rachel were declared man and wife, give or take the random blowing of a nose or the quiet weeping of an overwhelmed female relative. I watched and sighed wistfully as Rachel folded back her veil and Simon bent down and kissed her to the sounds of a few cheers and euphoric sobs, a little ripple of applause, and Marbles and Alex shouting out 'Go on, my son,' a little too loudly. Nadine noticed my eyes clouding over and started fidgeting, pulling at the neckline of her dress and rubbing at her blistered heels where her new shoes had rubbed.

'Pull yourself together, Abi,' she said with a smile, 'you're just too damn romantic for your own good. All this lovey-dovey stuff is vomit-inducing.'

'Don't be so cynical.'

The thunderous organ erupted into song, the guests started filing out, Simon and Rachel looked at each other as if to say 'Is that it?', and the minister sloped off into the vestibule, shaking his head and smiling bemusedly.

'Right, now that's over, I'm off to get absolutely obliterated on free booze,' I declared. I tried getting up but Nadine pulled me back down, gripping my arm and looking at me with a serious frown. 'Oh what *now*?' I asked huffily.

'You know Marbles is in love with you, don't you?' she said, too loud and too assured. Then she excused herself before giving me a chance to respond, mumbling something about having to go and throw up somewhere.

The post-wedding piss-up was of unsurpassed lunacy; more blazing inter-family arguments than you can shake a toaster at, incestuous snogging, glass-smashing, hat-stamping, floor-to-ceiling vomiting, tacky disco music, screaming children, food fights – you name it, Rachel and Simon and their families had it covered.

'You see, this is what marriage is really about,' Marbles philosophised, as a seafood vol-au-vent whizzed past his ear. 'Sod the together for ever part, it's the fucking great piss-up afterwards that makes the whole damn thing almost seem worth it.'

Alex voiced his agreement, downing his umpteenth glass of champagne while trying to shake off a middle-aged woman who had adhered herself, whelk-like, to him. (It wasn't until later that I discovered the woman was in fact Rachel's mother.)

'The best thing about wedding parties,' said Garston, unbuttoning a starchy white shirt to reveal a Talking Heads T-shirt underneath, 'is that all the birds are well up for it.'

Nadine brought me over a paper plate stacked high with buffet food, but I left it on the table in front of me and told her I wasn't hungry.

'Fair enough,' she said, tipping it all on to her plate and tucking in. I caught Marbles's eye from the other side of the table, but he looked away and deliberately struck up a conversation with Simon's sister, a petite blonde GCSE student whom Alex had sensitively described as 'a barely legal bit of fluff'. The disco started relentlessly thumping out eighties pap pop, and I decided to go outside and find a quiet spot to smoke and wallow by myself. Having already consumed the customary vat of wine, a few hours in the giddying glare and blare of the disco lights and pulsating music had started to make me feel nauseous. And intensely anti-social. I garbled something incoherent at Nadine, who was too preoccupied with repulsing the advances of an overweight, avuncular man with a moustache. I took a chilled and uncorked bottle of wine from the end of a long buffet table and stepped outside into the garden. By myself, away from the barrage of competing stimuli, the babble of chattering voices, the world suddenly seemed grey again. I found a secluded patch of grass at the back of the garden and sat down next to a rose bush, watching fireworks ascend and burst into colourful sparks, sputtering out into embers as they cascaded back down. I drank wine from the bottle and chain-smoked and shivered, masochistically enjoying being cold and miserable and on my own. My inability to get on with life, to feel human again, was beginning to make me feel inadequate. People die all the time, and the people who loved them get over it. It's a fact of life – I was told: just give it time. Time heals. But there was always something gnawing at me, something coiled up tight in the pit of my stomach, a horrible, cold feeling that wouldn't go away – an absence, a void, a colossal sense of loss.

Since starting back at university, my approach had been the reversal of what it was in the first year. I had completely immersed myself in studying, sometimes up to ten hours a day, and I hardly ever went out. Nadine had, of course, been wonderful, but there's only so much patience even a saintly best friend can have. As for Marbles . . . I had well and truly messed things up with him. It was so difficult for him to know how to act towards me – I knew he resented me, probably despised me, but at the same time he felt sorry for me and didn't want to continue holding the circumstances of our untimely break-up against me.

As if on cue, I heard his voice behind me. It sounded far away, but when I turned around he was standing just a few feet away.

'Is it OK if I sit down?' he asked.

'Sure,' I said, untying my cardigan from around my waist and shrugging it on.

'Cold?' he enquired, kneeling down next to me and taking a swig from my wine bottle.

'Not really. I'm just . . . watching the fireworks,' I murmured weakly, pointing at the stone sky and watching my breath frost the air in front of my face.

'Here,' he said, taking his jacket off and placing it around my shoulders. He hesitated and then started to rub my back, an action that caused me automatically to flinch as it was the first time he had voluntarily touched me since Jasmine's funeral.

'Sorry,' he mumbled, retracting his hand, thinking he had offended me. I desperately tried to think of something to say to put us both at ease. I couldn't think of anything at all. Eventually, he said, 'It was a lovely wedding.'

'Yes,' I agreed, too readily, 'it was wonderful.'

'Shame about Rachel's old man, but . . . still, great party.'

'Yes,' I said. 'Great party.'

I mentally cursed myself for sounding like such a cretin, but still I couldn't think of anything intelligent or interesting to say. He took another gulp of my wine and then stood up, saying, 'Well, see you later then.'

I found my voice, at last. 'Please don't go.' I shocked myself with the force and desperation with which I said it, but it had the desired effect. Marbles sat back down immediately, nearer to me this time.

'Are you all right?' he asked. I looked over at him and felt like bursting into tears. Instead I just nodded. He fumbled for his cigarettes.

'I've stopped smoking, you know,' he told me, lighting one up.

'Really?'

He smiled his captivating smile as he inhaled deeply, his cheeks flushed with cold and alcohol. 'What do you think?'

I smoked my own cigarette, pulling up grass with my other hand. 'It's been a good day, anyway,' I said eventually, in a small, timorous voice. 'I've really enjoyed myself.'

'Good.' He nodded, cleared his throat, mumbled, 'That's good,' then, subconsciously mirroring my actions, started nervously pulling up grass himself. Together we created two small bald patches on the lawn, side by side. The next silence was so long that I actually jumped when Marbles finally spoke again.

'I miss you.'

Those three simple words were like a tonic. I met his gaze, shyly at first and then full on, before admitting, 'I miss you too.'

He finished his cigarette before he said anything else, and when he did, he talked rapidly and didn't look at me. 'It's been hell living under the same roof as you and not being able to . . . be with you. And with all that's gone on, I couldn't even . . . I mean, I didn't think you'd want me to talk to you about how I felt, and I didn't even know myself.'

I waited before responding, not wanting to make a crass verbal blunder. 'I'm sorry,' I murmured finally, for want of something more original, more substantial. 'I've been so selfish.' I moved as close to him as I possibly could and put my head on his shoulder. To my indescribable relief, he put both his arms around me and kissed the top of my head, pulling me close.

'No you haven't,' he said. 'I'm just not very good at handling emotional situations. What I'm trying to say is . . . I don't suppose . . . you'd be willing to give it another go? Us, I mean?'

I sobbed quietly as I told him, in all honesty, 'You could do so much better than me. You deserve better.'

'Yeah, that's true, but I can't be bothered to go out and find someone else.' I looked up at him and he wiped away my tears as I laughed feebly at his characteristically crap wit. 'Anyway,' he continued, kissing the end of my nose, 'we're living together now so there's no escaping from each other.'

'Is that a good thing?'

'For me, yes. For you, absolutely not.'

I gazed up at him in awe, feeling more drunk than I was. We held each other there for what could have been hours, drinking wine and sharing cigarettes until the last of the fireworks had died.

The first Christmas without Jasmine was not nearly as dreadful as I thought it would be. I went with Dad to visit her grave on Christmas Eve, armed with bundles of flowers: lilies, freesia, gypsophila, carnations, winter jasmine; a rainbow of colours she would have loved. I had been worried about Dad for a long time – he barely ate, he never smiled, he rarely even talked. But that evening, as we laid the flowers down, he unexpectedly pulled me towards him, burying his face in my hair.

'I don't know if I can ever let her go,' he mumbled tearfully, as I hesitantly returned the embrace, afraid of his new fragility. 'Life is just not the same without her.'

'We'll get through this, Dad,' I said. 'We need to be strong. For Floyd. For each other.'

'I just . . . can't bear to think of how unhappy she must have been . . . to want to . . . how could I not have seen it? I should have . . . somehow . . .'

'Dad, just stop it, will you? How can you feel responsible? Do you really think Jas would want you torturing yourself with these thoughts?'

'I just *miss* her. I miss her so . . . so much, I can hardly stand it.'

He moved away from me and sank to his knees by Jasmine's grave, forlorn exhaustion crumpling his pale face. I sat beside him and looked up at the sky, which was purple – not a cloudy, watercolour mauve, but a deep, amethyst purple pinpointed with stars. I dug my hand in my pocket, feeling for a joint I had prepared earlier.

'It still doesn't seem real,' Dad said, distractedly plucking the petals from a lifeless flower. 'I still can't get my head around it.'

'Maybe this will help,' I offered, lighting the joint and holding it out to him.

He blinked at it for a moment, not knowing whether to accept it.

'I suppose it can't hurt,' he reasoned, taking it after a few seconds. We sat in silence for a while and then he handed it back and said, 'Well, it's just you and me now, kid.'

'Looks like it.'

'That's what Jasmine said to you when your mum died, you know.'

'Really?'

'Yeah, she sat you on her lap and looked at you in that serious, protective way, and she said, "Well kid, it's just you and me now, and that sad old excuse for a father".'

'She said that?'

'Yeah.' His smile was barely discernible, but I noticed the corners of his eyes crinkle and when he glanced at me his expression was more one of fond reminiscence than of sorrow. 'Sad old excuse for a father, she called me. Nine years old, and she'd already sussed me out!'

I put my gloved hand in his. 'She really loved you, Dad.'

'I know she did, Abi.'

We were quiet as we sat together, lost in our own private thoughts about Jasmine.

'She taught me so much,' I whispered, more to myself.

'Yeah,' Dad said. 'Me too.' Then he looked around at me and said, 'Gimme some more of that joint, will you.'

It had gone out, so I lit it again for him, shielding the flame from the bitter winter wind.

'Might grow my beard again, what do you think?' he mused, puffing contentedly.

'Hmmm . . . Jane told me to never trust a man with a beard.'

'Jas loved my beard. She used to plait it for me. Stuck daisies in it.'

He glanced over at me, winked as he blew out the pungent smoke, and his smile seemed genuinely happy this time. In that instant, I felt as if a massive weight had been lifted from me, a phenomenal sense of release. Jasmine had set herself free. There was nothing to feel sad or guilty or regretful about. Jasmine was *free.*

Silver blue moon slid over the trees and shimmered through the bare branches. We stood up and Dad put his arm around me as we ambled together down a winding path towards a clearing in the trees beyond the cemetery. We took the long way home, talking animatedly about our best memories of her, without a trace of sadness.

Acknowledgements

I am hugely grateful to the following people: my fantastic agent Rosemary Scoular, Vanessa Kearns and everyone else at PFD who believed in me and helped me to believe in myself. The team at Orion, particularly my wonderful editor Christine Kidney, whose dedicated patience, persistence and perfectionism helped me transform my original manuscript into something I am not ashamed to feel proud of. Jeremy Lee, just for being there and putting up with me right from the start. Ginger Ninja and the rest of the usual suspects from the unforgettable (but mostly forgotten) Warwick daze for remaining incurable students . . . All at John Murray for their professional advice and encouragement when I needed it most. Paddington & co. for showing me some of the 'real' Brighton and for various inspiration along the way . . .

And a special thank you to my extraordinary sister Lynette Steel. I hope you have found peace now; I miss you always.

For Lynette, 23 July 1962–8 December 1997